Praise for _New York ...
                                 Julia

'Charming, witty and warm. ...
Sarah Morgan, _Sunda..._

'_The Princess Plan_ made me fall in love with historicals again.
I couldn't stop reading, but at the same time, I didn't want to
get to the end. What a fabulous story and characters!'
JoAnn Ross, _New York Times_ bestselling author

'Julia London writes vibrant, emotional stories and sexy,
richly drawn characters.'
Madeline Hunter, _New York Times_ bestselling author

'The gorgeous characters and the wit and charm made this a
book I simply didn't want to put down.'
Nicola Cornick, _USA Today_ bestselling author

'Deliciously clever... London's flair for creating engaging
characters and her Austenesque sense of wit guarantee
historical romance readers will be lining up for the
latest in her Royal Match series.'
Booklist

'Secrets, scandals and steamy chemistry – this paperback
escape has it all!'
Woman's World

Julia London is the *New York Times* and *USA Today* bestselling author of more than fifty romantic fiction novels. She is the author of the bestselling Highland Grooms historical romance series, and the Lake Haven contemporary romance series. Julia is the recipient of the RT Bookclub Award for Best Historical Romance and a six-time finalist for the prestigious *RITA*® award for excellence in romantic fiction. She lives in Austin, Texas.

Also by Julia London

A Royal Match
Last Duke Standing
The Duke Not Taken
The Viscount Who Vexed Me

A Royal Wedding
The Princess Plan
A Royal Kiss and Tell
A Princess by Christmas

The Highland Grooms
Wild Wicked Scot
Sinful Scottish Laird
Hard-Hearted Highlander
Devil in Tartan
Tempting the Laird
Seduced by a Scot

The Cabot Sisters
The Trouble with Honour
The Devil Takes a Bride
The Scoundrel and the Debutante

For additional books by Julia London visit her website,
julialondon.com

AN
INCONVENIENT
EARL

JULIA LONDON

MILLS & BOON

Mills & Boon
An imprint of HarperCollins*Publishers* Ltd
1 London Bridge Street
London SE1 9GF

www.harpercollins.co.uk

HarperCollins*Publishers*
Macken House, 39/40 Mayor Street Upper,
Dublin 1, D01 C9W8, Ireland

This paperback edition 2024
1

First published in Great Britain by Mills & Boon,
an imprint of HarperCollins*Publishers* Ltd 2024

This book is produced from independently certified FSC™ paper
to ensure responsible forest management.

For more information visit: www.harpercollins.co.uk/green

This book is set in Times New Roman

Printed and Bound in the UK using 100% Renewable Electricity at
CPI Group (UK) Ltd, Croydon, CR0 4YY

The year 2023 marked the twenty-fifth anniversary of the publication of my first historical romance, *The Devil's Love*. This book is dedicated to all the readers who have picked up my books through those years. To the readers who reached out to let me know my books resonated with them. To those who wrote to correct a historical fact. To those who tagged me with what they didn't like (and for a few, that was every page). To those who have shared reviews and comments on social media, in shelf talkers and in book clubs. I'm grateful to every one of you. You've all made it possible for this dream career to come true. Thank you for simply everything.

Julia London

'I thought an hour ago that I loved you more than
any woman has ever loved a man, but a half hour after that
I knew that what I felt before was nothing compared to
what I felt then. But ten minutes after that,
I understood that my previous love was a puddle
compared to the high seas before a storm.'

William Goldman, *The Princess Bride*

CHAPTER ONE

Butterhill Hall
England
1871

EMMA CLARK WAS thinking of taking a lover. She had an itch that could not be scratched, one that was causing her to look at men—*all* men, whether short or tall, lean or round, old or young—with lust.

A sinful, and probably unpardonable, but undeniable fact.

After surveying the nearest candidates, she'd settled on Mr. John Karlsson, the new stablemaster at Butterhill Hall. He looked to be somewhere in the vicinity of her thirty-two years, had flaxen blond hair, arms as big around as her thighs, and an easy smile that sparkled in his blue eyes.

She'd made a habit of going down to the stables to watch him exercise the horses. She would call out to him. "*That* mount is full of vinegar today." He'd laugh. "Toby would run straight to the sea if I let him." Or she would note the excellent grooming of the horses' coats. "They're so shiny," she would say approvingly, and he'd say proudly, "Aye, ma'am, I've a new lad in the stables."

Sometimes, when one of the stable hands was putting a horse through its paces around the paddock, Mr.

Karlsson would stand with his back to the fence, his elbows propped on the railing as he watched. He would remove his hat and drag his fingers through his hair. He smelled of horse and sunshine and salt.

On the opposite side of the fence, Emma liked to step onto the bottom rail and lean over the top one beside him. She'd attempt to make small talk. She'd run through various scenarios in her mind, different ways she might ask him if he would like a lover. She dismissed most of them as impractical or cringe-inducing. Propositioning a man didn't come naturally to her, and she continued to be bewildered by what might be considered offensive versus what might be considered enticing. She'd even thought about consulting her very married sister, but she imagined Fanny would be appalled and spend an entire afternoon lecturing her why she could never *ever* do such a thing.

Then Emma decided that it ought to be *his* idea and mulled over ways to lead him to it.

After days of chatting about horses, she'd decided it would never come to fruition if she didn't take the reins. Ironically. She came up with a scheme that seemed the least egregious of all she'd imagined—she would ask him to saddle a horse for her. She was not the best rider, but she was competent enough, and she thought she could manage to dislodge herself from the horse and fall—Lord knew she'd done it before—but in a manner that would necessitate her rescue.

She just hoped it didn't hurt. Or that she didn't break an arm or leg. Worse yet, her head.

On the day she was set to carry out her plan, she made her way to the stables. But Mr. Karlsson was in the company of a young girl, perhaps seven or eight years old. She had the same flaxen hair as he, the same lean build. Emma watched as he picked the girl up and swung her around so that her braids flew out like wind streamers. That laughing girl was the spitting image of him. Which meant, with a high degree of probability, that he was married.

Alas, so was Emma.

Ah, well. She changed course and walked away, leaving behind her dashed hopes of taking him as her lover.

Granted, there had been other obstacles besides marriage that she'd not yet established how to overcome. For example, the cumbersome business of her being the Countess of Dearborn, and thus, Mr. Karlsson's employer. Ethics and morals were probably involved in a way she preferred not to think about.

She trudged on in disappointment. What was a woman of her age to do when her estranged husband was in Africa or some other far-flung place for months on end with no sign of ever returning? Not that she wanted that intolerable human being to return. But that didn't mean she'd given up personal desires.

Emma hadn't always thought Albert intolerable. Years ago, when he was wooing her, he'd been the perfect gentleman. He and his mother would come for supper, and he'd charm her and her family by reading a sonnet after the meal or singing along with Fanny to some tune. He escorted her to church and back and picked wildflowers for her along the way, which he would insert into her bonnet or her hair. He would call on her and Fanny with his friends and they'd play cards and laugh.

It had all been cordial and exciting and precisely the

sort of thing Emma's mother had promised her love would be.

Her parents were thrilled when Albert Clark, the Earl of Dearborn, asked for her hand in marriage and had happily trundled her off to holy matrimony unto death with a modest savings in the event she ever needed money of her own. Emma had been so sure of her and Albert's mutual affection that she believed she would never need it. The sum had been tucked away, quietly collecting a small interest.

She'd expected marital bliss with Albert. She imagined evenings spent with him reading sonnets as she quietly did her needlework. She imagined they would entertain on occasion but would catch each other's eye across a crowded room and realize they preferred their own company to anyone else's. She imagined they would take long walks around the lake and travel to London and spend long winter nights tucked away in bed, making love.

The problem with expectations, she discovered, was that they rarely lived up to reality.

Curiously, from the start, Albert had seemed indifferent to their intimate relations. Which was precisely the opposite of what Fanny had said she might expect. Fanny said she'd spent the first few months of her marriage fending off her husband several times a day. Not Emma. At times, Albert had seemed downright annoyed with the prospect of it. And when he did perform his marital duty, he was not a man to take his time—he wanted it done as quickly as possible. Emma had tried everything she knew to make it more pleasant for him, which, in truth, was not a lot. And when she attempted to make things better, or more pleasurable, he said she made them worse.

And yet, Albert was obsessed with producing his obligatory heir. Unfortunately, human biology required that he have a working appendage, and increasingly, he did not. Every time he failed, he grew angry and verbally abusive. Every month that Emma didn't conceive, he blamed her. Every month they tried again, but the coupling was rougher and devoid of affection. She'd begun to feel like a cheap vessel, misused and unappreciated.

He soon began to blame her for everything inside and outside of the marital bed. He belittled her and dressed her down in front of family and friends. Everything she said was open to ridicule. He avoided her presence and told others he found her company unendurable.

Emma sincerely believed she'd tried as hard as one might, but she came to loathe her husband. On the day he announced he was going on expedition to Africa, she could not have been happier. He said he needed to go and "clear his head" and didn't know how long he'd be gone.

Emma secretly rejoiced and imagined being widowed in the event he was gored by a rhinoceros. His family, on the other hand, was distraught. What of the estate? Who would manage his wife? How could he leave them there alone with her?

His older sister Adele was a spinster who looked after his fourteen-year-old brother, Andrew. The boy needed Albert, Adele said. And really, wasn't it Albert's duty to remain in England until he'd sired his heir? "Your wife has passed her thirtieth year, Albert," she'd said. "You haven't long before she's no longer any use to you."

"She's no use to me now," he'd said sharply.

"I'm sitting right here," Emma had reminded the siblings. "You do know that I am a person and not just a womb, don't you?"

She'd received a tongue-lashing for mentioning her supposedly barren womb.

In the end, Albert turned a deaf ear to the pleas of his sister and prepared to leave. Emma was secretly giddy with happiness. She said she hoped the wind would always be at his back and privately hoped the winds would blow him all the way to China and he'd never return.

And indeed, it had been a beautiful ten months since Albert had left. Emma had begun to feel herself again, free to be who she was without fear of disparagement. She didn't miss him in the slightest or wish for his return. What she wanted was love—physical, emotional, consuming love—and she would never have that from him.

She was beginning to fear love would not be hers to have. She was biding her time, waiting for her husband, wandering through her life, playing the role of countess and, in her husband's absence, estate manager. She dined alone, slept alone, spent nights before the hearth alone. And while that was infinitely more desirable than spending that time with Albert, it did make for loneliness.

She reached the hall in something of a mood and tossed her hat carelessly onto a console as she walked into the foyer. Feeney, the butler, appeared from another corridor to take her hat. "You've a caller, my lady," he said. "Mr. Victor Duffy."

She so rarely had callers. "Who is that?"

"He did not say. He said he has news for you."

News for her? How odd. It probably had something to do with the town house in London. A tax or something like it. "Thank you, Feeney. Whatever it is, I'll dispose of it quickly and send him on his way so do stay close by."

"Very good," Feeney said.

The man standing in the receiving room was wearing a coat that had faded, the sleeves and hem frayed. His collar appeared to have a ring of dirt around his neck. His waistcoat strained across his paunch, and he'd combed his thinning hair over as much of his head as he could. He coughed as she entered, obviously trying to swallow it down, but as coughs were wont to do, it escaped him. "Lady Dearborn," he said, and coughed again.

Emma unthinkingly took a step back. "Good day, sir. How may I be of help?"

He suffered a fit of coughing and removed a crumpled handkerchief from his pocket and dabbed at his mouth. "I do beg your pardon. I am perfectly well, but I think I've gotten a bit of road in my throat." He dabbed at his forehead, which, Emma noticed, had broken out with perspiration. "I've have come from Egypt." He coughed again. "With news of your husband," he rasped.

"Albert?" Just her luck. "And how does he fare?"

Mr. Duffy reached into the interior of his coat and withdrew an envelope and held it out to her. From where she stood, she could see her husband's distinctive handwriting. She didn't move to take it straightaway. "That's from Albert?"

He nodded.

"You've come from Egypt to deliver it?"

He nodded again.

Emma sighed. "He might have posted it and saved you the trouble, Mr. Duffy." She gingerly took the letter from him.

Mr. Duffy suffered another short fit of coughing. "Unfortunately, madam, I am the bearer of distressing news. You may want to sit."

Well, now he had her attention. What could be more distressing than the news Albert was coming home? "I'm sturdier than I look. What news?"

He coughed again. He was starting to look a little gray.

"Would you like some water, Mr. Duffy?"

"No, no. Please don't trouble yourself. I do beg your pardon. As I was saying, it is my solemn and distressing duty to inform you that your husband has…died."

Emma froze. She was certain she'd misheard him. *"Died?"*

"Died. Yellow fever."

She was stunned. So stunned that she didn't believe him. "What?" Could it possibly be true? Could Albert really be dead? "Are you certain?"

"Quite." He reached into his pocket again and withdrew a small leather pouch. He opened it and out dropped Albert's signet ring. "He was buried immediately, as is the custom there."

"Buried?" She was gaping at this man, her mind racing. Albert was dead? Her belly began to churn with confusion and sorrow and joy all at once. "Have you been to his sister?"

"No, ma'am. I have come to you first." He tried to stifle another cough.

"Oh my," she said, and turned away from him, her mind struggling to comprehend.

Mr. Duffy coughed and said hoarsely, "Shall I ring for your butler? Someone to help you?"

"No, no. I… I will manage." She pressed a hand to her forehead. *Would* she manage? She stared at the wall, thinking. What did this mean? How would they memorialize him? What would happen to her? Had he left a will? How ridiculous of her to never have asked.

A sudden and tremendous thud startled her, and she whipped around. Mr. Duffy was lying facedown on the rug. "Mr. Duffy!" she cried and rushed to his aid. It took all her strength to roll him onto his back. His eyes were bulging, and his face was turning a shade of blue. Emma shoved the letter into her pocket and ran to the door, shrieking for Feeney.

The butler came running. Then came two footmen. One of the footmen fought with the knot of Mr. Duffy's neck cloth to release it, but it was no use. Mr. Duffy was dead.

They carried the man to a bedroom and laid him out there until they could determine what to do with him.

In the chaos and days that followed that untimely death, no one asked why Mr. Duffy had come to call. Emma was grateful for it, because it gave her a chance to breathe, and when she did, she realized that had Mr. Duffy made it to Adele's house, or had he gone there before he'd come to Emma, Albert's little brother would be the earl now.

And she'd be…what? Out on her arse, that's what, with nothing but her savings to lean on. She had no illusions about Adele's regard for her or what she'd force Andrew to do.

And then it occurred to her: she was the only person who knew Albert was dead. No remains of her husband were going to suddenly appear, and apparently, his sole personal effect was in that leather pouch.

If everyone assumed Albert was alive, Emma could carry on as she had for the past ten months, living life on her own terms.

The letter Mr. Duffy had delivered had been one Albert had written presumably before he'd taken ill. He curtly informed her he'd be home by Christmas.

Emma tucked the signet ring where no one could find it. She burned Albert's letter in the fire in her room. She said nothing to no one. Not even Carlotta, her lady's maid and friend.

Emma was very good at keeping secrets.

CHAPTER TWO

Cairo, Egypt
Two Months Later

THE *SUQ*, the Cairo market, felt so crowded that Luka Olivien found it overwhelming. It reminded him of when he was a child and his governess would take him to the Christmas markets in the central square of St. Edys, Wesloria. He would cling to her hand, fearful of being swept into a sea of humanity and carried off to God knew where. This was much like that, only bigger and more crowded.

He was exhausted and covered with the grime of travel. He'd been with a nomadic Bedouin tribe in the desert for months. He'd been working under the tutelage of an English scholar, an Egyptologist, whom he'd met several years ago. He had written Professor Henley about his interest in Egypt, and Henley had encouraged him to take up study, had even said he would help shape the book Luka hoped to write. So Luka had come to Egypt to document the intersection of trade and migration to better understand desert economy and migration infrastructure of wadis, oases, and ancient routes. He was an anthropologist, introduced to the science when he was at Eton, trained by one of the best anthropologists in St. Edys.

The science, and his study of various cultures, was afforded him as a man of privilege. In other words, when he was not engaged in anthropology, he was the Weslorian *Comte ve Marlaine*, the son of the Duke of Astasia.

He caught a glimpse of himself in the reflection of a glass window and inwardly recoiled at the sight of himself. He had returned to his Western clothes when he reached Cairo. He'd kept them tucked away for safe-keeping, having worn the traditional Bedouin garb of the *thwab* and *keffiyah* these last many months. And still, somehow the red dust of the desert was baked into his buckskins. A dark, permanent stain of perspiration ringed the crown of his hat. His leather boots had begun to form cracks. He had a beard that itched like the devil, and he couldn't wait to be rid of it—but he'd broken his razor at a stop along a wadi. His shirt sported dried blood from a brawl he'd had the misfortune of being drawn into in one oasis town. Sometimes, men in this part of the world didn't like the look of men from his part of the world. Who could blame them? It seemed like Europeans were coming in droves to question their way of life and put their stamp on a culture that had done well enough without them for a very long time.

The *suq* crowd was oppressive, but Luka mean-dered through, stopping at different stalls to bargain for gifts to take home. He bought a gold bracelet for his younger sister, Dagna. An ivory comb for his older sister, Ester. He bought some saddle oil to apply to his cracked leather boots. For the Gunkopfs, his friends and gracious hosts in Cairo, he bought silk for Heda and, at the next stall, cigars for her husband, Boris. The man said they were American. Luka had his doubts.

He and Boris, a German, had met at Eton more than a decade ago, where many European aristocratic and wealthy families sent their young men for polishing. Boris and Luka became fast friends and had remained such all these years. Boris was a banker now. He'd been living in Cairo for several years, lending money to Egyptian businessmen. He'd apparently lent enough of it—he lived quite well here.

Luka made one other purchase, a piece of jewelry that resembled the star-shaped blue lotus flower. It was made of diamonds and sapphires, with an amber at the center. For ancient Egyptians, the blue lotus was a symbol of life, resurrection, and immortality. Luka had no one in mind for the piece. But he liked the symbolism and bought it as a souvenir for himself.

His purchases made, Luka continued, past beggars to whom he tossed a few coins, past braying donkeys with baskets strapped across their backs. A pair of camels in repose. Young men playing illicit betting games in darkened doorways. He turned up a long, uncomfortably dark street, and from there, turned into a quieter street where the houses grew bigger and the sounds of the market farther away. This was *Shabah Ziqaq*, or Ghost Alley, which felt aptly named. It was so dark Luka was convinced he heard footsteps behind him and quickened his step.

At the end of the alley was a three-story rectangular house with painted cornices above the windows. He could see an elaborately carved wooden entry door through the gates. The house had four small towers at each corner, and atop the towers were sculptures of falcons. Between the falcons, a colorful, cloth canopy stretched across a rooftop veranda.

He entered through the iron gate and walked through the courtyard. Several tropical plants he'd not seen elsewhere in Egypt were arranged around and between two fountains. He moved across the granite path to the door and knocked.

A dark-skinned man in a turban, his face weathered by sun, answered. It was Mustafa, the houseman.

Luka bowed. "*Masa alkhayr*," he said. "Good evening. Is Herr Gunkopf in?"

Mustafa did not speak—he rarely spoke at all to Luka's knowledge—but beckoned him in. He began to walk in the direction of the main salon when Boris suddenly appeared, grinning. He was wearing the traditional Egyptian *galabeya*, a long white robe, generously cut. Boris's blond hair was uncovered. "Luka!" he said, casting his arms wide as if he meant to hug him. "A *wunderbar* surprise. We weren't expecting you for another month."

"I hope it's not an imposition—"

"Nonsense! Of course not, my friend. Come, come," he said, gesturing for Luka to enter the salon.

"Luka is here?" His wife, Heda, popped into the tiled hall, too. Unlike her husband, she was wearing a gown in the style of European fashion. They made for a very odd couple in some ways. "We're so glad you've come!" she warbled and came forward, grabbing his shoulders and forcing him to bend down to her.

"Heda, I'm filthy—"

"I don't care," she said, and kissed both cheeks. "We've so many letters for you!"

The Gunkopfs were the most gracious people he'd ever known. Boris had insisted that Luka keep a few items of respectable clothing here and have his post directed here. "Let this be your base," he'd said.

"I'll get them," Heda said. "One of them seems very important!"

"You must be hungry," Boris said. "Mustafa! Our guest is hungry. And by the look of it, he'll want a bath. You want a bath, no?"

Luka desperately wanted a bath, but before he could answer, Mustafa was gone, off to do Boris's bidding. "I'm filthy, Boris. I can wash in the alley. Please don't go to any trouble—"

"Nonsense," Boris said again and dragged him into the salon.

It was furnished in the Egyptian style, with low divans and rugs and pillows. The one nod to Boris and Heda's homeland was a cuckoo clock that chimed a German nursery tune.

Boris strode to a small brass cart, his *galabeya* billowing around him. "Wine from Italy," he said as he poured. "Quite good."

"Thank you," Luka said, accepting the glass with a surprising amount of gratitude. He sipped and sighed with contentment. "One forgets how much one enjoys wine after weeks in the desert. I apologize for arriving—"

"Smelling like a skunk?" Boris laughed.

"That bad?"

"Worse, my friend. But never mind that. You are always welcome here. How long will you be in Cairo?"

That was the question. Luka pondered his answer as he sipped the wine. His stomach was winning the war of thoughts—he thought the wine would complement a hearty beef stew perfectly. The thought made his stomach growl.

"How long has it been since you've eaten?" Boris asked, curious.

How long *had* it been? "I couldn't say," Luka said. The wine was going straight to his head. "I'm on my way to England to review my work with Professor Henley."

"You and your studies. But you can't run off so soon," Boris said. "You must remain for a time. We are desperate for guests and diversions."

Luka snorted. "I'm not much of a diversion, friend. And I wouldn't like to impose on your hospitality."

"On the contrary, you are terribly diverting," Boris insisted. "Your tales of the desert are remarkable."

"Here we are!" Heda sailed back into the room carrying a surprisingly thick stack of letters. He hadn't been gone that long, had he?

"So many!" Heda said, and handed him the stack.

He glanced at the exquisite script of his name on the top letter, then turned it over. It had been sealed by the Duke of Astasia, his father. Generally, it was his mother who wrote. His father was too embroiled in politics to be bothered with it.

"Go on, then," Heda said. "You must want to read them."

Yes and no. Luka smiled a little. "I probably should."

Mustafa entered with a tray of unleavened bread, hummus, dates, and olives. He bowed. But before he could set it down, Boris stopped him. "Take it to his room, Mustafa, please. He can dine after his bath." He looked at Luka. "I don't think I can bear the stench a moment longer."

"I do apologize," Luka said.

"We'll have all your news at dinner," Boris added, hopping to his feet.

Heda smiled at Luka. "We dine at nine."

Luka sheepishly followed Mustafa out of the salon and toward the back of the house. The guest room had a towering wardrobe where his clothes were stored. He waited for two young boys to bring steaming pails of water to his bath, then gratefully shed his clothes and sank into the water. When he'd bathed and sawed off his beard, he sat by the fire to read his post.

The first letter he read was from his father. After the salutation and greeting, his father wrote to say the family was well, that his sister Dagna was expecting another child. To which he added, *More's the pity, as this country has lost that which brought us out of the dark ages, and now the situation is hopeless for our youth. I know you will agree with the need for change, for without it, we will not prosper.*

"Bloody hell," Luka muttered. His father, his father—he sighed and looked at the ceiling for a long moment. The old man had changed much in the last years.

There had been a time, when Luka was a child, that his father and King Maksim were friends. But when King Maksim became gravely ill several years ago, he abdicated and put his young daughter, Justine, on the throne.

Queen Justine was a dear friend of Luka's. They were similar in age and as children had often been at the same events, shuttled off with nannies and governesses while their parents dined. But when Justine acceded to the throne, his father had begun to change. He found fault with her, and her advisers, at every turn. Luka discovered that some men did not want a female monarch—and definitely not a young one. Fantastic stories, leaked by the queen's detractors, said that she was a witch. Or she had drained the country's coffers. Or that she had approved a sentence of death for a man with whom she'd had an affair and was through with him. His father believed it all.

"The queen is not involved with any sentence handed down by the courts," Luka would point out. "Therefore, logic says it can't be true." Or "The newspapers report that our economy is robust. What are you talking about?" But it never mattered what he said. His father believed everything he heard about the queen and her advisers and that his own son was refusing to see the truth. He developed a group of like-minded men, and they would meet in a local tavern, drink ale, and talk about how the country was falling apart.

Then, he'd begun to talk real nonsense. "We need to take back Wesloria from her liberal ways," he'd complain.

"What liberal ways?" Luka would ask. "And take it *back*? How, Papa?"

"I have some ideas," his father would say ominously.

Luka had considered it the talk of disgruntled old men. Still, his father had expected his son to fall in line. He accused Luka of being a pacifist, a coward. Luka had implored his father to use reason and facts. He accused him of being mad. They'd reached a point where there was no discussion between them, only shouting. That's when Luka began to plan his extended trip to places far-flung to pursue the data for his book.

He'd seen Queen Justine just before leaving, when she'd come to Marlaine to open a new pavilion. She was with her husband, William, a strong Scot who watched over her like a hawk. In private, Justine told Luka that his father's actions and public statements had hurt her. "I thought he was our friend."

"So did I," Luka had lamented. "I've been terribly disappointed and confused by the things he's said."

She'd winced and asked apologetically, "Is it senility, do you suppose?"

Luka had considered it but shook his head. His father's problem, he believed, was that he was fearful of change. The queen and her prime minister had instituted some social changes, such as doing away with the poorhouses. She'd led an effort that had resulted in a parliamentary victory of setting a standard living wage for everyone who sought employment. She'd championed avenues for women to find meaningful work other than marriage and child-rearing if they desired.

Luka's father saw those actions as threats to the Weslorian way of life, to his own title and legacy and estate. Change to him meant that the privileged few would become as unprivileged as the vast majority of Weslorians. That's what was whispered, anyway—the queen would do away with titles and legacies and divvy up the land among the poor.

I should like to see you home soon, his father continued. *Your mother misses you, and you've gone long enough ambling about the world with savages. You should be here as the* Comte ve Marlaine *for what comes next.*

What did the old man fantasize would come next? Luka put the letter aside. He moved on to a letter from his sister Ester, who also informed him of Dagna's happy news, but without the lament that the child would never prosper. He had three letters from his estate manager in Marlaine, a pair of letters from tenants, and a letter from Professor Henley, suggesting that Luka come to England to review the research he'd sent along so far.

The last item in his pile was a small package from one M. Lapont. Lapont was a Frenchman by birth, an Englishman by education, and an Egyptian by his choice of a home. He owned a gentlemen's club for ex-patriots in Cairo.

Inside the package was a diamond-encrusted pocket watch. Luka turned it over. There was an inscription on the back: *May the wind be at your back. Emma.* He read the letter that had come with the watch.

> *My lord, kindest regards. I believe you are acquainted with Mr. Victor Duffy. He had the unpleasant task of carrying the effects of the late Lord Dearborn to his widow in England. Unfortunately, once he had departed, I found in my possession this pocket watch, which was to have been included with the other items. It seems to have sentimental value, and I do so regret that I overlooked it.*
>
> *Mr. Duffy informed me that he intended to return to Cairo and meet with you to offer his assistance in the writing of a book. As of the date of this letter, he is overdue. I will soon be departing for Istanbul and ask that you kindly deliver this watch to Mr. Duffy upon your reunion.*
>
> *Sincerely, M. Lapont*

Mr. Duffy had presented himself as a sort of man-servant for any gentleman who needed one. He was a man of many talents and was agreeable to practically anything anyone asked of him, if it paid. He and Luka had struck up a conversation one night before Luka had embarked on his months with the Bedouin tribe, and Mr. Duffy had offered to help him in the compilation of his book. As Mr. Duffy's Arabic was excellent, Luka was interested in a potential arrangement.

As for Lord Dearborn? Luka hardly knew him. He'd run across him once or twice and had found him off-putting in that way some men had of trying desperately to be relevant to whomever he was speaking to. He'd heard about his death from yellow fever. He'd heard Dearborn had been in Alexandria at the time, up to no good, as they said.

He looked at the watch. It was expensive, and the inscription touching. Any wife would want it returned, he reckoned. Unfortunately, he wouldn't be able to wait for Duffy to return from wherever he was now.

Luka wrote his father and told him he would be home after a short visit in England, hopefully in Wesloria by the end of the year. There was no question that he *would* go home—his return was, by necessity and by birth, inevitable, and he couldn't put off the inevitable forever. But he didn't mind delaying it as long as he could. He wasn't looking forward to renewing tensions with his father.

Feeling clean and renewed, Luka joined Boris and Heda for supper and an evening of tall tales—mostly Boris's, but Luka tossed in one or two of his own.

A few days later, he made his way by train to Alexandria to book passage on a clipper headed west.

CHAPTER THREE

Butterhill Hall
Three Months Later

ADELE WAS PERTURBED AGAIN.

Emma could see it in the way her sister-in-law was striding over the hill and across the meadow in her practical boots, wielding a walking stick like a sword, ready to fight as best a lady could when one considered herself a lady.

Emma had intended to walk outside and oversee the construction of the musician's platform that would be erected on the west lawn for her party this weekend, but the sight of Adele's indomitable figure prompted her to groan and then go in search of Feeney, her butler, to ask that tepid tea be brought into the solarium. Adele didn't like her tea too hot.

Adele and Andrew lived in the dower house that was just over the hill from Butterhill Hall. It had been built for Adele's great-grandmother, and Adele swore that the scent of all the tinctures and salves once liberally applied to old people still lingered. She constantly complained that it was drafty, it faced the north and never warmed, it creaked at night, it was damp. To Emma's eyes, the dower house was a lovely building, larger than her childhood home and in better repair. Andrew seemed to like it there. What Adele wanted was to re-side at Butterhill Hall again, just as she had all her life.

In truth, Butterhill Hall was very large—certainly large enough to host the entire Clark family and a few stragglers. But Albert had never extended the invitation. He had asked his sister and brother to move shortly after he and Emma married. Adele had been caught off guard. She had argued, tried to reason. But Albert had insisted that now he had a wife, the house was for his family.

Emma and Adele had been friendly before then, but after, Adele began to distance herself. Emma sensed that her sister-in-law somehow blamed her for the move. When Albert left, Emma had suggested to Adele that she and Andrew come stay at the main house while he was away, but Adele wouldn't hear of it. "Albert has spoken," she would say with a sniff.

Andrew wasn't with his sister today. Emma guessed he didn't much care to march across the countryside like soldiers across Crimea during that war. He might be young and sickly, but he was smart.

When Adele had at last stormed the castle, she was seated in the solarium. Her hands were wrapped around the cup of lukewarm tea as if she sought to warm her fingers. It was early summer, the day bright and blue. Adele was dressed in a drab brown gown, her brown hair pulled back in a severe bun. She was pale, and dark circles shadowed her eyes. To look at her, one would think the dead of winter was upon them. She wore her bitterness like a cloak.

Emma remarked on the fine weather. Adele put aside her cup. "Enough of that," she said, as if Emma had been droning on about the fine summer day. "I have come to inquire, as I always do, if you've had any word from Albert?"

Every fiber in Emma tensed; she had the terrifying thought that, somehow, her sister-in-law knew something. It was impossible, but still. "Not recently, no," she said, and smiled serenely.

"Why doesn't he write?" she asked, eyeing Emma suspiciously. "It's not like him not to write."

As Albert had never, to Emma's knowledge, traveled very far from Butterhill Hall until he'd impetuously struck out, she didn't see how Adele could possibly know if that was true. "Well...he does write," she said carefully, "to me."

"To you, maybe, but I've not received a letter from him in several months."

"Really?" Emma tried to look surprised. "I hadn't realized. I had one—"

"May I read it?" Adele asked instantly.

"Oh." *Blast it.* Emma tried to blush, but to no avail. "I think not, dearest. It's rather personal...of a marital nature." She smiled shyly.

Adele's brows dipped. "Why is *that* necessary? And why doesn't he ever write to *me*? We are very close, the two of us. He's always kept me informed."

She was getting riled. Emma carefully put aside her teacup. "I think because he's busy exploring. And...and I understand it's not easy to post letters from that part of the world. He assumes I am passing along his news. Which I am," she hastened to assure her. "I'm careful to pass on all the news fit to share."

Adele pressed her lips together in a tight, thin line that clearly relayed her skepticism. "Then, pray tell, Emma...what is his news?"

Emma was good at keeping secrets, but she was not very good at lying. "It's rather boring! His news is that he loves exploring the corners of the world."

Adele stared at her.

"And that he likes the camels. See? Boring."

Adele folded her hands primly in her lap, much like Emma imagined a cat crossed its paws as it considered how it would go in for a kill. "Camels, is it? So where, exactly, is he exploring just now?"

"Pardon?"

"Where—*is*—he?" she enunciated.

"I've told you, darling. He's in Egypt. I can't remember the name of the town, precisely, as it was a very difficult name to read. Wadi…something. There are some ruins near there."

"Ruins of what?" Adele asked, her brown eyes narrowing.

"Of…a temple." Seemed a safe bet. Didn't all the ancient empires have temples that still stood? She picked up her tea again, but her vague anxiety caused her to bobble the cup just enough that a drop of tea fell onto her skirt. "I'm sure we'll hear all about it when the time comes." She felt a slight stab of pain just above her right eye. She hadn't quite worked out how she would eventually extract herself from the predicament she'd created. But she didn't intend to do any extracting today.

"And when will that be?" Adele asked.

This was terribly uncomfortable. Emma kept smiling and cast her gaze to the window that overlooked the gardens. "I hope by the end of the year." Fair enough. At the end of the year, she would cross the treacherous bridge she'd built.

Adele swept up her cup of tea and drank it like water,

then banged the cup against her saucer as she put it down. "I only hope you haven't bled us all dry by then."

Emma laughed with surprise. "I beg your pardon?"

"You're obviously planning yet another party. I saw them erecting a stage as I came in."

"It's not a *stage*, it's a small platform."

"The same thing. What's it for? A church service?" She laughed roundly.

"No, Adele. I'm having a party. You and Andrew are invited, of course." They were always invited, always welcome.

"Does Albert know of your extravagances?"

They'd been around this before—Adele thought that Emma was being untoward by hosting supper parties and soirees in her husband's absence. Emma pointed out that it had been his choice to go off and leave her. "Extravagances," Emma repeated.

"Yes, Emma, your *extravagances*. These…*evenings* of yours can hardly be affordable. At the last one, you hired a man who did circus tricks on the back of a pony!"

"He was very entertaining, wasn't he? Can you imagine standing on your hands in a saddle as a pony canters along? What talent that requires!"

"One cannot say the same for the high-wire walker who fell and broke his ankle before that."

"I was assured that he'd done the high-wire act hundreds of times," Emma protested.

"You are willfully missing my point. You're draining the family coffers with your entertainment, and there will be nothing left for Andrew."

It rankled Emma that Adele assumed that any inheritance would flow to Andrew. Andrew had his own inheritance. Adele never seemed to consider Albert's future heirs. Not that there would be any now, but Adele didn't know that. Emma wondered what Albert had told his sister about their inability to have a child but could never bring herself to ask.

Nevertheless, soon after her first real party, when Adele had looked on with shock at the ice sculptures Emma had purchased and cried about the waste, Emma had invited Adele to look at the estate books so she could rest assured that the money was still there. She hadn't yet.

And really, it wasn't just the money. What really seemed to antagonize Adele was Emma's presence at Butterhill Hall without Albert. Adele had never agreed with her brother's decision to see the world, not without having sired an heir, and took out her displeasure with her brother's absence on his wife.

At first, Emma had tried to play the dutiful wife, the one left behind to keep the home fires burning. She'd done it for as long as she could bear it. But a few weeks after Mr. Duffy's unfortunate demise, and an unusually rainy period, and roaming endlessly about her grand house, reading novels and needlepointing to the point of utter distraction, Emma decided that what she needed was a proper diversion. Something fun. She was lustful, bored, and desperate for some titillating company.

What she wanted was a lavish supper party. The sort that was written up in newspapers and that people would talk about for weeks afterward. She had the money to do it, too, because over the long nights of last winter, she'd studied the estate books. She was amazed by how much money the Clark family had. The gift of some savings her parents had given her when she'd wed was paltry in comparison—it might last her a year on her own. But the Clark fortune, well…she would be quite comfortable all her life. The estate turned a respectable profit, although straightaway Emma had a few ideas of how it might earn more. Estates of this size were difficult to manage, that much she knew after listening to Albert's complaints. It seemed to her it could do with a bit of modernizing. But it earned enough that Albert could wander across the globe without worrying about funds. Enough that she could have a party or two. Or three. Or more. If she liked.

When the rain ended, Emma was ready to host a supper party. Feeney was reluctant, but he slowly helped her make a list of people to invite, mostly from the area, and mostly people who knew her husband. She didn't think anyone would come, not really, but if even only one couple came, she would be delighted.

She planned for a meal of venison and ham. She enticed some musicians in the nearby village of Rexford to come and perform. She invited Adele and Andrew, too, of course, although she had desperately hoped they wouldn't attend. No one could stomp the life out of an evening quite like Lady Adele Clark.

On the evening of her party, she'd dressed in a buttery-yellow gown with tiny seed pearls embroidered into the bodice and sleeves. She'd checked in the kitchen that everything was proceeding as it should. She reviewed the table Feeney had set. Satisfied that all was in order, she'd waited for the guests who would or would not show up.

Feeney had said to expect a few to return a favorable reply and then for whatever reason, not attend. To her great surprise, everyone she'd invited attended. Footmen brought more chairs from the staff dining room. Wine flowed freely, there was laughter and singing.

Emma had thoroughly enjoyed the evening. She'd laughed like she hadn't in ages. She drank too much, she warbled alongside Mr. Kent and Mrs. Perkins, she played charades badly. The night was the perfect antidote to her months-long bout of loneliness, the perfect medicine for melancholy. One gentleman said, "We had no idea you were such a bright light, Lady Dearborn."

Because Albert had not allowed her to shine in any way. Well, she was such a bright light that she'd immediately planned another evening.

Adele had said this sudden desire to entertain was no way for the Countess of Dearborn to act and that people would talk.

"Let's not care just yet, Adele," Emma had playfully begged her.

"You must show some decorum, Emma. Particularly as your husband is not here to oversee things."

Emma didn't need a husband to oversee things.

She next hosted another soiree, then an evening of music, and after that, two supper parties.

Then she planned a party in London, far from Adele's prying eyes. Now *that* was a party—there were two threatened duels that she knew of (which were forgotten by dawn), a ballroom so crowded that the dancing spilled out of doors, and a proper and terrible scandal that arose when Miss Flora Raney was caught in a flagrantly compromising position with Mr. Daniel Woodchurch. People talked about that for *weeks* afterward.

That party was so rowdy that Adele heard about it all the way back at Butterhill Hall. "It's obscene! You shouldn't be at events where scandal is introduced! And how can you possibly afford it all? I think we both know Albert wouldn't approve of your spending his money in this way."

"Really?" Emma pretended to blink with surprise. "I think his outlook has probably shifted completely." Truthfully, one couldn't have gone on to the great beyond and care much about how much a party cost, could one? "He would want me to be happy."

Adele had snorted her opinion of that, and to be fair, she had a point.

Fanny, known to the world as Mrs. Yates, said Adele wouldn't be upset if the estate was earning more. "It's a simple matter of having something come in to cover what goes out," she'd said sagely as she bounced her baby on her knee during one visit.

Emma considered this. She went back to the books to look. They were still rich, but…her entertaining *was* costing quite a lot. That's when Emma decided to pay a visit to Mr. Donald Horn, the estate accountant.

Mr. Horn was reluctant to speak to her. He said he thought he might require permission from his lordship to review the books with her. He said that financial matters were difficult to understand.

Emma pointed out that his lordship had been gone longer than anyone had expected and that certain financial matters required attention. That she, in Albert's absence, and for all intents and purposes, *was* the earl. That she was as capable of understanding financial matters as he was of understanding how to plan a menu, but if he didn't feel comfortable speaking to her, perhaps he would feel more comfortable speaking to Lady Adele Clark, the earl's sister.

Without hesitation, Mr. Horn sat down and opened the books to review with Emma.

He very kindly pointed out a few things that were draining the family coffers. He said it was unfortunate and she should not let disappointment disturb her.

Emma didn't see disappointment—she saw opportunity.

She took her sister's thinking to heart. She never wanted to be on the receiving end of an accusation from Adele that she had burned through the Clark fortune, so she began to study how the estate was managed and how she might increase profits.

With Mr. Horn's help, she began to get rid of dead and unprofitable ventures, such as the fishery project where Albert had seeded the lake with trout. The trout were the size of minnows. She shored up other endeavors to increase efficiency and, thus, profit, such as turning their sheep business from one that produced food to one that produced wool. That change was already showing a better profit. She had ideas, so many ideas, not only to increase the income but to modernize the estate that Mr. Horn advised her that they would need more than a meeting or two to discuss it.

Her parties continued to grow in popularity, and invitations were highly coveted. Fanny said that everyone wanted to be invited to a Lady Dearborn event. Emma was having the time of her life. There was still the issue of wanting a lover, but she had to be careful about that. So she flirted and lusted and toyed with men, as it was better than nothing. She secretly considered herself a merry widow, living grandly without the albatross of Albert around her neck. Oh, she knew it wouldn't last forever, but she intended to enjoy every moment of it while she could.

Speaking of which, she hurried the tea along so that Adele would take her gloomy disposition and carry on with her day. Emma had so many things to do before her next party.

CHAPTER FOUR

LUKA HAD ARRIVED in London a week ago. He'd met
with Professor Henley three times, the two of them
spending hours talking about his research and notes,
about the luxury of exploration and expedition, about
the creativity and cleverness of humans as a whole. He
could have spent weeks in the professor's company, but
he had to finish his business in England and be on his
way to Wesloria.

One last item of business was the pocket watch, and
Luka set out one bright morning for Butterhill Hall. He
arrived by train at the village of Rexford that afternoon.
He walked to a nearby public house, bought an ale and
a steak-and-kidney pie, then asked the barmaid how to
get to Butterhill Hall.

She leaned across the table in a manner that dis-
played her bosom and pointed at the road just outside
the establishment. "Follow it five miles or so. Can't miss
the hall. Twenty chimneys if there's one."

Five miles. He winced inwardly. Not a terribly long
walk, but still.

The barmaid smiled. "Need a conveyance, love?
Have another ale. When I'm through here we can hitch
my mule to a cart, and I'll take you wherever you need
to go." She smiled suggestively.

"A very kind offer, but I don't mind the walk." He

minded the walk. He could have hired a horse, he supposed, but with no real plan, and no way to stable it, well…he'd walk.

He filled his canteen at a communal water pump and set out, formulating his plan as he strode along. It was too late in the day to call, so he decided to camp in the forest, hoping for a good stream where he could wash and shave in the morning, then call on Lady Dearborn. The weather was perfect for sleeping under the stars—the air was warm, but not too warm. The sun bright. The sky a deep shade of blue.

He'd been walking for a time, watching the sun position itself for a slide into dusk, when the first carriage passed him, the driver going so fast that Luka was almost knocked from the road. Several more carriages followed, all of them filled with finely dressed people.

Butterhill Hall came into view a short time after that—or more accurately, the twenty chimney tops did—and Luka veered into the forest and followed a game trail to a lake. Here he made a small camp. He collected enough wood to keep a fire burning low through the night and spread his bedroll over some pine needles. From there, he walked down to the water's edge and fashioned a fishing line with some twine he had in his bag and was lucky enough to catch his dinner—a trout that was surprisingly small. He had to catch three to make a small meal of them.

Luka liked being in nature. Even in the middle of the desert, he'd liked the feeling of openness, the vastness of the world above and around him. Here, he liked the monuments to God's creative glory—tall beech trees, wych elms and ash, an abundance of violets and cowslips, nightshades and foxgloves blanketing the ground. His grandmother had used the latter to cure headaches.

When he'd had his fish, he settled back onto his bedroll. As the fire turned to embers and a patch of sky overhead revealed the stars, he could hear the faint sounds of music and laughter coming from the hall.

In the dying light, he took out his journal and made an entry about the day. As an anthropologist, his own movements and habits were as interesting to him as the Bedouin tribe he'd accompanied in Egypt. He liked to keep a record of his adventures.

As he drifted to sleep, he could still hear the music and the voices drifting over the treetops.

The next morning, Luka washed in the stream and dressed in clean garments. He didn't have the most proper of clothing with him—his trunk was at his hotel in London—but he had clean buckskins and a lawn shirt, and a presentable coat and hat. He looked, he thought, like a country squire out for his morning stroll. He squatted next to the stream and shaved with a small mirror, combed his hair, packed his things and hoisted them onto his back. When the sun was above the trees, he carried on to Butterhill Hall with his condolences and the earl's pocket watch for Lady Dearborn.

As the house came into view, he was impressed with its grandeur. One long expanse of house, with wings on each end. He realized he was approaching from the back, as he could see the garden, the large central fountain, a smattering of furniture on the terrace. As he drew closer, he noticed that several of the chairs were overturned. Colorful paper streamers were strewn across the ground, as if they'd been pulled from the rafters and tossed aside. A man's neck cloth had been tied in a bow around the neck of the sculpted rearing horse that spouted water into the fountain. A recently constructed platform, judging by the fresh lumber, was littered with confetti and scattered wineglasses.

There was no sign of life, which he thought unusual for a house of this size. He looked around for a path that would wend around the house and take him to the front door when he noticed a pile of blue and pink clothing on a bench. As he moved closer, he noticed a slender foot sticking out from the pink. He realized the pink was a blanket, and the blue was a gown. And the gown was on the body of woman. She was either fast asleep (he hoped) or dead (he feared).

Luka glanced around, seeking anyone he might alert to this figure on the bench. Seeing no one, he moved closer, prepared to render aid if necessary.

The woman was lying on her side, a curtain of auburn hair covering half her face. He leaned over to see if she was hurt, or breathing, when she suddenly snorted and rolled onto her back, her eyes closed.

Assuming she was rousing, Luka shifted back, not wanting her to wake to a man looming over her. But she didn't move. He cautiously leaned forward again. The woman had fair skin, and her hair was half in its coif and half-down.

Suddenly, her eyes flew open and locked on him. After a moment that seemed interminably long to him, she shrieked and came up with a start, both feet hitting the ground, one covered in a blue slipper. She stared at him, then stared at the pink blanket she was clutching.

"I didn't... That was there," he said clumsily, gesturing at the blanket.

She squinted at him, as if trying to place him, while

she pulled some leaves from a tangle of hair. She must have concluded she did not know him, because she let out another cry of alarm.

"Whoa, wait," he said, throwing up both hands. "I should have... My apologies. I didn't intend to frighten you."

"Frightened! I'm not *frightened*. Who—" She surged to her feet to confront him, the blanket slipping from her lap. But the moment she was standing, her lovely face screwed into a pale grimace, and she pressed a hand to her forehead. "Ow, ow, ow," she muttered and slowly lowered back down to the bench. She swallowed, removed her hand, then squinted at him again. "Who *are* you?" she demanded, wincing still.

"Are you all right?" he asked.

"I am perfectly fine. Why do you ask?"

Why did he *ask*? She was wincing, she was missing a shoe, her hair was half undone, and she'd been sleeping on a bench under a blanket she seemed not to recognize. He shifted his gaze to said bench. She pushed hair from her face and looked at the bench, too. Then at him. She stood up—carefully—and folded her arms across her body. "It was a perfectly lovely night to sleep under the stars. Not that it's any of your affair."

"I would never say that it was. And I agree, a lovely night." He didn't believe she'd simply chosen to sleep here. She was clearly suffering the effects of having been pissed drunk the night before... Having been in that state a time or two himself, he recognized all the signs.

He tilted his head to one side to study her. Her gown had a stain down the side of it. Her hair was remarkably lustrous, her eyes an appealing shade of blue. She was, in every which way, an attractive woman. "I have something that might help you," he said. He dropped his bag and went down on one knee to take something from it.

"Help with what?"

"It's a tonic for your ills, as they say."

"What ills? Who says?"

He found the bottle he was looking for and showed it to her as he came to his feet. "This will help ease the pain in your head. And...settle your stomach if that's necessary as well."

She stared at the tonic. "Are you a doctor?"

"No."

"Why are you dressed like that?"

He blinked. He glanced down. "Like..."

"I don't know. A highwayman. Or a pastor."

What was she talking about? "I don't... I wasn't aware—"

"And really, it's none of your business how I feel."

One would think a woman, having been discovered in this state, would be a bit more agreeable. "I offer it all the same."

She squinted at the bottle. "Does it really work?"

"It does." He held it out to her.

She stared at it longingly but shook her head. "I don't need your help, thank you. I am perfectly fine. And I'd wager there is some unwritten rule that one must never take bottles from strangers. What is your accent?"

An abrupt change of topic. He lowered his arm and slipped the bottle into his pocket. "Weslorian."

Her eyes moved from his face to the patch of green on his collar. It was a habit of Weslorians to wear the bit of green somewhere on their person to signify their nationality. They were a proud people.

The woman was frowning again, as if trying to place

him. She pushed the hair aside that had fallen in her face again. "I don't remember you. Were you in attendance last night?"

"I was not." He glanced back at the platform. "It looks to have been a lively evening."

"In the best way. What are you doing at Butterhill Hall?" she pressed.

"I have something for Lady Dearborn."

She hesitated. Her eyes darted to the house and then back to him. "She's not here."

"She's away?" That didn't ring true, given that there had been a party here last night.

"She's away," the woman said. "May I ask what it is you have for her?"

That was either terribly rude or terribly shrewd, depending on who this woman was. "I'm afraid that is for Lady Dearborn to know."

"I know her very well, and she'll want to know what it is before she will speak to you. Believe me."

That sounded like a woman avoiding creditors or a solicitor, carrying a suit or petition from someone who wanted a piece of her estate, now that her husband was gone. He didn't think he ought to tell anyone but the countess about the pocket watch, but in the interest of moving things along… "What I have comes from her… husband," he said carefully. "Hence my reluctance to say more." That ought to do it. No one would keep a widow from news about her late husband.

And indeed, something shifted in the woman's blue eyes, but the glint in them did not convey understanding, really, but something else. She stepped away from the bench, in the direction of the house, slowly backing away from him. "If you'd like, I'll tell the butler you've come and that you might be expected again."

Why was she acting so...suspiciously now? And what did she mean, expected again? "*Je*—well, I—"

She suddenly surged forward, grabbed the pink blanket, then turned and began to walk briskly toward the house. "I'll tell the butler." She practically sprinted away from him, the blanket and her skirt billowing behind her.

"You didn't ask my name!" he shouted after her.

"You may tell the countess yourself when you see her!" she called back, then picked up her skirts and raced away.

A thought occurred to Luka... That woman couldn't possibly have been the countess, could she? *No.* He couldn't imagine any circumstance that would cause the lady of the house to sleep on a bench in the garden overnight. A friend, then? Cousin? Sister? Maid? Escaped from an asylum?

Whoever she was, he watched her disappear behind the shrubs.

It suddenly dawned on him: she probably feared being discovered in whatever she'd been about last night. That had to be the reason for her escape, and given that, he didn't trust her to pass along any message at all.

He carried on in the direction of the house. He found the path he was looking for, one that led to the front of the house. The entry was covered by a portico for carriages; he walked up the steps and knocked several times.

After a few moments, the door was opened by a footman. Behind him, a man in a dark suit with a bald pate came forward. "Good day, sir," he said. "How may we be of service?"

"Good day. I have come with a message from the late Lord Dearborn for his widow."

The man blinked. "Widow?"

"The countess," Luka prompted.

"I beg your pardon, sir, but she is not a widow. And the earl is not *late*." The butler seemed peeved by the suggestion.

But that made no sense. Luka and the butler stared at each other, clearly muddling through their respective confusion. Was this a language issue? Luka's English was quite good, but it was not his native tongue. "I don't understand. Has she remarried?"

The butler's eyes widened. "Of course not."

Did he have the wrong *house*? "This is Butterhill Hall, is it not? I am looking for the Countess of Dearborn."

"This is indeed Butterhill Hall, sir, but the countess is not a widow. Her husband has not passed. He is abroad. You are mistaken."

Luka's stomach sank on a bad feeling. Something was very wrong here. Looking back on it, he hadn't really questioned Monsieur Lapont's note to him, because Luka had heard of the passing of the English earl. Even Boris had confirmed it was true. But now he wondered if he'd been misled somehow. But why? How?

Whatever was happening, all he had to do was deliver the watch, and then he could leave this strange place behind. "I must have misunderstood," he said. "I have something that belongs to... Lord Dearborn. I have been entrusted with it to see it safely home."

The butler eyed him, sizing him up. He seemed to accept the explanation. "Your name?"

"Luka Olivien."

"If I may show you where you might wait while I see if the countess is available." He gestured for Luka to come in.

So, the countess was not away, as the woman in the garden had said.

Luka stepped into the foyer and removed his hat. The hall was quite impressive, with a soaring, domed ceiling. A grand staircase swept up then split and curled in two directions to the floor above. Luka followed the butler to a small receiving room. The furnishings were lush: thick velvet drapes were held back with gold cords. The carpet underfoot was an Aubusson weave, the same that graced the rooms of the palace in St. Edys. Porcelain figurines adorned the mantel, and a pair of ancestral paintings graced the walls. A large urn of freshly cut flowers stood at the center of a table.

The room, intended only for reception, was splendorous. In contrast, his estate in Wesloria was an old castle. His ancestors had been warriors who had routinely lost, and the austerity of defeat suited them. His castle was terribly drafty and impossible to heat in the winter. This house seemed as if it would be warm year-round.

"I am Mr. Feeney, at your service," the man said, and with a quick bow, he went out before Luka could think to speak, to ask him about the earl.

Nothing made sense. Why would Lapont have the pocket watch if the man wasn't dead? And what about Mr. Duffy? Hadn't he come as he'd said to deliver the rest of the man's effects? Luka shook his head. He was being too analytical, particularly as it hardly mattered. His task was not to understand but to give the woman her husband's keepsake and be on his way.

So he waited.

And waited.

He wandered around the room, examining the paintings and the furnishings.

At some point, a young footman brought in tea and left it. Luka helped himself to a cup and a biscuit. When he was done with that, he walked to the window to have a look at the grounds. The view was of a meadow, a tree line just beyond. The meadow was covered in yellow flowers. Cowslips or buttercups. He could see men cleaning up from the event last night, carrying away glasses on trays, raking the lawn, rolling up the colorful streamers that seemed to be everywhere.

Out of the blue, a rider went thundering past the window, onto the drive, and then to the main road. And not just any rider—it was the woman from this morning. He knew her instantly by the auburn braid of hair that ribboned behind her. She was bent over the horse's neck, riding like a band of thieves were on her heels. "What the devil?" he muttered as he watched her veer into the meadow and disappear over a rise.

A moment later, Feeney entered the salon. He bowed. "I beg your pardon, my lord, but her ladyship requests you come another day. She's a bit under the weather."

He stared at the butler. Was the woman on the bench—the rider—Lady Dearborn? What in God's name was going on here?

"Did you come by foot?" Feeney asked.

"Pardon?" He mentally shook himself into the moment. "*Je.* I walked from Rexford."

"Walked?" Feeney repeated, sounding either impressed or confused. "I would be happy to arrange a carriage to take you to Rexford."

"If you would be so kind." So much for his plans to deliver the watch and leave this area. He was curious now—the anthropologist in him was intrigued by what had happened here.

The carriage ferried him to the Rexford Arms in the village. Luka took a room for two nights. He dined on shepherd's pie in the dining room, then walked across the village green to a haberdashery. There, he bought a ready-made suit of clothing and had it marked for altering. He asked that a patch of Weslorian green be added to the lapel. The shopkeeper assured him the suit would be ready in two days' time.

That night, as Luka lay in bed with his journal, one arm propped behind his head, he wondered if it was even remotely possible that the people here truly didn't know that Dearborn was dead. Was it possible that something had happened to Mr. Duffy on his way to England? Had he never arrived to deliver the news? Or was M. Lapont mistaken about Dearborn's demise, and it was some other poor Englishman? After all, Dearborn had supposedly been in Alexandria at the time of his death. But then, how would Lapont be in possession of his pocket watch?

Even more curious was the countess. Or at least the woman Luka thought was the countess. His instincts told him she didn't want to speak to him, and it wasn't because she was under the weather. Perhaps she'd been embarrassed that he'd discovered her on the bench.

He thought of her blue eyes and her lustrous hair. He thought of her foot, dangling off that bench. He thought—and this was really diabolical of him—that she was the most intriguing part of this mystery.

He was unacceptably eager to see her again.

CHAPTER FIVE

EMMA'S OLDER SISTER was in her garden with her youngest child, Tommy, who had just begun walking. Fanny squinted up at Emma when she abruptly jumped over the low hedge that served as a fence around her garden, catching the hem of her skirt on it and yanking it free.

"What are you doing?" Fanny exclaimed as she came to her feet. "Why are you hopping around like a goat?"

"That was hardly as agile as a goat. But it seemed a more efficient way in than going around to the gate." Emma was still breathing heavily from her race away from Butterhill Hall. She'd left behind a disaster of what could only turn into enormous proportions, which is exactly what she deserved, having drunk as much as she did last night. She'd awakened on that bench, with only a vague recollection of insisting to someone—her friend Lady Sarah?—that she wanted to sleep under the stars. She suspected the blanket had come from her lady's maid, Carlotta, who was five years her senior, the eldest child of eight, and born to care for others. Emma was the second born, and apparently her purpose in life was to seek a diversion.

Her sleep under the stars had been terribly unsatisfying. Her back ached, her head hurt, and she awoke to that man towering over her. At first, she thought he was the Angel Gabriel come to deliver her, what with his longish golden-brown hair, his kind hazel eyes, a chiseled face bronzed by sun. But in the next moment she realized he was wearing buckskins and an old-fashioned coat. Gabriel wouldn't come for her dressed like that, but a highwayman would.

When she clambered to her feet, she noticed how tall he was. And very well built with terribly appealing muscles. *Weslorian*, he'd said. She'd thought him and his accent incredibly attractive, and the idea that perhaps *he* was the one she ought to take as a lover had flitted through her wine-soaked brain. But he'd ruined any hope of that by uttering the fateful words *late husband*.

He had shocked her. How could he possibly know? No one knew! But he seemed to, and she didn't know what to do in that moment. So, she did what every good coward would do and ran.

"Efficient though it may be," Fanny was saying, "I'd prefer you not give Tommy or Theo any ideas."

"Pardon?"

"Jumping the hedge."

Theo, her sister's four-year-old son, was not in the garden, but Emma quickly discarded the notion to point that out. "I apologize." She curtsied.

Fanny rolled her eyes, but she was smiling. "What is the matter with you? Here, take your nephew and come in. I've made some bread." She handed her child to Emma and picked up her basket. Emma followed her inside as she cooed and made faces at Tommy. This was a good decision. If she hadn't come, she'd still be pacing in her room, gnawing on her fingernails, frantically trying to think what to do. But Carlotta had come in and said, "Feeney says a gentleman has come to see you."

Well, she knew that. She'd presented her back to Carlotta. "Will you unfasten me?" she'd asked and then, in a moment of terrible indecision and more duplicity, which was hardly fair, seeing as how Carlotta was perhaps her dearest friend, she'd blurted, "I promised Fanny I'd come by."

"You did? But yesterday you said—"

"I forgot. Be quick, please."

"Oh." Carlotta unhooked the back of Emma's dress. "But…what shall I tell Feeney?"

"Umm…" Emma didn't have a ready answer for that. She couldn't risk running into that man again and needed time to escape. "Nothing yet. Help me dress. Then run down to the stables and tell Mr. Karlsson that I need a horse saddled right away."

"Is everything all right?"

With her back to Carlotta, Emma grimaced. Carlotta was her friend, and she couldn't do without her. But she hadn't trusted her secret to anyone. Not even Fanny. "Yes, of course! All is well," she said brightly. "It's just that I remembered only a moment ago that I promised Fanny, and now I'll be late." God forgive her, but she had been prevaricating left and right from nearly the moment she'd woken up on the bench. She wished she could ask Carlotta to write it all down so she wouldn't forget all the ways she had lied. "Now, once you've told Mr. Karlsson to make ready a mount, please tell Feeney I had to rush off as I was expected at my sister's. Unavoidable, I'm afraid. Or…or tell him I'm under the weather."

Carlotta looked dubious and concerned, but she didn't argue. She'd helped Emma out of the gown she'd worn the night before, and Emma quickly dressed in riding gear. She sent Carlotta to the stables, braided her hair in a tail down her back, stuck an old hat of Albert's on her head, and raced down the servants' stairs and out the back door.

When she arrived at the stables, Mr. Karlsson was just finishing up with the horse and looked at her with the sort of surprised expression one might have when something very important exploded and people were being warned to flee. "Milady?"

"Just help me up," she'd said, and stuck her foot into his cupped hands and launched herself onto the horse's back. "Thank you!" she'd remembered to call out to him as she spurred the horse forward.

And now Fanny was eyeing her with suspicion in her kitchen as she cut thick slabs of bread and cheese and put them on a plate to share. "Are you going to tell me why you look as if you've seen a ghost?"

"Do I?" Emma asked, pressing the tips of one hand to her cheek. In a way, she had. "Alas, no ghosts. Just... company."

"Company? But you generally like company, don't you? I thought it was all the merrier at Butterhill when you had guests."

"I *do* generally like it very much. And it *is* merrier at Butterhill when there are more people. But sometimes company outstays its welcome."

Just then, Mr. Bart, one half of the couple who lived on Fanny's property and helped with the household, entered the kitchen. "Ah, good morning, Lady Dearborn," he said to Emma with a bow. "Shall I water your mount?"

"If you would be so kind. Perhaps put him to pasture, too?"

"Aye."

"How is your ankle, Mr. Bart?" Emma asked him. The last time she'd visited, he'd fallen and twisted it and was walking with the aid of a crutch.

"Healed, it has," he said, and held out his foot, twisting it one way and then the other to demonstrate before going out.

Fanny arched a brow at her as Mr. Bart left the kitchen. "The horse to pasture? Planning to stay awhile?"

"Do you mind?"

"Of course not. But I want the truth."

Emma's heart seized. "What do you mean?"

"It's obvious."

Now her heart sank. Fanny knew her better than anyone. "Is it?" she asked softly.

Fanny nodded, hands on hips. "You're avoiding Adele, aren't you?"

And just like that, Emma's heart bounced back. She laughed. Her sister knew her well. "Just for a short time," she said sheepishly.

"I thought so." Tommy held out his arms to his mother. She took him from Emma and walked to a door that led to an adjoining room. "Mrs. Bart, I think Tommy is ready to nap."

Mrs. Bart emerged into the kitchen, wiping her hands on her apron. She greeted Emma, and took Tommy from Fanny, cooing to the baby as she went out with him.

"All right, what's your sister-in-law done now?" Fanny asked as she put a kettle of water on the cast-iron range to heat.

Emma's heartbeat was finally beginning to slow. She was desperate to confide in Fanny, but it was unthinkable. Her lie about her husband had gone on so long now that it felt impossible to broach it. She couldn't bear

Fanny's disappointment in her. And what was Emma supposed to say? *My terrible husband is dead and I forgot to tell you?*

Fanny looked at her with curiosity. "Emma? What is it, darling? You look...strange," she said. "Has something happened?"

"What? No, no. It's only Adele. Again." At least it wasn't a complete lie. It was always Adele. "She's complaining again about money," Emma said, and helped herself to some bread.

Fanny clucked her tongue. "For someone who has quite a lot of it, she certainly seems to worry about it. Haven't you told her about the profits you're seeing?"

"Of course. But it's so hard to tell her anything, really. She's in constant search of disagreement, and she never believes me." Her conscience was tweaked with the knowledge that perhaps she should not be believed when it came to important things.

The door to the kitchen suddenly burst open, and young Theo raced into the kitchen with a wooden bowl on his head and a wooden sword in his small fist. "En garde!" he shouted and pointed his sword at Emma.

Emma grabbed a wooden spoon off the table. "You'll never take me alive!" Theo raced forward, and Emma caught the child and swung him up in the air before wrapping her arms tightly around him and smothering him with kisses until a giggling Theo wiggled out of her arms. He grabbed a linen napkin from the table and held it out to Emma to tie around his neck like a cape. When he was properly dressed for a fight, he raced out of the kitchen again, one hand on top of his head to keep his bowl from falling off.

The days spent at her sister's home always left her

feeling nostalgic. Emma missed being surrounded by family and warmth. She and Fanny were only two years apart and had had the same upbringing, same education…but they'd married much differently. The truth was that Albert had wanted to marry Fanny. But Fanny had her heart set on the farmer, Phillip Yates, and had since she was twelve years old. Emma's parents were firmly against a union with Phillip—they'd wanted both daughters to marry men of titles and wealth. But they finally relented when Fanny calmly but firmly informed them that if they could not see their way to accepting her marriage to Phillip, she intended to elope with him.

To this day, Fanny was still quite in love with him. Emma could see why: he was a strapping man, handsome, a furniture maker and a farmer. They had cattle and sheep, they grew wheat and vegetables. They had two beautiful sons and a wish for more. It was a lovely, simple life. It inspired Emma's deepest longing and envy.

Emma, on the other hand—Albert's second or third or fourth choice, who knew?—now lived in an empty mansion with a dead husband and a hostile sister-in-law. She wasn't complaining—she had so much to be grateful for. But she was lonely.

"How was the party?" Fanny asked as she picked up a bowl and some flour. She and her husband had come to two of Emma's events but preferred their quiet life.

"Marvelous! It was the perfect night for Irish dancers and merriment." For some reason an image of the Weslorian popped into her head. "What do you know of Wesloria?" she asked idly as she helped herself to cheese.

"Wesloria? Nothing. Why do you ask?"

Emma shrugged. "They wear a patch of green, you know. The Weslorian people."

Fanny paused for a moment. "I think I did know that." She cracked some eggs into the bowl. "Like a tartan, isn't it, some form of identity? It reminds me of the yellow-striped dress you had when we were girls that you refused to take off."

Emma laughed at the memory. The dress had been passed on by a distant cousin, and Emma had loved it. She'd worn it until her mother threatened to burn it if she wouldn't allow it to be washed. "I wonder what happened to it?"

"In the scraps bin, I'm sure," Fanny said.

"Hallo!"

They both turned to the door. Phillip walked in, doffing his hat and tossing it artfully onto a coat-tree. "What a lovely surprise, Emma." He first went to his wife and embraced her tightly and kissed her. The sight of the couple both titillated and saddened Emma. She would give anything for that sort of affection with someone. Just about anything.

Phillip came around the table and hugged Emma, kissing her on top of her head. "Visiting for the day? You must stay for supper."

"Do you mind?"

"Mind? I insist. Your sister has grown weary of my tales, and I need a fresh audience." He winked at her. "I'll go and have a look for your bowl, darling. Theo has determined he fights better without a helmet." He left the kitchen.

"I'm glad you're staying," Fanny said. "I don't see enough of you."

Over supper, they laughed until tears fell at Phillip's

recounting of his attempts to remove a bucket that had
gotten stuck on a curious sheep's head. Later, in the drawing room, he showed Theo how to advance his sword.
Fanny worked on her needlepoint, her gaze straying to
her husband and son, and Emma sat on the couch with
Tommy in her lap. For those few hours with the family,
she first felt terrible guilt for keeping such a monumental
secret from her sister. Fanny would be so disappointed in
her. But as the day went on, she slowly forgot the terrible
secret. She forgot poor Adele, pining for her brother and
Butterhill Hall. She forgot Andrew, with the gray skin
and dark circles under his eyes.

But she did think of the Weslorian. She thought of
how uneasy she felt for what he knew. She thought of
how physically attractive he was. She thought that she
had to avoid him at all costs if she wanted to keep disaster from darkening her door. Just how she might
manage to do that, she didn't know.

CHAPTER SIX

SOMETHING STRANGE WAS happening in the village of
Rexford. It was the seat of the Dearborn earldom as far
as Luka could gather, but no one seemed to know the
earl was dead. But the man had to be dead, didn't he?
Why else would Luka have the watch?

After being dispatched from Butterhill Hall, then
wandering around the village, Luka had come to the
only reasonable conclusion: that for whatever reason,
Mr. Duffy had not arrived in Rexford. He'd obviously
not delivered the news. What else could explain it?

But that notion was dispelled later that afternoon at
the Rexford Arms. The innkeeper, noticing he was Weslorian, struck up a conversation with him. When Luka
said he hadn't arrived from Wesloria but from Egypt,
the innkeeper said he was the second man to have come
from Egypt in the space of a year.

"Oh?" Luka had asked.

"Aye. Man named Duff. Or Duffy. One or the other.
Bit dusty on the outside, but good for a laugh."

"What brought him here?" Luka asked.

The innkeeper shrugged.

"Where did he go?"

"Can't say, milord," the innkeeper said. "Struck out
for Butterhill Hall one morning and was not seen in
Rexford again."

So Duffy had come to Rexford. Then, how was it that no one seemed to know about the earl?

He spent the next day rummaging around the village, waiting for his suit to be altered. He visited a barber and had his overly long hair trimmed, his face closely shaved. He picked up his suit and a new hat and, satisfied, hired a horse that looked dangerously close to permanent retirement in the big stable in the sky. But the proprietor of the village stables swore the old mare could still make the five-mile trek to Butterhill Hall.

Luka planned to go the following afternoon. That evening, in the pub attached to the inn, he casually inquired of a few people about the earl and countess of Dearborn. He heard that the countess was pretty and visited the orphanage regularly.

As for the earl, well…no one had much to say about him. Frankly, what Luka heard most about was the lavish parties that occurred at Butterhill Hall. Some seemed to think that was a curious choice while the woman's husband was away. "No good can come of it," said the innkeeper's wife as she swept past, laden with empty plates.

Apparently, the party Luka had heard that night was not unusual.

The closer he looked at the hall, the odder everything seemed. He'd always thought the British people were a strange lot. When he'd been at Eton, he'd found the strict rules of high society—who was above who, who might speak to who, who might call on who—confusing and often nonsensical. But as a people they had never failed to fascinate him.

The next day, dressed in a new suit of clothing, and looking more presentable than he had the first time he'd visited Butterhill Hall, Luka saddled Esmerelda and started out. He guessed the trip on horseback would take an hour or so…but he hadn't figured in his mount's unwillingness to trot. A canter was out of the question. Instead, they plodded along with the sun beating down. By the time Luka arrived at the hall, he wished he was a bit fresher.

As they meandered into the drive, a footman came out to take the reins of his horse. Luka swung down and tugged at his uncomfortable waistcoat—he hadn't worn one regularly in quite some time—and walked to the front door. Feeney met him there and bowed. "My lord," he said, and then waited for Luka to state his business. As if he needed to be reminded.

"Good day, Feeney. Is Lady Dearborn at home this fine afternoon?"

Feeney gave him a quick once-over, then with a nod of his head indicated she was. He opened the door wider. "If you would please come with me, I will inform her you are calling."

He led Luka back to the same room he'd been in before. This time, Luka positioned himself at the window so he could see if she fled when she was told he'd come. If she did, he would attempt to follow her, but one look at Esmerelda, who'd been laced to a hitching post and was eating grass, and he had to accept that he'd not catch her. He was certain Esmerelda would race for no one.

He watched a breeze ripple the cowslips in the field and wondered how long he'd be made to wait. He twirled his hat in his hands. It was too stiff, this hat. He liked the hat he'd worn to England. It looked like it had been trampled by a few camels, but its utility in keeping the sun off him was unsurpassed.

He was pondering the small marble table sculpture of a bare-breasted mermaid stretched across a rock when the countess entered the room. He'd suspected it, but now it was confirmed—she was most assuredly the same woman he'd found on the garden bench, the only difference being that she looked well-rested and, well...beautiful.

He was caught a bit off guard by it, frankly. She was dressed in a simple dark brown gown with lace at the sleeves. Her dark auburn hair had been pulled back from her face and knotted elaborately on top but then fell in soft curls to the middle of her back. Her eyes were clear blue, her skin glowing. She smiled at him as if they were old friends. "Good afternoon!"

He bowed his head. "Good afternoon, milady. Thank you for receiving me."

"Of course. Now, what may I do for you?"

Surely she remembered what he'd said when he'd first come. Then again, given her state that morning, perhaps she didn't. "I, uh... My name is Luka Olivien. I failed to give you my name when we met a few days ago."

She laughed as if it was entirely unnecessary to identify oneself. "All right."

He'd been in her presence only a minute, and she'd already knocked him off balance. "You're feeling improved, I hope?" he asked.

"I'm feeling wonderfully well, thank you. Why do you ask?"

Because the last time he'd seen her, she'd looked like she'd been trampled. "I was recalling our previous meeting."

"Right," she said. "Oh dear, I have forgotten my manners. Are *you* feeling improved?"

He blinked. What did that mean? "I am very well, thank you."

"I'm so glad to hear it! Now then, how may I be of service? Are you wanting a tour? That can certainly be arranged. I'll call one of the footmen for you." She moved in the direction of a bellpull on the wall.

"A tour?" he repeated, confused.

"Of the estate. Isn't that why you've come? Everyone wants to see it. They say Henry VIII slept here when it was only a manor house. The manor house is no longer standing, obviously, but I suppose it's the atmosphere one wants to feel." She paused her step. "Well, gentlemen might want to feel it. I can't imagine any lady with the slightest knowledge of history would want to feel that particular air."

What was she talking about? "Madam... I've not come for a tour."

"Oh." She turned away from the wall. "Then...?"

Had she truly forgotten? Was she toying with him? Had he dreamed the whole thing? "I have something that I think you might want. Something that belonged to your husband."

Curiously, Lady Dearborn's smile brightened at the same time she seemed to pale. "Belongs to Albert?" she repeated. "Goodness! On my word, I don't know why he shouldn't just post whatever it is instead of troubling you to come all this way." She rolled her eyes. "It's quite inconsiderate."

Not only did she not ask what it was, she gave no indication she knew about her husband's demise. "I think, given the circumstances, it would have been difficult for him to post," he said carefully. Surely it wouldn't be left to him to tell her that her husband had died. He had misunderstood her, or she had misunderstood him. Surely, *surely*, he had not found himself in this predicament.

"Perhaps," she said with a shrug. "I've not been abroad, so I've no idea. In England, you can post anything to anywhere and trust it will be delivered promptly. Well, sir, I appreciate your diligence. You may leave it with Feeney, and he'll see that it's dealt with."

Why was she intentionally trying to avoid knowing what it was? His instinct told him she was playing a strange game with him, but he didn't understand the rules. She seemed to be working very hard not to hear any news of her husband. She hadn't even asked after the man. "I really think I ought to hand this delivery directly to you, milady," he said solemnly. Once she saw the watch, she would inquire about her husband.

But she blinked at him, looking a bit like a startled deer. "But I'm just on my way out."

"It will only take a moment, and then I will leave you to your day."

She glanced at the bellpull, then at him. He could practically feel her desire to escape. But instead of bolting, she folded her arms rather defensively across her middle and eyed him. "All right. What is it that couldn't be posted?"

Luka reached into his pocket and withdrew the watch. When she made no move to come forward, he came to her. "A pocket watch I think you will recognize. Your inscription to him is on the back."

"Oh, *that*," she said. And still, she made no move to take it from him.

He laid it down on an end table. "Lady Dearborn, there is something I must tell you. It is—"

"You look different."

He paused. "Pardon?"

"You've cut your hair."

He resisted the urge to run his hand over his head. "*Je*. Lady Dearborn, I—"

"I rather liked it long and untamed. It gave you a mysterious air." She smiled.

He didn't think his hair had been untamed. Maybe a bit windblown.

"Like a highwayman, as I might have mentioned. Or a doctor. Perhaps even a preacher. You hear about them from time to time, wandering the countryside and bringing lost souls to their flocks."

Luka was losing his train of thought.

"But today, you look very much like a country gentleman. A Weslorian country gentleman."

He didn't know what to say to that. And really, why would he say anything? The sooner he could announce her husband's demise, the sooner he could leave. "I... Thank you?" he said awkwardly. "Lady Dearborn, I'm afraid—"

He was interrupted by Feeney's sudden entrance into the room, causing Luka and Lady Dearborn to start. "Beg your pardon, milady, but Lady Adele and Master Andrew have come," he announced.

"*What?*" Lady Dearborn said. "Now?"

"Yes, now," said a voice in the hall. A moment later, that voice appeared in the form of a woman with a dour expression and severe bun. She sailed in behind Feeney, dragging a boy along with her. He was pale, terribly thin, and had dark circles under his eyes that made it seem he hadn't slept in days.

"Good afternoon, Adele! Andrew!" Lady Dearborn said brightly, gliding away from Luka. "What a lovely surprise."

Neither caller spoke; they were staring at Luka.

"Oh," Lady Dearborn said, as if just noticing him. "Yes. Adele, Andrew, allow me to present Mr...." She glanced at Luka.

Luka looked back at her with disbelief. "Olivien."

"Mr. Olivien."

The visitors didn't move, kept their gazes locked on him.

"My sister-in-law, Lady Adele Clark, and my brother-in-law, the Honorable Andrew Clark."

Dearborn's siblings? "How do you do," he said with a bow of his head.

"Who are *you*?" Lady Adele demanded, and the temperature in the room seemed to drop a few degrees.

Luka didn't understand the tension or why Lady Adele would look at him and the countess with such suspicion.

"Mr. Olivien," the countess reminded her. "He just said."

"Are you Weslorian?" the boy asked.

Luka shifted his gaze to the boy. "I am."

"I noticed the green," he said proudly. "I've read quite a lot about Wesloria. I should like to go one day."

"Not now, Andrew," said his sister, before Luka could utter a word.

"I have wonderful news, Adele!" Lady Dearborn said brightly. "Mr. Olivien has brought us news of Albert."

Lady Adele gasped. "What? When did you see him?"

Luka felt as if he'd been punched in the gut. Would he have to tell the entire family the man had died? "Well, I—"

"Recently!" Lady Dearborn blurted. "Isn't that wonderful? Albert sent his pocket watch with Mr. Olivien to us for safekeeping. He was afraid of it being stolen."

Lady Adele looked at her. So did Luka. Why would she say that? Did she believe that? Or was this part of her crazy, elaborate game?

She was holding out her hand, appearing to examine her fingertips. "He said so in his letter."

Letter? Luka didn't have a letter, and he'd said nothing of the sort. Had there been another letter? And why was Lady Adele looking at him as if she suspected he'd murdered her brother? "He sent a watch?" she asked.

"Well, he…" Luka swallowed, confused as to what his role was in this mad little tableau. "Yes," he said.

"It seems a rather strange thing to send all this way for safekeeping when he might have put it in a safe, does it not?"

"That's what *I* said!" Lady Dearborn chirped.

"Did he send more letters? Perhaps one to his sister? Or were they all addressed to his *wife*?" she asked, slanting a look at her sister-in-law.

"Oh, Mr. Olivien didn't bring me the letter," Lady Dearborn cheerfully corrected. "I received it in the post. Didn't you get one, too?"

"*No*," Adele drawled, her gaze filled with ire now.

"I'm so sorry, darling. Letters are forever getting lost with the mail, aren't they?"

Not five minutes ago, she'd been singing the praises of the English postal system. No wonder Luka could sense Lady Adele's suspicion as strongly as if it was a pungent scent. Moreover, he shared her suspicions.

Lady Dearborn obviously picked up on the doubts swirling around the room, because when Lady Adele asked Luka how he knew the earl, she interjected again. "I beg your pardon, Adele, but Mr. Olivien was just on his way out, and so was I."

"I beg your pardon, Emma, but this man has seen my brother, and I should like to know a thing or two. I'm sure he won't mind staying a bit longer to answer a sister's questions."

Yes. Yes, he would mind terribly.

"Of course! But might you ask him another time? I've invited him to stay at Butterhill."

Luka was so surprised, he snorted. Not that anyone noticed—suddenly, all eyes were on Lady Dearborn. She smiled serenely as if it had all been arranged and posted in the banns.

"I beg your *pardon*?" Lady Adele said shrilly.

Lady Dearborn gave a little laugh. "Are you surprised? The gentleman came all this way on Albert's behalf. I mean to have a party in his honor."

"Pardon?" Luka blurted. "That is—"

"No need to thank me, Mr. Olivien. You know very well Albert wouldn't have it any other way."

"*Albert* wouldn't have it any other way?" Lady Adele exclaimed.

"I like parties," young Andrew added. "May I come?"

"I *insist* you come," Lady Dearborn responded.

Luka was speechless. For the life of him, he could not unravel what was happening in this room. Something was amiss, and he was a bit player. Why was she lying about a letter? Why the sudden party and invitation to stay at Butterhill Hall? A party? For *him*?

"I'm inviting everyone from London," Lady Dearborn went on, clearly warming to the idea of a party for a total stranger. "It's the perfect time of year for a house party, don't you think? It will be my first weekend affair. And here we are, with our eighteen bedrooms and all this land! We'll have games and walks and boats—and a ball! We must have a ball. Won't it be the perfect diversion?"

"Yes!" Andrew said with great enthusiasm.

"Quiet, Andrew," his sister snapped. "Emma. Be reasonable. You just this week hosted a party. How can you possibly host one for an entire weekend so soon? Have you considered the cost?"

"I have an entire fortnight to plan it. And I have covered the costs. Will a fortnight suit, Mr. Olivien?"

He was speechless. Just a few minutes before, she'd been eyeing an escape from him. But now she'd done a complete turnaround, although how exactly this country house party fit into her scheme was a mystery. Well, he had no intention of being here in a fortnight. He'd tell her just as soon as her sister- and brother-in-law left that he planned to be in Wesloria in a week. He could imagine how she'd explain his absence: she'd say he'd left in the dead of night or received a letter from Albert and had raced back to Egypt.

"This is madness!" Lady Adele cried, echoing his thoughts. "You don't need to host another *party*. Especially not for a stranger—"

"Please don't be unkind to Mr. Olivien," Lady Dearborn said. "And really, one can never have too many parties, can one? Everyone loves them, Adele—why don't you? Life is too short without a rousing good time on occasion."

"I like them," Andrew volunteered.

"*Thank* you, Andrew," Lady Dearborn said.

Lady Adele, who'd been momentarily distracted by the talk of a party—and who could blame her, which was perhaps the point of it all along—swung back around to Luka. "How do you know my brother?" she demanded.

The change in subject was jarring. "I made his acquaintance in Cairo. There is a small community of European ex-patriots there."

"And I'm to believe you are his dear friend when I've never heard of you?"

"I didn't say that." He felt like he was on a rickety canoe that was listing either left or right, depending on who was speaking. "We are acquaintances," he added carefully, unwilling to swamp his boat.

"Why would my brother send his prized pocket watch to England with you?"

"It wasn't prized," Lady Dearborn said as she fit a loose curl around her finger. "And I already told you, Adele. Albert didn't want it to be stolen."

"It wasn't prized, and yet, he didn't want it to be stolen," Lady Adele huffed. "Did he send anything else?" she asked, her eyes narrowing on Luka. "Is that the only thing he feared would be stolen? What of his purse? What of his diamond-studded tiepin?"

"Adele, darling! You are badgering our guest," Lady Dearborn said. "Feeney!"

The butler almost instantly appeared, bowing to the room. "Please show Mr. Olivien to a guest room. I think one in the east wing. The sunrise is spectacular from there."

Feeney looked slightly stunned. His gaze shifted to Luka. Then to his mistress.

"You know the room I mean," she said.

"Ah…yes, madam." He bowed low and stepped back, waiting for Luka.

Luka was generally a self-assured man. He knew himself, made decisions quickly and decisively, and was rarely, if ever, caught flat-footed. But for once in his life, he didn't know what to do. He suspected that whatever he did would be perceived as the wrong thing by one of the women—the balance of power in this particular tribe felt volatile.

What was the easier path for him? To follow the butler? Explain he was only passing through? Tell them both their loved one hadn't sent the keepsake but had died, and his friends thought she might like to have it? Or did he ignore all the above and allow the anthropologist in him to rule? He found the interplay between people, and particularly families, rather fascinating. Particularly the British. The unwritten rules, the struggle for supremacy, the secrets that were kept. And, he would admit, he was feeling a little desperate to know what this woman was about and what would happen when her ruse was discovered.

After a moment's hesitation, with all eyes on him, he awkwardly stepped forward to follow Feeney.

He could hear the two women arguing as he followed the butler across the marble foyer and up the grand staircase. Their voices receded into silence when they proceeded down a very long hall and turned right into another long hall. The bedroom Feeney eventually showed him to—it seemed to be a half mile from the main drawing room—was quite large, with a high bed, a chiffonier, a commode, and an expansive view of rolling hills. He imaged the sunrise here was indeed quite spectacular.

"Have you any luggage?" Feeney asked.

"I do...at the Rexford Arms." As soon as the coast was clear, he would untie Esmerelda and convince her to carry him back to Rexford.

"Very good, sir," Feeney said, and, with another formal bow, left him in the room.

Luka slowly sank onto the edge of the bed and looked out the window. Whatever he'd imagined or expected when he'd come to England, it was nothing like this wild turn of events. A dead earl who was not dead to his family. A widowed countess who was not a widow who slept on garden benches. A spinster whose expression was one of murderous desire, easily cast around the room to anyone. A ghost of a boy who wanted to visit Wesloria.

Now what?

He fell back on the bed and spread his arms wide and sighed. Now?

Now, he got to the bottom of whatever the devil was happening here.

CHAPTER SEVEN

EMMA WAS NOT without a conscience. Despite Adele's unlikable manner, Emma understood that Albert's sister loved and worried about him. She understood why Adele was eyeing her with a look that suggested she wanted to strangle her.

Emma felt truly awful about her deception and would admit that there had been nights it had kept her up. But in that moment, with her lie about to be exposed, she couldn't think what to do. She needed a plan, and really, she could kick herself for not having thought of one before today. If Adele so much as dreamed Albert was gone, she would toss Emma out of Butterhill so fast that she probably wouldn't have time to collect even her shoes. Andrew would be kind to her, but he was only a boy, and Adele practically had him on leading strings as it was.

Still, this...*lie* (she hated to use that word, particularly applied to herself, as she had always considered herself to have excellent moral character) had taken on a life of its own. And if she doubted it, Adele had just moments ago accused her of playing with fire and said she didn't believe for one minute Albert approved of anything Emma was doing in his absence and, furthermore, intended to inform him of all Emma's doings the moment she saw him.

"I understand," Emma said calmly. She really did. If Albert could have come back, Adele should do precisely that, because Emma was a horrible person to have done this to her. And as if to prove just how horrible she was, her mind soon thereafter wandered to the house party as Adele continued to lecture her. She wasn't being rude, really—but she'd heard everything Adele would say a hundred times before, could probably recite it along with her. A party was much more pleasant to think about.

Why hadn't she thought of this before? What a wonderful idea! If she was going to go to the trouble of arranging a lavish party, shouldn't her guests enjoy it for a few days? She hadn't really intended to rope Mr. Olivien into it—Adele was right in that he was a perfect stranger. But she'd spoken in panic, and the moment the words *country house party* had left her lips, she'd been utterly in love with the idea.

There was much to do, of course, and she could hardly wait to get started. Which she did, by slowly moving Adele and Andrew along to the door, promising she'd send a messenger just as soon as she heard from Albert.

Adele rolled her eyes. She pushed Andrew out the door ahead of her, then glared at Emma. "I don't know what you're about, Emma, but I mean to find out."

"The only thing I'm about is planning a house party, and I sincerely hope you'll come," Emma said. She meant it. There was still a part of her, that naive young woman who had married Albert, who hoped that she and Adele could be friends again.

When Adele and Andrew had left, she sighed and pressed the tips of her fingers to her temples in a futile effort to clear her head. Now she had a more immediate problem: explaining herself to Mr. Olivien. Or, rather, coming up with something that sounded plausible. If that was possible. Lord, but she'd really knitted herself into a corner, hadn't she? What was she going to do with that rugged, striking man, who looked at her with such interest, such curiosity? Besides entertaining the fantasy of taking him as a lover—*that* was certainly not possible, as it would be terribly wrong.

But would it?

What are you thinking?

She was appalling herself. She shook her head and walked to the window, her hands on her hips, taking in deep breaths to stop herself from traveling down any other rabbit holes.

One thing was clear, she had to get rid of the man before he ruined everything. Because Mr. Olivien had obviously wanted to tell her that Albert was dead—she could see it in his pained expression, the look of sympathy and confusion in his eyes. She hated when sympathy and confusion made her feel so intolerably guilty. Which she was, quite obviously, but she didn't care for the way guilt made her feel a bit nauseous.

Anyway, she didn't have time to ruminate in her guilt. *Think, Em.* All right…if Mr. Olivien informed her that Albert was dead, she would thank him for the news and send him on his way. Except…she couldn't trust that he'd not mention it to someone else. Feeney, a footman, someone at the inn.

Think. How exactly would she convince Mr. Olivien of her need to stay silent with the news he would inevitably give?

She couldn't let him and Adele meet again. *What if*

he was an inspector? Sent by the bank? The government? She really didn't know who else knew of Albert's demise. What of Cairo and London and all points in between? Who had Mr. Duffy told?

Her heart was beating with anxiety as she thought things through. Mr. Olivien wouldn't dare accuse her openly, would he? But he might very well mention Adele's suspicions and use that to suggest he suspected Emma knew Albert was dead and was spending his fortune. No, she had to think of a way to dismiss him without him uttering a word to anyone.

What if she simply acted shocked and demanded proof? Her husband's remains! Simple.

But...what if Mr. Olivien knew Albert was buried in a grave somewhere? Of course he must—he'd just come from Egypt and would know.

Then she'd say she needed something more, that she'd only just made his acquaintance and couldn't trust his word on this. How did she even know he was who he said he was? Exactly, and that's what she'd say. Perfectly reasonable, practically expected.

Except she probably shouldn't have invited him to stay in her house if she found his word so suspect or presented him as a dear friend of Albert's to her sister-in-law. Blast her impetuosity.

She was being ridiculous. He'd given her the pocket watch. He'd obviously been trying to do a kind thing. And she generally prided herself on her good judgment of character (well, except for Albert) and had detected nothing suspicious about the man.

She walked around the drawing room, one hand on her waist, one hand on her forehead, thinking. This was a bit of a tricky—

"Madam?"

Emma jumped what felt like a foot and whirled around. Feeney had come into the room, his steps silent on the new Aubusson carpet. "I beg your pardon. I startled you."

She gave a little laugh and pressed her hand to her heart. "I suppose I was quite lost in thought. What brings you?"

"The guest," he said. "Is there any information—"

"He's a friend of Albert's," she said quickly, before Feeney could question her. "I've asked him to stay on for a time. He came all this way, after all."

"Yes, ma'am," Feeney said carefully. He, too, looked suspicious of her. "He informs me he has been a guest at the Rexford Arms and his things are there."

"Oh. We should fetch them for him. Mr. Barnes, the proprietor, will be happy to help collect his belongings and send them."

"Shall I return the horse as well?"

"The horse?"

Feeney gestured to the window. Emma followed him over, and they both looked down to where a horse was sleeping standing up. "Is that…Esmerelda?"

"It is," Feeney responded.

The mare had been one of the utility horses at Butterhill, until she grew too stubborn for her own good. "I thought she'd been put to pasture somewhere."

"Indeed, she had been," Feeney said, "but I understand the pasture didn't suit her. Mr. Karlsson sold her to the stablemaster in the village. It would seem he hires her out occasionally."

"Hires her *out*?" Emma laughed with disbelief. "She can hardly be persuaded to allow anyone on her back, much less walk. I do hope Mr. Olivien didn't pay much for her."

"Shall I return her when I send one of the lads to fetch his bags?"

"I think so. And perhaps with a warning to the stablemaster that she is not suitable for hiring." She turned from the window. "Is our guest in his room?"

"He is. Shall I ask him to join you?"

"No, no. I'm very much occupied this afternoon." She would think of something to occupy her.

"Shall I invite him to dine this evening?"

"Umm…" Emma's preference was to avoid him, but Feeney was already eyeing her warily. It didn't help that she dined alone most evenings and had complained more than once to her butler that she was bored by her own company. "Yes," she said. "Of course," she made herself add, as if she'd not hesitated, as if it hadn't even been a thought. She smiled.

"Very good, madam," Feeney said, and took his leave.

She would think of a way to avoid being alone with Mr. Olivien. A massive headache, perhaps? She could feel one building in her neck and rubbed her nape. It was the sort of pain she often felt in Adele's company, when she found herself gritting her teeth. Well, she couldn't sit around here, waiting for Mr. Olivien to show up and tell her Albert was dead. Or anyone else for that matter. What she needed was to clear her head and think seriously for once how she was going to solve the problem of Albert.

She retreated to her room and changed to a walking gown and pulled on her walking boots. She went down the servants' staircase in the event Mr. Olivien was ambling down the main one and escaped through a side door before Feeney or anyone else could interrupt her progress.

Much better. There was something about bright summer sun and cloudless skies that always made her feel happy and thankful to be alive and residing at Butterhill Hall. Her darkest thoughts were pushed back into the shadows the moment sunlight entered her brain.

She strode along a familiar path to the lake and then around it, her arms swinging. She walked forty minutes or more, interrupted only by a few geese who were in no hurry to cross her path. She walked and walked, but by the time she turned toward the house, she had not come up with any solutions. Still, she was optimistic that a solution would present itself. She hadn't done anything terribly wrong, after all—she'd simply failed to mention a few things.

Which was a notion so absurd that she couldn't help but roll her eyes.

She turned up the narrow path to the gardens and was startled to see Mr. Olivien striding toward her with purpose. She made a sound of alarm and pressed both hands to her heart. *Now* what?

"Did I startle you?" he asked. "I do beg your pardon—I thought you saw me here. I've been looking for you."

"Me?" She sucked in a breath. *Get hold of yourself. Don't act so guilty.* "Were you looking for me here, or did you mean to stroll? You really ought—the lake is quite lovely this time of day."

"Your butler said you'd gone missing—"

"Missing?"

"No." He shook his head. "Forgive my poor use of

English. He said he didn't know where you'd gone. And I was looking for my mount."

"Oh, you're looking for Esmerelda."

He opened his mouth as if he intended to speak but then closed it. His beautiful hazel eyes shone beneath frowning brows. "How do you know her name?"

"Esmerelda? She once belonged to us, until she wasn't much use. Mr. Karlsson—he's the new stable-master here—sold her to the public stables in Rexford. I was aghast that the village stables hired her out to you. She's ridiculously stubborn."

He looked at her like he didn't trust this information. "I need her," he said simply.

"Why?"

"Why?" He sighed. He removed his hat and pushed his fingers through his hair, then settled his hat on his head and his hands on his hips. "Lady Dearborn, you've been very kind to invite me to stay—"

"It was my pleasure! Albert would insist."

"*Je*, well, I was a bit caught off guard in the moment, didn't know what to make of it, really, as we are not acquainted. And at the time, there seemed to be a domestic storm brewing in your drawing room."

"A domestic storm!" She laughed. "How apt. And correct. There is *always* a storm brewing between me and my sister-in-law. We have very different views about most things, as you may have gathered."

"*Je*," he said, and once again took his hat off and dragged his fingers through his wonderfully thick hair. He seemed uncertain how to proceed.

"What is *je*, by the way?"

"It means *yes* in Weslorian."

"Weslorian sounds lovely to the ear," she said.

Mr. Olivien was looking down at his hat. He was so...*virile*. Masculine, exuding strength with his muscular build. He was wearing a fine suit of clothing, the bit of Weslorian green sewn into the cuff of his coat. His hair had been trimmed since the first time she saw him, and it occurred to Emma that maybe she didn't want to avoid him like she thought. "I wish I understood your language. How interesting it would be to speak more than English, to open parts of the world that I've never seen."

He suddenly looked up from his study of his hat. "Madam... Lady Dearborn. We need to talk."

Oh dear. "And we will," she said reassuringly as she began to inch her way around him. "Tonight, at dinner. I'm afraid I can't now, as I'm expected." She wasn't ready to face him just yet, needed all her wits around her, and edged past him. "You really should walk along the lake path. Oh, and Feeney sent Esmerelda to Rexford with a footman who will collect your things while he's there."

"I beg your pardon?" he asked, turning around as she passed him.

"Butterhill Hall is much more comfortable than the Rexford Arms. At least I assume it must be," she said, walking backward. "I never had the pleasure of staying there. But Mr. Barnes was a true friend when my father died. He's the proprietor, you know. Hordes of relatives came to pay their respects, and he accommodated them all. And do you know, my mother passed not six months later?" she asked as she continued moving away from him. "My sister said she died from a broken heart...but then again, Fanny can be terribly romantic about such things. I'm far more practical. I think our mother's death had more to do with the amount of whisky she drank each day. She was convinced of its healing properties. Poor thing lingered for *weeks*."

He was staring at her, seemingly at a loss as to what to say.

"Dinner at eight!" she called cheerily. She turned away from him and strode as fast as she could without running.

He thought they should *talk*? Well, she could talk with the best of them. She could fill empty air without batting an eye, and that's what she would do to keep *him* from talking.

You might have something there, old girl. In her panic to keep him from saying what he so obviously wanted to say, before she knew how to best respond, it occurred to her she could be like the Persian queen, Scheherazade! Not to keep her head on her shoulders but, more realistically, to keep him from speaking. Stories! She would tell him tales of everything she knew. She really could talk about anything.

Well, except about her husband, of course. The irony struck her as both amusing and disturbing.

It was settled then, at least for the moment, at least until she could think her way through this debacle she would avoid him as best she could, and if she was cornered, she'd talk until his head spun and his eyes bulged and hope he'd give in and go on his merry way. And if he insisted on having his say, she would be ready with her response.

Not an ideal strategy, admittedly, and there did seem to be an argument for honesty here. But Emma didn't have time to think about that right now. She had a party to plan and a man to avoid.

CHAPTER EIGHT

LUKA FOUND HIMSELF STUCK. Or, not stuck precisely, as he could make an escape from Butterhill Hall on foot. But stuck in a rather metaphorical manner. Apparently, at the very least, he'd be forced to wait for his things.

He thought longingly of his trunk in London. He'd told the hotel he'd be away two days at most, and he was a few days past that. The practical side of him advised that he corner Lady Dearborn, explain her husband had died, and begin the long walk to a train that would take him back to London.

But—and this was generally his downfall when it came to attractive, engaging women—he was intrigued by her. Attracted, curious, a little dazzled—all the things he felt when a woman caught his undivided attention. He knew she was toying with him, avoiding the subject of her husband by nattering on, the few times he could catch her, filling the world around him with a cascade of words so breathlessly delivered that he could not possibly speak. He found it endlessly fascinating how masterfully she could steer a conversation to her desired path and so breezily avoid hearing him say anything she didn't want to hear. He appreciated the skill that took.

But why did she do it? What was she hiding?

Instead of following her now and demanding her

attention, he took her advice and walked around the lake. It was indeed beautiful—tall, stately tree canopies shaded the path. Forest flowers were blooming, giving the appearance of a colorful carpet of purple, yellow, and white. The walk gave him the space to think about what he would do next. He couldn't simply linger here—he needed to be in Wesloria. He had no doubt Lady Dearborn would redouble her efforts to avoid him, because the moment he'd said they ought to talk, she had ratcheted her game. Every hour that passed made it clearer there was nothing for him to do here.

His personal fascination and anthropological interest aside, he recognized that this was none of his affair and acknowledged that he was allowing himself to be diverted to avoid an unpleasant situation at home. He'd lingered long enough and decided, by the time he'd walked the whole of the lake, that when he received his things from Feeney, he would inform Lady Dearborn of the tragic news and return to London straightaway.

But that didn't mean his curiosity about the secrets she was hiding was in any way satisfied. What would make her go to such great lengths to avoid hearing what she clearly already knew? Or was she truly ignorant of her husband's death?

He supposed he'd learn the answer tonight at eight o'clock.

LUKA DID NOT learn the answer that night, because after his things had been brought to him, and the dinner hour had at last arrived, and Luka presented himself in the dining room at exactly eight o'clock, there was no Lady Dearborn.

"I'm afraid she has taken her meal in her room,"

Feeney said. He presented a silver tray to Luka with a single glass of wine.

Stunned, Luka stared at the butler. But she'd said… "In her room?" he repeated.

"A headache, I believe," Feeney said stoically.

A headache, his arse. "What am I to do, then?" he asked, looking at the long dining table set with fine china and crystal, an enormous floral arrangement, and a pair of silver candelabras.

"The cook has prepared venison this evening," Feeney said.

Luka's stomach rumbled at the suggestion of meat. He hadn't eaten since this morning. He sighed with frustration but took a seat at the table nonetheless. One had not wandered about the desert for months without learning not to pass up any chance at a meal.

He dined on vermicelli soup, venison, and apricot comfit. It was the best meal he'd had in a very long time. He was feeling quite mellow by the end of it. "The wine," he said to Feeney as he cleared the table around him, "is excellent."

"It is Italian," Feeney said. "Her ladyship appreciates fine wine."

A point in her favor.

Luka retired that evening completely sated.

The next morning, he rose with the sun. A footman brought him coffee and opened the windows to the cool morning air. Luka took a seat at the small table near the windows to write in his journal. As he sipped his coffee, Luka felt the brush of a morning breeze, stood up, and walked to the window with his cup to view the day. But it wasn't the day he noticed, it was Lady Dearborn. She was on the long lawn that went down to the lake, seated on the ground, her back to him, her legs beneath her skirt. Her hair was unbound, hanging nearly to her waist. Next to her were two sheep dogs, curled up, resting back-to-back. Her head was bowed in a way that made him think she was reading a book in her lap. Or possibly praying, but for some reason, that didn't seem as likely to him.

He watched her until she stood up a few minutes later. She shook out her skirts, revealing her bare feet. She had indeed been reading: she tucked a book under her arm and spoke to the dogs, who both quickly came to their feet, tails wagging. She began to stroll up the lawn to the house, the dogs trotting on either side of her.

He assumed she was heading in for breakfast. He packed away his journal and his few things and fastened his bag. He went down to breakfast with the intention of taking his leave immediately after he told her about her husband.

A footman directed him to the breakfast room. He walked in, fully expecting to see Lady Dearborn at the table.

She was not there.

A moment later, Feeney swung in through a servants' door with a tray. "Good morning."

"Good morning, Feeney. Is Lady Dearborn... Will she come to breakfast?"

"I'm afraid not," Feeney said, and pulled out a chair for him.

"No? Still indisposed? Shall I venture a guess? A headache?"

Feeney avoided eye contact. "She didn't say."

"No, I'm sure she didn't. Could you pass along to

her ladyship that I should like a word the moment she feels able? And then I'll take my leave."

"Very good." Feeney went out.

Luka ate again with gusto. The breakfast of eggs and black pudding was as delicious as last night's meal. One could be convinced to stay on indefinitely at Butterhill Hall for the food alone.

When breakfast was done, he wandered around the hall, taking in all the fine furnishings and art. There was an endless parade of rooms, some formal, some small and cozy, and all of them grander than anything he or his family owned.

He eventually bored of touring the house and sought out Feeney to ask if the lady's health had improved.

Feeney gave a quick but unmistakable roll of his eyes. "I have not been informed," he said calmly as he bustled about the foyer.

This game of cat and mouse was beginning to grate on Luka. The day felt too warm, and he was too idle.

He went outside, to the back terrace and down the steps to the long lawn that led to the lake. There, he followed the lake path, feeling like an utter fool for having stayed on as long as he had, tricked by the countess.

As he neared the water, he could hear voices. Feminine voices. He followed the path around the boulder and saw them then: one woman in a maid's uniform was sitting on a rock, her chin propped in her hand as if she were bored. Next to her, a discarded gown. And in the water, up to her waist, wearing only a chemise as far as he could tell, was Lady Dearborn.

He was so startled that he stopped walking. When Lady Dearborn spotted him, she looked just as startled. "Oh," she said.

The maid turned to see what had her attention, and when she saw Luka, she shrieked. She leaped to her feet and picked up the yellow-and-white gown and held it aloft, blocking his view of Lady Dearborn.

"Carlotta, it's our guest, Mr. Olivien!" Lady Dearborn called from somewhere behind the gown. "Good morning, Mr. Olivien! I have been remiss in not inviting you for a swim, I think."

Is this what *indisposed* meant in this corner of England?

"I'm getting out," she said. "May I have a towel, Carlotta?"

"Not at the moment," Carlotta insisted. She was glaring at Luka, and he could hear Lady Dearborn splashing toward shore. It alarmed him, not because she had the daring or audacity to present herself in this manner but because of his body's instant reaction to the few curves he'd just seen. He felt suddenly very hot, the sun beating down on him harder than it ever had in the desert. He lifted his hand. "I beg your pardon!" he called out and took several long strides on the path, away from her, out of sight before she could emerge completely from the water and set him on fire.

When he was at a safe distance, he shrugged out of his coat and draped it over one arm. This business was carrying on far too long. He meant to tell her today, preferably when she was not *en déshabillé* in the middle of a lake.

She would have to return to the house eventually, and Luka decided to head her off at the terrace before she could escape. He climbed up the steps; from this vantage point, he could see anyone coming from the lake. He waited a quarter of an hour before he began to wonder if he had somehow missed them. Just when he was about to give up and go in search of Feeney, he heard voices that were suspiciously coming from the walled garden on the west side of the lawn.

He came down from the terrace and went to the open door in the stone wall of the garden. When he stepped through, he was greeted with beds of flowers: roses and foxgloves, peonies and phlox. At the back of the garden was a stone arch that led into another section. He wandered through the colorful and fragrant display and passed under the arch and into a vegetable garden. At the far end, bent over some plants, was a woman with a large sunhat on her head. Luka didn't want to startle her, so he said, from a distance, "Good afternoon!"

The woman stood up and twirled around. "Goodness! Mr. Olivien, it appears we meet again!"

Even from this distance, Lady Dearborn's smile radiated. Her hair was tucked up under the hat. And she was barefoot again, her slender feet covered with leaves and garden debris. "I thought perhaps after our last meeting you would have fled Butterhill." She laughed at her remark.

The minx was trying to chase him off with these ridiculous antics, that much was clear. In that moment, with his gaze on her bare feet, Luka decided he was not going to go. Furthermore, he was not going to mention her husband until she did. Two could play at this bizarre game.

Another woman suddenly stood up. It was the maid; he hadn't seen her behind Lady Dearborn.

"May I introduce Miss Carlotta Davis? She's the one that shrieked at you at the lake. She's been with me for an age. Haven't you, Carlotta?"

"For all of my youth and more," Carlotta said.

Luka bowed in the direction of Carlotta. He was feeling a slight undertow, a force tugging at him. Lady Dearborn was a beautiful woman, and it left him feeling terribly conflicted, caught between frustration and attraction. Moreover, she smiled as if she knew exactly how he was feeling and was enjoying it. "I missed you at breakfast," he said.

"Oh, I rarely have breakfast."

"What?" Carlotta said, seeming surprised.

"Not when I've so much to do! Didn't you say just this morning that you don't know how I possibly manage with all I must do?"

"Did I?" Carlotta asked, frowning uncertainly.

"I'm certain you did." Lady Dearborn smiled again.

The undertow dragged Luka a little deeper. "Nevertheless, madam, I was hoping to have a word with you this morning and be on my way. Perhaps we could speak now."

"Now? I'm afraid that's not possible." She suddenly removed her hat, and her damp hair tumbled down over her shoulder. "I was just going in after my swim. Why don't you tell me your news this evening, at dinner?"

"I beg your pardon, but I don't trust that I would see you at dinner."

"Whatever do you mean? Of course you will!" She said it as if she had been at every meal and he was ridiculous to ask.

"Will I? I am beginning to wonder if you eat at all."

"I have a very healthy appetite for many things. I do indeed eat, sir. I would say cake is my downfall. What is yours?"

It certainly wasn't cake, he thought, his gaze flicking over her. "I think it best we speak now, if you wouldn't mind. It won't take but a moment. You understand." He gave her a pointed look. "In fact, I feel quite certain you understand."

"I do. And I adore hearing news," she said. "If I may be a bit selfish, I hope the news is about your travels, Mr. Olivien. I have forever longed to travel, but unfortunately, my presence is needed here. It's quite a large estate. You can't imagine how much goes into the management of it." She reached into a basket she was holding and withdrew a carrot. She wiped it on the side of her skirt as she observed him, then casually bit off the tip of the carrot and chewed. "Would you like a carrot? I find they are best straight out of the earth. It's the soil here at Butterhill, someone once told me. Who was it that told me?" she pondered, squinting at Carlotta.

Carlotta's eyes widened. "I don't know."

"It will come to me." She took another bite. "I should tell you the story of how this garden came to be. It was once considered the perfect spot for a graveyard. But not just any graveyard—a graveyard for *criminals*."

Luka had to admire her tenacity—she was throwing everything she had at him to avoid the news. He couldn't help but wonder just how far she'd go.

She turned to Carlotta and handed her the basket. "Would you please take them to Mrs. Hawley?" she asked sweetly.

"Now?" Carlotta asked, staring at Luka.

"Now, please," Lady Dearborn confirmed. "I think she would like them to prepare for tonight. Mr. Olivien will be awestruck at how good they are."

Carlotta took the basket and eyed Luka suspiciously as she passed him. He held up his hands in surrender. He'd done nothing but come into the garden.

Carlotta's mistress took another bite of the carrot
and began to saunter toward him. "She's rather protec-
tive of me." She moved with some suggestion that surprised him. She stopped a foot or so before him, took
another bite of the carrot, and casually munched it as
she studied him.

He could tell her now. All he had to do was utter the
words *Your husband is dead* and be on his way. But for
whatever reason, his tongue refused to work. Maybe because her gaze was on his mouth. Or her mouth was on
the carrot. Or there was a sparkle in her eye. "You're a
curious man, Mr. Olivien," she said, pointing her half-
eaten carrot at him.

"I beg your pardon? Of the two people in this garden, *I'm* the curious one?"

Her gaze fell to the patch of green on his cuff. "I've
never met a Weslorian before. Are they all like you?"
She lifted her gaze, and the pool of her eyes tried to
suck him into the dangerous eddy he knew was just
beneath the surface.

"Like me. Like everyone. Like you."

"*Really,*" she said, as if she found that fascinating.
"I've been told that there are very few like me. Mostly
by people who don't approve of me." One corner of her
mouth tipped up in a lopsided smile.

"Why would anyone not approve of you?" he asked
her lips.

Her blue eyes shimmered with delight. "Come to
supper and find out."

He narrowed his gaze. "That sounds like a challenge,
Lady Dearborn. Which I will readily accept. But can I
trust you to appear? I certainly hope so, as I think your
butler has grown weary of me."

"Nonsense. Feeney loves company."

"Debatable. You didn't answer my question."

"Yes, Mr. Olivien, you can trust me. To a point, anyway. You should really ask yourself if any of us can trust anyone completely."

He arched a brow. She was good. She was *very* good at derailing him. "What does that mean?"

She shifted even closer, her body nearly touching his, her head going back a bit so that she could smile up at him. "It means…" She hesitated, her eyes a little heavy, her lips slightly parted, and for a moment, a slender moment, Luka thought she meant to kiss him. It was as preposterous as it was titillating, and he felt himself tense like a cat, ready to spring. "That I suppose you'll find out at supper." With a soft laugh, she shifted back, took another bite of her carrot, and stepped around him.

Luka stood rooted to his spot, the scent of her perfume overwhelming his senses in her wake.

He'd just wasted his opportunity. He'd been quickly and thoroughly defeated.

He heard her humming as she left the garden. He could feel his body humming, too. He could still feel the magnetic pull of her when she'd stood close to him. That look in her eye, as if she wanted to kiss him. If he'd been a young man, he might have acted before he thought, might have taken advantage of the opportunity he sensed she was presenting. But he was not such a young man anymore, and there was a practical side of him that couldn't believe that could have possibly been her intent.

He did not understand what the devil was happening at this hall, but he was tantalized.

CHAPTER NINE

THAT FLASH EMMA saw in her mind's eye was none other than herself, marching into madness. Not only could she not seem to avoid her restless guest but, shockingly, she didn't want to. Somewhere between his arrival and that moment in the garden, she'd become obsessed with his handsome face and his hard physique. She'd relished how he looked at her, as if she was from another world. And she'd positively simmered when his gaze skimmed her body at the lake before Carlotta blocked his view.

Carlotta had scolded her for her behavior. She'd been against Emma swimming as it was, certain someone would see and disapprove. "What if your sister-in-law had seen you like this? You're practically naked. You're tempting fate, swimming in the sunlight where anyone can see you."

"I've nothing better to do in this heat than tempt fate," Emma had replied indifferently. And while she wouldn't disagree that she was behaving a bit indecently, she wasn't *practically naked* at all. She'd had on a corset and chemise and drawers, all the things she wore under her gown every day. And it was so bloody hot. No wonder women fainted in the heat.

But Emma would accept that she had been tempting fate a little too earnestly in the garden later. She'd stood so close to him while nibbling a carrot and smiling suggestively. She had no defense for herself, other than she was driven by a force greater than her conscious will: undiluted desire and years of want. She'd contemplated kissing him, and there was something about his demeanor that suggested he wanted to be kissed, a gleam in his eye that excited her. The way he looked at her made her feel exposed, both in body and in mind. But curiously, he had not told her his news. He'd let her walk away.

It was all very thrilling and provocative, and even though she knew she was getting mired deeper and deeper into her deceit, she was enlivened by his presence and this strange game she was playing.

After she'd left Mr. Olivien standing there, she'd come back to her suite of rooms and asked Carlotta to draw her a bath. "I believe I'll dine with him this evening," she said as casually as she could manage.

Just as she expected her to, Carlotta gave her a look from the corner of her eye. "Is that wise?"

These days, nothing about her life seemed particularly wise. "Oh, I'd wager not," she said cheerfully. "But he intrigues me. Aren't you intrigued? He has the most arresting eyes."

"Aye, he's handsome, I'll give him that," Carlotta agreed.

With her back to Carlotta, Emma smiled. "He doesn't compare to Albert, of course." Which was not an untrue statement—Albert's good looks were far inferior to those of Mr. Olivien's. Frankly, she doubted few men could compare to Mr. Olivien. It wasn't so much that he had a perfect face, because he didn't. It was rather everything about him taken as a whole. He was robust. Muscular and bronzed by the sun. He could probably pick her up with one hand and toss her onto the back of a horse.

She imagined he had a wife somewhere who was eternally grateful for that.

She didn't know if he was married or not, and unforgivably, she didn't care. She was glad he was staying another evening, despite Carlotta's words and disapproving looks. Despite the danger he posed to her way of life. Despite having avoided him just so that he'd go. But Emma's restlessness had done her in. Over the last couple of years, she'd forgotten how to be prim and proper and always above reproach.

She was thoroughly reproachable now.

After she bathed, she chose a soft blue gown with a pleated low-cut bodice. Gold tassels dangled from the elbow-length sleeves. Carlotta wove her hair at the back of her head and framed her face with soft, wispy curls. Emma was pleased with the effect—she was as fashionable as any lady from London. She was looking forward to flirting, that delicate dance between her desire to be admired and to have the evening not ruined with any word of Albert.

She had no hope that she'd be able to avoid the latter. But she did hope it would, at the very least, be a diverting meal.

As she made her way to the drawing room, she passed through the wide main corridor that connected the east and west wings. A cold wind shot through an open window, lifting her hair and causing the wall sconces to flicker. A storm was brewing—unsurprising, given how hot it had been the last few days.

A moment later, she heard the distant rumble of thunder and could feel a change in the temperature. She smoothed her hair and carried on, pausing to instruct a footman to close the north windows.

Mr. Olivien was already in the drawing room when she entered. He turned, his gaze skimming over her before he bowed low. He was dressed in a dark, formal suit of clothing. His hair was brushed back, his neck cloth perfectly tied, his beard neatly trimmed. He looked less rugged, but still quite powerful. Like a king. A prime minister. A lord. Her attraction sizzled in her.

"You came," he said simply.

"Yes, of course I came," she said breezily. She smiled, pretending that she hadn't avoided him the last two days.

A sudden, closer rumble of thunder caused them both to turn to the massive windows that overlooked the long lawn. A gust of wind lifted the drapes, followed by another thunderous burst, this one even closer. "It would seem we are in for quite a storm," she said, and hurried across the room to shut the window. The wind had picked up dramatically, and another gust tried to suck the window out of her grasp. Mr. Olivien was suddenly behind her. He reached around her and caught the window, pulling it to a close so that she could latch it.

With the window closed and her hands on the sill, she was aware of him at her back. She stood perfectly still, her gaze on a darkening, swirling sky, which seemed to mirror what she felt in her body. She willingly sank into the solid feel of a man at her back. She liked that feeling, longed for strength to surround her and lift her up and hold her close and protect her. "Does it storm like this in Wesloria?" she asked.

"It storms like this everywhere," he said softly into her ear, then moved away from her.

Disappointing. She was hoping he'd lean over her shoulder to have a look at the skies raging outside. She was hoping he'd press against her back, put his arm around her middle, and draw her against him. But when she turned from the window, he'd retreated to the center of the room again. "It must be terribly cold in Wesloria. It's rather mountainous, isn't it?"

"The winters can be brutal," he agreed. He sounded bored.

Of course he was—he did not seem like a man given to small talk, and here she was, nattering about weather, one of the small topics of conversation she could hardly abide herself. When she met someone, she wanted to get right to the meat of things. Who were they, how had they come to have married this or that person, did they find the rector's sermon on Sunday to be a bit too preachy? He was probably chomping at the bit, desperate to tell her about Albert and carry on. She didn't know what to say, how to keep him talking, how to keep him from the subject of her husband.

Scheherazade. Start with a story. And perhaps not one about a graveyard.

She was saved from having to start just then by Feeney, who suddenly burst into the room, his eyes immediately darting to the window she'd just closed, and then to the carpet beneath it. The few hairs on top of his head had been blown out of place. "I beg your pardon, madam, but I was helping to close the windows. A terrible storm is upon us."

As if they hadn't noticed.

He strode to the sideboard and quickly poured wine, placed the goblets on a silver tray, and hastily presented them to Emma and Mr. Olivien. His breathing was labored, as if he'd sprinted to the drawing room.

Emma took the wine from the tray. She knew her butler, knew he'd worry about rain coming in and ruining the floors. "Take all the time you need to batten down our hatches, Feeney," she said cheerfully. "We'll be fine. Won't we, Mr. Olivien?"

Mr. Olivien smiled faintly, took the other glass of wine, and said, "We will."

Feeney gave a curt nod. He returned the tray to the sideboard and exited the room as quickly as he'd come in, like a captain trying to save his ship from going down.

Emma and Mr. Olivien looked at each other. She was reminded she needed to talk so that he wouldn't. "I have an amazing story to tell you." She turned away from him, grasping for a suitable tale to keep him occupied. She took a seat on the settee, relaxing against the back of it instead of sitting primly on the edge with her back ramrod straight. She never saw the point of perfect posture. Why shouldn't everyone be comfortable? But her mother, and then her husband, had pressed upon her the importance of sitting straight, and never with any good explanation why.

"Won't you have a seat, Mr. Olivien? You look as if you mean to bolt at the first sign of trouble."

He looked at her curiously. "Are you expecting trouble?"

"One never knows, does one?" She gave a breezy wave of her hand. "But if we have it, I've no doubt you will conduct yourself splendidly. One doesn't simply hie oneself off to Egypt without being prepared for a bit of trouble, does one?"

"What has led you to believe I *hied* myself there?"

"Well, then, what took you there? Were you desperate to see the pyramids?"

Mr. Olivien remained standing, his gaze on the window, where great flashes of lightning were periodically illuminating the room. He looked so terribly elegant that she wanted to sigh.

"I am an anthropologist."

It took a slight moment for Emma to refocus her brain. She would have rather he'd admitted traveling for love or to catch a fabled beast. "An...anthropologist." She repeated the word carefully. She thought she knew what it was, but she wasn't entirely certain.

Mr. Olivien shifted his gaze to her. "Anthropology is, in short, the study of humanity. I've been studying and collecting information about the migratory habits of the Bedouin tribes with the goal of writing a book about the infrastructure of trade routes." He smiled a bit sheepishly. "It's not a particularly interesting subject to anyone who is not an anthropologist, I'm afraid."

On the contrary, Emma was delighted by this unexpected news. "You're a professor!"

"Alas, I am not. Mine is more of a hobby, I suspect. However, I have spent time with Professor Henley of Oxford. He is a renowned anthropologist."

"A *hobby*?" Her delight deflated. "I can't imagine anyone choosing to study the migratory habits of Bedouin tribes as a hobby. But..." she sat up now, curious "...how do you then earn your living if it's only a hobby? You must be paid for your research, is that it? Is it rude of me to ask? I confess I'm suddenly dying of curiosity, so please do forgive me if my question is improper."

"It's not improper. My true occupation is…" He looked around the room. "I suppose it's the same as yours."

Except that she had no occupation, and she laughed at what she thought was a joke. "It must be vastly different in your country, sir, but I am a countess, and as such, my occupation is to support my husband, tithe generously, and entertain the *haut ton* in a manner befitting the Dearborn seat. That's all." What a lush existence. Comfortable and dreadful at the same time.

But he smiled wryly, his gaze warm. "You have just described my occupation. I would add to that list the responsibility of siring an heir."

What was he saying? Was he teasing her? "I'm afraid I don't understand."

"I should have mentioned it when we first met. Frankly, I should have mentioned several things when we first met and then been on my way. But I'm an earl, Lady Dearborn. Or, the equivalent of an earl in my country. I am *Comte ve Marlaine*, the son of the Duke of Astasia."

This news astounded Emma. To this moment, she'd thought of him simply as a man walking the world. She put her wine aside. "You're a Weslorian *earl*? Why on earth didn't you say so?"

He shrugged in a way she found endearing. "I suppose for one, it's been a bit difficult to gain your attention," he said, one brow arching slightly. "And it didn't seem particularly germane, quite honestly. I meant only to pass through, and my title…my title only matters in Wesloria."

"It matters to me. I've called you Mr. Olivien—"

"Which is quite acceptable as that is my name."

"Yes, but, you're a *comte*, or whatever you said. How *fascinating*," she said, and meant it. "I've never known a gentleman who didn't like to hear his title loftily used with every other breath." In fact, Albert had once dressed down a poor man at the pub for not recognizing him as Lord Dearborn.

Mr. Olivien laughed at that. "Neither have I," he agreed.

"Now I must know how you came to discover your interest in anthropology."

He thought about that as he sipped his wine. "When I was a child, my tutor noted my interest in some of his books. A few years later, he suggested Eton to my father. I was educated here, in England."

"No wonder you speak English so flawlessly. That must have been quite a long way from home for a boy."

"*Je*, it was. But most of the Weslorian aristocracy sent their children away to be educated. It's seen as a mark of wealth to be able to educate one's children in England or France or even as far as Harvard in America. It pains me to admit that even schools in neighboring Alucia are better than those in Wesloria. You've probably heard as much."

"Me?" Emma laughed. "I haven't the slightest notion. My formal education ended when I was fifteen, at which point the real education began—how to curtsy properly, how to dance, serve tea, do good, charitable works, and count linens." At the time she'd been perfectly content to do what everyone else did in her position—learn all the skills necessary to marry at a higher social circle. Unfortunately, she'd not been a clever girl who thought too much about her future. She'd thought of young gentlemen and parties.

She was still that girl, she supposed, but fortunately with more interests. Her involvement in the management of the Dearborn estate had made her regret her lack of formal education. It seemed men learned so many more interesting things than women.

She realized Mr. Olivien was eyeing her shrewdly.

"It's a pity you didn't introduce yourself as the *comte*...earl. Feeney would have shown you to a better room, had we known."

He smiled faintly. "It's only a title. The room you've so graciously provided me is lovely."

Emma shook her head. "Only a title to you, but the difference between this life and poverty for me."

"Poverty!" He laughed. "I can't imagine you in any state of poverty, Lady Dearborn."

"No? Can't you imagine what my situation would be, without the Dearborn estate to provide for me?"

He looked around the room. "I see. I suppose I am thinking of my own circumstances. For me, the title can be a bother. A bit too political at times."

"Ah, politics," she said with a sigh and flicked her wrist as if to swat it away. How many times had she listened to Albert and his friends argue about politics? "Live and let live, I say."

He gave her an indulgent smile. "Do you really say so?"

"Sometimes." She kicked off her slippers and tucked her feet under her gown. Another breach of protocol, but she didn't care.

Mr. Olivien looked at the floor where her feet should have been, and his indulgent smile faded. He put aside his wine. "Speaking of *live and let live*, Lady Dearborn, I really must—"

"You haven't heard my story!" Emma suddenly interjected. Her heartbeat ticked up—he was on the verge of telling her about Albert before they'd even had dinner. But she was enjoying her evening. She'd envisioned an entire meal, just the two of them, her flirting shamelessly, and him continuing to look so appealing. Couldn't she have this one thing? Couldn't she have just *one* dinner with a handsome man before everything went to hell?

Her feet suddenly found the floor again, and she leaned forward before he could form his thoughts. "Do you know what I like?"

"Pardon?"

"I like parties," she said.

He snorted. "I have gathered as much."

"I adore it when people dress for the evening and laugh over good food and dance and play. I can't wait to introduce you to my friends. They'll be fascinated by your work! I'd wager none of them have ever met an anthropologist. I made the invitation list just today." She'd really only started it, but she meant to finish it tonight.

He stared at her with an expression of disbelief. "You're not really planning a party."

"I am! Everyone who is anyone will be here for it."

"Not I, madam. I won't be here."

"Why not?" She knew perfectly well why not. "Once, I had a party in London, and *everyone* came. The invitations were highly coveted. You'd be amazed at how wonderful—"

"I'm needed in Wesloria," he interrupted, before she could fill the room with more words. "I never intended to be here for more than a day or two."

"That's a terrible pity, Mr. Olivien, and we'll soldier on. But don't you think you could stay just a little while longer? Don't you *want* to be here? I would want to be here if I were you. The grounds are spectacular. We are a short distance from London. Do you know, you could take one of our horses and go to London if you like. Not Esmerelda, obviously." She laughed. "But we have other horses. You needn't stay here *every* day. In fact, I'm going to tell Feeney to arrange it for you tomorrow. Why don't you—"

"*No*, Lady Dearborn," he said with a quiet firmness that made her spine tingle. "I can't fathom why I've stayed as long as I have. There is a part of me that is intrigued by you and the estate, but I need to be home." He slowly leaned forward, holding her gaze. "I sense something is terribly amiss here."

Emma's heart skipped a beat or two. She laughed and hopped to her feet. "Your imagination has got the best of you, Mr. Olivien. What could possibly be amiss?"

He stood, too. "I think you know. I think you understand that I know your secret."

Her palms felt damp. He was ruining her hopes for this evening. And her life, although that was a bit down the road. She shrugged insouciantly. "Which one? I am a woman. I have many secrets."

"I would offer that some of your secrets are more consequential than others."

She stared at him. He stared at her. She was surprised that they had come to be standing like this, so close. She didn't know how to convince him he ought not to say what he wanted so desperately to say. "You seem to know a lot about secrets."

"I know when I suspect a big one." His gaze bored into her, like he was trying to see the truth inside her. The intensity of it made her feel warm and crackling inside, like the first fire of a winter's evening, too hot to begin, but settling into a slow burn.

She very foolishly moved closer to him, her gaze locked on his. "And just what do you think is my very big secret, Mr. Olivien?"

His gaze fell to her lips. "I was hoping you'd tell me," he said, his voice shiveringly low.

Despite the loud voice inside her head bellowing at her to stand back, Emma took another step toward him, so that they were almost touching. But the man didn't move; he stood as solid as a tree. He looked at her with a mix of amusement and interest, as if he didn't believe she had the courage to stand so close. She could kiss him if she wanted to. And she wanted to—her body was thrumming with anticipation. But she didn't have the best idea of how to go about it.

A blinding round of lightning was quickly followed by a loud crack of thunder. It felt like the storm was in the room with them and pushed her even closer. And still Mr. Olivien did not move.

"I think," he said, his gaze maddeningly on her lips, "you know more about your husband's watch than you've admitted."

His lips looked so plush. She could imagine the soft feel of them, could almost imagine the taste of them. "Are you really thinking about a pocket watch just now?"

"I am thinking about a woman who, for whatever reason, refuses—"

She did the only thing she could do to stop him from speaking. She rose on her toes and kissed him. She had to grab onto his arm to keep herself from losing her balance, which pitched her forward in a way that pressed her chest to his. She brazenly kissed him like that, her lips moving softly on his.

And she regretted nothing. Scheherazade would be proud.

He made a sound of surprise, deep in his chest. His fingers curled around her elbow, steadying her. Emma brought her hand to his face, felt the stubble beneath her fingers. The fire was ignited in her, blistering at her core. He put his hand on her waist and pulled her closer—

But then she heard the unmistakable squeak of a door.

She leaped back and away from him, grabbed up her glass of wine, and turned to the window just as Feeney opened the door to the drawing room fully and stepped inside.

"Madam, Lady Adele and Master Andrew have arrived."

He could not be serious. "Pardon?" She was not expecting them. Was she *ever* expecting them? It was almost as if Adele had an unworldly sense for the absolute worst time to make an appearance. Emma suddenly wanted to violently gouge a pillow with sharp scissors. She tried to force a smile, but she could see the way Mr. Olivien was looking at her with a hint of a wolfish smile. It wasn't the kiss that put that smile on his face.

She knew *that* smile was because he'd guessed her darkest secret.

CHAPTER TEN

THIS WOMAN.

This impossibly unpredictable, beautiful woman had just kissed him, without warning, as brazenly as you please, and he'd bloody well allowed it. More than allowed it—he'd been a willing participant.

He'd never claimed to be a saint.

And still, he was stunned. Aroused. *Madly* intrigued. In fact, his intense interest was sluicing through him, drowning out more pragmatic thoughts. Every time he was in her presence, she surprised him again.

A simultaneous crack of powerful thunder and a shock of lightning rattled the windowpanes and went right through him, mirroring a raging storm inside—a squall of desire and dismay and confusion. He could feel a gnawing hunger—for food, for drink, for a woman's touch.

She'd *kissed* him.

He didn't know what to do in the moment. He watched her hurry to the window, pressing the heel of her hand against her cheek. Did he end the game she was playing with him? Was this at last the moment he exited and went home to see what havoc his father had wrought? Or did he keep playing?

He wondered why he even bothered to ponder. He

knew he would keep playing, at least for now. He was too captivated to do anything else.

And it hardly mattered what he might have done because Lady Adele and her brother entered the room. The lady was still shaking rain from her clothing.

"Andrew! Adele! What are you doing out in this storm?" Lady Dearborn exclaimed.

"It's a *terrible* one, isn't it," Andrew said excitedly and raced to the window to look out.

"It's not as if we planned it," Lady Adele said as she made a show of swiping rain from her face with one finger and then flicking away the drops. She had a way of speaking that made everything sound like an accusation.

"I'm glad we're not at sea," Andrew said. "We'd be tossed to our deaths if we were at sea! How will ships hold up? Do you think they will sink?"

"As we are not at sea, we will never know," Lady Adele said curtly. "We were on our way home from Rexford when we got caught in this awful deluge. It's a wonder we weren't washed off the road!" She paused to drag a hand over her head, at which point she seemed to fully notice Luka. Her hand dropped. She forced a smile. "Oh. I didn't realize you were still here, sir."

He bowed his head in acknowledgment that yes, he was still here.

She turned back to her sister-in-law. "Naturally, I apologize for any inconvenience we might have caused you, but I'm sure you won't mind that we've sought refuge here, will you, Emma?"

Emma. Luka tucked that away.

"Of course not, darling!" Lady Dearborn trilled. "I'm

thrilled you're safe and dry. Feeney, show Adele to a room so that she might—"

"No need," Lady Adele said, throwing up a hand. "I'll dry off before the fire. Andrew, come," she commanded and gestured for her brother to join her at the hearth. With a loud sneeze, Andrew went to stand beside his sister. He was bony and thin, with a gray complexion, a young man who was not still a child but not yet an adult. But he had a beaming smile and obviously enjoyed a loud and precarious weather event.

Lady Dearborn moved across the room and tried to slip on the shoes she'd carelessly discarded without being noticed and failed miserably. Lady Adele looked at her aghast. "Are you *barefoot*?" She made it sound as if Lady Dearborn was completely naked.

"Only for a moment. Feeney? We'll need more wine to warm Adele and Andrew."

Andrew sneezed again.

"Shall I have rooms readied?" Feeney asked.

Lady Dearborn gave her butler a pained smile, and Luka couldn't blame her for it. He would not like to play host to Lady Adele for long. "You absolutely must," Lady Dearborn said. "I wouldn't *dream* of sending them out tonight. We'll wait for tomorrow's sunny skies."

Another bolt of lightning and crack of thunder hit, and the boy said eagerly, "Lightning can explode trees, did you know? Just *pow!* and a tree can erupt into flames."

"I didn't know that," Lady Dearborn said, settling on the settee again—this time with prim posture and both feet planted firmly on the carpet. "When I was a girl, a house near our family home was struck by lightning, and it burned right to the ground."

Andrew gasped. "Did anyone *die*?"

"Alas, no," Lady Dearborn said with an apologetic wince, because she clearly understood how a boy's mind worked. "I think they moved to Bethel-on-Sea after that," she added thoughtfully, as if trying to recall.

More thunder rattled the rafters. "It's so loud," Lady Adele said, and covered her ears with her hands. "I can scarcely hear myself think!"

She only lowered her hands when Feeney presented her and Master Andrew with a glass of wine. Lady Adele immediately took the wine her brother had accepted from his hand and placed it back on Feeney's tray, with a glare for the butler.

"Andrew, come and sit by me," Lady Dearborn said, patting the settee cushion beside her.

Luka rather doubted the lad would be able to slip out of the invisible tether his sister had him tied to, but lo and behold he did, moving awkwardly to sit beside Lady Dearborn.

Lady Adele, who had somehow managed to persevere in her thinking despite the loud thundering, eyed Luka. "Mr. Olivien, you must sincerely enjoy Butterhill Hall. How long do you think you will stay?"

"Adele!" Lady Dearborn interjected before Luka could even open his mouth. She laughed nervously. "I told you I mean to host a gathering in his honor."

Lady Adele ignored her. "But I'm pleased to find you here," she said to Luka, moving away from the fire toward him. "May I inquire, how well do you know my brother?"

"Adele, please!" Lady Dearborn said, sounding a bit alarmed. "There is no call for interrogating our guest."

"It's quite all right," said Luka. He didn't intend to

give Lady Dearborn away, but he wouldn't mind seeing just how much she could squirm. "Our paths crossed on occasion."

"On occasion?" Lady Adele repeated. "I believe I have misunderstood the situation. I thought you were so well acquainted with my brother that he would insist on a fete in your honor."

He didn't know of anyone who would insist on a fete in his honor, and that included his own parents. "In Egypt, most Europeans are friends," he said.

"Did you know that Mr. Olivien is a Weslorian earl?" Lady Dearborn asked and stood up from the settee, as if she meant to block her sister-in-law should she attempt to make a run at Luka. In this house, he guessed anything was possible. "What did you call it, my lord?"

My lord. She'd elevated him. *"Comte ve Marlaine."*

"Yes! That's it."

"A what?" Lady Adele sounded skeptical.

"I am, in Wesloria, what you would call an earl here. My father is the Duke of Astasia, and I hold the title of *comte* for the Marlaine region."

"Astasia is where they mine for coal," Andrew announced.

His remark drew the attention of the adults. The lad looked around at them. "I've read the history of Wesloria. Weslorian rebels attempted to overthrow the King of Alucia once. They kidnapped his baby, and the baby was never seen again."

Lady Dearborn beamed. "Andrew has so many books," she said proudly.

"It's a very bloody history," Andrew added enthusiastically.

"Like most countries, one would think," Luka muttered.

"Yes, but *very* bloody. Once, a long time ago, a duke chopped off a queen's head and put it on the dinner table before the king."

"Oh dear," Lady Adele said.

"That doesn't sound very nice," Lady Dearborn added.

"But the king didn't like her, and he tossed the bones of his fish into her hair," Andrew said.

"If I may," Luka said, "that particular incident is not the most flattering historical anecdote from Weslorian history. It happened ages ago. A lot of marital strife in that era."

"Please don't take it personally, Mr. Olivien," Lady Dearborn said. "English history has a bit of chop-chop marital strife, too, doesn't it, Andrew?" she asked cheerfully.

"*Quite*," Andrew agreed, just as cheerfully.

"Could we please turn our attention to something more appetizing?" Lady Adele demanded.

"We certainly may." Lady Dearborn turned to Feeney. "Have you something more appetizing?"

The butler perked up. "I will learn if dinner is ready to be served."

"Please," Lady Dearborn said, before Feeney had even managed to leave the room, as if she expected to be called to dine in the next few seconds. "Why don't we go through?" She gestured to the door.

"Shouldn't we wait for Feeney to announce?" Lady Adele asked. "My mother always waited for him to announce."

Luka was learning that whatever Lady Dearborn

suggested they do, Lady Adele would suggest the opposite.

"I'm sure the table has been set. Feeney is terribly efficient. Your mother would have agreed." Lady Dearborn started walking in that direction at a pace that suggested she did not want to be in this drawing room a moment longer.

Andrew hopped up from the settee with an energy one would not think he possessed by the look of him and scampered after her.

Lady Dearborn paused at the door to wait for Andrew. She took his hand, then glanced back at Luka and her sister-in-law. "Aren't you coming?"

Luka looked at Lady Adele and very reluctantly offered his arm. "Madam?"

"No, thank you," she said primly, and with an upward jab of her chin, she lifted her skirts and marched after her brother and sister-in-law.

Luka hesitated only a moment. He was too ensnared by the tribal dynamics to cower now.

CHAPTER ELEVEN

THE DINING ROOM had been formally set with the sort of decorative porcelain china that heads of state might expect. Four places had been laid with a variety of stacked plates and silver arrayed in fans, candles lit, a fire at the hearth behind an iron screen with a floral pattern. With the storm still blowing and rain lashing against the windows, the setting was surprisingly agreeable. Cozy and warm.

Luka sat across from Lady Dearborn, and brother and sister sat across from each other. Lady Dearborn asked after Andrew's reading. "Andrew reads the most interesting books, Mr. Olivien. Tell him, Andrew."

"I'm reading a book about Japan," the lad said proudly.

"Japan!" Lady Dearborn exclaimed. "Do you know what I especially like about Japan? The art."

"What do you know about Japanese art?" Lady Adele asked. Luka silently seconded her question, but unlike Lady Adele, he was genuinely interested in Lady Dearborn's answer.

"Oh, nothing," Lady Dearborn said breezily. "But I should like to. Albert has the painting of the dragon done by a Japanese artist in his study. Have you seen it? We could all have a look after dinner. It's quite impressive and very large and a bit erotic when viewed in a certain light." She laughed. So did Andrew. Lady Adele gasped audibly. "Emma Clark!" she said sternly.

"I beg your pardon, Adele," Lady Dearborn said, although she didn't seem the least bit apologetic to Luka.

Her breezy abandon was as alluring as it was vaguely alarming. He didn't know why he thought so, exactly, other than he'd never been around a woman who didn't tend to lean toward a prim and proper air. Or perhaps it was that kiss that had alarmed him. He kept thinking about it. He couldn't shake it. It had been two years since he'd been with a woman. Maybe his abstinence had been the reason the kiss had rattled him so, but he wanted to know her. He wanted to understand how she moved through this world. Alas, he was expertly thwarted by Lady Adele, who meant to dominate the conversation.

"I don't know why you're so interested in Andrew's books, anyway," Lady Adele said. "It's not as if you intend to read them."

Luka was slightly taken aback by the implication in that remark. But Lady Dearborn laughed without rancor as she set her wineglass down with a bit of a thump. "You know me well, sister! That's why I rely on Andrew to tell me what I ought to know." She beamed at her brother-in-law, and the lad beamed back.

"There are any number of occasions you may quiz Andrew about his books, but we've Albert's esteemed friend at our table. And as I have never heard of him until he arrived at Butterhill Hall, I should like to know more." Lady Adele looked pointedly at Luka.

"What would you like to know, madam?"

"How did you become acquainted with my brother?"

"In a friend's salon to begin," Luka said. "He and I were among the guests."

"But you must have become better acquainted with him," Lady Adele insisted. "I never understood why Albert was so determined to see the East. I'm curious, sir, why you were in Egypt."

"I am an anthropologist, Lady Adele. I've been working on a study of the nomadic migration routes in a particular part of Egypt as they relate to the trade infrastructure in the area."

"Really?" Andrew asked.

"Whatever for?" Lady Adele asked.

"It helps our understanding of international economics. I've been working under the tutelage of Professor Edward Henley of Oxford."

"Oxford!" Andrew repeated excitedly.

Lady Adele shot him a look. "That's all well and good, I suppose, but don't you have a family? People who rely on you? Who are your father and mother?"

An odd question. "The Duke and Duchess of Astasia."

Lady Adele was not done—she continued to ask questions. He told her that he'd been educated at Eton and then at the Sorbonne in France. He told her he'd been away from Wesloria for more than two years, but that he was expected home soon. She said that seemed an awfully long time to be gone, and if her parents were alive, she'd seek to be near them.

She didn't know his parents and, therefore, couldn't rightly say if she'd want to be near them. But he kept that to himself.

She asked about his siblings, if they were married, if they had children, building up to the fundamental question of why *he* hadn't married. He'd been a guest at too many dinner tables not to understand where the conversation was leading.

"Adele, dearest! That's a terribly personal question," Lady Dearborn said. "What if he has something terribly, *terribly* wrong with him? Would you force him to tell us?"

All eyes turned to him. Andrew particularly looked eager for a terrible, *terrible* answer.

"I wish I had something gruesome to share," Luka said with a chuckle, "but alas, I am perfectly healthy."

"And how pleased we are to hear it!" Lady Dearborn said. "As they say, if you have your health, you have everything."

"And yet, in spite of excellent health, he's never married," Lady Adele said with a snort.

The pot had just called the kettle black. "I think there is a season for everything. Wouldn't you agree, madam?" he asked and lifted his glass in toast to the other unmarried adult in the room.

Lady Adele reluctantly lifted hers. "Another question, if I may," she said.

Lady Dearborn pressed her forehead into her palm.

While Luka was somewhat amused by the lady's tenacity, she was proving herself to be a formidable dinner-table opponent. She wore them all down with her insistence that she approve any topic of conversation that was not her own. She did this in the form of questions, fired at an amazing rate. After a time, even the irrepressible and always cheerful Lady Dearborn could not talk over her sister-in-law or redirect the conversation.

Moreover, the tension in the room was as thick as the flies in the desert camps. Whatever had happened in this family, whatever the reason for Lady Adele's animosity toward him, it was palpable. Luka wished he had a notebook in which to record observations.

"Please tell me once more how it is you know my brother so well."

What exactly was making her so suspicious? "I'm not sure what more I can say," Luka said evenly.

"It's just that I don't understand why he'd entrust his watch to you," Lady Adele said, watching him carefully. "Seems an odd thing to ask."

"I thought so, too," Luka said. "But as I was—"

"Do you know, I think the storm has passed," Lady Dearborn said suddenly, in another attempt to turn the subject. "There you are, Andrew. No need to worry about ships at sea." She smiled fondly.

"Have you heard?" Andrew asked. "There are pirates invading vessels near Yorkshire again."

"Really? How exciting! At a distance, of course. I'd not like to be on a ship that was pirated," Lady Dearborn said, and clinked her glass to Andrew's. "Tell us everything. How many pirates, of what stripe, and what have they managed to steal?"

"Emma, dearest, do you really mean to imply that you find pirates more exciting than news of your husband?" Lady Adele countered. "What of the *exciting* moment Albert comes home from this godforsaken sojourn? Perhaps Mr. Olivien can help us determine when that will be. Albert trusted his watch to the man. Perhaps he trusted the date of his return, as well." She looked at Luka. "Of all of us gathered here, you were the last to see him, after all," the woman pointed out.

As if he needed to be reminded. Luka put down his

fork and dabbed at his mouth with his napkin as he thought of how to answer. But he didn't have to—Lady Dearborn answered for him.

"But didn't I tell you? I recalled a conversation Albert and I had before he left, and now I have every reason to believe he'll be home in time for Christmas." Lady Dearborn put down her wineglass, picked up her fork and knife, and began to saw on her meat as if this revelation was old news, as if it was the sort of thing one might tell an elderly, senile parent over and over again. But it clearly was *not* old news, judging by the looks of shock from her family.

"What?" Lady Adele sputtered.

"I think he'll be home by Christmas. I've worked it all out." Lady Dearborn popped a piece of meat in her mouth and chewed. "Isn't that wonderful?"

Lady Adele was beside herself. She dropped her utensils and sat up. "Have you had a letter? Some word from him? What do you mean, you recall a conversation? How could you sit there and not say?"

"I beg your pardon, Adele, I really thought I had. I've been so busy planning the party that I can hardly keep a thought in my head these days," she said, fluttering her fingers at her head. "Forgive me."

She did not think she had told anyone that outrageous lie—Luka could tell from the bit of color rising in her cheeks. Couldn't her family see it?

"It's remarkable," Lady Dearborn said, pausing to take another bite of beefsteak and chewing thoughtfully a moment. "It popped into my mind one day. I had forgotten it, but I suddenly recalled that a few nights before Albert left, when he was putting the finishing touches on his packing, he said he would be home in winter, before the turn of the new year. And I said, 'Oh, I so hope you are, as Christmas wouldn't be the same without you.' I thought he meant *last* Christmas, but when I began to think on it, I realized he must have meant *this* winter. It all makes perfect sense, really. He didn't leave until August."

Lady Adele looked dumbstruck. "How does any of that make perfect sense? Wouldn't he have written to confirm? Wouldn't he have mentioned it to me? The only thing he ever said was that he would be back before I knew it. And why winter? Why not return now?"

"The winds," Andrew said. "The prevailing winds aren't suitable for sailing west just now."

Amid this unfurling disaster, Luka had to marvel that the lad was a walking encyclopedia. Had he read *every* book in the library?

"Stop interrupting, Andrew!" his sister snapped. "No one cares about wind. Emma, you might have mentioned this!"

"I do apologize," Lady Dearborn said. "I really thought I had."

The lady did not for a moment really think she had mentioned anything. Furthermore, Luka had the distinct impression that she was avoiding his gaze, looking everywhere around the room but never at him. Because she knew that he knew that *she* knew her husband was dead.

He could honestly say that this family was at least as riveting as the Bedouins.

Lady Adele sighed wearily, as if she'd heard every possible date for her brother's return now. "Well. Then, I suppose this is wonderful news, isn't it, this new recollection of yours. At least we have some idea of when.

We should plan to welcome him home properly, Emma. A *big* party. We'll invite everyone for miles and from London, too, just as you like. Mr. Olivien, perhaps you'd agree to forgo your party so that we might—"

"*No!*" Lady Dearborn cried. "Why would we forgo his party? Christmas is *months* away. I intend to honor Mr. Olivien, our very own Lord Marlaine—"

"Wesloria's Lord Marlaine," Andrew clarified.

"Wesloria's Lord Marlaine," Lady Dearborn quickly corrected, "in a manner in which Albert would be proud." She lifted her wineglass in toast. "To Lord Marlaine. Or...Mr. Olivien." She paused. "We ought to sort that out."

Andrew lifted his glass, too, and turned eagerly in Luka's direction.

"This really isn't necessary—" he began, but Lady Adele interjected herself.

"Emma, you can't mean to host *two* very large parties. And if you must choose one over the other, it must be Albert. I'm certain Mr. Olivien understands." She suddenly laughed, the sound of it jarring coming from such a sourpuss. "I can't tell you how relieved I am to hear that Albert may be home soon. We've all gone quite round the bend without him, haven't we?"

"We haven't!" Lady Dearborn protested. "We've been perfectly well without him. What are you talking about?"

Luka could guess a dozen different ways, starting with the fact that Albert's wife was keeping his death a secret.

"You really don't know?" Lady Adele said. "Mr. Olivien, please forgive us all for being so untoward as to talk about money, but Emma, you can't continue to spend as you have. Albert left the estate to itself! I grant you, Mr. Horn is a capable man, but without a hand to guide him, Butterhill Hall could turn to ruin."

"That's what happened to Hornsby Gate," Andrew said. "They didn't have the funds to keep it up and left it abandoned, and now they say it's haunted. I know! We should go there at night and see if it is."

"Butterhill Hall has not been left to turn to ruin," Lady Dearborn said, sounding a bit peeved. "Or without a hand to guide it. You know very well I've kept a close watch on everything, Adele."

Lady Adele laughed.

"Why are you laughing? I review the ledgers with Mr. Horn every week. I make decisions." She leaned forward slightly. "I would love to show you, darling, if only you would come and see."

"Yes," Lady Adele said carefully. "No doubt, Albert will commend your efforts. But I think it hardly matters what you might have to show me, as you can't possibly look after Butterhill Hall in the same meticulous manner he can."

Luka had been in enough dodgy places in his life to know when a duel was brewing, and he feared one lady might challenge the other. As if reading his thoughts, Lady Dearborn sat up, fisting her hands on either side of her plate. "Why can't I? I'm not a half-wit."

Lady Adele's smile turned into a bit of a sneer. "But you're not exactly schooled in the details of managing an estate, particularly of this size, are you? I didn't want to tell you just yet, but… I've been so concerned, I have written to our cousin, Mr. Timothy Longbottom, and asked him to come and assist until Albert's return."

Lady Dearborn's mouth gaped. "I beg your pardon. You did *what*? You wrote *who*?"

"Our cousin. I wrote him," Lady Adele said, enunciating every word.

"I've never heard of him!"

"You've never heard of Timothy Longbottom, our second cousin on our mother's side? How odd that Albert never mentioned him. He's a financier, and I think he could be very useful to us. Frankly, I wonder why Albert didn't think of it before he left."

"Adele?" Lady Dearborn's voice was low and dark. "How—"

"Ladies, if I may," Luka interjected, hoping to de-escalate a deteriorating situation, "this conversation is reminiscent of a few I've had in my own home. Perhaps you'd like to discuss this matter without Mr. Clark and myself present?"

"A splendid suggestion," Lady Dearborn said.

"Not at all!" Lady Adele said. "Mr. Olivien, you are our guest, and I was wrong to mention Mr. Longbottom at the dinner table." She smiled thinly, straightened in her seat, picked up her wineglass, and sipped. "But may I say again, I'm so *relieved* my brother will be home soon."

Lady Dearborn forced a smile. "As are we all." She tucked a curl of hair behind her ear before slowly sinking against the chair back. She looked like her thoughts had skittered ahead, out of this room to some dark corner of her mind. If Luka had to guess, he'd say she was contemplating one Mr. Timothy Longbottom. That was a new wrinkle for her.

"Shall we play whist?" Andrew asked, looking hopefully between sister and sister-in-law. Not only was he the most well-read young man Luka had ever met, he was also a budding diplomat. And it worked: both women looked at him, considering the idea.

"I should warn you, sir, I'm quite good," Luka said, following the lad's lead. "And I can think of nothing more delightful." He then proceeded to think of at least fifteen things that were more delightful.

Starting with that unexpected kiss.

CHAPTER TWELVE

TIMOTHY LONGBOTTOM? Who in bloody hell was he? Not a distant cousin—Emma did not believe that, not for a moment. She'd never heard of him. Albert had never said to anyone, much less her, "Remember when Cousin Timothy…" or "my cousin Timothy lives…" or "my cousin Timothy is a rat bastard."

Adele was lying. What was she plotting? Emma didn't like being on the receiving end of a scheme—but she couldn't very well challenge her given the magnitude of her own lie.

Things were spiraling out of control so fast that Emma didn't know what to do.

Except drink champagne. That seemed to be the thing now, and she waved her glass at Feeney, and he filled it up without batting an eye. The two of them had developed a certain understanding and rhythm with each other over the last year or so. Feeney silently disapproved of many things she did, and she did not ask him why.

Adele, however, was fond of eyeing Emma's glass disapprovingly. Nothing new there, as Adele was always looking at something disapprovingly. Generally, Emma felt entirely confident and nonchalant when Adele peered down her nose. Tonight, however, she felt strung as tight as Fanny's harp. She might bust apart at any moment. Maybe she'd confess all and remove this weight from her chest. But then what? Give Adele the satisfaction of tossing her out? Ensuring that she never kissed Mr. Olivien again? She was not willing to risk either of those things.

They played whist. She partnered with Mr. Olivien because Adele said so. Emma was a bit tipsy and trying not to feel too terribly guilty about kissing him. How ironic was it that one of the worst things she'd done was also one of the best things she'd done? The thought caused her to chuckle softly to herself, which of course drew the attention of the others. "I love this game," she said.

Adele rolled her eyes. Andrew said he loved the game, too. Mr. Olivien arched an inquisitive brow in her direction.

Emma tried to focus on the game and enjoy the reverie. She knew that the odds she would never have fun again were rapidly increasing. Unfortunately, her conscience kept interrupting her—she was distracted by her thoughts and champagne and Mr. Olivien, and as a result, she and Mr. Olivien lost twice in a row. He was a gentleman; he showed no signs of distress or irritation with her careless play.

Why did she have to say Albert would be home by Christmas? Why couldn't she *ever* keep her mouth shut? Because she'd feared Mr. Olivien would say then and there that Albert was never coming home, and there she'd be, cast out in a driving rain.

Andrew suddenly laughed. "You played a heart, Emma! The suit is a club."

"What?" Emma bent over to have a look. "Well, will you look at that." She corrected her mistake.

"It shouldn't be hard to remember what suit, darling," Adele said. "After all, there are only four." With that, she trumped Emma's card with one of her own. Adele played card games with the efficiency and attitude of an assassin. She didn't care for banter or delays in play. She'd said more than once in the last few years that she didn't understand why any person was not ready to make a play when it was their turn. She was as charming at the gaming table as she was anywhere else, which was to say not at all. When had she become so bitter? There was a time when Emma had believed they could be dear friends, and she'd believed Adele had wanted that, too. But when she married Albert, things had changed. It was as if Adele was startled to find that she was no longer mistress of Butterhill Hall.

Mr. Olivien trumped Adele's play. She snorted.

Emma crowed with delight, but what she really needed was for them all to go to bed. Better yet, to leave Butterhill altogether. She wanted to wander the halls while she tried to think what to do. She needed to come up with a real plan to stop the unveiling of her debacle. She'd been so *foolish* to think she could get away with pretending Albert was alive. In her defense, she hadn't meant it to go on forever—she'd meant only to prolong the inevitable. But…she'd been seduced by her freedom and happiness and had begun to believe she could somehow continue.

Damn her folly.

She needed more champagne and held out her glass again.

Adele disdainfully eyed the refill then turned to Mr. Olivien. "My brother Albert is an excellent card player."

Rubbish, thought Emma. He'd been mediocre at best and petulant when he lost.

"But as his friend, I'm sure you're well aware," Adele continued. She laughed gaily. "He is merciless with his friends, is he not?"

"Speaking of friends," Emma said, committed to turning the attention from Mr. Olivien and feeling just enough of the champagne to do it. "I'm quite amazed to learn of your cousin. I'm wondering why Albert never mentioned him."

"Maybe he mentioned him while you were drinking champagne," Adele said.

Emma laughed. "I can be forgetful after some evening reveries. But I don't think he did," she said pleasantly. "Was he not a friend of Mr. Longbottom's? I feel certain he would have mentioned him if he was. You know that some of my fondest memories are of my cousin. Particularly Cousin Darwin. He once tricked my sister and me out of the silver pieces our grandfather had given us."

"How?" Andrew asked.

"He claimed to know magic."

"Devil's work," Adele muttered.

"He said he could make the silver magically disappear and then reappear. True to his word, he made the silver pieces disappear. But when it came to the magical reappearance, something went awry." She giggled at the memory.

"What happened to the silver pieces?" Andrew asked.

"I can't say for certain, but I believe they ended up in Cousin Darwin's purse."

Andrew gasped. "Did he do that to anyone else? He must be rich now."

"Oh dear, no, he's not rich. He is a vicar now," Emma said. "As far as I know, he tried his trick only on his young female cousins. We went straight to our grandfather and told him the woeful tale of our lost silver pieces. And do you know what he said?"

"What?" Andrew asked eagerly.

"That two young fools are soon parted with their money."

"That is the very point I've been trying to make," Adele said curtly. "Shall we play another round?"

Lord, not another round. Emma couldn't bear another moment in this bit of nightmare. "I'm rather tired. Perhaps we all ought to retire for the evening."

"Just as well," Adele said. "Andrew and I will rise at dawn as is our custom. Should we wake you before we go?" she asked slyly.

"No, thank you," Emma said. She stood from the table and went to the window under the pretense of drawing the drapes, but really, she just wished for some air. The rain was still falling steadily, but with much less ferocity than earlier in the evening. She heard Feeney come in and offer to show Adele and Andrew to guest rooms.

"That won't be necessary, Feeney," Adele said with a sniff. "Andrew and I are as familiar with Butterhill Hall as is your mistress." She never failed to mention that she and Andrew had lived here until Albert had sent them over the hill when he married. "Perhaps you might escort Mr. Olivien?"

"Thank you," the Weslorian said, "but I know my way as well."

"Very good," Feeney said. "Lady Dearborn?"

"I'll be along shortly. I'm just going to…" she looked

around for a reason to keep her from walking with the others "...choose a book to read."

"A *book*?" Adele echoed.

"Yes, darling, a book. I do read, you know." Not very often, as reading was not her favorite pastime. Was she to be blamed that she preferred dancing and needlepoint and games to reading?

Her excuse seemed to work. While Emma perused the bookshelves, the rest of them filed out of the drawing room. Once she heard the door close quietly behind her, she sighed with relief, kicked off her shoes, and wandered back to the window. It was so dark she couldn't see anything but her own reflection. She was a bit light-headed from the champagne but felt as if she could sing or dance or just go to sleep. She wasn't sure which activity spoke to her more.

Maybe her desire to sing and dance and sleep was the problem—she was always wanting something other than what she had. Perhaps now was the time to turn over a new leaf, to begin to read for pleasure like a proper countess. To become the countess her sister-in-law thought she ought to be. But to what end? She wouldn't be a countess much longer by the look of things.

She went back to the bookshelves and looked at the titles there. Albert had loved to read, and books had arrived with some frequency. One or two titles leaped out at her as potentials, and she chose one that looked intriguing, mainly because she recalled it had come just after Albert left. *The Mystery of Edwin Drood* by Charles Dickens. She tucked it under her arm and left the drawing room, dimming the lights as she went. When she reached the door, she dimmed the last wall sconce and opened the door—and gasped.

Mr. Olivien was standing with his back against the opposite wall, his arms folded, one ankle casually crossed over the other. "Lady Dearborn."

"You startled me," she said, pressing a hand to her chest.

"I apologize for that. I didn't want to disturb you in your quest for a book. A good one, I hope?"

"It's a mystery." She held it out for him to see.

He moved away from the wall and took the book, read the spine, then opened it to the first page. After a moment, he handed it back to her. "Interesting."

"Would you like to choose a book, too?" She stepped back from the threshold, to allow him to pass. "I've dimmed the lights, but I can put them up again if you—"

"Actually, I wanted to speak to you, if I may."

Dread knotted in her belly, mixing uncomfortably with champagne. Her light-headedness was turning to headache. "Is there something wrong with your accommodation?"

He smiled lopsidedly. "The accommodation here is perfect."

"How kind of you to say. We do pride ourselves on our guest rooms." They had never, to Emma's knowledge, said a word about the guest rooms. That was Feeney's domain.

"I thank you for your generous hospitality."

"Please don't mention it. The pleasure is mine. We pride ourselves on our hospitality, too." Which was something else they did not particularly take pride in. Why did she keep saying so? "Please, do find a book. If you will excuse me—"

"Lady Dearborn, I really—"

"Emma," she interrupted out of desperation now.

He paused. "Pardon?"

"My name is Emma. Please, just…call me Emma." She meant it. It suddenly felt very important. She wanted this man, of all the men she'd met, to say her name. To take the countess out of it. "You don't seem to put much stock in titles, and neither do I. I would prefer it if you would call me by my given name."

"All right, Emma. My given name is Luka."

"Luka," she repeated. She liked the sound of it. "Is it short for something? Lukas? Lucien?"

"Just Luka." He glanced down the hall. "Might we step inside for a moment? There is something I must say."

No. "Luka Olivien, the Earl of Marlaine. It sounds almost like a name from a Shakespearean play, doesn't it?"

He looked at her blankly.

"One of his happier plays, I should think. No dead fathers or conniving daughters for a Luka Olivien."

He smiled.

"And now, Luka Olivien, you have met my family. Not quite what you expected, I'd wager?"

"Your family seems like any other family to me."

"Oh. How dreadful for us all."

His smile broadened.

Emma pivoted and walked back into the drawing room. She turned up the first lamp and dropped the book she'd chosen on an end table. If he was going to tell her, he could tell her in here. "Adele hates me, which you might have gathered. Since Albert left, it's as if she believes I am slowly and methodically stealing the silver, one spoon at a time."

Luka frowned. "She surely doesn't hate you. But perhaps she'd be kinder if you were more truthful with her."

Emma's heart started to skip around in her chest.

Here it came, and alas, her thinking was not as sharp as it normally was. She *knew* she should have stopped with the champagne. She couldn't keep him from saying it this time. With her back to him, she said, "I am as truthful as I can possibly be."

He didn't speak for a moment. Her curiosity got the best of her, and she turned. She was surprised that he looked slightly confused. "What do you mean?"

"I mean exactly that, sir. It's difficult to explain to an outsider, but it has much to do with marriage and entailments and all those things. Quite complicated, really." She was watching his expression. He had a kind face. A very kind and handsome face.

"I don't follow."

She stepped closer, better to see him in the dim light of a single lamp. "Do you ever wish, Luka? Do you ever find yourself wishing and wishing and wishing for things that are far out of your reach?"

He gave her a funny smile. "Have you had too much champagne?"

"Oh yes. But in some ways, not enough. Which is my point, really. So much depends on one's perspective. Does anyone's life unfurl perfectly? Doesn't every experience result in a wish for more or different or better?"

"Has your life unfurled in a way you don't care for?"

"No, but what I mean is…" She didn't know what she meant. His presence, the shine in his eyes were undoing her. "For example, when you kissed me, did it not result in a wish?"

Luka's expression changed from confusion to consternation so quickly that he looked almost ill. "I did not kiss you—"

"You did. In this very room."

He stared at her in disbelief. She could hardly believe herself. "I don't know what you are implying, Emma, but I did not kiss you. You very definitely kissed me."

"No. You kissed me."

He shifted forward, his gaze on her mouth, his eyes smoldering. "I did not, madam. If I had kissed you, I wouldn't have been so abrupt about it."

"Abrupt?" She was abruptly insulted. She was brazen, she'd admit to that. But *abrupt*?

He leaned closer. "If I had kissed you, I would have made certain you were as open to the suggestion as I was." He lifted his hand and slowly, gently, caressed her cheek with his knuckles. "I would have tucked your hair behind your ear," he said, as he tucked a sliver of hair behind her ear. "I would have looked at you with intent. I would have moved as close to you as I could without touching you, like I am now."

He was indeed very close. She could feel the heat of him. "And then what?" she asked, her voice hardly above a whisper.

"I would have looked in your lovely eyes, and I would have asked if I might kiss you."

She felt her lips part in anticipation.

His gaze moved to her mouth. "You would say yes, I think, and still I would not kiss you." Emma felt his arm go around her waist and yank her to his body in a manner that thrilled her. "I would ask you if you were certain and remind you that no one really knows where a kiss may lead, is that not so?"

"Is it?" she murmured and laid her hand on his chest.

He brushed his thumb across her lips. He touched her face again, and she felt a deep tremor spread through her, radiating out through her limbs. His fingers curled around her ear, then settled on her neck, warm and firm against her skin. "And you would not answer but look at me as you are now, with longing in your eyes, and I would relent and kiss you."

He lowered his head to hers, the scent of cologne intoxicating her more than even the champagne had done. She opened her mouth to his, felt his tongue slide in between her lips and tangle with hers. Emma could feel herself falling down a familiar path of desire, but this was different. She wasn't seeking just a physical release, but something deeper than that. Her heart began to race with the pleasure his kiss gave her, with the feel of his hands on her skin, with the anticipation of what was to come. She slid her hands up his chest, beneath his coat. She wanted to remove his clothing, one piece at a time. She wanted to lay herself bare before him. She wanted him to do anything he could imagine, anything that would bring her the pleasure she had craved for months now.

She pressed against him, crushing her breasts into his chest. She sank her fingers into his hair. Her skin was hot; she could feel the heat spreading from her core to between her legs.

And then it was over. He lifted his head. He stroked her brow. He said, "If I had kissed you, that's how I would have done it."

She couldn't move. Her body felt frozen, held up by his arm around her waist. But then he released her and stepped back. Emma swayed a little and stared at him, her body warring with her thoughts. She wanted to launch herself at him, toss him on the divan, and do what she pleased to him. But she also wanted to retreat, to *think*, damn it. She had let this spin so out of control that she was about to explode the world she had created for herself.

"I... Excuse me," she said, and with a hand on her nape, she brushed past him, nearly sprinting for the door. She expected him to call her back. *Wait! I haven't yet told you your husband is dead!*

She was up the stairs and locked in her room before he could have even dimmed the single light in the drawing room.

This was bad. This was very, very bad. But it was so *electric*, so fascinating! But *bad*. Terrible, awful, the worst.

Emma was in desperate need of advice.

CHAPTER THIRTEEN

AFTER A RESTLESS NIGHT, Emma woke just after sunrise. Waking so early was unlike her and left her feeling cross and confused.

She sat up, fluffed the pillows, and leaned back, her gaze locked on the circular crown molding on her ceiling. She was in too deep, completely submerged in her own shenanigans. Who could possibly help her out of this morass?

Fanny. She needed to talk to Fanny.

Emma got up and dressed in riding clothes. She put her hair in a long tail—she'd never been very good at properly dressing it—and was walking out the door just as Carlotta was coming in with a cup of tea. The poor thing tiptoed in as she normally did, so as not to wake a sleeping countess, who could be unreasonably cross in the morning, but stopped so quickly when she saw Emma that she spilled a bit of tea into the saucer. "Is something wrong? Are you ill?" She quickly set the tea aside and hurried forward with both hands free to commence an examination if needed.

"I'm fine!" Emma chirped. "I mean, besides a terrible headache and a bit of a sour stomach."

Carlotta put her palm to Emma's forehead. Emma pushed her hand down. "I never seem to remember that champagne doesn't agree with me until it's too late."

"You should be in bed," Carlotta said, and put a hand on her arm to guide her in that direction, but Emma shook her off.

"I'm fine, really. I'm up because I must speak to my sister. Something's come up." She grabbed her hat and started for the door.

"At this hour? But what of Mr. Olivien?" Carlotta cried, sounding desperate, as if she feared she'd be forced to entertain him.

It was a good question, Emma mused. What *of* Mr. Olivien? She mulled it over for the entire length of a few seconds. "He'll have to wait, won't he? Send him up to the ruins. Tell him I said there is some anthropology there he might like. Good day!" Emma darted through the door before Carlotta could begin to ask questions and scurried down the servants' stairs and out to the interior courtyard.

It was quite cool this morning. The mist was just rising from the fields, the sun barely above the trees. One had to appreciate the beauty of an English morning, particularly when one rarely saw them. But Emma was too frantic to appreciate much other than a desperate need to get away.

Mr. Karlsson was at work mucking out the horse stalls. He started when Emma burst into the stables and looked past her, as if he thought she was being chased, or maybe Jesus had come for them all. Emma realized she must look half-mad. "Good morning!" she said brightly, as if this was a normal morning. As if she wasn't at all breathless like she was.

"Madam? Is everything all right?"

"Absolutely! But I need a horse, Mr. Karlsson. The pony, preferably."

He frowned. "Do you mean to go far? It looks like a red sky, and that means rain is likely. Perhaps a carriage—"

"Oh no, no." A carriage would require too much time. "A bit of rain doesn't frighten me. I am riding to my sister's house. Just over that hill." She jerked her thumb over her shoulder to indicate the hill north of Butterhill Hall. "A mount, please?"

Mr. Karlsson looked as if he might argue but reluctantly did as she asked. A quarter of an hour later, he was helping her onto the saddle. Emma no longer used a side saddle, having given up that contraption once Albert had left. She felt more secure astride and didn't care that the lower part of legs—covered in stockings and boots—showed. If Mr. Karlsson had an opinion of her choice of saddle, he hid it well.

Adele had a very vocal opinion about it. She said Emma was risking her ability to ever give birth, bouncing around on the back of the horse as she was. Emma said she didn't see how bouncing could possibly make a difference to giving birth, particularly when she was not carrying a child. Adele said she was being obtuse.

"Thank you, sir!" Emma said, once she was in the saddle, and gave the pony a dig of her heels. Out the paddock they went, Emma leaning over the old girl's neck, riding like fire was at her heels. She could almost feel Butterhill Hall growing smaller and smaller behind her, finally disappearing.

Fanny's house was only thirty minutes over the hills, twenty if the horse was spirited, and when Emma crested the last one, she could see smoke curling out of one of the four chimneys. She'd never seen a more comforting sight. She and the pony raced down the hill and up to the fence. Emma leaped off the horse, wrapped the reins around the hitching post, and strode through the gate into Fanny's garden. It was bursting with color and scent and instantly made Emma long for simpler times. When she and Fanny were girls, they would spend weeks with her mother's parents, in their little cottage on the river with the luscious garden. Funny how nostalgia crept into your heart when you were least expecting it.

Emma hopped up on the landing beneath the eaves covered in climbing roses and knocked on the door. "Fanny!" she called. "Fanny, open the door! It's me!"

A few moments later, Mrs. Bart yanked open the door, her eyes wide with surprise. "Lady Dearborn?" She squinted past Emma just like Mr. Karlsson had done, as if she expected someone was chasing her.

"Is Fanny home?"

"I'm here," Fanny said, appearing behind Mrs. Bart. She was wiping her hands with a towel. "What has happened? Has someone died?"

The irony. "No! That is, not recently."

"Why are you shouting? What are you even doing here? It's not even nine o'clock."

"Was I shouting?" Emma said, and not only did she sweep by the other questions, she swept in through the door past Mrs. Bart. "I hadn't thought of the time. Was that rude of me? Is this an inconvenient time?"

"Of course not, darling," Fanny said, looking at her curiously. "But it's a bit peculiar."

If her sister thought this was peculiar, she would really be surprised in the end. "Where are the children?"

"They've gone with Phillip to visit his parents."

"You didn't go with them?"

"Obviously not, as I am standing here." Fanny put her hands on her waist. "What is the matter, Emma? *Has* someone died?"

The question was so on point that Emma couldn't help but laugh like a crazed woman. "Yes, Fanny, someone has died. Do you have some tea? Better yet, some whisky?"

"Whisky! Certainly not—it's too early for that. Come into the dining room. Mrs. Bart, will you bring us tea?" Fanny took Emma firmly by the elbow and steered her into the dining room and sat her in Phillip's chair. "Now," she said, "what on earth is the matter?"

So much that Emma didn't know where to begin. She sighed wearily. She removed her gloves and her hat, then leaned forward and pressed her fingertips to her eyes to keep from bursting into the sobs that were suddenly clawing at her throat.

"Oh, Emma," Fanny said, and Emma felt her sister's hand on her back. "What's wrong? Is it Adele? I swear on our mother's grave—"

"Surprisingly, it's not Adele," Emma said, and lifted her head. Fanny handed her a handkerchief. Emma dabbed at her eyes. She gazed at her sister, her brown hair and blue eyes. The same eyes that used to peek at Emma when they were in bed, supposedly sleeping. They were as close as two sisters could be, which made Emma's omission of truth even worse. "Do you remember the gentleman who came to Butterhill Hall and died in the drawing room?"

Fanny blinked. "How could I possibly forget it? Mr....?"

"Duffy," Emma supplied.

"Yes, Mr. Duffy. That poor, dear man, to die in a stranger's drawing room. And you! You've never known why he called, what news he supposedly had for you. A tragedy all around." She suddenly leaned forward. "Emma…you're not blaming yourself—"

"No," Emma said. "But…" She was beginning to feel ill and a bit dizzy. Like she needed to expunge a rotten piece of her before it poisoned the rest of her.

"The truth of it is, Fanny… I do know why Mr. Duffy came to Butterhill Hall."

Fanny frowned. "I don't understand. Wasn't the poor man struck down before he said more than a few words?"

"That is…true," Emma said carefully. "The poor soul died before he got very many words out…but he did manage a few more than I've let on."

Something changed in Fanny's expression. Her frown turned a bit darker. "Such as?"

"Such as…he'd come from Egypt."

"Egypt," her sister repeated, although she was staring at Emma as if she couldn't make sense of the word. "Why have you never said so? What did he say?"

A heaviness settled on Emma's chest and made it harder to draw a breath. The weight of terrible guilt, she suspected. "I never said because…well, because I'm an awful, *terrible* person who will surely rot in hell." This, she announced just as Mrs. Bart came in with tea.

"Emma!" Fanny cried.

Mrs. Bart looked stunned.

"Pay my sister no mind," Fanny said. "She'll not rot in hell, no matter how hard she might try." A look of unspoken understanding passed between the two women who spent their days together. "Or at least she won't before I get to the bottom of things." She took the tray from Mrs. Bart. Mrs. Bart stood rigidly, staring at Emma.

"I beg your pardon, Mrs. Bart," Emma said. "I did not mean to imply I will begin to rot today."

"*Goodness*," Mrs. Bart said, and with a blink, she went out, closing the door firmly behind her.

Fanny placed the tea on the table and began to pour. "All right, Emma, if you can refrain from scandalizing Mrs. Bart for the time being, will you start at the beginning?" She set a cup of tea in front of her sister. "You said Mr. Duffy claimed to have come from Egypt?"

"Yes. He said he had a message from Albert. Well—not *from* Albert but *about* Albert. Oh, and he had a letter. *That* was from Albert."

Fanny shook her head. "You're not making sense. Try again."

"Albert had written me a letter, and Mr. Duffy brought it along with his message."

"Why? What did it say?"

"The letter? Oh, that Albert expected to be home by Christmas."

Fanny fell back in her chair and stared hard at Emma. "You're going to have to help me understand because none of this is making sense. What was the man's message? Why haven't you told us all about the letter? Why didn't Albert come at Christmas, if that's what he wrote you?"

"You're getting too far ahead," Emma said. Her mind was spinning, and she could only handle one question at a time. "The message Mr. Duffy had for me—and you should brace yourself, Fanny, because it really is quite astonishing—Mr. Duffy had come all that way to tell me..." She paused to draw another short breath, during which Fanny leaned forward, all ears.

"Tell you what?"

Emma swallowed. "That Albert had died."

At first, there was no sound, no movement from Emma's sister. But then Fanny's voice exploded at the same moment her hands flew up in the air, and she shouted, "*What?*"

"Of yellow fever."

Fanny shrieked, then quickly covered her mouth with her hand. "*Emma!*" she hissed.

"And furthermore, that…that they had buried the body within a few hours as is the custom there. It makes a good deal of sense when you think of it."

All the color had drained from Fanny's face. She stared agape at Emma as a range of emotions flashed across her features. Disbelief. Anger. Disbelief again. Sorrow. And more disbelief. In fact, she began to shake her head. "Is this a joke? A trick? Because you can't *possibly* be serious, Emma Clark. You cannot convince me that you learned of your husband's death several months ago and never breathed a word of it to anyone!"

"Well…" Emma wanted to say something to appease her sister, but of course, there was nothing she could say.

Fanny sprang to her feet and began to pace. She could be very demonstrative with her emotions when she was highly agitated, and Fanny was highly agitated.

"This must sound so mad to you," Emma said apologetically. "It does to me, too, but—"

"Who have you become?" Fanny shouted at her.

"Hear me out, Fanny—"

"Hear you out? Emma! Have you heard the words you've uttered here today?" She was moving at a clip now, a palm pressed to her forehead, her skirt kicking out when she turned violently to pace the length of the room again. "That poor man died months ago. And all this time—" She suddenly gasped again and pressed both hands to her abdomen. "Dear God, what about Adele? Does she know?"

"God, no," Emma said, squirming uncomfortably in her seat. "She's the reason I never said anything."

Fanny gasped. "It's even worse than I thought! How could she possibly be the reason to keep such news to yourself? How could you keep it from her? From *me*?"

"Fanny, please...will you sit down and listen?"

Fanny ignored her, her gaze wild. Emma got up and went to her, put an arm around her shoulders, and dragged her back to the table. "Please. Sit. Just listen to me."

Fanny sat, but she wouldn't look at Emma. She was clearly appalled and unable to speak and gestured impatiently for Emma to speak, then clasped her hands tightly on the table before her, giving the impression she was trying to keep them from going around Emma's throat.

"What I did was wretched, I know that. But Fanny, you know the state of my marriage to Albert."

Fanny frowned, but she didn't argue that point.

"And you know how Adele feels about me. Do you think if she knew Albert had died that she'd wait even a day before she had Andrew declared the earl and living at Butterhill Hall? He's not ready to be an earl—there is too much to learn. And I've... I've made some good changes to Butterhill. I've been working to modernize it. Adele is opposed to any sort of change and would undo it all before Andrew understood. And the kindest thing she might do to me is lock me in the attic."

"That is more than you deserve, Emma! How could you? Albert is her *brother*."

"Was," Emma said with an apologetic wince.

Fanny glared at her. "You've never been one to not speak. How did you manage to keep it to yourself?"

Emma was afraid to admit that it hadn't been very hard at all until recently. "You know how I felt about him. Honestly, Fanny, after the initial shock, I was relieved. For months, I had lived in dread of his return."

"Oh, Emma," Fanny moaned. "I know. He was terrible to you. But you didn't wish him *dead*."

"Of course not! Never!" Except occasionally when she was hurt or angry or both. But only in the fantasy of her thoughts. She'd imagined a fall from a horse, or even a train accident, but she'd decided that would involve too many others. "When Mr. Duffy told me, I... I was so stunned. I didn't know what to say, and before I could think, the poor man was dead, right in front of me, and then all the chaos that followed. It was a *wretched* day, Fanny."

Fanny softened a little. "I know."

"Days rolled by before I realized I hadn't mentioned the letter, or Albert, what with all the conundrum about Mr. Duffy's body. No one ever prepares you for a body in your drawing room. And it...it felt easy to carry on as if the man had never uttered a word. Then, more days passed, weeks even, and I realized that I very much enjoyed being a merry widow. I was finally free of Albert. I was free to be myself. My secret didn't seem to harm anyone, not really, and I had every intention of confessing the truth, but the time never seemed right, or Adele vexed me to no end, and really, weren't things going along just exactly as they had before Albert died? In some cases, even better! You know that with Mr. Horn's help, I've changed our sheep management from producing food to producing wool, and we've already seen an increase in profits. I ended that dreadful idea that the lake could somehow become a fishery, and we are building a small shop to sell goods from the estate. That's just a few of the things we plan to do. I'm proud of what I've done for Butterhill Hall."

Fanny didn't look impressed or even convinced. "Is any of that a reason to keep Albert's death a secret? One doesn't seem to have anything to do with the other. You could have talked to Adele. You could have had Mr. Horn talk to her."

"Fair. But I convinced myself there was no harm. Until…" She winced.

"*Until?* Until when? Until what?"

"Until Mr. Olivien came with Albert's pocket watch." Fanny glowered at her.

"I think he thought I'd be grateful that he'd come all this way to return Albert's watch. But I wasn't grateful at all, I was rather vexed that he'd come and ruined everything. I meant to avoid him—"

"Wait," Fanny said, holding up a hand. "Who is Mr. Olivien?"

Emma blinked. She was so discombobulated she forgot that Fanny knew nothing about him. "Oh! The Weslorian."

"The *Weslorian*? What Weslorian?"

Emma told her. How he'd come from Egypt to deliver the watch and seemed confused when Emma didn't mention her late husband. And that she probably could have sent him on his way then and there, but then Adele had come, and Emma had foolishly said she'd invited him for a country house party and what went on from there.

Fanny looked as stunned as if she'd run straight into a wall.

"I did try to avoid him," Emma promised.

"How could you possibly? You're hosting a weekend gathering for him!"

"Not for him, really. But you're right, I couldn't very well avoid a guest in my house, and then…well, Fanny, I might as well tell you everything. I kissed him."

Fanny's arms slid out along the table as she slowly lowered her forehead to the surface with a groan. "Don't tell me more."

"I kissed him twice. And Fanny?"

"I beg of you—"

"I'm thinking of taking him as a lover before this all collapses around me. He's very well-formed."

Fanny drew a long breath that lifted her up off the table. And then she screamed.

"Don't do that!" Emma cried. She hopped up and went to her sister, put her arms around her.

Fanny screamed again.

Mrs. Bart burst through the door. "What is the matter? What's happened?"

"I've upset her," Emma said, squeezing her sister tight. "But we're fine. Perfectly well. We're fine, right, Fanny?"

"No! We are not *fine*, Emma!" She angrily shrugged out of Emma's embrace and stood. "I have collected myself," she said to Mrs. Bart. "Please, don't concern yourself. It's a quarrel between sisters."

Mrs. Bart hesitated. "Sounded a bit more serious than that."

"It's really quite all right," Fanny said, and sighed heavily.

Mrs. Bart pressed her lips together. "As you please," she said, and backed out of the room and slowly shut the door. When the door latched shut, Fanny whirled around and punched Emma in the shoulder.

"Ouch!" Emma cried, her hand going to her shoulder.

"*Now* what, Emma? Now what? You must fix this! Adele and Andrew deserve to know the truth. And the more you keep silent, the bigger and more convoluted your lie becomes. Don't fool yourself—in the end, this lie *will* be discovered, and *then* what? If Adele was in any way inclined to help you, she won't be after this. Don't you *see* that?"

"I do, Fanny, of *course* I do. On my life, I never meant for everything to get so out of hand. But I don't know *how* to fix it. I was hoping you'd help me."

Fanny folded her arms and looked away for a long moment. When she returned her gaze to her sister, her look was cold and dark. "The first thing you must do is get rid of this man."

"Get rid of him?" Emma asked uneasily. Before she'd had a tryst with him?

"Yes, Emma! He obviously must go."

"But the house party—"

Fanny punched her again, only harder, and Emma cried out. "He has to go!" Fanny said loudly. "No wonder Mother always said that you do more harm to yourself than anyone could possibly do."

Emma blinked. "She said that?"

"Never mind," Fanny said, waving a hand at her. "We've enough to think about without adding a discussion about Mother."

But as Fanny started to talk, Emma was thinking of Mr. Olivien. Apparently, she hadn't learned anything, other than she was clearly addicted to bad behavior. Because she did *not* want to get rid of him.

Not yet.

CHAPTER FOURTEEN

LUKA SPENT WHAT felt like a good portion of the morning pacing his room, peering blindly out the window, his thoughts swirling. He didn't recognize himself, had never known himself to be held in thrall by a woman to the point of ignoring all the warning signs and playing a game with a widow who would not admit she was a widow.

He had new resolve to end this nonsense today before he lost his mind and his dignity completely.

Unfortunately, confronting her would once again prove impossible, as she was nowhere to be found. And it wasn't from a lack of searching. He'd looked in every common room on the ground floor, assuming she'd be at her breakfast, or in her drawing room, or even in the kitchen cooking something—even that didn't seem terribly far-fetched for this countess. But the kitchen staff was startled by his appearance, and when he asked after her ladyship, they looked at him as if they weren't quite sure who he meant. The cook informed him her ladyship did not visit the kitchens except on Sunday afternoons to discuss menus for the week ahead.

Outside he went, through the gardens, down the lake, and around. When he couldn't find her there, he returned to the house. The hunt for her was making him cross. He decided he'd write some letters home to inform his father he'd been delayed a week. When that was done, the letter addressed and sealed and in his pocket, he headed for the stables.

On his way, he noticed quite a lot of activity around the orangery. Feeney was there, directing footmen and others as they hauled pots from the building, and others carried chairs and tables inside. Luka paused to watch a moment. He noticed Lady Dearborn's maid hurrying down the path to Feeney. When she said whatever she'd come to say, she turned to go back up the path.

Luka intercepted her. "Good afternoon, miss. Carlotta, is it not?"

Carlotta blinked. She glanced surreptitiously over her shoulder at the butler.

"I won't keep you but a moment. Your mistress doesn't appear to be…here. Can you tell me where I might find her?"

"No," she said instantly. "That is…her ladyship has gone to visit her sister. She said you might like to visit the ruins up that hill." She pointed to a place over his shoulder. "She said you might find some ant-apology."

Luka turned to look in the direction her finger was pointing. He could only see a hill, but no ruins. He turned back to the young woman. "Anthropology?"

"*Ant*-apology," Carlotta insisted.

"Do you perhaps mean archaeology?"

Her dark brows knit into a frown. "I do not. Something *apology*, I'm certain of it. I suppose you'll know when you see it, sir. She seemed to think you would."

"I would imagine she did," he muttered. "When is your mistress expected home?"

Carlotta shrugged. "Tonight? But sometimes she stays the night. Sometimes, she stays two days. She used to stay three or four, but with the earl away, she must be here to see after things."

"Thank you." He tipped his hat. Carlotta scurried past him like she thought he might be infected.

This was his own damn fault. He thought for the thousandth time that he should have shown some strength of character, tamped down his curiosity about her, and been on his way. What was it about this woman he found so impossible to turn away from?

He carried on to the stables and introduced himself to the stablemaster. He explained to Mr. Karlsson that he was a guest and needed to go to Rexford to post some letters. Mr. Karlsson, after ascertaining Luka's proficiency with a horse, offered him Lord Dearborn's former mount. He was a stallion and had the look of a horse that wanted to run. "I don't... I wouldn't presume to borrow his lordship's horse," Luka said awkwardly.

"You'd be doing Cicero a service," Mr. Karlsson said. "Her ladyship refuses to ride him, given his size and spirit, and he spends too much time alone in the fields." He stroked the stallion's nose. "He is lonely here, I think."

Luka looked at the horse. Maybe this was the least he could do for the late Lord Dearborn, whose hospitality he'd abused by staying too long and kissing his wife. Not once, but twice. "All right," he agreed.

Cicero was indeed eager to be given his head, and Luka gave it to him, letting him gallop along the road, then veering into a meadow and letting him run there. When the horse had settled, Luka rode into Rexford and to the post office. He dismounted and tied the reins to a hitching rail. From the corner of his eye, he noted two gentlemen studying him and the horse. He nodded.

"It's Dearborn's horse, isn't it?" one of the gentlemen called.

A small buzz, a warning, slipped down Luka's spine. "It is. I have the good fortune of borrowing him."

The two men exchanged a look. One of them came forward, peering curiously at Luka, as if he thought he ought to know him. "Have we met?"

"No, sir. I am from Wesloria."

"Wesloria!" The man looked at his companion again. "How did you come to borrow Lord Dearborn's horse?"

It was none of the gentleman's concern. "Is Cicero so well known?" He stroked its nose.

"Aye. That horse is one of the finest racing animals in this part of England. I've won a fair amount wagering on him. Curious, however, as no one has seen him since Dearborn took his leave."

Luka could feel their curiosity rolling over him in waves. A mysterious foreigner on the missing earl's mount. "I wasn't aware of the horse's history." He patted the stallion's long neck. "I'm a guest at Butterhill Hall, and the stablemaster offered him this morning as the horse needed exercise."

"Ah." The man extended his hand. "Allow me to introduce myself. I am Mr. Donald Horn. And my friend, the Reverend William Thompson."

"Luka Olivien." He shook the men's hands.

"A guest, you say?" Mr. Horn asked.

"A guest," Luka confirmed.

"Forgive my surprise. I do a bit of work with her ladyship, and she hadn't mentioned a guest."

What sort of work did he do for Lady Dearborn that would entitle him to know of her guests? Luka stepped away from the horse. "Perhaps because the visit is quite short." He looked at his pocket watch. "Gentlemen, I'm afraid the time has gotten away from me. If you will excuse me."

"Of course," Mr. Horn said. He tipped his hat as Luka passed. But Luka could feel the men's eyes on his back as he walked.

He posted his letters with the clerk there, and when he'd finished, he unhitched the horse and rode out of Rexford with the uncomfortable feeling that many eyes were on him.

When he arrived at Butterhill Hall, Mr. Karlsson thanked him for giving the horse some air. Luka returned to his rooms and bathed. Later, as he dressed, he heard something through the open window on the east wall that sounded like humming. He went to have a look.

Below him, in a walled rose garden, Emma was seated at a small wrought-iron table with several papers before her. Next to her on the ground was a basket of cut flowers. She wore a hat with a wide brim so that he couldn't see her face. But he knew it was her because she was barefoot, and the long tail of auburn hair was draped over her shoulder. She would hum, jot something down, hum again.

She was a country tableau, a comely lady at her leisure in a beautiful garden. He felt a slight tug in his chest, a familiar pull of happiness that someone he knew had come into his day. But he had to ignore that, push it down, stomp it out. It was time to speak to her. He couldn't put it off another moment.

Luka combed his hair and straightened his neck cloth, then made his way down to the rose garden. But he was too late—the garden was empty. With a sigh of exasperation, he turned back to the house. She could not have gone far. And indeed, when he entered the hall, he could hear her laughter coming from one of the reception rooms. He strode in that direction...but as he neared it, he heard more feminine voices. Carlotta?

He went to the open door of the reception room and peered inside. Two women, dressed as if out for calls, were seated on the settee. Emma had removed her hat and put on shoes and was casually braiding her long hair. She was in the middle of telling a story, clearly, as the two women were laughing. But then Emma spotted him standing there, and they turned.

"There he is, the man of the hour!" Emma chirped. She stood up. "My lord Marlaine, may I introduce you to two dear friends of mine, Lady Carhill and Mrs. Westwood?"

He was Lord Marlaine again. The ladies stood and curtsied.

"This is Albert's special friend," she added.

He shot her a quick look. "Acquaintance," he clarified.

"You're too modest, my lord," Emma said.

And she was too cheeky. "A pleasure to make your acquaintance," he said to the ladies, and bowed.

"How fortunate we are to make *your* acquaintance, my lord," said Mrs. Westwood and appeared, at least to Luka, to elbow her friend very subtly. "We've heard quite a lot about you."

He didn't care for that and looked at Emma.

"My friends have come to help me finish the invitation list to your party," Emma said. "Would you care to join us?"

Her cheek was unparalleled in the history of mankind. Did she really think he would join them to create an invitation list for a party he would not attend? "Thank you, but I've some tasks to complete."

"Tasks! My good man, you must make better use of a fine afternoon!" she declared. "We will take our tea on the terrace. At least join us for that."

"I'm afraid I must decline."

The two women exchanged a sly look.

"Very well, then," Emma said with a shrug. "But you'll miss all the gossip, you know." Her friends laughed, and then all three feminine gazes were fixed on him. Luka murmured a good afternoon and walked on. Marched on, really, as he was fuming that she seemed to have put him off yet again. She was masterful at playing games.

He could hear the fluttering about and the whispers as he moved down the hall. Apparently, the gossip had already begun.

Later, he could hear their laughter rising up from the terrace, and then again coming from the drawing room as the dinner hour approached. When Feeney came to him with a dome-covered plate that contained a meal, he understood that the ladies meant to stay for dinner.

Later—much later, after he'd come precipitously close to finishing off a bottle of wine—he heard a ruckus on the drive and went to the window that overlooked the rose garden. Just beyond the garden wall, he could see a carriage had been brought round, the lanterns lit and illuminating the drive and team of two. The ladies were leaving. It was half past eleven.

Once again, a full day had passed and he'd failed to tell Emma about her husband, or force her to admit the truth, or come close to understanding his fixation.

This was the height of absurdity, he thought in his state of semi-inebriation. There were any number of moments he could have done it. What the bloody hell was he waiting for? Another kiss? What sort of man had he become in the last few days? A pitiful one, that was what. A coward or a weakling or an imbecile— the English language had a colorful roster of words to choose from.

Luka fell into his bed, thoroughly disgusted with himself.

The next morning, he was up at dawn, dressed and his few things packed. Again. He was determined that today was the day, to use whatever moment he had to deliver the news and then be on his way.

It was early yet, and he went outside to breathe in cool morning air and dispel the headache he'd awakened with. He took his last walk around the lake, his thoughts moving ahead to the task of collecting his things in London, booking passage to Wesloria. Tasks he should have taken care of days ago.

When he had made the circuit, he walked up past the stables and saw Mr. Karlsson in the paddock with horses. "My lord," the man said cheerfully. "Fancy taking Cicero for a turn about the fields?"

Luka glanced at the horse and with a pang of regret, shook his head. "I'm afraid not. I'll be taking my leave this morning. In fact," he said, glancing at his pocket watch, "would you know what time the train leaves for London?"

"One comes through every day at two o'clock."

Luka nodded. He had time to gather his things and speak to Emma one last time. "If you'll excuse me— I'll pay my regards to her ladyship and be on my way."

Mr. Karlsson slipped a bridle over one of the horse's heads. "Best be quick, sir—I've readied the coach and taken it around for her. She's to Rexford today."

Bloody hell. She was not going to avoid him again. Luka wished the stablemaster a good day then strode to the drive. The coach was still there, a coachman waiting for the lady. Luka strode through the front door, prepared to demand of Feeney that he see her ladyship at once, prepared to refuse to take no for an answer. But that would not be necessary, as Emma stood in the foyer, dressed in green and adjusting her elaborate bonnet in a mirror over the console. She turned slightly when he entered. "Ah, good morning, Mr. Olivien!"

He almost smiled at her cheerfulness but would not give her the satisfaction. "Good morning, Lady Dearborn. I see today I am Mr. Olivien and no longer Lord Marlaine?"

"Isn't it delightful to have more than one name? I wish I had more."

"You do have more. You have as many names as I have."

She seemed surprised by this, but after a moment, she smiled. "So I do!"

"Madam—"

"*Emma.* Remember?" She smiled, and it sparked a little fire in him.

Je, he remembered. He remembered everything about her.

She leaned forward in the mirror as she tied her bonnet strings.

"I insist that I must have a word. I intend to take my leave—"

"Oh! I nearly forgot. Some things have come for you," she interrupted.

He knew what she was doing, quite obviously, but he was unbalanced by the idea of *things*.

"Pardon?"

"Letters and what-not."

Letters and what-not? He didn't believe her. He folded his arms. "Is that so? And where are these letters and what-not?" he asked, looking around. "You may think me a fool, but I know what you are attempting to do."

"I really don't know what you mean. Your things aren't here at Butterhill Hall, but they are *here*. In the vicinity." She held up a finger and traced a circle in the air, then turned back to the mirror and made a small adjustment to her hat.

"Could you elaborate?"

"On which part?"

He narrowed his gaze. "Emma? Where are they?"

"I am confusing things a bit, aren't I?" She dropped her hands and turned to face him fully. She was smiling at him as if they were old friends. "At the Rexford Arms. Mr. Barnes, you remember him, the innkeeper? He sent a messenger this morning. It was early, and I told him you were sleeping."

"Sleeping?"

"And therefore unavailable, and he said, well, he'd wait, and I said that was hardly necessary, that we were perfectly capable of passing along the message, and surely the poor man couldn't afford to wait. What of your wages, I asked him." She paused to look at him. "Wages are something I am very interested in refining. Here at Butterhill, we are reviewing them all. People should be fairly compensated for their work, wouldn't you agree? But that's another story for another time. *This* story is about your things at the Rexford Arms. I won't even tell you the story of how dear old Mr. Foster came into possession of a new dog, which I heard just this morning from the same young man. I am delighted for him. Anyway, I told the messenger that I was on my way to Rexford, to the post office, and would see to it that your things were collected. Didn't you say you wrote some letters? I'd be happy to post them if you like. Better yet, you should come to Rexford with me. I should probably mention that Mr. Barnes insisted some of the letters seemed rather important. He said they had an official seal and were written on the thickest paper he'd ever held." She widened her eyes slightly and leaned forward to whisper, "You're not in any trouble, are you?"

Yes, he was in trouble, but not the sort she meant. He was distracted by her blue eyes and her smile, and the way she could natter on about anything, and something was stirring in his chest that seemed to happen with alarming frequency when she was near. And who was Mr. Foster? He was troubled by the kissing they'd done, and the letter that seemed important. To add to that was the not insignificant problem that he could hardly form a cogent thought because she looked so beautiful to him, so bloody appealing, all fresh and dewy.

She picked up a cloth bag and hooked it over her arm. Just then, her maid came into the foyer in a similar bonnet to Emma's and stared at Luka as if she thought he meant to kidnap them. Right behind her was Feeney, who hurried past them and out to the drive without a word to anyone.

Emma was still smiling at him. And her smile was

entirely too self-satisfied, because she knew that she had foiled him again. He wanted to kiss that bit of a smirk right off her face.

"Will you come?" she asked.

He needed that letter. And his things. But he didn't want to be in a coach with her superior little smile or her scowling maid. But he couldn't let her think she'd won. *Again.* "I, ah... I will ride."

"Yes, of course you can ride if you prefer. But I understand one of the things for you is a trunk. Isn't it a trunk, Carlotta?"

"I couldn't say," Carlotta said coolly.

Emma said to Luka, "I think she *could* say, but she prefers not to." She smiled with fondness at her maid, then said to him, "Shall we?"

Luka didn't answer straightaway because he realized he had another problem—he hadn't sent for his trunk. What was it doing in Rexford? How was he to haul it back to London? And just how long had he been away from London that someone thought it necessary to forward his trunk?

The two women started for the door. Emma looked over her shoulder at him. "Are you coming, Mr. Olivien?"

Luka sincerely hated himself in that moment, because of course he was coming.

CHAPTER FIFTEEN

IT WAS QUITE obvious that Emma's guest was perturbed. He hardly said a word on the way to Rexford, probably vexed that she'd managed to evade his announcement once again. She would be if she was in his shoes.

Or maybe he wasn't vexed at all but simply couldn't find a moment to speak because she kept a running stream of conversation moving along with Carlotta, recounting the many, *many* things Lady Carhill had said. She even made up a few bits and pieces to fill in the gaps of things she couldn't recall. Lady Carhill was a magpie, and Emma had lost her train of thought more than once during the day with her friends.

Furthermore, she couldn't really judge his mood because she'd hardly spared him a glance, fearful that if she gave him the slightest opening, he'd launch himself at it and blurt his news. She was so fearful, in fact, that she pretended to forget he was even in the coach sitting directly across from her by keeping her body turned to Carlotta and her shoulder to him. She *hadn't* forgotten, obviously, as his mere presence seemed to fill the interior and press against her in a pleasant way. And then again, not entirely so, because…because why did he have to be so determined to tell her about Albert? He knew she knew. Did he think it the noble thing to do?

It *was* the noble thing to do, but really, his dogged determination was throwing a spanner into *everything*.

By the time they reached Rexford, she felt coiled up like a spring, her head aching—symptoms that her inner turmoil was coming to full boil.

She couldn't avoid Luka any longer. Fanny was cross with her, so she couldn't decamp there without a lecture. She wouldn't, anyway, because there was so much yet to be done for her country house party. Yesterday, she'd spent two hours with Feeney in the throes of planning. And then, she and her friends Lady Cargill and Mrs. Westwood, had finished the invitation list and created the invitations—Mrs. Westwood had perfected the art of calligraphy.

This morning, when she'd been deciding which hat to wear, Feeney had been beside himself, insisting they couldn't bring acrobats from London, as there was no place to put them. Emma insisted she was confident he would think of something, which wasn't fair, she knew, but her thoughts were so crowded she couldn't figure it out for him. She knew her butler longed for the day Albert would return and he could resume his usual rhythm of working, unbothered by what he surely thought were her frivolous demands. Emma loved the stoic and steadfast old Feeney, but she wished with all her heart that he would loosen his necktie a smidgen and enjoy life alongside her instead of seeing everything as an obstacle to the way things were generally done.

Today, she would post the invitations, then go to a fitting for three dresses she'd commissioned that were almost ready, all while devising stories to launch at Luka if he tried to tell her about Albert. She was Scheherazading her way to...what? Now Fanny knew her secret. Obviously, the time had come for Emma to tell the truth. But couldn't she have her last party before she did?

No wonder she was so tightly wound.

As they pulled into the village center, Emma stole a glimpse of Luka. His indefatigable gaze was fixed on her, his expression suspicious. Like he expected her to leap from the coach and run from him. Which, come to think of it, was not a bad idea. Maybe, when the coach stopped, she would leap through the open door and hurry into the post office before he could speak. It would be easy to do—Carlotta was so slow in getting in and out of the coach she would block his progress while Emma ran.

But when they reached Rexford, he was the one who was quick to alight and turned to help them down. He was being a gentleman, but on the slim chance he was going to take her hand and pull her aside, Emma said to Carlotta, "You go" and gave her a bit of a shove toward the door. And as Carlotta carefully put her foot on the step, then took Luka's hand and carefully took the next step down, Emma sprang out behind her, hopping down so awkwardly that she only narrowly avoided a stumble to the ground, startling both her guest and her maid. "Thank you, sir!" She grabbed Carlotta's hand. "Mr. Barnes has your mail and trunk from London." She yanked Carlotta into a brisk walk.

"Why are we running?" Carlotta asked, trying to pull her hand free.

"We are not running, we are walking with purpose."

"The *purpose* feels like running," Carlotta said, already breathless, and managed to free her hand. She yanked up her glove. "You needn't walk so fast. The post coach won't come until the afternoon. There is plenty of time."

Emma couldn't explain why there was no time. She felt a sense of urgency, as if the personal storm that was coming would blow in from the darkest skies and sweep her all the way to the sea.

The urgency was her desire to avoid the inevitable. Interestingly, Emma had never been one to put off the hard things in life—she'd always preferred to walk right into them, to face the pain or discomfort as quickly as possible so she could move on from it just as quickly. But with Luka, something was different. She didn't want him to leave. And yet she did. She didn't want to unburden herself with the truth about Albert. And yet she did.

Nothing made sense.

Her first order of business was to post the invitations to the party. That went quickly enough, even though Mr. Kettleman, the postmaster, was keen to talk. From there, Emma and Carlotta walked to Mrs. Porter's dress shop, where Emma tried on the gowns she'd commissioned. It seemed to be taking quite a long time to mark the hem on the last one, and Emma felt a desperation to hurry the seamstress along, but she was engaged in a lively conversation with Carlotta, and it wasn't until Emma shot Carlotta a look that the task was completed.

When she and Carlotta left the shop, Emma turned in the direction of the waiting coach, but Carlotta stopped her. "You're going the wrong way," she said.

"Pardon?" Emma said.

"My mother, remember? We promised we'd call when we came to town this week. We'll be a bit early, but she won't mind."

No, Emma had not remembered. They'd made plans last week, before her life had begun to unravel. "Right." She pursed her lips. Another conundrum—she thoroughly enjoyed Carlotta's mother, a jovial, quick-witted woman who made the most delicious apple cake she'd ever had the pleasure to eat. She regretted not having the opportunity for a thick slice of that, but she couldn't afford to spend the afternoon laughing.

Carlotta noticed her hesitation. "Is something wrong?"

"No, not at all."

"Mama is always so happy to see you."

"And I am always delighted to call." Emma smiled.

Carlotta frowned. "But...?"

It's just that...that I forgot, and I have so much yet to be done for the house party. You should have heard Feeney this morning! I fear he will find another position if I put him off any longer."

"Oh." Carlotta looked longingly in the direction of her parents' house.

An idea struck. "You go, Carlotta. I'll send the carriage back for you. Better yet, stay overnight!" *Perfect.* Carlotta deserved the time with her mother, and Emma would be busy with various things.

But Carlotta looked surprisingly appalled by the suggestion. "No!"

"Why not? Won't you enjoy the time with your mother?" She glanced anxiously toward the coach. There was no sign of Luka, but she did realize that it would be the only the two of them in the coach, and the perfect opportunity for him to speak.

"I couldn't!" Carlotta said. "Mr. Feeney hasn't said I might stay overnight. He'd have my head."

It was true that Feeney ruled the household staff

with an iron fist. "I'll speak to him," Emma said. "He can't disagree then, can he?" He would, undoubtedly. But the more immediate problem was Luka. She could say she had a terrible headache and ask him to ride with the driver.

"Oh, but he can," Carlotta said darkly.

"Carlotta, take this time with your family. If Feeney has anything to say, he may say it to me. I would not rest easy if I kept you from seeing your mother when I'd promised."

Carlotta looked away, as if debating it. Over her shoulder, across the village green, Emma saw Luka come out of the inn.

"You're certain?" Carlotta asked.

"Quite! Really, you don't see your mother enough. You'll give her my warmest regards, won't you? And a promise that next time I will come." She put her hands on Carlotta's shoulders and turned her in the direction of her mother's home.

"It's true I've not seen my sister in a fortnight—"

"Then it's settled!" Emma said before her maid could ponder it another moment. "Have a wonderful visit." She gave Carlotta's shoulders a squeeze, then a friendly little nudge to carry on. "I'm off!" she said, and began to stride toward the coach. Out of the corner of her eye, she saw Luka step off the walk and start to stroll across the green in the direction of the coach, too. Behind him, two men carried a large trunk.

A coachman opened the door for her. "Thank you," she said. "I'm feeling unwell, so if you might ask Mr. Olivien to sit with the driver?"

"Yes, milady." He helped her in, then shut the door behind her.

Emma sat on the edge of her bench and pushed aside the curtain from the small window. She couldn't see Luka now, couldn't see much of anything, really. But in the next moment, the coach sagged to one side as someone climbed up to the driver's seat. The conveyance began to move. Slowly. But it was moving.

Emma fell back against the squabs with a sharp sigh of relief.

And then, quite abruptly, the coach came to a halt. She bolted upright, her eyes wide. She could hear voices behind the coach, followed by a jostling that very nearly knocked her off her seat, as if men or things were being moved around.

"What is—"

The door suddenly swung open, and she raised her hand to block the brilliant sunlight from hitting her square in the eyes. She saw one boot hit the floor of the coach, followed by a leg, and then his entire being. She lowered her hand. "You," she said.

"Me," he said curtly. He dropped onto the bench across from her, his legs sprawled, frowning darkly. "Your plan didn't work."

"What plan?"

"To send me to ride with the driver. You failed to account for my trunk, which has taken up all the available spots on the back of the coach, which means the coachman must ride up top." The door closed, and Luka knocked on the ceiling as if this was his coach, signaling the driver to carry on.

"But we were moving."

"The driver was positioning the coach so that the trunk could be properly lashed."

The coach picked up speed.

"Why are you in such a rush, Lady Dearborn? You seem to have forgotten your maid."

"I didn't forget her, I intentionally left her to visit her mother."

"And your headache? Vastly improved?"

"That depends," she said.

Anxiety was most decidedly creeping into her neck and squeezing at her temples. This was it, then, the pinnacle moment had arrived, unless she started talking. "My apologies," she said, and smiled sweetly. "I suppose I'm a bit single-minded today, what with all there is to do. But now I am dying of curiosity—were your letters as important as the messenger made it sound?"

One of Luka's brows lifted with mild surprise. "That's a rather personal question, but *je*, they were. And before you ask, because I know you will, the most important are from Her Royal Highness, Queen Justine."

Emma perked up at that. "From a *queen*! I've never known anyone to receive a letter from a monarch. What good company you must keep in Wesloria, Mr. Olivien, sir. Or should I call you Lord Marlaine in this instance? Are you acquainted with her? Or was it written by a minister? Was it a tax bill?"

"They are personal letters. We've been acquainted since we were children. She is my friend and my queen."

"Oh." She was desperate to know what she'd written.

Luka smiled a little. "I haven't read them yet."

"Does she write you often?"

"Never before."

"What do you think it means?"

One corner of his mouth tipped up. "I think it means I am likely needed at home."

Home. Emma thought she ought to be inwardly celebrating this good news, but the idea of this intriguing man leaving now struck her as all wrong—the wrong idea, the wrong time, the wrong everything. An utterly mad thought! How confusing that she *wanted* him to leave without announcing his news, but she didn't want *him* to leave.

"And while I appreciate your hospitality, I must do as the queen asks."

"Well, of course you must! She's your queen. If Queen Victoria summoned me to London, I'd jump on a horse and ride there straightaway."

"On horseback? All the way to London?"

"Or in a coach. Whichever would be more readily available."

"I see. Because nothing would stand in your way, if you were summoned by your queen."

Emma snorted. "Nothing."

"*Je*, and nothing should. Frankly, I find myself wondering why I've lingered here for as long as I have." His gaze moved over her so casually that her skin tingled.

Luka suddenly sat up and braced his elbows on his legs. He looked at her—looked into her eyes, really. "Emma...there is something you should know—"

"No!" She threw up a hand in a panic. "I beg you don't tell me anything that I must know or remember or act upon. My head is simply filled with—"

"You really must listen—"

"—all the news that Lady Carhill has given me, and I can hardly squeeze in another—"

"Lady Dearborn, people in Rexford are whispering that you are having an affair," he announced loudly before she could interrupt him again. "By God, you are a challenge."

Emma had opened her mouth to shout over him, but she quickly closed it again. That was most decidedly *not* what she thought he would say, and if he was going to blurt something out, why that? Why not the other? And who was saying that about her? She was caught completely wrong-footed. "I beg your pardon?"

"I heard it myself, in the public room of the inn. Two gentlemen were talking, and one said his wife had heard you're engaged in an illicit affair while your poor husband is abroad."

"My poor *husband*?" Emma blurted. "He was hardly conscripted!" Her husband had never done or accepted anything less than precisely what he wanted. *She* was the one who had been left behind as prisoner. Which she would have loved to point out, but given the circumstances, she thought not. "And just who is my paramour? Because I assure you, I don't have one. Believe me," she said adamantly and gave a huff of bitter laughter. If only the gossips knew how badly she *wanted* to have an affair.

"I know you're not engaged in any such thing," he said, in a kind manner that sounded like he thought it was out of the realm of possibility, "but—"

"But I want to," she snapped. There, she'd said it. And Luka looked stunned, as if she'd slapped him. She decided then and there that it hardly mattered what she said now. This man was leaving England. She could say whatever she pleased. "Well? I do! I *yearn* for an affair of the heart. Why must you look so shocked? Everyone wants the same, you must admit."

"I *am* shocked. Even if it is true that everyone wants an affair of the heart, they don't go blurting it out."

Emma shrugged nonchalantly.

Luka turned his gaze to the window and stared for a long moment. And then he turned back to her. "One question?"

She indicated with her hand that he should let his question fly.

"Thank you. What is the *matter* with you?" he demanded. "Are you mad?"

"No!"

"I think you should consider the possibility that you might be, at least a little! You speak of affairs of the heart when your..." He suddenly surged forward. "What I've been trying to tell you, what you *surely* must—"

"Say no more!" she cried. Her heart was racing, her palms suddenly damp. She couldn't avoid it any longer; her secret was ready to burst out of her like a bad appendix.

"Emma, I—"

"*Luka*, I know! All right? I *know*." And with that admission, she felt something in her crumble. Not in a terrible way, as one might expect, but more like a dam had burst and the terrible task of holding it together had thankfully washed away. Like a massive stone she'd been carrying in the pit of her stomach had finally crumbled into dust. "I *know*," she said again, softly.

She didn't expect him to be surprised by her admission, but she thought he would at least thrust his finger skyward and shout *I knew it!* or offer some other display of vindication. But he didn't do any of that. His gaze narrowed and fixed on her. He studied her face. He said, "You'll need to be more specific."

What? She'd just confessed her deepest, darkest secret, and he wanted her to amend it? *"Why?"*

"Why? Because we've a lack of trust between us.

I wouldn't be the least bit surprised if you meant that you know I am vexed, and not something else."

"Mr. Olivien!" He obviously wanted a full confession.

"Je?" He was looking at her contemplatively, like he couldn't quite make her out, like she was moving in a mist and he could only catch a glimpse of her. He lifted his chin. "Say it," he demanded. But at the same time, he seemed slightly uncertain. An exciting idea popped into Emma's head. Maybe, just maybe, Luka Olivien was the one who didn't know Albert was dead.

What the devil? Just a moment before, she'd been feeling as if everything she'd felt in these last many months—the freedom, the joy—would be coming to an end. But now she wondered if she'd misread the situation completely.

"Say it," he said again. "I would hear it from your lips."

They had turned onto the drive to Butterhill, and Emma suddenly leaned forward. "I'll say it, all right. I'll say it all. But at dinner."

"Dinner?" He shook his head. "No. You won't come, and moreover, I don't think you understand. I mean to leave, Emma. I've done what I came here to do—a favor to a friend on my way to Wesloria. I've stayed too long." He leaned forward, too, so they were just inches apart, their gazes locked. "So I really need you to say what you know."

"But you can't leave! I just today posted invitations to my weekend country house party in your honor."

"You did *what*?"

"You can't be surprised! I told you I was hosting a party in your honor."

"You said that as a ruse—"

"But then I discovered I really liked the idea, and I've gone to a great deal of trouble now. It would be exceedingly rude of you to leave me in the lurch."

"Emma... *Satamna*," he muttered.

"Pardon?"

"Never mind. It's not polite." Luka dropped his face into his hands and rubbed his forehead. After a moment, he lifted his head. His eyes moved over her face. "For the love of God, you confound me."

If she hadn't been so flattered—she rather liked being confounding—she might have felt sorry for him. "I know," she said gently. "You must think the absolute worst of me, and who would blame you? All I can say is that it will be the grandest party of them all, and no matter that you are friends with your queen, you will never have another party quite like this in your honor. You really must stay."

He gave a laugh that sounded both sad and bedeviled. He began to shake his head. "I just want you to admit what you know. That's all."

"And I will," she assured him. "At dinner."

"Emma, you—"

"Insist," she said quickly and leaned forward, putting her mouth on his, curling her fingers around his lapel.

Luka went still as death. But when she touched the tip of her tongue to the seam of his lips, she felt his fingers graze her face. And then he pulled her into his lap and kissed her in return. A fully vibrant kiss. A kiss so thorough that her head spun and her skin prickled with excitement. She pressed against him, wanting more, feeling the wave of need rush over her, her heartbeat racing with anticipation. She felt the madness of desire, that feeling that nothing else could matter…

But Luka lifted his head and stroked his thumb across her lips. "You really must stop kissing me, Lady Dearborn. I can't think properly. In fact, the only thing I can think is that you have surely lost your mind."

"I may have done," she whispered back. "Do you mind terribly?"

"Not at the moment."

She kissed him tenderly, stroking his face with the tips of her fingers.

Luka moaned and took her head in his hands and returned her kiss with a tender one of his own, his lips softly demanding. But he was pushing her back to her side of the coach as he did, and when she was seated on her bench, he put his hands on her shoulders and held her there. "I have never in all my life met a woman like you. I've had the privilege to know some strong and determined women, some interesting and curious women. But you?" He shook his head.

She sounded intriguing when he put it that way. "You'll come to dinner, at least?" she asked. "Allow me to say…*it*? You may be surprised by what I say. You may be surprised that nothing is simple or obvious. I have a story to tell you, one that, I think you'll agree, shows that really, all we care about in the end, each of us, is survival."

One corner of his mouth tipped up in a sardonic smile. "I haven't the slightest notion what you're talking about, but I would agree that nothing about you seems simple."

"Thank you."

"It wasn't meant as a compliment."

"But taken as one." This man, this beautiful man, was her hope. Hope of what, she didn't know, as there didn't seem to be a logical reason for so much hope spilling out of her right now. But it was there in buckets, sweeping through her like a tide.

The coach rolled to a halt before the house. The door swung open, and the coachman put a step down for her. Emma moved to the opening and paused to look back at Luka. "Will I see you at dinner?"

"I don't know," he said, his gaze moving over her, his expression one of fondness. "Will you be attending?"

"I will." She would be there, all right, as if a queen had summoned her. Nothing would keep her from it.

She stepped down and floated away from the coach, not looking back, content to revel in the warm, fizzy feeling in her blood. She picked up her skirts to climb the few steps to the house, aware that she was smiling. She was currently imagining Luka Olivien naked in her bed, which was such a pleasing image that at first, she didn't even see the short, round man standing in her foyer.

She handed her hat to Feeney and started to say something about supper when she heard Adele's unmistakable voice from the receiving room. "Is that you, darling?"

Emma's head snapped up; she saw the man then. He beamed at her, then came bouncing forward, not unlike a balloon. "Good afternoon, Lady Dearborn. I am Mr. Timothy Longbottom, at your service." He bowed low and made a grand flourish of his hand.

Oh, no.

Oh, bloody hell, no.

CHAPTER SIXTEEN

HOW WAS IT possible that Luka could come so close to hearing the full truth from Emma and be interrupted so many times? And furthermore, how could he look forward to this evening's meal against all better judgment? Because he was actively convincing himself that this would be the end of it. She would finally acknowledge what they both knew, and then he could be on his way. He *would* be on his way.

And then the Longbottom fellow appeared. In the company of Lady Adele, naturally, who was glaring at Luka as if he'd intentionally ruined her surprise.

The introductions were made, with Mr. Longfellow effusively shaking hands and bowing before Emma. As Emma removed her hat and set it aside, Lady Adele turned her ire to Luka. "My lord Marlaine, it seems you are in the company of my sister-in-law more than anyone of late." She tried to sound as if she was teasing him, but her insinuation was clear. "One would think you were her husband instead of my brother!" She laughed shrilly, as if she'd said something genuinely funny. No one else laughed.

Luka pointed to the trunk two footmen were struggling to carry inside. "Lady Dearborn very kindly offered me a way to retrieve my trunk, which was sent to Rexford by mistake. And now, if you will excuse me,

I will see what can be done with it." He moved to help the two footmen, hoisting the trunk onto his shoulder with them. As they began to go up the stairs, Emma called after him.

"Dinner at eight, Mr. Olivien!" She sounded a bit desperate. Understandably so—he couldn't imagine much worse than dining with Lady Adele and the overly cheerful Mr. Longbottom.

Once in his rooms, with the trunk set aside and the footmen gone, he withdrew the letters from Justine. One had been forwarded with a brisk note from Boris, who wrote that it had arrived shortly after Luka left Cairo.

From Her Majesty the Queen Justine
To the Honorable Lord Marlaine

My friend, I pray this letter finds you well. I have no wish to impose on your adventure.

Adventure. Why was it when a lord undertook an actual occupation, others made it sound like he was on a lark?

I am in need of your help. Forgive my lack of civility as I come straight to the point. I am writing you, Luka, in the strictest confidence. I am requesting, as your queen, that you return to Wesloria at your earliest convenience. I have reason to believe that your father, the Duke of Astasia, is plotting against me.

A rock of dread settled in his gut. He recalled the letter he'd received from his father in Cairo, the ominous tone of it.

My advisers have warned that his plan is to disrupt the lawful elections of our parliament next summer, particularly in the Astasian region, where, I am sure you know, support for my reign is not high. I hope that you will agree with me that this can only be viewed as treason.

That feeling of dread began to press painfully against Luka's ribs. *Treason* was a heavy, irretrievable word. The letter went on to say that she hoped he would send word of when she might expect him home.

The second letter was written some weeks after the first, when apparently, she'd learned he was in England from his sister, Dagna.

I've not had your reply to my last letter and pray that you are well. I must regretfully inform you that since writing the last letter, I've received reports of men being trained in the art of combat in the Astasian mountains, and my advisers believe a threat against the throne will be made within six months. I believe you will be instrumental in negotiating with the duke. And if he is not involved as we suspect, perhaps you might help persuade him to help us. No matter what, you are key to a solution, as your father has thus far resisted any communication with me or my envoys.

I am sending an escort to see you safely returned to Wesloria at once. Expect them Tuesday, the last week of the month.

Justine R

Luka folded the letter carefully and put it aside. He tried to scrub the tension from his face with his hands, but it was pointless. There was no other option—to prolong his return any longer was unthinkable. His queen had asked him for his assistance. His father had at last lost his fool mind. He knew his father was unreasonable, but a traitor? Surely that wasn't true. He was a disgruntled old man, but he had never acted on his feelings. It made Luka sick to consider the possibility.

This changed everything, of course. They were at the end of the second week of the month. Which meant he had less than two weeks.

He ought to be on the train to London tonight. He ought to be booking passage, telegraphing that he was on his way. But for some reason this thing, whatever he might call it, between him and Emma was not finished. Why wasn't it? Yes, she knew her husband was dead. No, she hadn't admitted it aloud. But what did it matter to him if she did? What could her life here possibly have to do with him? Nothing!

And still, he couldn't walk away, not until he absolutely must. He didn't know what he was waiting for, didn't understand how she'd managed to completely captivate him as she had.

He stood up and walked to the window and stared out without seeing anything. He was being egregiously stupid. He wanted to stay for a woman, but his loyalty was always to his country, his queen, his family. So he would go.

His stomach soured even more. He'd found something at long last, a holy grail that struck him as vital.

He'd found a woman who intrigued him like no other. But he'd found her at the worst possible time.

THE SOUR FEELING carried into dinner. Luka had very little appetite, particularly considering the company. He wished that it had been only him and Emma.

Emma was likewise subdued. She kept stealing looks at him. Sometimes, she looked apologetic. Other times, she looked as if she needed rescue—or was utterly bored. Little wonder. Mr. Longbottom was a jovial fellow who exclaimed over every bite he took and told long-winded stories about his work in finance. He had a curious way of introducing a variety of tangents to very simple statements.

"I didn't know Albert had a cousin," Emma said idly.

"Oh yes, we are cousins," Mr. Longbottom said eagerly. "But by a rather circuitous route, which, I suppose, seems rather hard to fathom unless one can trace the family tree for generations. We had such an illustration that hung right above the hearth when I was a lad. An entire family history at one's disposal or, at the very least, a tree above the hearth—" here he laughed "—but in this case, we needn't go so far."

"Second cousins, actually," Andrew offered, as he was the only one at the table who seemed to follow Mr. Longbottom.

"Second?" asked Emma.

"Second," Andrew confirmed.

"Well, perhaps that is so, as our relation is distant in some ways and yet a true one. Blood runs thicker than water, as they say."

Did anyone say that bombast ran thicker than blood? Because Luka was beginning to believe it was so.

"It is your good fortune that I am a financier. When your sister wrote to me and asked for help, I was more than happy to oblige. Estate books are a lot of mathematics for a young wife, I should think."

"I beg your pardon?" Emma asked.

"All those numbers, dear," Mr. Longbottom said.

"I shouldn't worry about that, Mr. Longbottom," Emma said with false cheer. "I have my nursery slate and chalk." And then she stabbed her fish with her fork.

Thankfully, Mr. Longbottom turned his attention to the history of the house, and Andrew was able to commandeer the conversation with a litany of anecdotes. The boy was extremely knowledgeable, his facts going back five hundred years, to when the original hall was a warlord's keep. Mr. Longbottom seemed truly interested in the details and fired questions at Andrew, who handled them deftly. It appeared that Emma was attempting to listen to Andrew's details, but her wistful gaze kept sliding to the window.

Somewhere in the recounting of the Napoleonic Wars, when one of the Dearborn earls had gone off to fight on the Continent and the house had fallen into disrepair, Emma suggested that perhaps they retire to the drawing room.

"I should retire to bed soon," Mr. Longbottom said, patting his belly. "I've quite a lot of work to do on the morrow. One can't simply start with the latest book of accounts and make heads or tails. One must go back a few years."

Emma, who had risen from her chair, turned to look at him. "Pardon?"

Mr. Longbottom waved a hand. "I beg your pardon.

I'm nattering on, aren't I?" he said amicably. "I want to be fresh for my meeting with Mr. Horn in Rexford."

"You've arranged a meeting with Mr. Horn without telling me?" Emma asked, sounding confused.

"I arranged it for him," Lady Adele said.

Emma gaped at her. "That was hardly necessary," she said, trying to keep her voice light. "I would have been happy to make the arrangement. Mr. Horn and I have a good working relationship."

"Yes...but Mr. Horn did admit to me that he wouldn't mind some oversight. It's a large estate, after all."

"I met Horn today," Longbottom said, seemingly unaware of the tension in the room. "Lovely chap. Had a pint at the Rexford Arms."

"Well," Emma said with forced cheer, "a lot of things happened today, it appears. I predict your visit will be a short one, Mr. Longbottom." She kept her gaze on her sister-in-law. "Mr. Horn will show you that the estate is running perfectly and that in fact we have turned a profit."

And with that, Emma walked out of the dining room.

The rest of them followed like sheep.

"He did mention a cistern in need of repair," Mr. Longbottom said as they moved down the hall to the drawing room. "Said his lordship was never keen to do it because of the expense, but now it was a more urgent matter."

"I know all about the cistern, Mr. Longbottom, and I *am* keen to do it," Emma said over her shoulder, as if it were a trifling thing.

"Oh yes, Mr. Horn told me the same. But I don't think he feels comfortable with such a large expenditure without the earl's approval. As a general rule, I think gentlemen are uncomfortable with large expenditures. It is the curse of our sex, I think, to have the financial care of our loved ones upon our shoulders, and even though Mr. Horn is not one of your family, he feels the weight keenly. He would prefer to wait, of course, until Lord Dearborn returns."

"That's because Albert is very exact in everything he spends. He feels the burden quite keenly," Lady Adele agreed.

"But he also delights in profit," Emma said airily as they entered the drawing room. "We've been able to turn some healthy profits with a few simple changes and modernization."

"Well, fortunately, when Albert comes home, you won't have to worry over the estate any longer, dearest," Lady Adele said as they filed in behind Emma. "You may return to the privilege of being the wife of the earl."

Emma paused in the middle of the room. She looked around, at the soaring paneled ceilings, the massive hearth, the two separate groupings of chairs and sofas at either end of the room, at the rich carpets, the floor-to-ceiling windows, and heavy velvet drapes. "It has been a privilege," she said softly. "But my interest and care for the hall extends beyond my marriage."

"I don't see why," Lady Adele pressed as she lowered herself to the settee. "You are well provided for. What does that leave?"

"The spiritual?" Andrew asked hopefully.

Emma smiled at him. "Something like that, Andrew." She looked again at her sister-in-law. "This is all so unnecessary, Adele. You might have eased your concerns if you'd come to look at the books when I asked. I feel like we are wasting Mr. Longbottom's and Mr. Horn's precious time."

"Oh, my time is not that precious," Longbottom said. "I'll tell you what is, however—family. Even distantly related as we are, it's a treat for this old gentleman. And I've nothing to occupy me at home, not with Mrs. Longbottom away with her sister."

"How long do you anticipate the review to take, sir?" Emma asked.

"Oh, a few days, that's all. Unless I find something egregiously wrong, in which case, it would necessitate an even closer look. Not that I expect to find a single thing wrong, mind you, but one must always be prepared for the possibility. Possibilities are the thing that keeps the mind sharp, in my opinion."

"I hope you won't mind, Emma, but I've taken the liberty of inviting Mr. Longbottom to your weekend affair," said Lady Adele.

Emma, much to Luka's surprise, suddenly smiled. "Wonderful! The more the merrier. I hope you will attend, Mr. Longbottom. Unless you need to get home to your wife?"

It was remarkable to Luka that Emma could so readily extend an invitation to basically an interloper.

"I would be delighted," Mr. Longbottom said. "I'll send word to Mrs. Longbottom."

"Wonderful. Speaking of the house party, there is so much yet to do in a matter of days," Emma said. "Thank you all for a lovely evening, but I am feeling a bit tired." She stood up. Luka, Andrew, and Mr. Longbottom did, too. "Please excuse me. Feeney will see you out. Or in. Whatever you would like."

The three men bowed as she went out. When a footman had closed the door quietly behind her, Lady Adele stood. "I suppose we ought to be on our way, Mr. Long-bottom. I replied to Mr. Horn that we would meet him at his offices at ten o'clock."

"Very well," the man said, and shoved his hands into his pockets.

"Good night, Mr. Olivien," Andrew said.

"Good night," Luka said, and watched the three of them quit the room, leaving him alone with his thoughts and the sour in the pit of his belly.

CHAPTER SEVENTEEN

EMMA DID NOT leave her rooms until after lunch the next day. She couldn't possibly—she was still fuming about Adele and feared she would unfairly snap at a maid or a footman. Adele was supposed to be more of a sister to her than a foe. There were expectations about family ties! Entire generations had forged bonds between sisters-in-law, but hers acted as if she was a criminal!

Where had it all gone so terribly wrong between them? In the months before Emma and Albert married, when he was courting her, when speculation throughout the area was that he would offer for her, Adele would come for tea. The two of them, separated by only a few years, would laugh and whisper and share gossip about the ladies and gentlemen they knew. Emma had thought they were friends. But when she married, Albert sent Adele and Andrew to the dower house. Then their marriage began to worsen, and her relationship with Adele deteriorated right alongside.

Maybe it was the loss of the siblings' parents, their father having died a few years earlier, their mother dying soon after the wedding. Maybe it was jealousy or contempt that filled Adele when Albert asked her and Andrew to move to the dower house. Or maybe, possibly, Adele had never really liked her at all, had been playing the part of a dutiful sister for the sake of her brother. Whatever the reason for Adele's animosity, she clearly longed to catch Emma at something that would give rise to banishing her from Butterhill Hall altogether. And she clearly thought the answer was in the estate books. Well, Emma was not worried in the least about Mr. Longbottom's examination of the accounts. If anything, he would find them vastly improved.

Nevertheless, the audacity! To assume Emma was dishonest (well…she could see the argument that perhaps she was) or incapable of math (how insulting), was too much to be borne! Yes, all right, there *was* something Emma was doing wrong, and Adele would be justifiably angry when the truth was revealed. But she was not a thief, and the circumstances, as they say, were extenuating. And really, did Adele have nothing better to do?

And Luka! What was she to do with *him*? That kiss—the kisses, all of them—were deliriously stimulating. She'd felt as if she was melting inside, had wanted to melt right out of all her clothing. The slightest touch from him singed, and the heat he radiated enough to warm all of Butterhill Hall. Her head was filled with so many questions about him, so many desires to taste him, to feel his skin, to feel him inside her. But every time she was near him, the unspoken truth was hanging over her head. It would lead to her destruction.

She did not like to think about where she would land when she was sent away, but she was finding the possibility increasingly hard to ignore.

The morning of brooding about her troubles left Emma feeling low. She needed to shake herself awake, to put on her happy face. After all, she had a massive party to host in only a matter of days. She decided to walk around the lake. That always enlivened her.

She donned a skirt she often wore for gardening, a blouse, and her gardening hat and was pulling on her walking boots when Carlotta came in. "There you are! Did you find your mother well?"

"I did, thank you," Carlotta said. "She missed you." She glanced over her shoulder to the open door and moved to close it. "Mr. Feeney very nearly had my head."

"But I told him I'd given you leave."

"Not that," Carlotta said. She said something else, but the words were lost over the sound of sudden hammering coming through the open window. "That," Carlotta said, pointing to the open window.

With only one boot on, Emma hobbled to the window to have a look. Carlotta joined her. "It's the tent," Carlotta said. "I said to him, 'You ought to put it elsewhere, as the wind always comes off the lake,' and he said I should return to my duties of scrubbing floors and ironing unmentionables."

"Oh dear, he *is* in a mood." Emma sighed. The pavilion tent, lying on the ground as it was, did seem enormous. Like a sail that could take flight at any moment. There were stakes positioned around, as well as men who held the ropes and stared at the canvas, the stakes, and the sky.

"But the party is days away," Emma said. Just then, she saw Feeney stride to where the men were standing about. Her head groundskeeper, Mr. Stanton, walked over to meet him. And then the two engaged in what to Emma looked like an argument, judging by the gesticulations.

"I'd steer clear if I was you," Carlotta said as she went to Emma's bed to make it. "He can be quite unreasonable when he gets like this."

Emma knew that to be true, but she had no intention of ignoring him. She pulled on one of Albert's old frock coats, which she had repurposed for blustery days. "I'm off for a walk, Carlotta. If anyone comes looking for me, I am indisposed." And with that, she went outside and walked down to the orangery where work was underway to prepare for the house party.

The wind was terrible today, and she could see the few strands of Feeney's hair standing on end. He and Mr. Stanton were quite agitated, neither of them seeing her approach until she was in their midst. Her appearance startled Feeney, and she could have sworn that he cast a glance skyward like he was praying for strength. She was not daunted. "Gentlemen? Is there a problem?"

"Not at all, madam," Feeney said crisply. "We are agreeing on where to raise the tent."

"Disagreeing," Mr. Stanton muttered.

"It's all settled," Feeney said.

"With all due respect, sir, I don't think it is," Mr. Stanton said.

"But the party is days away," Emma said.

"Yes, milady, but Mr. Feeney thought we ought to determine where it will be erected, and how, for the sake of efficiency. Don't want to be disagreeing about where on the day your guests arrive."

Feeney responded with a sharp intake of breath and said that Mr. Stanton was being stubborn, and Mr. Stanton said he was being thickheaded, that the wind was making it impossible, and then the two of them argued for a few more moments while Emma watched what was happening behind them. Luka had appeared on the scene, dressed in buckskins, boots, and a linen shirt without a neck cloth or coat. He looked like he might be on his way to fish or dig in a field.

He was discussing the tent with the other men. He was sketching something with his hands in the air that she didn't understand, but the other men did. They began to pick up stakes and ropes. More men gathered the tent and turned it a bit clockwise.

Feeney then raised his voice to a point that Emma reflexively put her hand on top her hat in the event his expulsion of air blew it off her head. She'd never seen the butler lose his temper, but she feared he might explode all over them.

"Gentlemen! It seems the problem has been solved," she said loudly.

"I daresay it has not until we can agree on the construction," Feeney returned.

"But look," Emma said, and pointed to the raising of the tent.

The two men turned around. Mr. Stanton took off his hat. "What the...?"

Luka was directing the tent erection. But instead of the tent being open on all sides, the men were pulling one side down to the ground. From where the stakes were positioned, it looked as if the massive tent would be tacked to the ground on the windward side and open on the lee side. Luka watched them for a moment, nodding, then walked over to where Emma stood with Feeney and Stanton.

"Mr. Olivien!" she said cheerfully. "Are you an expert on tents?"

"Not an expert, but I've seen my fair share of tents

the last several months. This one is quite large. The wind should ride up the slant." He looked at Mr. Stanton. "I hope you don't mind the change in plans, but that wind is formidable. I learned this technique in my travels with nomadic tribes in the Sahara Desert. The wind blows like the devil there, and the sand gets into everything. They've devised a way to stake the tent to keep out wind and sand."

"It's an interesting idea," Mr. Stanton said, and began to ask Luka several questions about it.

Emma smiled up at Feeney. "There you are, one less thing to fret about."

Feeney attempted to smile, she could see that he did, but the effort was too much for him. "I'm afraid there is no lack of subjects to worry about. If you will excuse me, madam?"

She watched the butler walk toward the house. He hated the idea of this party, but she was committed. It would be her last fling. Perhaps her last chance at frivolity and happiness for the rest of her life. Who knew where she would be a year from now? Only eight more days until the party. Eight days of being a countess, of living her best life. After that, well… Luka would leave, she would be found out, and then…

No. She wasn't going to think of that now. She turned back to the work on the tent. Luka and Mr. Stanton were examining how the tent was staked to the ground. Emma watched as they and two other men stretched the tent canvas over the poles and put in more stakes. The effect was immediate—no wind, no flapping. Quite pleasantly still on the other side.

All right, then, she was going to think of other things today besides her eight days of freedom. Pleasant things. Salacious things. She would think about seducing Luka, particularly how to do that while refusing to admit the truth. Goodness, what a complicated little world she'd created for herself!

CHAPTER EIGHTEEN

THERE HAD BEEN a few moments, back at the tent, that Luka feared old Feeney would be struck with angina pectoris and expire before them all. But he did not. He went off to argue with Mr. Stanton, and during *that* argument, the tent problem was solved. Luka hadn't solved it, although he'd had the idea. But the men working to erect it knew a thing or two about wind and tents, too. The only one who didn't seem to know was Feeney.

After Luka explained the theory to Mr. Stanton—who was relieved to have a solution—he looked around for Emma. She was, as usual, nowhere to be seen. She'd flitted into the melee and danced out like a butterfly. But she'd been dressed as if she meant to hunt some fowl or paint a barn. He had a feeling she was taking her daily stroll around the lake. He left the men and walked down to the lake.

He made his way to the place he'd seen Emma swimming that memorable afternoon. There was the flat rock where Carlotta had been sitting, and a gradual slope into the water. Moreover, he could see the path from both directions. She would eventually pass by.

When she didn't appear immediately, Luka lay on his back in the sun, covered his face with his hat, and allowed himself to drift to sleep.

It was the shallow sleep of midday, and it wasn't long

before he became aware of something. Another presence. He removed his hat and blinked into the bright sunlight. Emma was standing above him, hands on her waist, a long tail of her hair over her shoulder. "Mr. Olivien," she said pertly.

"Lady Dearborn."

"What on earth are you doing here?"

"Napping," he said, and pushed himself up to sit. "While I waited for you."

"Really?" Her face lit with a warm smile. "How delightful! I was hoping you'd say that." She suddenly dropped down beside him, bent over, and began to unlace her boots.

"What are you doing?" he asked.

"I'm going to put my feet in the water. Do you mind? Are you a prim and proper gentleman who thinks women should not show their feet to anyone but their husband? It's too late for that sort of modesty between us." She glanced up at him with a bit of a smirk.

"I suppose it is."

"You should do the same. I am not scandalized by feet in the slightest. My sister says she can't bear to look at her husband's feet. But I've never been bothered. My father's feet were a sight to behold, and yet, every night, I removed his boots and his stockings."

"What a good daughter you are."

"Was. Alas, both of my parents are gone now. What about yours?"

Luka glanced at the water. He didn't want to be reminded of his father in this moment, but he was never really out of his thoughts. "Both very much alive." He watched Emma slide one delicate foot toward the water. Then the other, until her toes were wiggling just above the surface. He had an image of kissing those feet, but suddenly, into the water they both went. She smiled at him with a bit of a dare shining through.

What the hell.

He removed his shoes and stockings and shifted his gaze to the water as he rolled up his trouser legs.

"My, sir, what big feet you have," she teased him.

"It's a matter of physics, madam," he said as he slid his feet into the water. "The size is necessary to support my height and weight."

"What an amazing anthropologist you must be! You know all about tents and feet."

They sat a moment, swirling their feet in the cool water. He had to admit it was invigorating. "Aren't you curious why I was waiting for you here?"

"I couldn't possibly guess, but I'm so glad you did. As it happens, I want to speak to you."

"You do?" That was a surprising development.

"Mmm," she said, nodding her head. "I *like* talking to you. Have you ever noticed how you meet certain people, and no matter how hard you try or what you say, you have the most ridiculously boring conversations? I have experienced none of that with you. You are *always* interesting, Luka."

He smiled. "Not always."

"Well, you are to me. I should like to be as interesting as you, to engage people in ways they find exciting."

He wasn't aware he engaged people in that way. "I find you interesting in ways that I couldn't possibly have predicted."

"You're being kind. That's another thing about people I've noticed. There are those who are unfailingly kind and those who are terribly unkind. There never seems to be much in between, does there? But anyway, enough of that, I want to tell you something."

She was so good at seizing the subject and controlling it. Where had she learned that? It seemed effortless, and he rather admired it—it was a skill that could come in quite handy. "Pray tell, what could it be? The story you meant to tell me last night?"

"Last night," she said with a roll of her eyes. "It was a bit of a disaster, wasn't it? But no, my good man. I don't mean to confuse you. This story is an entirely different one."

"I would characterize my state as *curious* rather than *confused*. I've come to expect stunning turns of subject from you. Are you ready to tell me the truth?"

Emma grinned and swirled her feet in the water. "Doesn't it feel wonderful? One can never underestimate the simple pleasures of summer. In the winter, this lake is frozen at the edges. One winter, the entire lake froze. People would come and walk across it or skate. I never did. I feared falling through."

"You're stalling, Emma. Go on, tell me why you think I must be confused. I've been waiting ages to hear you tell me the truth."

"I know you have, but it makes no sense to me why. I should think it's obvious."

"It *is* obvious," he agreed. "But I would like to hear you say it all the same."

"Why?" She looked directly into his eyes. "If it is so terribly obvious, why must I say it? It makes me a bit uncomfortable."

It was a good question—and a mystery to him, too. "I don't know," he said at last. "I suppose I could say it now and spare us both, and that would be the end of it.

But I think you should admit the truth, if for no other reason than to admit it to yourself."

"I see your point," she said with a nod, presumably in agreement. She put her hand on his knee; he looked down at it. "But I disagree," she said, surprising him. "It won't help anyone if I say aloud what is painfully obvious to us both."

He lifted his gaze. "Say it."

"Very well, then. Here it is." She pressed her lips together. She swallowed. She squeezed his knee, then blurted, "My sister-in-law is a difficult and exasperating woman. There, are you happy?"

He stared at her. "No. No, I am *not*. That is not the truth I want you to admit, and you know it."

"Yes, but it's the *start* of the story," Emma said, looking entirely innocent and sincere. Once again, he had to ask himself if she was mad as a hen or perhaps too clever for him. To think she could outfox him was disturbing enough, but even more alarming was the fact that he had come to enjoy this game they'd played for days now—him insisting she tell him what she knew to be true, and her avoiding it so artfully. "And it's certainly not *all* the story. You've noticed my brother-in-law is very well-read, haven't you?"

"Yes, but…but what's that got to do with anything?"

"Nothing yet. But it will. Luka—" she leaned forward, her hand pressing into his thigh "—you don't believe her, do you?"

"Believe her?"

She slid her hand a little higher on his thigh. "You don't believe I have swindled the estate or mismanaged it to the point she practically had to invent a cousin to come and see what I've done?"

"I… No, I don't believe that," he said as Emma's hand crept higher. "But I don't know what to believe if I'm honest. Emma?" He caught her hand before it slid between his thighs and laced his fingers with hers. "Are you trying to seduce me?"

Her eyes sparkled. "I'm trying to tell you a story."

"Then, forgive me, as I find it quite impossible to follow with your hand on my thigh." He did not add that he hardly cared about her story just now. She was looking at him with her gorgeous, shining blue eyes— it was like swimming through a sea of bluebells and he was eager to get to the other side.

"How interesting. Because I find it impossible to tell my story with my hand on your thigh."

"Then perhaps you ought to remove it," he said, without making the slightest move to let go of it.

"I will, I promise. But first I must beg your forgiveness for how long the story is."

The length of story had nothing to do with her hand on his leg. "How long?" he asked and brought her hand to his lips, kissing her knuckles.

"Impossible to say. Not as long as the *Iliad*, but longer than the *Odyssey*."

He kissed her hand again.

Her eyes moved to his mouth. "It begins about thirty or so years ago."

"Thirty years? Does it begin with the coronation of Queen Victoria? Seems a good place to start a story."

"No, that was 1837. My story starts well after that."

"Before or after the Crimean War?" He turned her hand over, kissing the inside of her wrist.

Emma drew a slow breath. "Much before that."

"I've exhausted my knowledge of notable historical events."

"Think a little harder," she said.

He began to trace a line of soft kisses up the inside of her arm. "I hesitate to voice my next guess, as it doesn't reflect well on your government, but are you speaking of the Irish potato famine?"

"No!" She gasped as he flicked the tip of his tongue against the crease in her elbow. She slipped her free hand beneath his chin and forced his head up. "I am speaking of the birth of Emma Robbins Clark."

"Oh, *that* important date. Are you certain your story goes as far back as that?"

"Very certain. It goes back to July twelfth of that summer. It was a very hot day." She stroked his jaw with the tips of two fingers.

He smiled. "You remember how hot it was?"

She curled her fingers behind his ear. "No, but my mother told me many times. 'Hot as Hades,' she said." Her fingers sank into his hair. "I was born on a very hot day, and I suppose it took me a moment to breathe, and everyone believed that I might not survive, but I did." She shifted forward, her lips hovering just above his for a long moment. "And the funny thing is, I'm still surviving."

She kissed him.

Luka was a terribly weak man, for the moment her lips touched his, he not only welcomed it, he moved his hand to her back and twisted her around, putting her on her back beneath him on the rock. He kissed her thoroughly, angling her head as he moved from her lips to nuzzle her neck. He liked the way she tasted. The way she smelled. "Where were we?" he muttered against the soft skin of her throat.

"I was telling you a story," she said, and took his head in between her hands and kissed him to the point he felt a bit dizzy.

Luka lifted his head, needing to get his bearings. "You were born on a very hot day. Then what?" He kissed her again, but it felt like too little, not enough to appease the craving that was spreading in his chest and pounding in his veins.

"I was croupy," she said, then nibbled at his lips. "A lot of coughing and what-not."

"A sickly infant," he said against her hair as he slid his hand up her rib cage.

"But by winter, I was as hale and hearty as they come. A survivor."

"Mmm," he said, and cupped her breast. "And then what?"

She sighed into his hair. "And then I became a precocious child."

"Entirely predictable, when one goes from croupy to hale and hearty." He trailed a line of kisses down her chin to her neck. "And while the anthropologist in me is enthralled by this tale of a hot summer birth and hard winter, I'm not sure of the point."

"That's because I haven't gotten to the best part yet," she said, and drew open the neck of her blouse. He moved his lips down her chest, between her breasts. He listened to her breathing, felt her body moving beneath his. This unexpected tryst on a flat rock on the shores of a picturesque lake was the most brilliant thing he'd done in ages. He was sizzling inside, his body responding to the feel of her, to the slightly floral scent of her, to her curves and yielding flesh and sparkling blue eyes and lips and everything, *everything*. He couldn't remember feeling this heat in him, couldn't recall being quite so dazed. He forgot everything else, forgot that she was hiding, forgot that she was married or a widow, depending on what you knew, but in either case not his to kiss. He caught her chin in his hand, held her still to kiss her deeply, and the desire poured through him.

Emma grabbed a fistful of his shirt and pulled him to her, flicking her tongue against his. His heart raced almost uncomfortably; he sat up, dragging her into his lap. His body had sprung to attention, ready and willing to do whatever Emma wanted and would allow.

He thought she responded to the thoughts in his head because she made a sound of desire in her throat, and he took heart that something utterly captivating could happen by chance on this sunny afternoon. They'd been caught on this rock by some celestial intervention and—

And she abruptly slid off his lap and braced her hands against the rock. She was breathing hard, gasping for air, her eyes locked on his. Her skin was flushed, her lips plumped by kissing. She slowly licked her lips and then deliberately took in his body.

"And then," she said, "I began to dream."

"What?"

"I dreamed of things. Big things. My father took me and my sister to the fair, and I saw the most inspiring acts of heroism."

He was trying to shake his brain back to the present moment, to her story. He didn't know if it was possible in his current state. "A duel? Swordplay?" he asked, dragging his fingers through his hair.

"Even braver and more exciting than that. I saw a

man stand on the back of the horse, without falling, as it ran around the ring. With his arms held wide. And acrobats who would toss their bodies into the air, twisting and turning, as if it was nothing. I thought I would be excellent at such things."

"At acrobatics?" he asked, still confused.

She slid her thumb across his lip. "And standing on horses. But alas, that dream ended when I broke my arm. See?" She held up her right forearm. The dip in the bone was still visible. "I was forbidden from horse acrobatics after that."

"For your own good by the look of it."

"But I still had a taste for adventure," she said, lowering her arm.

He pushed her hair over her shoulder and caressed her jawline with his knuckle. "And now you will tell me that you longed to explore the world, but were likewise forbidden, because you were a girl, or they feared more broken limbs, or—"

"Not at all. I hadn't even begun my education at this point. There is much more to go before those dreams."

As much as he would like to hear it, she was stalling. He cocked his head to one side. "Are you telling me this story to keep me from talking? Or asking questions?"

"No. I just want to tell you my story, but it's a bit involved. I haven't even come to the most exciting parts." She moved away from him, sat on the rock, and began to put on her stockings and boots. "I almost died once. When I was twelve. But we aren't there yet."

"You almost died?" He reached for his shoes.

"Can you guess how?" she asked as she laced up one boot.

"Tricks on a horse?"

She grinned at him.

"You must have challenged your sister to a duel," he said, and pulled on his shoes.

"Never! She would have won."

He paused in what he was doing just to look at her. He wanted to kiss her again, to hear her laugh. He wanted to tell her about the trouble at home, how he shouldn't be here, how he was only here because he needed to hear her say it. But that wasn't the reason, he knew. It was because he was irretrievably smitten. "I can't possibly guess."

"I nearly hanged myself." She got up from the rock. "By accident, of course. A quick-thinking footman saved me. It's a rather long story, though, so I'll tell you later."

"And how many times have you almost died?"

She pretended to think about it as she stepped up to the path. "Figuratively? Or actually?"

He laughed. "Either."

"You'll have to wait for the answer," she said, and began to back away from him.

"What? Where are you going?"

"Home."

"Emma, wait. You—"

"Come to supper, and I'll tell you more. I swear it." She smiled, then turned and began to run up the path as he fit his second shoe on his foot.

She had disappeared again. Luka stared out at the lake. *This woman.* This utterly fascinating, exasperating woman.

CHAPTER NINETEEN

EMMA WAS TRAIPSING up the path to the house, giddy from a very satisfying kiss. She was considering her early childhood years and what she could mine from them to keep a man engaged just like Scheherazade had to do. How clever the Persian queen had been! A more skilled storyteller, Emma assumed, but she was holding her own. She was smiling to herself, thinking of how she would keep talking, when she heard her name.

"Emma! Emma Robbins Clark! Halt where you are right now!"

Emma turned to see her sister striding forward, the hem of her skirt kicking up around her. She was without her children or her husband and held something in her hand. She looked, even from a slight distance, quite murderous.

"Oh dear," Emma muttered to herself. She smiled as Fanny sallied forth. "Fanny, darling, what's the matter?"

"Don't you dare *Fanny, darling* me," her sister said, breathless from her onslaught. She held up the thing she was holding and waved it in Emma's face so aggressively that Emma had to back up. "I got the invitation, Emma! The invitation to your weekend house party honoring Mr. Olivien!"

Emma caught Fanny's wrist and pushed her hand down. "Oh," she said.

"*Oh?*" Fanny shouted. "I told you to tell him the truth! I told you that you were playing a dangerous game! I told you to get rid of him, Emma! He can't possibly still be here!"

Emma swallowed. She looked over Fanny's shoulder where Luka was strolling up the path, looking at them with some interest. "He is."

"Emma!" Fanny cried with great exasperation. "How *could* you?"

"And here he is now!" Emma said brightly.

Fanny gasped. She whirled about just as Luka walked up to them. He smiled. Fanny stared at him. Then at Emma. "What have you been doing?" she whispered hotly.

"Not what you think," Emma whispered back. "Mr. Olivien! May I please introduce my much-loved sister, Mrs. Fanny Yates. Contrary to appearances, she is not a madwoman."

Fanny shot her another murderous look.

"Mrs. Yates, it is my pleasure," he said, and offered his hand.

Fanny seemed to think about it, then hesitantly took it. "You're Weslorian," she said, glancing at the patch of green on his cuff.

"I am," he said.

"You don't speak with much of an accent."

"He attended Eton," Emma chirped.

"Ah," Fanny said. "A pleasure to make your acquaintance, Mr. Olivien," she said, and then turned her gaze to Emma. Rather, her glare. "Emma, darling, might I have a word?"

"Yes, of course! We'll all have tea—"

"I haven't time for tea," Fanny said. "Just a quick word. You will excuse us, won't you, Mr. Olivien?"

"Of course." He bowed his head. "I wish you a good day, Mrs. Yates." Clasping his hands behind his back, he moved on.

Emma discovered in that moment it was just as entertaining watching him walk away as it was when he was approaching her.

Fanny slapped her arm, grabbed her elbow, and marched her back down the path. She glanced over her shoulder, to make sure Luka could not hear them, then said, "Emma, you have lost your bloody mind."

"I have not!"

"Can you not see how this—" she gestured wildly to the path and, presumably, Mr. Olivien "—looks to everyone near and around Butterhill?"

"I don't care how it looks."

"Don't *say* that—"

"Fanny." Emma lay her hand on her sister's shoulder. "Stop. I am hosting a weekend house party for my adieu. After that, I will tell the truth. But I have no place to go once I do, and I want to enjoy my time as countess while I can."

"Emma," Fanny said, softening considerably. "You'll come to us, of course."

Emma shook her head. "I will not. I will not burden you and Phillip with your diabolical sister who caused such a scandal that no one will touch her—and then, by association, you."

"You are not a diabolical sister, and we love you—"

"And I love you, and therefore, I will not do it. It's not fair to you and your family, Fanny."

Fanny sighed. "Then what will you do?"

"I don't know. I hope to think of something before Adele pushes me out. But I can't think of it just yet—I've so much on my mind. Will you come to dinner?"

"What?"

"You and Phillip and the children. Please, Fanny. Come and meet him, at least."

"I don't see the point."

Emma grinned. "So you won't feel so bad about him when I seduce him."

"Stop *saying* that," Fanny groaned.

Emma laughed and looped her arm through her sister's. "Then, come only to look at him. You must admit he is very handsome."

Fanny frowned as she allowed Emma to pull her into a walk.

"Go on, then—admit it."

"Fine!" Fanny said, annoyed. "He's as pleasing to the eye as Adonis! *Quite* handsome, with eyes like summer grass and a hint of an accent that makes him even more appealing! There, are you happy?"

"Completely," Emma said, and laughed as she and her sister strolled toward the house.

CHAPTER TWENTY

EMMA DRESSED IN her new pink satin gown with the velvet flowers embroidered along the edge of the skirt's apron. The bodice was square, and the bustle and corset so tight that she accused Carlotta of trying to prevent her from eating any cake that night. "It won't work," she warned her. "I never refuse cake, no matter how uncomfortable I am."

"Eat an entire cake if you like," Carlotta said, and yanked at the bottom of the corset, trying to fasten the last hook and eye. "I'm trying to fit you into this *dress*," she added with a huff of exertion at her success.

The dress was indeed tight—Mrs. Porter had warned her it would be so—but the effect of her discomfort was stunning. Emma's breasts looked ripe and as if they would spring free of their entrapment at the slightest breach. Her waist was as slender as when she was a girl and had been less interested in cake and fine wine than being outdoors. And the pink, she was pleased to see, went very well with her complexion. She could hear her mother's voice, warning her to stay away from bright colors because of her auburn hair. She'd been dressed in drab colors all her life because of it. Perhaps that was the reason she gravitated toward bright colors now.

"Well," Carlotta said, standing back to admire her, "you look like a dream."

"I do, don't I?" Emma *felt* like a dream, like a princess, as pretty as she'd felt the day of her wedding.

She just hoped she wasn't the only one to notice how lovely she looked. Her esteem of herself was robust, she would be the first to admit. But it wouldn't hurt if Luka's esteem washed over her.

Earlier, she'd asked an increasingly strained Feeney to inform Mr. Olivien that her sister and family would be joining them for dinner, and then asked if he wouldn't mind informing the cook as well. "Of course," Feeney had said, and had marched away as if he couldn't believe she would ask this of him in addition to all the other things he had to do for the weekend house party. Or maybe she'd imagined that was his demeanor, but she found herself wondering often how long it would be before he was plotting with Adele to see her removed and the quiet days of Albert's reign returned to Butterhill Hall.

A few more days, Feeney. Please bear with me, and then you and Adele may while away the hours with your books and needlework and polishing of silver.

Carlotta draped a diamond necklace around her throat that had belonged to Albert's mother. Emma had already donned the matching earrings. When her dressing was complete, she smiled at herself as she twisted one way, and then the other, to view herself in the mirror. "I ought to be in a palace, don't you think?"

"Like a queen?" Carlotta asked.

Emma laughed. "If the crown fits, darling."

Fanny, Phillip, and their sons, Theo and Tommy, were already in the drawing room when she arrived. Theo, nearly five, was following his little brother, Tommy, wherever he waddled, grabbing the figurines and books before Tommy could put them in his mouth. Phillip was dressed in his formal suit, which he wore every time he was invited to dinner at Butterhill Hall, as if he expected Queen Victoria to be in attendance. He came forward at once, his hand outstretched to her. "Emma! How beautiful you look tonight." He took her hand in his and leaned forward to kiss her cheek. "I understand you've a distinguished guest."

"I do. He is a friend of Albert's who's come to call." She could see Fanny from the corner of her eye, could see her disapproving frown at Emma's characterization of Luka.

"I look forward to meeting him," Phillip said. He moved aside so Fanny could greet her sister for the second time that day. She was still frowning, and Emma knew why. Fanny didn't like to keep things from Phillip, and she clearly hadn't told him about Luka. Emma doubted Fanny had told him anything at all, probably torn between the desire to protect her sister and her desire to tell her husband everything. It was very unfair to Fanny, and Emma felt truly ghastly for having put her in this position. She'd never intended for it to come to all this.

Goodness, a lie that had seemed so simple at the outset had sprouted tentacles that were attaching themselves to everyone she loved. "Thank you for coming," she said to Fanny as Phillip went to keep Tommy from pulling on the drapes.

"I didn't want to, but I felt like I had no choice. *Someone* should keep an eye on you before you make things even more impossible."

Emma smiled fondly. "Did you really think Adele would neglect her favorite hobby of keeping an eye on me?"

A hint of a smile appeared on Fanny's lips. "You know what I mean."

"Good evening."

The gentleman's voice was low and soft and accented just enough to send a tiny shiver up Emma's spine. They turned to the door to where Luka was standing just across the threshold. He looked quite handsome in his dark suit, the bit of Weslorian green pinned to his lapel, his hair combed behind his ears. His gaze went instantly to Emma. He smiled faintly as he took her in, his eyes moving over the length of her. The look in his eyes made her cheeks turn as pink as her dress. Though he gave no obvious outward sign, she could feel his appreciation of her.

"Mr. Olivien! So glad you could join us," Emma said, sailing forward to greet him as if he was any other gentleman come to call.

"It is my pleasure. Thank you," he said, and bowed over the hand she offered.

"I am Mr. Yates," Phillip said, coming forward, his hand extended in greeting. "I am married to Lady Dearborn's sister, whom I understand you've met."

"*Je*, I had the honor earlier today." Luka took Phillip's hand. "Luka Olivien, sir."

Phillip was quite at ease in any social situation and immediately engaged Luka in conversation. He pointed out his two young sons, then asked about Luka's journey to England. Tommy, having been deprived of a small porcelain bird, began to sob, so Fanny went to tend him, leaving Emma with Theo.

Theo had a very urgent message for her: he had caught a frog and put him in a box.

"A frog!"

"A *frog*," Theo said, and squatted down on the carpet to trace a flower with his finger. "Are these real?" He looked up at her, pointing to the woven flower on the carpet.

"No."

"I caught him in the lake. There are quite a lot of them there, but I only caught one."

Emma, who had lost any semblance of primness since Albert had left, came down onto her knees beside her nephew. "And what do you intend to do with this frog?"

"I mean to teach him tricks."

It turned out that Theo had a rather long list of tricks he intended to teach the frog, which he reviewed with her in detail. Emma added a few ideas of her own, which would never work—frogs didn't ride tiny unicycles—but she enjoyed the idea of Theo trying them.

She loved spending time with her nephews. She loved their innocent view of the world where, at least to Theo, everything and all things were possible. What a wonderful way to live. She loved being with her family, small though it was. How marvelous it would have been had Albert been a different person. Had he been able to sire a child.

But then again, how marvelous that he hadn't been able to. She couldn't imagine him ever warming to the intimate family tableau. She shuddered to think what sort of father he might have been.

When Feeney stepped in to announce dinner, Emma gestured for Phillip to help her up. "My corset has been set too tight," she said with an apologetic smile.

"Emma!" Fanny's eyes darted to Luka and back to her. "You have a guest."

Emma laughed as she hopped to her feet with Phillip's help. "I feel quite certain that Mr. Olivien is aware corsets exist in this world."

"I certainly am," he said. "Most notably because of my grandfather, who steadfastly wore one until the day he died. May I escort you into dinner, madam?" he asked, extending his arm to Fanny.

Fanny looked both charmed and wary of him.

After Tommy was whisked away by a doting Carlotta to the nursery—along with several instructions issued by Fanny—they proceeded into the dining room. Theo was allowed to dine with the adults, something Emma had insisted upon. Theo made certain everyone knew it was not his first time to dine with the adults. Emma laughed at his eagerness and glanced at Luka, expecting to see a bit of disapproval. It was her experience that earls and titled lords in general did not care to have children at the dinner table. But Luka laughed at the lad, too.

As the meal was served—onion soup, oysters, braised beef, and carrots—Phillip took charge of the conversation, complimenting the cook and even the harried Feeney, who seemed surprised by the praise.

Then Phillip asked Luka how he knew Albert.

Luka glanced quickly at Emma before turning his attention to Phillip. "We met on an expedition in Egypt. Or rather, as I prepared to set out on one from Cairo."

"I've always admired explorers," Phillip said. "Our Albert is an interesting man. I never knew he desired to explore the world until he announced he was going. He keeps his cards close to his vest, I suppose."

"That is true," Emma said, already disliking the direction this was going. Albert never hesitated to tell her how he despised her, but to others he was a bit of an enigma.

"But you found a way to penetrate his reserve, Emma," Phillip said with a fond smile. "Then again, I can hardly imagine the gentleman who could resist you."

Emma blushed. "Oh, Phillip. You flatter me."

Her brother-in-law smiled. "Mr. Olivien, you must have found your own way into Albert's good graces, as well. I confess it's not something I've been able to manage."

Emma panicked; she had to pull this conversation back from the subject of sullen Albert.

Luka looked down at his plate and cleared his throat. He was clearly uncomfortable with the conversation. "Perhaps to an extent."

"You don't give yourself enough credit, Phillip. You've managed it, too," Emma said quickly.

"I don't know that I agree. It's interesting, isn't it, how gentlemen befriend each other. Generally, it seems to be around sports or clubs, that sort of thing. I doubt I would ever have made Albert's acquaintance had he not tried to court my wife."

"Pardon?" Luka glanced up. He seemed quite interested now. "Your wife?" He looked at Fanny.

"Before I was his wife, he fails to mention," Fanny said.

"Yes, of course. I beg your pardon for the confusion. Albert is a man of honor."

Emma inadvertently coughed on a bite of carrot. If she didn't choke outright, she had to change the direction of this conversation before it turned disastrous.

"Phillip, you're jumping too far ahead," she said, and sipped her water.

"Pardon?"

"I promised Mr. Olivien a story, which is that of my life, and I haven't even gotten so far as to who might have been courted by who. I have only reached the point where I almost died."

"Oh, Emma." Fanny laughed. "You didn't almost die. I thought you'd stopped telling the hanging story."

"I want a hanging story!" Theo said excitedly.

"I think I do, too," Luka said.

"I *don't* tell the story," Emma said. "It hardly ever comes up. But when I was recounting my childhood to Mr. Olivien, I remembered it."

"I insist you tell it now," Luka said. "One cannot announce there is a hanging story and then not tell it. Theo and I will not sleep without it."

"Go ahead, Emma," Fanny said with a singsong voice. "Tell them all how foolish you were."

"With pleasure," Emma said with a smile for her sister and proceeded to recount how she'd been playing at being a pirate in the drawing room during a particularly wet winter.

"Pirates are boys," Theo said. "Not girls."

"I beg to differ," Emma said. "Girls can be pirates, too. And I thought that any good pirate had to have a proper boat." She told them how she'd used her mother's best tablecloth and some rope she found to rig a sail from the chandelier. She'd been standing on a footstool to knot the rope in a manner she'd learned from her father, but she'd slipped, gotten tangled in the tablecloth, and somehow, the rope had gone round her neck. "Had it not been for the heroic actions of a footman, I wouldn't be here today."

Theo gaped at her. Luka seemed amused.

"You would have survived," Fanny said. "You were standing on your tiptoes. And Gregory yanked at the rope, and it easily came away from the chandelier."

"But I didn't *know* that, Fanny," Emma argued playfully. "As far as I knew I was swinging five feet in the air."

"The worst of it was the shrieking our mother did when the chandelier began to swing and all the candles fell off."

"I was banished to my room without supper," Emma said. "If you hadn't brought me a bit of bread and cheese, I might have starved to death."

Theo gasped again.

"Theo, darling, remember what we've said about Aunt Emma and her imagination?"

"That I'm not to believe her unless you tell me it's true," Theo repeated.

Emma burst out laughing. "All right, so I may have exaggerated some things to my adorable nephew."

"Having survived the hanging, what happened next?" Luka asked.

"Next?" Fanny echoed.

"In the tale of Lady Dearborn's life, what happened next?"

"Oh, well if you'd like that accounting," Fanny said, "I'd be happy to provide it."

"Please don't," Emma tried. "I've been saving some of the more outrageous bits for rainy afternoons."

"Oh, darling, there's no reason to wait," Fanny said, clearly delighted with the chance to review Emma's life, and indeed she settled back and began to recount the many ways Emma had gotten into some sort of trouble during their upbringing. Emma half-heartedly tried to stop her from telling the story of when she put salt in the teacup of Mrs. Carter, the family housekeeper. Or how she rowed with their first tutor because he refused to teach them marine science. "I wanted to learn about the ocean!" Emma cried. "Is that so wrong?"

And when Fanny related how Emma had been caught kissing one of the grooms in the stable, Emma protested that "it wasn't as bad as that," and rolled her eyes. Phillip leaned over and covered Theo's ears.

"You needn't bother," Emma said with a sigh. "I've already told him."

"You didn't!" Fanny exclaimed.

"Well? We were in the stables one day, Theo and I, and it just popped into my head."

Emma tried, she really tried, to keep the entire story of her life from coming out, as that was the only plan she had left to keep Luka where she wanted him. But Fanny had no qualms in her retribution for Emma having dragged her into this and kept talking, right up to the days when Albert and Adele came to call on Fanny, with the clear intent of Albert courting Fanny.

"Now this sounds like an interesting tale," Luka said, shaking his head to the offer of cake from a footman. "How *did* your sister maneuver Lord Dearborn away from you, Mrs. Yates?"

"It was more that I maneuvered away from Lord Dearborn," Fanny said. She smiled so sweetly at her husband that Emma's heart squeezed with painful envy. "I was deeply in love with someone else."

Phillip dabbed at his mouth with his napkin and returned a fond smile to his wife. "And I thank the good Lord you were, darling. I could not have competed with Albert's title and all of this," he said, gesturing around them.

"He never had the slightest chance," Fanny said. "He could never compare to you."

"All right," Emma said, holding up a hand. "Before the two of you begin to list each other's impeccable virtues, I *did* marry the man who could never compare."

"That's right," Fanny said.

"Can't blame the bloke," Phillip said. "If he couldn't have one Robbins girl, he had the next best thing."

Emma snorted. "I wouldn't put it quite like that."

"Neither would I," Fanny said with a laugh. "Really, our parents were very keen on either of us marrying him. And Emma especially. What else were they to do with her?"

"What is that supposed to mean?" Emma asked. "That is not an entirely accurate assessment, Fanny. I would like to believe I would have stumbled upon a solution."

"Oh, I would like to believe it to, darling, I would. But I don't know that I can."

Luka laughed. "It's not unheard of for an earl, or a *comte* in my case, to carry on with the sisters when one isn't inclined. The family's connections and suitability have already been determined."

Emma and Fanny both looked at him with surprise. "My goodness, Mr. Olivien, what a romantic you are," Emma said. "I thought my marriage was a love match. Once he discovered my sister's heart was with someone else, he was frankly relieved, because he'd not known that I, the terrible sister, was available."

Everyone laughed.

"He courted you properly," Fanny said. "For *months*, remember? Far longer than necessary if you ask me. He wanted to be certain that you were the one."

He wanted to be certain he had to marry at all. In hindsight, she believed that when she thought he'd been so careful of her feelings, he was, in fact, putting it off as long as he could. She felt a painful twist of shame in her belly. She'd been so naive then.

"You must miss him," Phillip said to Emma, which, of course he would assume. If Fanny was gone an afternoon to the village, Phillip missed her terribly. What love like that must feel like, Emma mused into her glass of wine as she sipped. "Terribly," she said when she put the glass down. It wasn't a true lie, she reasoned. The way she didn't miss him in the least was truly terrible.

She could feel Luka's eyes on her, could feel the draft of her cold heart whipping down her spine. She shivered slightly. What must he think of her? And why did he have the right to think of her at all? He might know her husband was dead, but he had no idea what she'd suffered when he was alive. "What of you, Mr. Olivien?" she blurted. "Have you a fiancée?"

He smiled, as if he knew why she was asking. "No. Alas."

"How long has it been since you were last in your home country?" Phillip asked, perhaps sensing that the subject needed to be changed. He and Luka began to discuss the rumors of unrest there. Luka said he was headed home soon to see if he could be of any assistance in tamping down tempers.

"Oh?" Phillip asked. "What will you do?"

"The unrest is centered in the coal-mining region

of Astasia. My father is the Duke of Astasia. And the queen and I were childhood friends. I hope to be able to broker peace between the two parties."

Emma was surprised. She was used to thinking of him as an explorer, an anthropologist. This was a new side of him. Funny how when one did all the talking, other important details were left unsaid.

Fanny asked about his family. He said he had two sisters, both married, and had grown up in the mountains of Wesloria. He talked briefly about his interest in anthropology, and how that had taken him to Egypt and the Sahara Desert for further study.

When he mentioned the desert, Theo perked up. He asked about camels and sand. Quite a lot of questions about sand. Frankly, the entire Yates family seemed to hang on every word Luka said. So did Emma.

After dinner, they retired to the drawing room, and Theo retired to the nursery.

The four of them played hearts. They had a rousing good time, really, with lots of laughter, and it felt so odd to be laughing like this in this house, but so *nice*. It was exactly the sort of evening Emma had envisioned with Albert and their combined families when they'd married. She had imagined that Butterhill Hall would be the center of both worlds, that they would be together often. But it had rarely happened—Albert and Adele preferred reading to conversation. Emma would wander the room, looking for something to do. When she suggested they invite Fanny and Phillip, Albert almost always had an excuse. Too tired, a headache, did she ever think of anyone other than herself?

Eventually, Phillip said that he and Fanny would have an early start in the morning, as there were chores to be done. He extended an invitation to call on them before Luka left for Wesloria. Luka said he would like that, and he seemed very sincere.

Emma and Fanny went up together, Fanny with her arm around Emma's waist. At Emma's door, she took her sister's face in her hands. "Emma," she whispered and glanced down the hall where the men were walking on, still in conversation. "Don't do anything to make the situation worse."

"Could it possibly be worse?"

"*Yes.* And you know exactly how."

"Fanny."

"Emma." She quirked a brow at her.

"I promise you that I will do my best." And she would. But she knew herself, and she was not a paragon of strength.

In her room, Carlotta helped Emma out of her dress. Carlotta left, yawning, when Emma told her she didn't need her tonight. Alone, Emma absently brushed her hair, her attention on the window. It was black outside, but it didn't matter. The only thing Emma could see was Luka in her mind's eye, sitting at the end of her table. He was smiling and conversing, laughing and teasing Theo. He was precisely the sort of man she'd believed Albert would be. And then hoped he would become. Luka was the sort of man any woman would want.

Her mind wandered to other images of him, and she imagined his broad hands on her body, his hard body inside her. She imagined how his kisses, so lovely, would grow more urgent. She was on the verge of losing everything. Her place at Butterhill. Her reputation. Her social status. What was left after that? No one would touch her: she'd heard too many stories of women who had behaved badly to think otherwise.

She had nothing else left to lose.

She put her brush aside, stood up, and slipped her dressing gown over her nightgown. What was it her grandmother used to say? *You only have one life, only one chance to truly live it, so don't sleep through it.*

Emma stepped out of her room and very carefully closed the door. She moved quietly down the hall, avoiding those places where the floor squeaked. Down the stairs, across the cold stone floor, and up again to the east wing with the stunning view of sunrise. She made her way to the last room on the right, where she paused, pressing her ear to the door to listen for any sound. Hearing nothing, she put her hand on the handle and turned it very slowly, cracking open the door, and pausing to listen. Still nothing.

She slipped inside and quietly shut the door behind her. She turned, looked at his sleeping figure, turned on his side, facing away from the door. She was surprised to see that he was not wearing a nightgown. The skin of his broad back seemed almost to glow in the dim light of the dying fire.

She had clearly gone off her head, because the only thing she could think of with any clarity was touching him. Her body was already heating, her heart already racing.

If she could say one thing for herself, it was that once she committed to an idea, she did not back away. She walked across the floor, and at his bedside, she dropped her dressing gown. She pulled up the linens and coverlet and slid into the sheets next to him.

CHAPTER TWENTY-ONE

IT WAS A tress of silken hair sliding across his arm that woke Luka. Later, he would recall that he wasn't really surprised by it, that he'd somehow understood exactly what was happening in that moment of waking, almost as if his body and his heart had been forewarned and were waiting for her. He rolled over without a word, took her in his arms, and kissed her.

She giggled against his mouth, clearly surprised by his reaction, then molded her body to his, softening in his arms.

"Are you lost, Lady Dearborn?"

"No more than usual."

"Why are you in my bed?" he asked, stroking her hair.

"I haven't finished telling you the story." She kissed his chin.

"Haven't you? I heard quite a lot this evening. I can't imagine there is more."

"Oh, there's *much* more to the story than even my sister knows." Emma pushed him onto his back, then climbed on top to straddle him, the damp warmth of her body pressed against his abdomen. "I haven't told you the most exciting parts. Do you want to hear it?"

He caressed her cheek, wishing he could prolong these moments indefinitely. Before their joint reality began to burn them down, starting at the edges. "I'm not certain I do," he said honestly.

"Really? But there are many little twists and turns and dark alleys in this tale."

His eyes roamed her face and neck, her chest. Her hair, fragrant and falling freely around her shoulders. Surely she knew what it would mean once the truth was said between them. And yet, she smiled reassuringly, folded over him, her hair falling around him now, and kissed him tenderly before lifting back up. "I was married in May, when the blooms were at their finest—yellow and pink and blue flowers everywhere you looked. One would have thought they were an omen. But my marriage was…well, it was wretched, really. It was not the love match I had believed. It was torture, every single day."

"What?" He found this admission startling. What would have made it torturous? What man wouldn't have thanked the Lord for this wife every day? Emma's eyes, which had been glimmering in the low light of the embers, seemed to darken. "You don't have to say more," he said.

"That's very considerate of you. It would undoubtedly be wiser for me not to say more, but I can never seem to do that. A terrible character flaw, I think. I won't burden you with the details but will say as kindly as I might that we were emotionally and physically estranged."

Luka didn't want to hear this. The Countess of Dearborn was the most vibrant woman he'd met in a long, long time, and it was impossible to imagine anyone being unkind to her.

"And because of it, I was crazed with loneliness, well

before he left on his expedition. When he left, so did all the agitation in my life. I didn't wake up dreading his cruelty each day. I didn't fear upsetting him by merely breathing. And do you know what else? I discovered that I very much liked who I am when I wasn't trying so hard to be the wife he wanted. I began to enjoy my freedom immensely."

Luka guiltily realized he'd enjoyed her freedom, too. His gaze slid away for a moment as he tried to work out his warring feelings about her.

"And then, one day, a stranger came to my door." She began to caress his bare chest, her fingers sliding up to his neck, to his ears, then down again. "He said he had some news for me." She drew a long breath. The playfulness left her; her expression had turned sober.

"He said Albert had died of yellow fever and they'd buried him straightaway, and he gave me a pouch with his signet ring, and before I could even absorb this news, the poor man…" She paused, bowed her head. "The poor man dropped dead in my drawing room. His heart gave out."

Luka blinked. "Duffy?" He sat both of them up. "You're speaking of Mr. Duffy?"

She nodded. "Mr. Duffy from Cairo."

"Mr. Duffy is *dead*?" He didn't know why he was so surprised by this, but he tried to imagine that buoyant fellow, dead of a bad heart in her drawing room.

"I'm very sorry if he was a friend of yours," she said, cupping his face with her hand. "But he very much is. He's buried in the churchyard if you'd like to see it. We didn't have the slightest clue what to do with him. No one knew who he was."

"The poor man."

"The poor man indeed." She paused. "But the point is, Luka, that in addition to Mr. Duffy... Albert is also dead."

His attention snapped back to her. "You're finally admitting it."

"I am," she said somberly.

"How long have you known?"

"Some months."

"Months?"

She winced slightly. "It was perfectly fine until..." She gestured between them.

"Until?"

"Until you came with his pocket watch."

He stared at her.

"No one else knew until then."

"Emma—"

"I understand you must have many questions, and it may surprise you to know that I have a few of my own. For myself. You'll want to know why, and so do I. You'll want to know who else knows of his death, and I will have to say no one. Well... Fanny knows, but only since a few days ago. And you're probably quite perplexed by what is happening at Butterhill Hall, and I will tell you. I'll tell you anything you want to know."

Luka held up his hand. "You don't owe me an explanation, Emma."

She looked surprised. "But don't you *want* one? If *I'd* been trying to deliver such terrible news for days, only to find out that the person knew, I'd be ablaze with curiosity about why she made it so impossible."

"I didn't say I wasn't curious."

"I had my reasons, even if they were made in the moment and were very bad in hindsight, and I realize that one day I may regret them—well, *will* regret them, I think that is a given now—but honestly, at this moment? I don't regret anything."

Her impassioned bit of truth-telling made her sound a bit like a fugitive, running from the authorities and wreaking havoc as she went. "Have you... Have you done something?" he asked, uncertain what she was trying to tell him.

"No! I mean...nothing criminal. And I imagine that being a man of scruples, you'll want to pull Adele aside and tell her the truth and perhaps suggest that something must be done about her sister-in-law, and on my mother's grave I wouldn't fault you if you did." She sighed and looked away. "Adele would relish that sort of moment."

"Yes," Luka said firmly. "But this has nothing to do with me, Emma. *You* need to tell her. You can't hide something like this from his sister and brother."

"I know, I know," she said, and slid off his body to sit beside him, her shoulders slumped, her gaze on her lap. "I've meant to a thousand times before. It's just that in the beginning it was... There was so much chaos, and I didn't see the harm in pretending. It was so easy, so freeing. I felt as if I was meeting myself again after years of living in oppression."

"But why did you pretend at all?" he asked her. "What did you have to lose by telling your husband's family he had died?"

"Because...because I knew that Adele would install Andrew as the earl the moment she knew, which is her right. And that I would have nowhere to go."

"What are you saying? You would remain here, wouldn't you? As the widowed countess?"

"For a time, perhaps. But I think Adele would find a way to send me off to the dower house. I would be delighted with that arrangement, but it wouldn't last. She'd marry me off as soon as possible, to wash her hands of me. And then poor Andrew, whose health is not good. She'd have a countess of her choosing and press Andrew to produce an heir like she did Albert. Then she'd want the dower house for herself, and I would have nowhere to go. She would undo all the improvements I've made to the accounts and management of Butterhill Hall, because she hates change. And Andrew? He is a dear, but he's too young to understand and would have to be taught everything I've learned. So I... I pretended until I could think of what to do. And then I kept pretending because I enjoyed my life. I kept thinking I would tell her the truth, but time...just stretched on." She glanced warily at him. "I can't imagine what you must think of me. I swear to you, I never meant any harm to anyone. I meant only to enjoy my freedom a bit longer."

Luka shoved his fingers through his hair, his mind hurrying through all the ramifications. "You must realize that consequences will be much worse now, especially when your sister-in-law learns how long you've known."

"I do," she said. "Is it possible that she will send her unruly sister-in-law to the convent? Do we still send ladies to the nunnery? She might go so far as to have the men from the asylum come and tell them my nerves must be sorted out somewhere far from Butterhill Hall."

Luka sincerely hoped she was making light of the situation and wasn't serious. "What of your sister?"

Emma immediately shook her head. "I won't do that to her. I refuse to burden her family with another mouth to feed, another body to house. And with the scandal that will follow, she and Phillip would be pariahs when they've only ever been my greatest support."

He understood. He'd not want to burden his sisters, either. Both had managed to escape the rough-and-tumble mountains of Astasia. "What will you do?"

Emma sighed. "I don't know quite yet. But I will think of something." She smiled softly, and he wondered if she was trying to convince herself.

"When will you tell them?" he asked.

"After the house party," she said. "It's my last hurrah. And yours."

Despite his own troubles, he smiled. "*Je*, the honored guest. How can I help you, Emma?"

She twisted around so that she was facing him, her figure framed by the lowlight of embers in the hearth. "Do you mean it? You want to help me?"

Luka took her hand and interlaced her fingers with his. "As barking mad as it is, I do." He wanted to help her more than he wanted to help his queen. He wanted this unusual, remarkable woman to carry on living as she had.

"Then, kiss me," she said.

"I meant help with your dilemma."

"So did I," she said. "Kiss me. Then take my clothes off, but one piece at a time. It's a start."

"Emma," he began, but the suggestion was already a flame to his kindling of desire. His morals were sinking rapidly under the feeling he'd had about this woman the first time he'd seen her, wild and curious and beautiful. He sank his fingers into her hair and pulled her to him. "How would you like me to remove them? With my hands?" He nibbled her earlobe, then her neck. "Or my teeth?"

"Oh. *Oh*," she whispered and steadied herself with her hands to his arms as he continued to kiss her cheeks, her nose. "There are distinct advantages to both methods." She paused, bending her neck to give him better access.

"Quite. With my hands, I can touch you in all the places you want to be touched," he said, and slid his hand inside her chemise to her breast, squeezing gently. "But with my mouth, I can kiss you everywhere you dream of being kissed."

"Outrageously good options," she murmured. "How will I ever choose?"

He kissed her mouth, his tongue slipping in between her lips. Her skin was heating under his touch; he could see the flush of desire creeping into her face. She ran her hands down his arm and up his chest. "And then what?"

"And then…" He wrapped her in his arms, pressed his lips to her neck for a long, lingering moment, and whispered into her ear, "*Then*, Emma, I would slide into you so long and so slow that you would beg me for mercy before I could get all the way inside you."

Emma's breath grew short. She dug her fingers into his arms. "Then, I choose all the options. *All* of them."

Luka held her tighter, twisting her around onto her back beneath him, his erect member pressed against her. "Are you certain, Lady Dearborn?"

"Never more certain," she said, and rose to kiss him.

It was his undoing. A light flickered somewhere in the room, catching the blue of her eyes, and then his mouth was on hers. He felt a bolt of lightning streaking through him, igniting everything in him. He felt almost weightless, lost in a haze of hunger that had not gripped him in ages. As his hands moved over her body, lifting her chemise over her head, then shedding his drawers, it seemed as if the only thing tethering them to earth was this room and the ceiling above them. Everything else faded away.

The lady did not hold back, did not wait for him to take the lead. She pressed against his hardness, wrapped one leg around his back, anchoring him to her, her hands moving on him, feeling the contours of his body, her mouth open beneath his. The tension between them escalated quickly, almost too quickly—he was fighting the urge to plunge into her with a roar. But he had promised his hands and his mouth, and he loved the little gasps and moans of delight as he used them on her body. His hands roamed to her breasts, then her hips, his fingers digging into her flesh. He inhaled the heady scent of her, lavender and roses, and a bit of smoke in her hair.

He couldn't think coherently—he was moving from desire to an all-consuming need to be inside her. He shifted his body between her legs. She wrapped both legs around him, and they gazed at each other for one terrifying moment in which an entire conversation passed between them. *We are coming together, we are going to experience this with abandon, and we will deal with the fallout another time.*

"Now," Emma said.

"Now," Luka replied.

They took each other, together. His blood rushed with anticipation—his erection felt as thick and hard as a tree. Her hair spilled around her on the bed, her nipples were hard with want. She closed her eyes, dug her fingers into his shoulders, and arched her body hard against his.

He slid his hand between them, into her sex. Emma moaned and turned her head to the side. He could feel her body pulsing against his hand, and it was ripping him apart. He pressed the tip of his body into her, and her eyes flew open, locking on his. He silently continued, taking it slow, making her breath shorter and shorter. When he was fully inside her, he paused to take her breast into his mouth, nibbling at the peak. Emma dug her fingers into his hips, pushing him against her, moving her body against his. Luka sank a little deeper, then moved to the other breast.

Emma arched her back into his mouth, thrust her hands into his hair. She rubbed her leg against him, slid her fingers down his back, even reached between them, trying everything she could to spur him on.

But Luka was steady. His breathing was ragged, too, and she squeezed him, making him groan. He caught her bottom lip between his teeth, then kissed her hard before pressing his forehead to hers.

"I am crazed with desire," she said breathlessly.

"As am I." He kissed her neck, feathered her chest with kisses. And he began to move, sliding in and out of her. But his own desire was working against him. He reached his hand between their bodies and began to stroke her. He thrust into her as deep as he could, felt her body clench around him. She met each thrust, gasping with delight as they moved. He increased the tempo, and their gazes locked, their bodies working from some primal place, until her arousal reached its natural end.

He quickly pulled out of her just as he reached his

own thundering climax, rolling onto his back and panting as if he'd run to Butterhill from Wesloria.

It seemed to him as if the light in the room had grown brighter. The air was damp with perspiration. Her hand slid across his chest, and she buried her face in his neck. He wanted to speak, but he couldn't find his breath.

After several moments, he felt her lips on his shoulder. He turned toward her then, lifted her chin, and kissed her tenderly. With affection. With regard. With something so profoundly unplumbed in him that he was a bit afraid to know what it was. He could possibly love this woman. He could possibly love her deeply, with all his heart.

Emma smiled and rolled onto her back, flinging one arm across him in her abandon. "I should like to bask in this," she said. "*This* is what happens to desire when it is left unattended for too long—it turns spectacular."

"It was astonishing," he agreed softly.

She sighed and rolled into his side, her head on his shoulder, her fingers tracing patterns on his chest.

Luka couldn't think about what came next. He couldn't think about tomorrow, or the day after that, because those days brought him closer to leaving Butterhill. He toyed with her hair, winding a tress around his finger. He allowed himself to pretend that this was normal, that they were destined for a life together.

It was Emma who finally broke the spell when she rose and began to dress. She was a perplexing mix of whimsy and practicality, and he never knew which to expect.

When she'd dressed, she twisted her hair into a tail and left it draped over her shoulder. Luka reached for her hand and squeezed her fingers. "Emma...you must have a care for yourself. You've put yourself in a terrible position, and I fear there is no easy way out."

"I understand. May I just say that I'm very glad you came to Butterhill Hall?" She squeezed his fingers in return.

"I'm glad I came, too," he said.

"When will you go?"

His stomach began to knot with reality seeping back into the room. "A week from Tuesday."

She winced. "So soon?"

"I've delayed longer than I ought to have done."

"At least you'll be here for the party. Won't you?"

Oh, how the heart could rule when it wanted. He ought to leave tomorrow. He had tampered with lives he never should have touched. But he brought her hand to his lips and kissed it. "I wouldn't miss it."

Her smile was one of relief. "I'm so glad. I still haven't told you the whole story."

A snort of disbelief escaped him. "What could you possibly have left out?"

"Lord above, Luka, I am thirty-two years old. There is more." She smiled, leaned down, and kissed his mouth. Then went to the door. She glanced back at him, her gaze moving over his naked body on top of the bed linens. She opened the door and slipped out into the night.

Luka lay back and pillowed his head on his hands for a moment. Then he got out of bed, pulled on a dressing gown, and went to the table near the hearth where he'd left his journal. He had to capture the extraordinary latest chapter in his life.

CHAPTER TWENTY-TWO

London

LADY LILA ALEKSANDER was dismayed by the state of Lord Iddesleigh's library. He'd once been such a fastidious bachelor—where had that man gone? Stockings, shoes, and bonnets were strewn about, as if someone had dashed in and thrown off their clothes. There was a parasol or two, leaning precariously against the wall. There were fashion plates and ladies' magazines and a wicker basket full of some sort of silky floral material, its purpose indecipherable.

What man allowed five daughters to infiltrate his sanctuary in this way? This London townhome in Mayfair had eight bedrooms and at least two sitting rooms, not to mention receiving rooms and drawing rooms and a fine music room, all more suitable for the detritus of a large family's life than Beck's sanctuary.

Lila knew from her experience as Europe's premier matchmaker that if there was a single unifying question every father encountered, it was most assuredly how long his children would continue to live in his house. Beckett Hawke—Beck, as he was known by his friends—had five daughters, two of whom were of marrying age, another one quite close, and none who showed any inclination toward the happy state of matrimony. By the all-too-comfortable look of things, they might very well be content to live with their parents forever.

There was a commotion at the library door, and Beck entered behind a lumbering big brown dog. Lila knew this dog—he diligently tried to anticipate every step a person might make so that he could put his body in the way of all of them. It seemed as if Beck was always skipping around behind that dog, trying to pass him.

"Lila! What a lovely surprise." Once through the door, he bypassed the hound but paused as he reached the middle of the room and glanced around. "Lord deliver me," he said, then smiled sheepishly at Lila. "I beg your pardon, but you see before you an earl, a father, a husband, a walker of three useless dogs, and master of none and no one."

That wasn't true—Beck knew absolutely everyone in London and beyond, was considered friend by all, and had been a great help to Lila through the years. She was quite fond of him.

"Look at you," he said, coming forward. "You've slipped into London without my knowing. Generally, when you are in town, you are in my parlor straightaway, seeking my assistance, asking questions about the Season's diamonds and young stallions. What has kept you?"

She laughed. "Word of my presence travels quickly— I've only been in town a fortnight."

"Naturally. Everyone is eager to know who the next match will be." Beck went to the sideboard and held up a bottle of port. Lila nodded. "You've come to ask for help in making a match, I presume."

"I have not. I accepted only one new client this year, and I've already made the match."

Beck handed her the small glass of port, his expression one of surprise. "Only one?"

"Only one. Last year was rather intense, you may recall, with the match of Lord Abbott and Miss Woodchurch. After that, I needed a rest. Too much scandal for one Season! My only commission this year was a Hungarian prince. It was quite easy, thankfully. But I don't care for the Hungarian cuisine, I must say. Too many dumplings for my liking." She sipped her drink.

"You needn't remind me of last Season's scandal," Beck said with a shake of his head. "What a debacle that was."

Beck had helped her salvage the match. That sometimes happened with the sort of matches Lila made. She catered to royalty, aristocracy, and the unimaginably wealthy. She'd made some spectacular matches among many elite European families over the years, and last year, she'd made a match of Lord Abbot, a Santiavan duke who was also an English viscount, and the indomitable Miss Harriet Woodchurch. Most thought the match would be impossible given their disparate situations in life, but amid a sensational scandal involving Miss Woodchurch's brother, with Beck's help Lila had managed to bring it all together. She'd recently heard from Lord Abbot's mother that Hattie and Mateo were very happy, living in the small country of Santiava with their first child.

"Then, if you've not called for information on some poor, unsuspecting lad, shall I assume this is a purely social call?"

"Of course! But there is something I should like to ask you—"

"I haven't given it the slightest thought."

"Pardon?"

"A match for my daughters."

Lila laughed. "I haven't come to discuss your dazzling girls."

"Yes, well, perhaps you should come to discuss them. They are more than old enough."

She smiled at her friend. "You will know when the time is right. But I've come to ask for a recommendation. Valentin and I are looking for a home here."

"What, you're leaving Denmark?"

"Heavens no," Lila said. She and her husband, a Danish count, had lived in Denmark for ages. "Valentin would never. But we find ourselves here quite a lot and thought perhaps a pied-à-terre might be in order."

Beck grinned. "Now, this is the sort of problem I can help with." He took his port and went to his desk. "I have an excellent estate agent." He put his glass down and began to go through his things. The brown dog suddenly hopped on the settee where Lila was sitting and put his head on the lap of her new silk gown. Lila stood up and joined Beck at the desk.

The surface of Beck's desk was stacked with letters and estate correspondence, receipts, bills of lading.

"I have the gentleman's calling card just here," he said, searching through the stacks. One of the envelopes slipped off the pile and fell to his chair. Beck paused to pick it up and shook it in the direction of Lila. "Wildly expensive paper, this," he said. "I know, because my darling Maisie recently decided she would write a book and bought this sort of paper in such a quantity that my eyes very nearly spun out of their sockets." He tossed the envelope onto the desk. It slid across to where Lila was standing as Beck returned to his search.

Lila glanced down at the broken seal. *Dearborn.* "Wonderful!" she exclaimed. "You've received an invitation to the country house party at Butterhill Hall!"

"Don't remind me."

"Why not? I am eager to meet her guest of honor. A Weslorian, you know. The *Comte ve Marlaine.*"

"No, thank you," Beck said, turning his attention back to his search. "I refuse to be hoodwinked into buying new wardrobes for six women for the sake of a weekend, and that will be the first thing demanded of me if they get wind of it. It's hard enough to satisfy Blythe," he said, referring to his wife. "I can't bear the wailing. *I've nothing to wear!*" he said, mimicking a girl's voice. "*I can't possibly be seen in that! Why must you always make me appear in public in old rags, Papa?*"

"But think of the fun they would have," Lila said. "I hear Butterhill Hall is quite grand."

Beck shook his head. "I don't want to go. I'm getting older, Lila. I've just marked my fiftieth year." He paused in his search. "I recall when my sister, Caro, and I were orphaned, and I only sixteen years, I thought fifty was so terribly old that I'd probably never live to see it. Well, here I am, a stone heavier than I was then, with lines on my face that seem to have leaped there overnight, and a body that requires at least two trips to the water closet every night. There are days that I wonder if I ought to take out a page in the newspapers and announce that I am too old for frivolity and to stop inviting me to it."

"One is never too old for frivolity, Beck. What you need, if I may offer my opinion—"

"I'd rather you not—"

"Is a change of pace."

"No, thank you," he said, and, having found the calling card he'd been searching for, held it out to Lila.

She ignored it. "Your sister and her prince will be attending. So will Princess Amelia and Lord Marley."

"Marley?" Beck sputtered. Lord Marley's estate was neighbor to Iddesleigh House in Devonshire. Lila understood Beck's surprise—Marley had been a recluse for years until Lila managed to match him with Princess Amelia of Wesloria. They spent most of their time in London now. "Marley abhors that sort of thing," Beck scoffed.

"And yet he's going," Lila said pertly. *"And* Donovan. So if you find yourself too weary to handle your brood, Donovan will be there to do it for you."

Mr. Donovan, the mysterious, terribly handsome man who had served as a governor, nursemaid, confidant, and wrangler for the Hawke family for years. He was a true enigma, his tastes running to gentlemen, his past a bit cloudy, his attraction universal.

"Then perhaps he might take them all," Beck groused.

"In fact, Marley was the first to say yes," Lila continued. "And *then* Donovan."

"What? Why?"

"Because, as the invitation says, the party is in honor of Lord Dearborn's friend, Lord Marlaine of Wesloria. Princess Amelia knows him well. And you know as well as I do that any gathering engineered by Lady Dearborn is always a very good time. I heard there will be horse races, a ball, and even acrobats. Oh, and a gentlemen's strongman competition."

"A what?"

"A gentlemen's strongman competition?" Lila repeated uncertainly. She'd heard that from Princess Amelia. "You would enjoy it, Beck."

"I don't see how I possibly might. I'm not as strong as I used to be, and I never win any sort of competition. Mr. Heller took me for twenty-five pounds at the club last week." Beck took a seat in the chair across from Lila and flipped the agent's card between his fingers as he pondered her. "Don't you ever grow weary of life, Lila? Of the soirees and parties and social expectations? Of the unmarried daughters and endless bills?"

Lila had seen this sort of middle-aged malaise before. "Well, I haven't any children, as you know. But I do enjoy life, Beck. Life is for living, and you shouldn't give up on it. Once you have your daughters married, you'll see what I mean. You must come. It will be quite the diversion."

He shook his head. "I can't manage it. My girls will want new things for it, and I can't afford it."

Lila rolled her eyes. Beck was richer than most. "Then, you best tell your sister when she comes."

Beck jerked his gaze to her. "Caro? Why do you say that?"

"I just saw her with your three youngest. They were on their way to shop."

"Caro took them shopping?" Beck let his head drop to the chair back and groaned loudly. "Are you telling me that my daughters know about the Dearborn weekend?"

Lila grinned. "I believe they do."

"That's it, then. They will insist on attending. Everyone knows that Lady Dearborn's events are all the rage among the younger set."

"Beck!" Lila laughed. "In all the years I've known you, I've never seen you so misanthropic! Think of the love that will abound in the country."

He eyed her suspiciously. "And what love is that, pray tell?"

"*Any* love. These weekends are where attachments are made and bonded. What if one of your girls was to find love and wanted to marry? It seems entirely plausible to me. Wouldn't you like to see them married?"

"*No.* I mean, yes, of course I do. They cost a fortune, they eat all the food in the house, they are generally incorrigible…but I don't think I can bear to see one of them leave. Especially not at your doing. You'll match them to some foreign dignitary, and they'll leave England altogether, and I'll never see them again."

Lila laughed. "Your girls? I hardly think so. I think they will be near you for all your life. And your odds are much higher that they will meet a fellow countryman at a weekend event, thereby doing away with any need of me at all."

Beck seemed to perk up at that. "That is an excellent point, Lila. All right, then. We will attend."

Lila fluttered with delight and clapped her hands, pretending that he had made the decision, even though she suspected the decision had already been made by his daughters. "Wonderful! Now, about a house…"

CHAPTER TWENTY-THREE

AT LONG LAST, Emma Clark had taken a lover. She might even be falling in love. She suspected the fluttering sensation in her chest, the breathless wonder she felt when she saw him, the joie de vivre that filled her every waking moment was probably an indication of it. But as she had never quite experienced anything like it, she wasn't entirely sure.

Funny how she'd believed the comfort and security she'd felt when Albert had courted her was love. She had no idea that true love could be something so electric and exciting, something so ethereal and deranged. Wasn't it lovely that falling in love was simply mad? The very thought made her smile.

She supposed she ought to be grateful that there was so much to be done to prepare for her guests, or she might have grown obsessive about him. But even amid all the planning and decisions Feeney forced her to make—she really wished he'd just manage it all—Luka was a delight. They found time every day to walk around the lake, and she continued to be Scheherazade, telling him her life stories. She told him about the fight she and Fanny had had when they were girls and the poor doll whose porcelain face was smashed as a result. About the summer her beloved grandmother died. About a failed courtship with a gentleman she'd believed truly esteemed her, but who had been engaged to a woman in London the entire time.

Simply put, Emma told him everything. Why not? She had nothing to hide and certainly nothing to lose. She shared the best and worst of herself with Luka Olivien.

And every day, when they'd completed their circuit of the lake, he would look at his watch and say, "I'm afraid the rest of the story will have to wait."

Today, he said he had promised Mr. Karlsson a hand in the stables.

Another surprising thing about Luka was that he'd proved himself a man who was not afraid of work and didn't even care what sort of work it was. In that way, he was like her. Or rather, the new her, casting off all the traditional roles in favor of living. "You did?" she asked, surprised.

"I mean to show him how to hobble a horse."

"Pardon?"

"Or rather, he knows how to hobble a horse, but I learned a trick with camels that I thought he might like to see." He smiled at her blank look. "Stable talk. Pay it no mind."

"I *will* pay it mind, Mr. Olivien," she said. "I deserve to hear about camels."

"*Je*, you do." He looked around them and, seeing no one, kissed her quickly. "Maybe one day I will tell you about them. When you've come to the end of your story."

"Why would you make me wait as long as that? You do realize, don't you, that I haven't even told you about my first party. My goodness, when I think of how much more there is to tell!"

Luka laughed as they continued up the path. "As God as my witness, I don't know how there can be a single day of your life I've not yet heard. I could have filled volumes of anthropological journals." He touched her hand as they neared the house, and then veered off toward the stables.

The conversation between them wasn't as one-sided as it might seem to the casual observer, however. At night—*very* late at night, when the house was quiet—she would sneak to the east wing, avoiding the squeaky floorboards, and crawl into bed with him, and he would make love to her in a way that transported her. He took his time with her, casually exploring her body and encouraging her to explore his. And when they had satisfied each other, she would lie in his bed, as sated and relaxed as a working dog after a long day, while he told her about his life. About his travels, of course. His interest in different populations and customs. He showed her some of the artifacts he'd collected along the way, the gifts he would bring to his family. He told her about the caravansaries, the traders who traveled together, east to west and west to east, trading goods, like silk from China and textiles from Europe.

He described his estate, named Mont Blanc for the Frenchman who had built it many decades ago but sounded more like a medieval castle than a lovely chateau. He said it was at the base of the Astasia mountains on the main road to the capital of Wesloria, St. Edys.

He told her about his family, his sisters and their children and their happiness. His mother's relentless pressure on him to marry and sire an heir.

And he told her about his father, the man who was the cause of so much consternation for him. His mercurial ways, his desire to see someone on the throne other than a woman Luka considered his friend. He explained his dilemma with the queen and showed her the queen's letters.

The letters were sobering in a way Emma had not expected. She was not one for fantasy, but she had allowed herself to indulge in one about Luka. She'd imagined them on an expedition together seeing the world in all its amazing colors and people and scenery. She'd imagined them living to together at Butterhill Hall and taking their daily walks around the lake. Silly fantasies, the stuff of a young girl's dreams. But once she read those letters, she understood Luka was destined for something greater. He had something important to do, something that an entire nation needed from him, and here he was, stroking her thigh, one arm propped behind his head as he watched her read the letter. He had no time or use for a woman who had lied about her husband and was bound to be married to someone she didn't love as a means of survival.

When she'd finished reading, she set the letters aside and turned to him. "Luka? You must go home."

He didn't say anything. He didn't need to, as his agreement with that sentiment was clear in his sorrowful expression. He looked resigned. Unflinching. And terribly sad.

They remained that way for a long moment, gazing at each other. The words, unspoken, flowed between them. *I will miss you so.* And then he reached for her, pulling her to straddle him, and removed any thoughts from their brains with his hands and his mouth.

With each day that passed that week, Emma was convinced she would never feel this way with or about someone again. That thought didn't drown her in sorrow as she might have expected, but rather it filled her with a strange sort of gratitude. She was so very grateful she'd had a chance to know this esteem and compatibility with a man, even if for a short time. The regard between them was everything she'd ever dreamed a marriage could be.

Her time with Luka left her feeling so immeasurably happy that even visits from Adele and Mr. Longbottom could not daunt her. She hardly cared when the two of them arrived, twice unannounced that week, presumably with something Adele was convinced showed malfeasance or, at the very least, incompetence on Emma's part.

The first time, Adele had sailed into Emma's drawing room as if she was the mistress here, a paper clutched tightly in her hand. Emma was assigning rooms for her guests on a ledger Feeney had given her. She thought it was something he ought to do, but she didn't want to argue with him.

"Do you know what this is?" Adele asked breathlessly as Mr. Longbottom ambled in behind her.

"I don't, dearest, as you are holding it in your hand and I can't read it," Emma said. "Good afternoon, Mr. Longbottom."

"This is an estimate of how much it will cost to repair the cistern. Which, I might add, has not been arranged. You said you knew about it and were keen to see it done."

"I did and I am," Emma said with cheerful confidence.

"The repair needs to be done at once, Emma, but

instead, you have spent the money for this extravagant house party."

"It's not terribly extravagant," Emma protested, despite the party being a bit extravagant. "It could be much worse."

"That is hardly consolation."

"What's that they are building?" Mr. Longbottom asked, having made his way to the window.

Emma didn't have to get up from her task to know what he was seeing. "The pavilion tent. They will raise it the day before the house party begins."

"And here, below us?"

Emma looked up. He was looking at the west part of the lawn. "Ah, yes...they are also preparing the field for the strongman competition."

"The *what* competition?" Mr. Longbottom whirled around, clearly delighted by the notion.

"Something for the gentlemen to do," Emma said. "We've planned a footrace, an ax-throwing competition, and an archery competition. Oh, and some boxing for those who fancy themselves pugilists." She cocked her head to one side and considered the rotund man. "You look as if you might be a pugilist."

"Good Lord," Adele muttered. "What a waste of time."

"Really?" Emma said. "I think it sounds like great fun." She wondered what Adele would plan for a weekend house party. Knitting? Sitting about and staring at the clock? Emma returned her attention to Mr. Longbottom. "You must put your name in the hat to join the competition, Mr. Longbottom."

"Perhaps I shall," he said, rising like a balloon onto his toes, then back down again.

"Mr. Longbottom, we did not come here to discuss

the weekend," Adele chastised him. "We came to discuss the cistern, remember?"

"Oh, that," Emma said with an airy flick of her wrist. "It's all taken care of. I'm surprised Mr. Horn didn't tell you! Remember the pair of plows we had down by the lake? Albert had the idea of planting there, but we discovered the river bottom was unsuitable." She'd told him at the time it seemed implausible, as it was too marshy, but Albert had dismissed her.

"Women shouldn't be involved in discussions of land management," he'd said.

"Really?" Emma had asked, truly mystified by that notion. "Why not?"

"Shut your mouth, Emma," Albert had snapped.

It was amazing how much Adele could look like her brother when she was glaring at Emma as she was. "I sold them," Emma continued. "Rather, Mr. Horn sold them. Once the money from the sale is received, we will repair the cistern. And, I am happy to say, we have a bit extra to put in the family coffers. Isn't that wonderful?"

Adele jerked her gaze to Mr. Longbottom. The man tapped a finger against his lips as he thought about it. "Come to think of it, I do recall him mentioning the sale of the plows." He nodded. "It's a good plan."

"It's a good plan, is it, Mr. Longbottom?" Adele demanded, waving the paper in his direction. "Earlier today you seemed to think it was foolhardy to let the cistern go unattended for another day."

"Yes, well, I'd forgotten that they'd devised a way to pay for it. Problem solved," he said with a jaunty snap of his fingers.

The pair had left that afternoon, the paper crumpled

in Adele's hand as she fumed, and Mr. Longbottom excited about the strongman competition.

Adele was not deterred, however—oh no. She and Mr. Longbottom returned two days later, this time with a complaint about Emma's plans to open a shop on the property. The pair of them caught up to Emma at the orangery, where she was reviewing with Feeney where they ought to construct the orchestra's platform.

"I don't see why they can't be in the corner," Feeney said.

"The acoustics, Feeney," Emma reminded him. "They should be a bit above the dancers so the music carries all the way to the end of the orangery."

Luka had come along to have a look around but wisely stayed out of the Feeney fray. He was the first one to notice Adele's arrival.

"Lady Adele," he said, "Mr. Longbottom, how do you do?"

"Mr. Olivien!" Mr. Longbottom said while Adele ignored him. "Will you be entering the strongman contest this weekend? I'm thinking of giving it a go. I won't win a footrace, but I rather think I can throw an ax with the best of them."

"Mr. Longbottom!" Adele said sharply. "Once again, you seem to have misunderstood the reason for our call."

"Right you are, Lady Adele. Pardon, Lady Dearborn, but we'd like a word about your farm shop."

Emma was amazed by the gentleman—he appeared to pay not the slightest mind to the shrill tone of Adele's voice.

"Pardon?" Emma asked.

"The farm shop, Emma," Adele said. "Mr. Horn said you intend to build one."

"I do! Isn't it a wonderful idea?" Emma said brightly. "Mr. Horn and I have looked at the costs, and really, if we use the old groundskeeper's house—you know, the one up on the road that goes unused?—the costs to modify it into a shop would be minimal."

Adele gaped at her. "What is the matter with you? How can you possibly think Butterhill Hall needs such a vulgar thing as a *shop*? It's a piddling, embarrassing endeavor when one considers the grandeur of the Dearborn estate."

"Oh. How interesting you see it that way, darling," Emma said. "I thought you were concerned about the estate's income."

"I am," Adele said. "But I am equally concerned with the frittering away of estate funds."

"Of course I share your concern," Emma agreed. "Mr. Horn surely explained to you that we expect the shop will be making a profit in a year." She gasped. "Adele, darling! I just had the most amazing idea! You could sell your brambleberry jam in the shop!" She hadn't just thought of it, exactly. What she'd thought was that she'd do everything necessary to keep Adele from putting her fingers on any part of the shop.

"I beg your pardon. I am not a merchant," Adele said haughtily.

"I love a good brambleberry jam," Mr. Longbottom said wistfully. "Nothing better than a bit of bread with jam, is there?"

"You're in luck, Mr. Longbottom. Mrs. Foster, one of our local ladies, makes the best jam in this part of

England, and she's quite eager to sell it." Emma smiled sweetly at Adele.

"Now, what are we doing here?" Mr. Longbottom asked, gesturing to parts of the wooden platform men were bringing into the long, empty orangery to make a dais of sorts.

"That is for the six strings that will play at the Saturday night ball," Emma said. "Imagine, the room strung with candlelight, the windows open to the night air. I think it will be very romantic."

"You ought to put it there," he said, gesturing to the wall of windows. "Right in the middle where all can hear."

"It would be in the way of the dancing," Feeney said.

"Ah, yes, I can see that it would. Such a pity Mrs. Longbottom isn't here. She has such an eye for these things."

"For God's sake," Adele said. She turned on her heel and walked out of the orangery.

It was a moment or two before Mr. Longbottom noticed she'd gone and scurried after her. Emma risked a glance at Luka as she turned back to Feeney. His smile was hardly even detectable, but it was there. So was hers.

They understood each other.

Late that night, they delighted in Mr. Longbottom's enthusiasm for her house party.

Adele couldn't fluster Emma, but Fanny could. Fanny came the day before guests were scheduled to arrive. Emma and Luka were coming up from the west lawn, where they'd gone to see how the men's competition preparations were coming. Mr. Stanton and his men had almost finished erecting the thick wooden boards men would fling axes at. They urged Luka to try one of the boards to see if it held. He was happy to oblige them and hurled the ax, just missing the bull's-eye, much to Emma's delight.

"Sturdy as a church," Luka declared it.

As they walked away from the field, Emma glanced up at him. She could feel her happiness warm in her body, radiating out of her. She didn't want to miss a moment of him and was just about to confess as much when he said, "Isn't that your sister?"

"What?" Shaken from her reverie, Emma looked up to the terrace where Fanny was standing with her hands on her waist, in a manner that very much reminded Emma of their deceased mother. And her gaze, even from a distance, was piercing Emma's with swordlike precision. "This can't be good," she muttered, then followed with a cheerful "Good afternoon, Fanny!" She waved and said softly to Luka, "Perhaps you might like to carry on with your day. Far from me and my sister."

Luka, who lifted a hand to wave at Fanny, too, muttered back, "Are you in trouble?"

"I'm just coming in!" Emma called, and said, "I believe I am."

"Hmm," he said. "That's four times this week you've been in some sort of trouble."

"Four? I only count three. Adele twice, and now Fanny."

"You have forgotten Feeney's displeasure at the orchestra's platform."

"Right you are," she said, and started to walk away. "Make that five times this week," she said over her shoulder. "He was also terribly displeased with the discussion of the menu."

Luka was grinning as he turned in the opposite direction of the terrace.

Emma headed up the steps to Fanny, but her sister's gaze was fixed on Luka's retreating back. When he'd disappeared into the gardens, she slowly turned to glare at Emma. "What in damnation are you doing?"

Emma almost laughed. Her sister never cursed. "I don't know what you mean. I was having a look at the strongman course. Phillip means to enter the competition, doesn't he?"

"Don't change the subject. What are you doing with *him*?"

God help her, but Emma's grin was so instantaneous that it surprised even her. And Fanny, understanding that smile at once, gasped with horror. "Good *God*, Emma! What am I to do with you? Oh Lord, oh *Lord*, this couldn't possibly be worse."

"I can't help it!" Emma insisted. "He's lovely and astonishing, and Fanny, you must believe me when I tell you that I have never been held quite like that—"

"Not another word!" she cried, her hands going to her ears. "My heart will fail, and I have two small children." She groaned and dropped her arms. "I'm so glad our parents aren't here to see you carrying on like this."

"Well, obviously, so am I. I promise I won't say another word about him."

"Are you mad? I insist you tell me everything!"

"No. You protest too much, Fanny," Emma said, and tried to walk away. "I am a *widow*."

Fanny grabbed her arm. "Yes, but nobody else *knows that*," she shot back.

Emma sighed. She linked her arm with Fanny's.

"Don't *worry* so," she said soothingly. "I mean to confess everything to Adele after the weekend."

"But Emma—"

"Don't *but* me, Fanny." Emma stopped walking and turned to put her hands on Fanny's arms to hold her still. "You know the life I've led until now. And you can guess the sort of life I'll have after. I'll have to come to Rexford in the dead of night just to see you. Please let me enjoy this. *Please.*"

Fanny softened a bit. But she did not look convinced.

"It's *wonderful*, Fanny. I'm so happy! It's exactly as you always said it should be. He's kind, and he's interested in me, and he's tender and—"

Fanny suddenly gasped. "You're in *love*."

Emma's heart began to skip around in her chest. "I am."

"Emma, *Emma*," Fanny implored her. "You do know that you can't have him here, don't you? That he can't stay."

"Quite obviously he can't, and neither can I. He will return to Wesloria where he is needed, and I will head to a convent."

"A convent! No, you won't."

"You're right. Adele may kill me instead."

"Stop making light of it!" Fanny insisted angrily.

"I beg your pardon. I don't mean to make light of it, truly. But I am very clear on what will happen once I have told the truth, and I'm not afraid to face it." She pulled Fanny into a walk. "At least, I don't think I'm afraid to face it. I suppose at the moment of truth I'll find out. But never mind what will come—I have been living in a dream, and it will end with the celebration that begins tomorrow. So I beg you to indulge me, darling, because it is very likely I will never know true happiness again."

When Fanny looked at her this time, she wore an expression of something that looked a bit too much like pity. Emma didn't like it—she didn't want anyone to look at her like that. "Don't, Fanny."

Fanny blinked. "Don't what?"

"Don't pity me."

Fanny shook her head. "I don't pity you, darling. I fear for you."

Emma feared for herself, too. But not in the same way as Fanny did. Emma feared the shattering of her heart she knew was coming.

CHAPTER TWENTY-FOUR

LILA SUSPECTED HER HUSBAND, Valentin, might want to throttle her when all was said and done, as it had been her idea to join Lord and Lady Iddesleigh in their coach to Butterhill Hall after all. Donovan, who was also riding along, sat up top with the driver, having learned through years of experience that the ride was more pleasant there.

"Don't you want to come into the interior?" Lila asked him anxiously. Beck and Blythe were generally delightful, but if they were cross with each other, they didn't care who was around to hear it.

Donovan smiled in his gorgeous way and said, "Madam, that is the last place I should like to be." He winked at her and climbed up top.

At least the Hawke daughters were squeezed into another coach behind them. Valentin would have been beside himself if he'd had to listen to their squabbling for four hours. Fortunately, Lila and Valentin were taking the train back to London on Sunday, as Valentin had business the next morning. Most guests wouldn't leave until Monday.

Beck was lethargic, sprawled against the squabs, complaining of having eaten too much the night before. Blythe, with tiny shimmers of gray in her glorious red hair, pointed out that he had no one to blame but himself and that she had warned him this would happen.

Beck said no one ever liked to be told *I told you so*.

Valentin quietly took Lila's hand and squeezed a little, either to convey he was relieved that their marriage was not like the Hawkes's or to convey that he was going to get his revenge for this jaunt.

They stopped for lunch at a public house with boxes of flowers in the windows and smoke curling out its chimney. They were all delighted by the name, the Hawk and Fox, although Birdie, the youngest among them, pointed out that a hawk had nothing to do with a fox, and they should have named it the Fox and Hound, or the Hawk and Rabbit.

Meg, who was once affectionately called Peg-leg Meg by her family despite having two functioning legs, said Birdie didn't know everything, which prompted Maisie to add that neither did Meg, which in turn, caused Maren and Mathilda, the eldest, to tell them all to stop talking, that people were watching.

In the pub, Beck made his daughters sit at a table in the window, the egress from which involved passing by the table that the adults took. Their position might have stopped anyone from approaching the girls, but it didn't stop men from looking.

Beck kept his eye on the crowded room. A pair of young bucks were openly eyeing the girls, and the girls were eyeing them in return. Beck frowned. "I can't decide if I want to plant my fist in their faces or invite them to join us," he said, sounding genuinely unsure.

Donovan looked at the pair. "It would satisfy you to punch them, but you'd do just as well to ignore them."

"Don't do anything, Beck," Blythe said. "They might be someone important. Or rich. Or unmarried."

Beck looked at his wife as if she'd lost her mind. "What does that matter?"

"Are you blind?" Blythe asked as she dug through her reticule for something. "All our girls need to be married. And if anyone here is a potential prospect, you don't want Lady Dearborn to get her hands on them."

The entire table looked at Blythe, confused.

Blythe looked around at them. "Because of the affair?"

Lila perked up. "What affair?"

"Goodness, never mind," Blythe said. "They're just rumors, after all. Which I heard from Mrs. Langston, who just last week dined with Lord and Lady Priddy. Lady Priddy said that everyone in Rexford seems to believe that Lady Dearborn is behaving badly with her husband away."

"He's been gone forever, hasn't he?" Beck mused. "What can any husband expect when he leaves his wife alone for so long?"

Blythe leveled a look at him. "I would like to think he could expect her fidelity, darling."

Beck shrugged.

"So?" Lila asked, trying not to sound too eager. "Who is the, ah…person of interest?"

"I don't know," Blythe said.

"I'd wager it's the guest of honor. He's been at the hall a fortnight," Donovan said.

Now everyone turned to him. Donovan never ceased to amaze Lila with what he knew. "The Weslorian?" she asked.

"Lila," Valentin said gently. "We have come for a house party."

"Of course. I'm just curious, that's all." She was always curious about love. Lila had to suppress a smile. She had the sense that Emma Clark was a woman who was on the verge of bursting out of her countess's tiara. She hadn't guessed an illicit love affair, but still.

"How long has Lord Dearborn been abroad?" Blythe asked.

"Nearly two years," Beck said.

Lila laughed. "He's probably found a lover of his own."

"Good Lord, Lila, what a thing to speculate," Blythe said.

"Well?" Lila said. "What else would keep a man from his wife?"

"I'd not be surprised if that was true," Donovan said. "As for the gentleman, we might ask Lady Marley. They are acquainted."

"Childhood friends, I understand," Lila said.

"I don't know if they remain friends, however," said Donovan. "She didn't seem terribly enthused about him. She mentioned his family was behind some trouble in Wesloria."

"When do the Marleys arrive?" Beck asked.

"Tomorrow," Donovan said.

"How do you know so much?" Blythe asked.

"I saw the princess yesterday," Donovan said. "She needed help with a small matter."

"Really? What?" asked Blythe.

Donovan chuckled. "That is for Lady Marley to divulge, Lady Iddesleigh. Just as it would be for you to divulge if I was to help you."

"You're so coy, Donovan," Lila said. "We'll have it out of you after a whisky or two."

He bowed his handsome head. "I look forward to the challenge."

Lila laughed, but there was one thing she was very good at. Well, two—finding out things no one wanted to tell her and eating cake.

They reached Butterhill Hall two hours later. It was a lovely vista, with buttercups and cowslips in bloom everywhere they looked. The house, sitting at the entrance to a lake, was quite grand, the sort one could imagine princes and princesses might live in until they took the throne.

The two coaches pulled into the wide drive. Two other conveyances had arrived before them, and footmen were darting between them all, carrying bags, while guests milled about. A butler who introduced himself as Feeney showed them all to their rooms. Lila was delighted that she and Valentin seemed to be at the opposite end of the hall from the Hawke family. Donovan, as a single man, had been shown to a different part of the house.

A maid brought fresh towels, and when she'd gone, Valentin instantly fell back onto the bed. "The next time, my love, we hire our own carriage."

"Agreed," she said pleasantly. She dropped her shawl onto the chaise longue and went to the window to open it a little wider for some air. Below them was a long sweep of lawn. Several people were out, some of them headed down to the lake. But on the terrace below, Lila could see Lady Dearborn. She was wearing a sunny yellow-and-white gown. Her hair was swept up, and she held a parasol overhead.

She was speaking with several people, no one that Lila recognized. Among them was a particular gentleman, with hair a bit too long, his coat missing. She couldn't see that Lady Dearborn noticed him at all, but when she pointed to the lake, and the party turned to have a look, the man very casually reached up and touched her elbow. It was the briefest moment, and it could have been to steady her or to draw her attention. Interestingly, Lady Dearborn didn't respond. It was as if she had received the touch and that was enough.

Oh yes, Lila would be giving Donovan whisky tonight to find out what was going on with the irrepressibly lovely Lady Dearborn. She was dying of curiosity.

CHAPTER TWENTY-FIVE

WHEN EMMA HAD made her invitation list, she hadn't envisioned that so many people would answer in the affirmative. Or how so many people could be squeezed into Butterhill Hall.

She considered that she might have overextended her hospitality a wee bit this time.

Nonetheless, she was proud of herself for having corralled everything that needed to happen for the weekend. Flowers were carted in. Cheese, bread, jam, and soups were made in the Butterhill kitchen and supplemented by others from Rexford. Game hunters had stocked their larder with fowl and venison. Emma had sent to a purveyor of spirits in London for wine. It was all a dizzying expense, but Emma had made certain every cent was accounted for and there was a plan to replenish it. She and Mr. Horn were considering a banker's proposal to reopen the old copper mine in the northern sector of the estate. That could earn quite a lot of money for them, the banker promised. And even Mr. Longbottom had suggested she might employ the use of the land for paid pheasant hunts. "The lads in London are quite keen to do a bit of shooting," he'd said.

It was not a bad idea.

No matter what, Emma would leave the hall's finances in a better situation than she'd found them.

Her guests had begun to arrive around noon, even though the invitation had clearly stated two in the afternoon as the arrival time. "The roads were so fast!" Mr. Dirking said with joy as he craned his neck to have a look around.

There was a lot of rushing about to and fro, servants carrying bags and towels upstairs, Feeney and his footmen showing guests to their rooms. Feeney had requested they employ a few temporary staff, generally relatives of their existing staff. Emma hadn't minded in the least: the more men to carry bags, the better. Unfortunately, none of them knew anything about service, which lent to the chaos. Feeney's few hairs on top of his head were standing up; he looked every one of his seventy years, which Emma felt bad about. He would be very happy to see her go. She did hope for his sake the next countess would be quiet.

Speaking of which, the next earl, Andrew, was in great spirits despite a cough and looking a bit paler than usual. He was very excited about the strongman contest.

"Heavens, Andrew, you don't think you can actually participate?" Adele said. Emma wondered if Adele realized how cruel she could sound—it was obvious Andrew wanted nothing more. But he knew his limits. He said politely, "I know, sister. Emma said I could be a judge."

"The head judge," Emma announced. "I have decreed it."

Andrew beamed his gratitude at her.

Adele looked like she was set to say more, but Phillip and Fanny arrived then, without their boys. "But I have painting and games for the children," Emma protested, when Fanny said she'd left her sons with Phillip's parents.

"It will be better this way," Fanny assured her. "I expect the next two days to be quite lively." She gave Emma a sidelong glance, then looked apprehensively at the number of people gathering on the terrace below them.

"I should like to present myself for the strongman competition," Phillip announced.

Emma suggested Andrew show him the course. And then she sidled to her sister's side. "Stop looking like you'll be ill," she whispered.

"How can I when I *feel* ill? Disaster is looming," Fanny whispered back.

Adele, Emma noticed, was watching the two of them very closely. "Where's your sense of adventure?" she muttered through her smile.

"You can't be serious," Fanny muttered through hers.

But Emma was serious. She fully expected this to be the last time she was a hostess. The last time she would even be *invited* to a weekend house party or any other sort of party. She meant to enjoy every moment of it before her life, as she knew it, came to an end.

The day flew by as guests arrived from London and from the surrounding shires, all of them in good spirits, all of them remarking on how fortunate that the weather was agreeable. It was a gorgeously sunny day; the surface of the lake glittered, the sky was an amazing color of blue. Emma had asked for a buffet of finger foods and libations to be set up on the terrace. She greeted her guests, showed them around the grounds, fended questions from maids and footmen and Feeney, and finally went to dress for dinner.

Carlotta brought out one of Emma's new gowns. It was a midnight-blue silk and had been embroidered with dozens of tiny white stars. Mrs. Porter and her daughters had worked through the night to finish it on time. When she'd finished dressing, Carlotta affixed a diamond tiara with a large sapphire in the center into her hair.

"Oh my," Carlotta said. "You look like a midnight dream."

Emma grinned. "Tomorrow, I shall look like the sun. Isn't it all divine?"

Carlotta agreed that it was, but Emma was really speaking to herself. She privately congratulated herself for leaving this life in impeccable style. No one would forget the Butterhill Hall house party for many years.

Emma had planned dinner under the stars, which meant dining under stars painted onto the pavilion canvas overhead. It was a still night, a perfect night, and the guests had taken liberal advantage of the wine and spirits served by the footmen. A buffet of food had been set up. Some people took plates and sat at tables to eat, others moved around the pavilion to talk and mingle. The laughter floated up like a cloud from the tent; the flap that had been tacked to the ground for wind resistance had been rolled up. Floating candles in crystal bowls graced every table. Moths dipped in and around the flames, so many of them that it almost looked as if stardust was falling.

In one corner of the pavilion, Fanny's good friend, Helen Bristol, played the harp. Just outside the tent was a stage, also marked by torches, where four acrobats performed tricks for the guests. Emma was enthralled by their tumbling and twisting in the air. Many times this week she'd felt as if she were tumbling and twisting in the air, even when she was standing still.

The setting was perfection. Emma stopped in the shadows to observe her creation. Surely even Feeney was proud of their accomplishment. She would make a point of asking him.

She slowly became aware of another presence, and before she could turn, he spoke. "Where did you find them? The tumblers."

She smiled at the sound of his voice and glanced over her shoulder as he stepped to her side. "A traveling circus."

"Is that another story you mean to tell me?"

"Of course. But we've a long way to it, obviously. I've hardly gotten past my coming out."

"I am painfully aware. How did an English countess happen to run across a traveling circus?"

"The same manner I suspect anyone happens upon one. I had gone into Rexford and saw them packing up, preparing to move on. Two of the circus workers were clearly arguing, and when one of them stormed away, I intervened."

"You what?" Luka looked dubious. "With a stranger?"

"With a stranger. I swear it. I'll tell you everything in due time."

"No one on God's earth has the sort of time required to hear all of your story, Lady Dearborn."

"Perhaps not. But you can't deny you seem to be all ears."

His gaze moved over her, settling on her mouth. "I can't deny it. I'm fascinated. I hang on every word. I wish I could kiss you right now."

"I wish you could, too."

They contemplated each other for a long moment in shadow. Much longer than they ought to have done, Emma reckoned, but neither of them willing to turn away. He straightened his necktie, and when he dropped his hand, his fingers brushed against hers, slipping in between them, his forefinger hooking around hers for a moment. Emma smiled, acknowledging the furtive touch, and turned back toward the pavilion.

When she did, her gaze met Lady Lila Aleksander's. She was standing near the orchestra platform, a glass of wine in her hand, her gaze fixed on Emma and Luka. Emma made a note to be a bit more careful. She smiled and walked forward, pretending that Lady Aleksander hadn't seen a thing.

Lila returned her smile and gave her a nod, then held up her glass as if she was silently toasting Emma before turning away.

People could infer what they liked—it was human nature to assume the worst, Emma supposed. She didn't know what Lady Aleksander thought, but she knew the woman was discreet in everything she did. It was imperative in her role as a matchmaker that she keep secrets.

Emma moved deeper into the tent and began to greet her guests anew. She spoke to everyone. Caroline, Lady Chartier, Lord Iddesleigh's sister, had come with her husband, Prince Leopold Chartier of Alucia. The lady was quite eager for her husband to meet the Weslorian count. "There was such animosity between the two countries for so long, and he is wildly curious about him."

Emma gladly made the introductions and watched Luka and the prince move to one side, talking quite fervently about something.

Emma said hello to Lord and Lady Iddesleigh and their five daughters. Lady Mathilda, was speaking to Lord Caster, the son of Viscount Caster. The girl looked smitten. Emma remembered those days, when the slightest bit of attention from a handsome young man would leave her in that state.

She encountered Lady Lila Aleksander again, but with her husband, Lord Aleksander of Denmark. Lila was a cheerful woman who enjoyed her food. She mentioned the last time she'd seen Emma was at Emma's party in London.

"What chaos that turned out to be," Emma said with a laugh.

"I expect no chaos here, Lady Dearborn," Lila teased with a shine of amusement in her eyes. "Nothing but good behavior."

"That we know of," Emma said, and Lady Aleksander laughed.

"What are the plans for the weekend?"

"Tomorrow, there will be rowboats on the lake. Some of the villagers are coming to sell their wares on the north lawn. And we'll have the strongman competition, of course. You mean to enter, don't you, sir?" she asked Lord Aleksander.

"Depends on how much whisky you have," he said.

"Tomorrow evening, the ball, of course, just here, in the orangery," she said, pointing to the building next to the pavilion. "Sunday, church for those who need or want it, a late breakfast, and a bit of hillwalking before the weekend ends."

"Marvelous!" Lady Aleksander declared.

Emma moved on, almost colliding with Mr. Donovan. She knew him mostly by reputation, although he had been at her infamous London party last year. Everyone in London knew him by reputation, it seemed. He was known simply as Donovan, a man about town. He was astonishingly handsome, and his past, as she understood it, was a bit mysterious. Nevertheless, he was universally admired.

"You look beautiful, madam," Donovan said as he greeted her. "No one compares."

"How very kind, sir, although I did not take you for a flatterer." She grinned up at him.

"It is not flattery, it is a statement of fact. I can honestly say that just looking at you makes me wish I was a different sort of man."

"A rake? I have an affinity for them."

He laughed. "Something like that. Now, where is our guest of honor?"

Emma pointed Luka out across the room. He was speaking to a pair of gentlemen. She hoped he was enjoying the evening thus far.

Donovan thanked her for the invitation, said he looked forward to the rest of the weekend, and began to make his way through the crowd.

Emma turned, looking around for any guest she had not yet greeted. Who she saw was Adele, looking miserable as her dining companion, Mr. Longbottom, seemed to be waxing on about something that had him a bit animated. Andrew sat on the other side of her. The poor lad looked a little anxious. He kept putting a handkerchief to his mouth.

Emma did wish her sister-in-law would let go her animosity if only for an evening and enjoy herself. If she could manage it, Andrew would enjoy it, too. Why didn't she take a cue from Mr. Longbottom? Now, there was a man who enjoyed a party, she could tell.

Emma turned away, wanting to avoid them, and began to move through the crowd of tables. But as she did—pausing here and there to speak to friends and acquaintances—she began to grow aware of something. At first, it seemed to her that everyone was having a grand time of it, just as she'd expected and hoped. But there was a whisper blowing through her guests. Hardly a whisper, really, and yet she was certain she heard her name float by so quickly that she almost didn't catch it. Or a derisive bit of a snigger that seemed to happen just as she stepped by a group of ladies. And those looks in her direction? They were not inadvertent.

People were talking about her, and not with admiration or even envy. No, they were talking about her in a way that made her feel a bit queasy. She didn't know what they were saying, but she could tell it wasn't kind. She remembered Luka repeating what he'd heard in town—that she was having an affair.

She began to feel increasingly conspicuous and looked around for her sister. She needed confirmation of what she was feeling. It was entirely possible her imagination was running wild—mixed with her private fear of being discovered, maybe she was reading much into nothing.

She spotted Fanny across the room and started in her direction to ask her what she thought. But before she could reach her, a pair of women from Rexford intercepted her. "Lady Dearborn!"

Emma stopped before she plowed into them. "Mrs. White! Mrs. Terrance! I am so pleased you could join us." Mrs. White was a particular friend of Adele's. Emma was pleased she had come, for Adele's sake.

"The pleasure is ours," said Mrs. White, and the two ladies dipped into curtsies. "Everything is beautiful," the guest continued. "You are to be commended for it."

"Thank you." All right, she was imagining things. Here were two women who were very admiring of her.

"It's a pity his lordship is not here to see it," Mrs. Terrance said. "He's been away for so long, hasn't he? When do you expect his return?"

It was a common question, but the women's eyes were shining in a way that made Emma anxious. Just like that, she reverted to being wary. They looked like they already knew the answer and wanted to see what Emma would say.

"I'm not entirely certain, of course, but I desperately hope he returns by the end of the year."

"I should certainly hope so!" Mrs. Terrance said. "It's quite a long time for a man to leave his wife."

"He's an adventurer," Emma said.

"But it must be terribly lonely to host such wonderful parties by yourself," Mrs. White said. "It's good that you've had company. Perhaps your guest of honor was able to help you plan it?"

Emma's stomach was beginning to twist uncomfortably. "Mr. Olivien? No, he hasn't helped. He's been at his work. I don't mind the planning at all. It keeps me occupied."

The two women exchanged a look. "I suppose it must," Mrs. Terrance said smoothly. "And we are delighted to be invited. We were just remarking how wonderful it would be if the earl was to walk into our midst now. We could all celebrate his return!"

Emma's pulse began to race. Why were they taking such an interest in her husband? Was it possible they knew the truth? Good God, was someone going to make a surprise announcement? Did they *all* know? "I... I don't expect that will happen. I am certain he would have sent word if he meant to come home tonight."

"You shouldn't be so pessimistic, Lady Dearborn," Mrs. White said. "You must think positively and pray for his safe return. God is good."

"Your guest," Mrs. Terrance said. "I understand he's come from Egypt. Surely he has some idea when the earl might return?"

Panic was beginning to rise in her throat, and Emma attempted to swallow it down, hard. "Unfortunately, Mr. Olivien had not seen my husband in some time before he arrived. He's been on expedition, as well. But in the Sahara Desert."

"Oh. And where did Lord Dearborn's expedition take him?"

"The, ah...the Nile." She swallowed again. "But I do recommend that if you have the opportunity, you ask Mr. Olivien about his travels through the Saharan desert. It's really quite interesting."

The two women smiled as if they thought she was dissembling. Which she was not, at least in this. Luka's stories were very interesting.

"Emma, darling, there you are!" Fanny suddenly appeared at her side, her arm going around Emma's waist. To her rescue, as always. "You said something about fireworks, didn't you?"

"I did indeed, when everyone has had a chance to dine."

"I haven't. Ladies, do you mind terribly if I steal my sister away?" Fanny asked.

"Not at all," said Mrs. White, and she and Mrs. Terrance exchanged another knowing look.

Fanny began to pull Emma away, keeping her close.

"Oh, Fanny, I have a terrible feeling," Emma said.

"You should," Fanny said, glancing around them, and made Emma walk with her to the buffet. A footman handed them each a plate.

"They're talking about me, aren't they? All these people who have enjoyed my hospitality these last few months—they are speaking ill of me, aren't they?"

"Some of them," Fanny agreed. She nodded to a footman who put beef slices on her plate. "Even Phillip has asked me what the rumors are about."

"But…" Emma tried to make sense of it. How could anyone know anything? "I don't understand."

"Don't you, Emma?" Fanny asked as they moved down the table, selecting food for their plates. "It's what I've been trying to tell you. No one has seen or heard from Albert in a very long time. And then a dangerously handsome man shows up claiming to have known him and is staying here. But he knows nothing of Albert's whereabouts. Of *course* everyone assumes the worst. Which, I hesitate to point out, turns out to be an accurate assessment."

"*Dangerously handsome*," Emma murmured, her heart squeezing. "He is definitely so. What do I do?" she asked sheepishly as they walked to a table and took their seats.

Fanny shook her head. "I think the time for correcting it has come and gone. So now you do what you've always done. Pretend you don't hear. Pretend all is well. Be the perfect hostess as you always are. Enjoy yourself, as you said."

Why had she believed for a minute she might somehow devise a way out of her troubles? She looked across the tent to where Luka was sitting at a table with two gentlemen. He looked bored. Emma imagined this sort of existence did bore him—he'd had a similar one in Wesloria, and now he traveled the world. How wonderful to be a man of means and do what one pleased.

He turned his head slightly and caught her eye. It was as if he could sense her looking at him. She felt that magnetism between them, the unspoken words flowing between them. *Let's fly away.*

She smiled meekly and turned to her plate. There was no opportunity to fly away with him. She had fireworks to host later, and there was still some confusion as to who had what rooms, and everyone assembled was asking about tomorrow's schedule. She suddenly wanted to kick herself. She could have spent this weekend with Luka, these last few days, just the two of them. But no, she had to host a grand house party.

To make matters worse, she noticed that Adele had somehow been brought to life. She was flitting about, in the company of Mrs. White, leaning over tables of ladies, her hands on the backs of their chairs, imparting some news or greeting, gesturing to the lake. Emma guessed then that Adele had heard the rumors, too, and instead of being appalled by them, she was finally satisfied that she was right: Emma was up to no good. And she'd enlisted the help of her friends to help make sure everyone knew it. She would make sure Emma was gone, one way or another.

What was to become of her, then? *Really* become of her. Her last hurrah was the beginning of her end, as she'd feared.

She looked around for Luka, but she couldn't see him in the throng.

When she and Fanny finished eating, Emma let her sister go to Phillip. Emma latched on to Andrew, who was quite excited about the fireworks, wanting to know when they would start.

"After the sun goes all the way down," Emma said, noting the thin line on the horizon.

"Did you know that fireworks were used for the first time in England at the marriage of King Henry VII to Elizabeth of York?" he asked.

"I didn't!" She listened half-heartedly as her brother-in-law enthusiastically explained how fireworks worked.

On the other side of the pavilion, Lila caught up with Beck and Donovan. "Where is your lovely wife?" she asked Beck, linking arms with him.

"Apparently, young Lord Caster has gotten a bit too close to Tilda for good taste," Beck said. "My wife is forever talking about marrying those girls away, but the moment someone shows interest, she sweeps them away and out of sight."

"Caster is neither rich enough nor kind enough," Donovan offered. "I have known his father many years."

Lila glanced around them. Valentin was wandering on his own down to the lake's edge, where everyone was to gather for fireworks, having had perhaps one too many whiskies. "Is it just me," Lila began, leaning closer to Beck, "or are there certain looks flowing between Lady Dearborn and Mr. Olivien?"

"What?" Beck looked startled. "Certainly not. She is a fine woman. She would never. You mustn't pay attention to rumors, Lila."

"I've noticed it," Donovan said flatly.

"Have you?" Lila perked up. "I thought perhaps I was imagining things. It's my habit to look for love where it doesn't exist."

"Lila," Beck said. "The woman is *married*. You can't possibly mean to interfere."

"Not at all," she said. "I was merely wondering." She glanced at Donovan. He winked at her. She was right, then. There was a certain chemistry between two people who had no business having any chemistry at all.

Oh, how *interesting* this weekend was shaping up to be.

"Shall we go have a closer look at the fireworks?" Donovan asked.

"The fireworks under the tent? Or down on the shore?" Lila asked slyly.

"Lila, don't you dare," Beck said, and began to usher her down to the lake.

CHAPTER TWENTY-SIX

LUKA'S BED FELT big and lonely and surprisingly cold.

He'd grown accustomed to his auburn-haired vixen stealing into his room and sliding in next to him late at night. He'd gotten used to her making him laugh and then making him desperate with want. He found it impossible to fathom how this had happened to him, but it had, and he already missed her.

His thoughts kept returning to the vision of her this evening, in the dark blue gown with the embroidered white stars. The sparkling tiara. The irrepressible smile that charmed him every time. She'd looked like a goddess to him, desirable and untouchable all at once.

As much as it had pained him to do so, he'd kept his distance from her. The rumors he'd heard in Rexford had arrived as not-so-subtle whispers at Butterhill Hall. One gentleman even intimated to Luka that perhaps he'd been playing with the pretty little mouse while the cat was away. Luka had wanted to put his fist in the man's face.

He hadn't because he understood how people talked out of turn and created scandal from the most innocuous thing.

He hadn't because it was true.

He hadn't because, deep down, he supposed he deserved the man's tacit derision and the snort of disbelief when Luka denied that anything of the sort had happened here.

He kept his distance because her scandal would be big enough without him adding to it.

He rolled over and punched his pillow several times in frustration that sleep would not come and to quiet his thoughts. His mind was racing around the inevitable end of his time in England. He should have left when he first arrived, a fortnight ago, but frankly, he wouldn't have traded these days with Emma Clark for anything else in the world.

It felt to him as if these days had been the most meaningful of his life. Days he had known himself better than he ever had before, discovering facets of himself he hadn't known existed. He understood what love was now. He understood how one could recognize a kindred soul.

He was in love.

He was in love.

He knew that's what the feeling of joyful elation in his blood meant. How he knew it, he couldn't say: he'd never been in love before, but he knew what it was the moment he'd watched her rise from his bed the first time, don her dressing gown, and with her hair disheveled, glance over her shoulder at him with a sultry smile and slip out of his room.

There had a been a girl once, a long time ago in Wesloria, in Astasia. She was agreeable and pretty, and Luka had esteemed her. He'd thought she'd be a good companion to any man. And yet, there was something lacking, something he couldn't quite grasp. He knew now what it was. That young woman hadn't been particularly interesting or surprising or clever. Not like Emma. No one was like Emma.

He didn't know what to do with such intense feelings. He didn't know how they could exist in him if he was elsewhere, embroiled in his father's mess. There was no question that he would go home. He had no choice. Which meant he had no choice but to leave Emma behind.

Luka finally drifted off to a fitful sleep in the late hours of the morning. When he awoke, people were already on the lawn, wandering down to rowboats and to the green where the strongman contest had been arranged. Emma had insisted he participate in the day's contests. "Everyone will want to see the guest of honor," she'd said one night, twirling a bit of his hair around her finger.

"God save me."

She kissed his lips. "Aren't you happy you stayed?" She didn't allow him to answer as she climbed on top of him.

She knew him. In a very short time, she had come to truly *know* him.

By the time he'd dressed and made his way outside, the skies had cleared to a glorious blue. Artisans and merchants had arrived and set up tents on the north lawn to sell their wares. Honey and jam, embroidered linens, ladies' sun hats. Quilts and belts, knives and neckties, bread and pastries. It reminded him of the country fairs he'd attended as a boy, when his father would be called upon to judge the contest of the fattest pig or best calf. How had Emma managed it all in such a short time? It was remarkable.

He decided to walk around the lake and set out on the

sun-dappled path. But he quickly discovered it wasn't the same without her endless stories and her laughter. It felt like an ordinary path, the most mundane of walks.

He was a bit lost in thought when he happened on Prince Leopold and his wife. Luka had met the prince yesterday. He'd heard of Leopold from the time he was boy—the dissolute younger brother of King Sebastian. He'd left Alucia as a young man, had married an English heiress, the sister of Lord Iddesleigh, and the rest of the story was quite obviously a happy one. What struck Luka about the prince was that he couldn't take his eyes off his English wife. He affectionately called her Caro, and he couldn't keep himself from touching her—her elbow, her hand, her back.

Luka wanted that. He wanted to be so devoted to a woman that he couldn't take his eyes off her.

Prince Leopold was ahead of his wife on the path. His hair had turned silver, which made his good looks even more striking. "There you are, my lord," he said. "They've been looking for you."

"They?" Luka asked.

"People," the prince said with a shrug.

"Not just people, Leopold," his wife said, skipping to catch up and reaching for his arm. "Footmen. And Feeney seems quite keen to speak to you."

Feeney? Was he expected? Had something happened?

"Princess Amelia has come," Lady Chartier said. "Your queen's younger sister!" she added brightly, as if Luka didn't know who she was.

"Ami?" he said, surprised. "She is here?"

"Ami?" Lady Chartier repeated. "She is Lady Marley now."

"She was Ami when we were children," Luka said. "I have known the princess and her sister all my life."

Lady Chartier gasped with delight and shoved her husband's shoulder. "Did you hear that, Leopold? Our Weslorian friends are acquainted!"

"I did hear, love."

"Well, sir, she has come with her husband, Lord Marley. And when someone asked if she would like to make your acquaintance, she said that she would like that very much."

"Thank you. I'll go now."

"But where is your charming escort?" Lady Chartier asked, looking past him. "She's not been seen this morning, either."

"Pardon?"

"Lady Dearborn. Feeney said that the two of you often walked the lake. We thought perhaps she was with you."

Which meant, he guessed, that Feeney was suspicious of them, too. It was all unsurprising, really. When he thought about it, it was a wonder that a group of vigilantes hadn't come to cart him off and hang him. Luka smiled thinly. "I have not seen her ladyship today. I'll inform Feeney that she is not with me."

He made his way back to the hall, intent on finding Princess Amelia. More people were outside now. Rowboats lined the shore of the lake, some of them with cushioned seats for the more romantic among the guests. The strongman field was ready for the event, which was to begin in an hour. Men had gathered around to examine the field. Some held tankards of ale. Laughter rose from every corner of the lawn.

Luka carried on, away from the field, but someone

was shouting his name. He turned. Lord Iddesleigh was walking briskly toward him. The man had disposed of his coat, waistcoat, necktie, and hat. He had rolled his sleeves up to reveal his forearms. "Mr. Olivien! You can lend a hand, can't you?"

"Of course. What is needed?"

"I'll tell you what is needed, my good man," Iddesleigh said, and clapped his hand on Luka's shoulder. "I consider myself a sporting gentleman. Never shy away from it. But I haven't the slightest notion how to throw an ax and have it stick into that plank of wood. I have heard that you do." He pointed to the ax-throwing ground. "I don't know what possessed me to enter this challenge. I'm too old to be slinging such a weapon around."

"No one is too old to throw an ax, sir," Luka said, and walked with Iddesleigh to the start line, where several axes of various heft and length had been propped up along a fence. He selected a short, lightweight one. He showed the earl how to wrap his fingers around the handle and throw lightly, not with force.

Beck made a few attempts with Luka's coaching before he managed to put the ax into the plank of wood. He gasped with surprise and delight. "On my word, it worked! How in heaven do you know how to do such things?" he asked, picking up another ax.

By living his life out in the wide world, learning and studying different cultures. Anything that could take him from Wesloria and a father who was apparently hell-bent on destruction.

Luka looked around—he didn't see Emma or Princess Amelia. Where was Emma? Yesterday she'd been present everywhere. He needed to see her, if even across a crowd.

He stayed with Lord Iddesleigh—Beck, as the man insisted—until the competition began. The first round of ax-throwing eliminated several men, all of them throwing too hard and from too far away. Mr. Longbottom preferred to throw with one hand. But his throws were so wild and far afield that Andrew, as official head judge of the competition, insisted footmen clear the lawn all the way to the lake so that no one would be hurt.

Once he'd learned how, Beck turned out to be rather good at throwing and finished the competition in second place. He twirled around in jubilation to the gentlemen gathered. And pointing a finger at each one he said, "Did you see that, you sorry lot of axers? I'm better than you."

"Shut your trap, Iddesleigh," someone groused, but Beck was enjoying himself far too much. He'd already marched on to the archery field.

Luka hung back, still surreptitiously searching the crowd for Emma. He could spot her auburn hair anywhere, but that hair was not visible on the lawn this afternoon.

The archery competition took quite a while to complete. Here, all the gentlemen excelled, as archery was a sport known to the privileged. Luka imagined summer afternoons spent in houses this grand, practicing their release. They went several rounds. Footmen brought ale. The men downed tankards of it.

Amazingly, Beck was a surprising third in the archery and roared out his approval until his wife called out from somewhere among the onlookers for him to stop his wallowing. He congratulated Luka on earning second place in the archery contest.

From archery, the men moved on to the footraces. The course was near the pavilion. Ladies were crowded around tables under the tent to watch.

Luka declined to participate in the race and went into the pavilion hoping to find Emma. He didn't see her. He walked to the sideboard laden with platters of fruit and pastries, with some cheeses and meats under a dome, and picked up a plate.

"Comte ve Marlaine."

He turned around and smiled. It had been many years, but he would have known her instantly. "Ami," he said, and put down his plate, reaching for her hand.

But Princess Amelia did not return his smile or give her hand to him.

He dropped his. "You're as beautiful as ever, Ami. How long has it been?"

"It's good to see you, Luka," she said flatly.

He laughed a little. Something was amiss, but he couldn't guess what. "Are you certain?"

She said nothing.

Luka could feel eyes on them and said in Weslorian, "Is something the matter?"

"Is something…what?" she responded in Weslorian. She and Justine had grown up speaking English and it seemed her Weslorian had grown rusty.

"Wrong," he said in Weslorian. "You seem…troubled."

"Speak English, will you?" she whispered and looked around them, too. She sighed. "Offer me your arm."

"Pardon?"

"Your *arm*, Luka."

He did as she asked, and Amelia put her hand on it. "Now, walk out of the tent. Away from all these ears."

He did as she asked, leading her away from the race

on the field and the prying eyes. He covered her hand with his, giving it a warm squeeze. "It's good to see you, Ami. You've married, I've heard. Any children?"

"*Je*, quite a lot of them." She glanced away, as if weighing what she would say. Luka noticed she was not wearing a patch of green.

Amelia suddenly turned back to him. "Why haven't you gone home? What keeps you?"

The question startled him. "What? I am, Ami. I—"

"No. You're not there, Luka. Why didn't you go before you father could make such a mess of things? Surely you know what your father has been planning."

He sighed softly. "I did not. He didn't confide in me. But I *am* going, Ami. I will leave from London on Tuesday."

She stared at him as if he was obtuse. "It's too late! Your father has been arrested for sedition."

Luka felt the blood drain from his face. He tried to form a question, but Weslorian and English words mixed into a jumble of incoherent thoughts. "Wh… *When?*"

Amelia's dark expression began to soften. "You really don't know?"

"I…" He was shocked. He'd never imagined it would come to this. "No. I've known for only a little more than a week that he was suspected of plotting against Justine—she wrote me to tell me—but I'd already left Egypt and didn't receive the letter until last week."

Amelia folded her arms. "Plotting a coup. There is proof that he's amassed weapons and men to do it in Astasia. They meant to attack on Midsummer Eve, when Jussie was to present a new clock tower in Pulsorat."

Luka knew Pulsorat and knew that the queen would

be vulnerable there, in the open, in a very large town square.

"Men he recruited and who have admitted the plan. A cache of weapons and communiqués."

Luka didn't want to hear more, not from Princess Amelia. He wanted to hear the truth from his father's fool mouth.

"He's in a cell in St. Edys currently, but all of Astasia seems poised to fight for his freedom."

"*Dia*," he muttered.

Princess Amelia shifted closer. "Luka…you must go home. You owe it to Justine…unless your sentiments have changed?"

What was she implying? "*No*," he said sharply. "My sentiments are exactly what they've always been. Justine is an excellent queen and belongs on the throne. I am not my father—you know that."

The princess sighed. "I honestly don't know if I do, Luka. I don't know you at all anymore. It's been years since I last saw you. What I know is that Justine has asked you to come to her aid, and you ignored her letter and stayed away. And then I find you here, throwing axes in England." She glanced at the field where the competition was ongoing. "You did very well, however."

"I didn't know, Ami. I *am* going to her aid," he insisted. "I will leave Tuesday for Wesloria and do all in my power to stop the madness my father has started."

She returned her gaze to him, studying his face, as though she was looking for any sign he wasn't telling her the truth. "She sent an escort because she doesn't know if she can trust you."

Good God. "I mean what I say."

"I hope for your sake that you do. There are those who think you might be abetting your father."

His heart lurched in his chest; his face felt hot with shame for his father. "For what reason?"

"Because you've not come to help her! You've been noticeably absent, your estate shuttered. There are those around Justine who believe you're hiding in the mountains of Astasia, helping your father. Suspicions about you and your loyalty have been raised by her closest advisers."

Luka felt as if he might be sick. "Does she—"

"No," the princess said quickly. "She doesn't believe you would plot against her. But she doesn't know if you would help her, either. It is your father, after all. Do you see, Luka? You must help her or be accused yourself."

He saw it all, very clearly. Furthermore, he could imagine that his father had done nothing to dispel any suspicions directed at his son for the sake of his own neck. His heart climbed to his throat and lodged there.

Princess Amelia was right—he had to return to the capital of St. Edys immediately before any more damage could be done.

CHAPTER TWENTY-SEVEN

LILA WAS COMFORTABLY inebriated at the edge of the pavilion, thanks to Donovan's diligent efforts to keep her glass filled with delicious champagne punch and to arrange some chaises longues for their little party.

She was delightfully free of any obligation or responsibility, as Valentin had joined the strongman contest after all. She would periodically lift her hand and wave at him, shout an encouragement or two. Blythe and her daughters were walking through the crowd, presumably to catch the eyes of eligible young men. Blythe said that was not her intent at all, but then fussed over the girls' appearance and admonished them about their posture.

To Lila's right were Caroline and Leo, both in chaises. Leo had covered his face with a hat and was asleep. Caroline was humming.

To her left was Donovan, sitting on a stool, his glass dangling from his fingers.

It was the perfect sort of summer day. Not overly warm, lots to watch, and plenty of libations. She could conceivably sit in this chaise for the rest of her days, watching people mill about.

Donovan had just refilled their glasses and reported the arrival of brambleberry pie at the buffet when Beck suddenly emerged from a round of boxing with a busted lip and swelling under his right eye. He was exuberant. "Did you see me? Any of you?"

Lila, Donovan, and Caroline looked at each other.

"You didn't see? Well, I held my own." Beck gave a few air punches to demonstrate how he'd presumably *held his own*.

"Why?" his sister Caroline asked. "What, exactly, are you trying to prove?"

"That I'm alive, love. That I am bloody well *alive*."

Beckett Hawke had found his midlife calling in boxing.

"You don't seem to have gone very far," Caroline said, nodding to the men who were lined up to take on the winners. "Who sent you out?"

"Frampton," Beck said with a scowl. "He's got quite a punch."

"He's taller than you," Donovan pointed out. "Works to his advantage."

Beck said something in response, something about his agility that made Caroline laugh, but Lila was distracted by the arrival of Lady Marley into the tent. The woman's youth had not faded with time—she was as beautiful as she'd ever been. Earlier, Lila had watched her and her handsome husband step out of a grand coach, then five children tumble out after them. A harried-looking governess rushed after them, and they'd all disappeared inside. Now, Princess Amelia had come out on her own.

There was one difference about her, however; she was generally as gregarious as Lady Dearborn, but there was something about her mien that seemed almost agitated. She moved around the pavilion, then suddenly went briskly to the buffet. Lila followed her progress and watched her walk up to Mr. Olivien. She saw a brief exchange, and then the two of them left the pavilion.

A few minutes later, they'd returned. As Beck and Caroline argued over who would win the boxing games, Lila touched Donovan's arm and nodded in the direction of Princess Amelia and Mr. Olivien. "What do you think?" she whispered.

Donovan gave them a look. "Old friends?"

"Or old enemies? They seem a bit agitated, don't they?"

Donovan nodded.

They watched Mr. Olivien head away from the tent. At that point, the princess spotted them all sitting there and made her way to them. Donovan stood, offering his stool.

"Good afternoon!" she said, her smile returned. All of them greeted her, asking after her health and that of her family. Donovan and Beck had moved away, watching the men in the makeshift boxing ring.

"Where is your lovely husband?" Lila asked. "I've not seen him in an age."

"My husband," Princess Amelia said with a contented sigh. "Poor thing is with the children. They are perfectly capable of entertaining themselves, but he worries so about them that he's afraid to let them out of his sight."

Their children, Lila remembered, were in their teen years now. She often thought of Marley, who years ago had claimed to despise children. Nothing was ever as simple as it seemed on the surface, was it?

She shifted her gaze back to the boxing. She was surprised to see that Mr. Olivien had stepped into the ring. His expression was a mixture of agitation and determination, and he landed the first punch, much to the approval of the men gathered. And then he began to really punch. He was lightning fast, his fists flying at the other man. He looked as if he had something on his mind.

No, nothing was ever as simple as it seemed on the outside.

Speaking of which, where *was* Lady Dearborn?

CHAPTER TWENTY-EIGHT

EMMA HAD NOT intended to be absent from the afternoon activities. She had been excited to award the winner of the strongman competition, which included a paper crown and a dull hatchet painted red. But she hadn't counted on Mr. Horn arriving in the company of Mr. Charles McLeary, the banker who had a proposal to reopen the copper mine in the northern sector of the twenty thousand acres that belonged to Butterhill Hall.

"Today?" she'd said, when Feeney had informed her. "But the party…"

Feeney stoically informed her they were in Lord Dearborn's study.

Emma hated Albert's study. His things surrounded them—books and knives, a pair of crossed dueling pistols over the mantel. Why, Emma had never understood—Albert was not the sort of man to engage in a duel. He was not the sort of man to leave his study, until he one day decided to go on expedition. Even though his absence was fresh air to her soul, in some ways it felt as if he'd never left. His presence was baked into the carpet and drapes, his scent permanently settled in the air.

After the introductions were made, Mr. McLeary offered an apology. "I beg your pardon, Lady Dearborn, but I am called to London and didn't want to leave the area without the chance to speak to you," he said. She sat ramrod stiff, as if Albert was watching her, conveying through raised eyebrows his displeasure with her posture.

"Copper mining has been depleted in Cornwall as you may know," Mr. McLeary was saying.

Of course Emma didn't know that. Why would she know that?

"And yet there remains a great demand for it. The mine here, as I recall, was closed for reasons other than depletion?"

"His lordship felt it was unsafe," Mr. Horn said.

Unsafe? Albert had believed mining was beneath an earl. And he had never been overly concerned for anyone's safety as far as she knew.

"I understand," Mr. McLeary said. "However, new methods and technologies would make it possible to reopen the mine safely. Lady Dearborn, if I may speak freely?"

"Please," she said without hesitation. She had a party to attend to and didn't need anyone mincing their words just now.

"The estate would undoubtedly see a great profit. The demand would, of course, determine it, but my analysis suggests it would exceed expectations."

Mr. Horn looked uneasily at Emma, who sighed. "You're thinking of my sister-in-law, aren't you, Mr. Horn?"

"Lady Adele?" He seemed taken aback. "No, madam, I am thinking of your husband. I would not think he would want such a decision made without his knowledge or presence."

She rather imagined he would not. "Mr. Horn, has my management of Butterhill Hall given you any pause?"

300 AN INCONVENIENT EARL

He looked surprised by the question and cast a sheepish look at Mr. McLeary. "I don't know what you mean."

"I think you do. Since my husband has been gone,
I thought we had managed the estate quite nicely together."

"We have, but—"

"I've been a bit impressed with myself. You remember how you didn't think I could possibly grasp the
nuances of the estate management? Or numbers." She
laughed sardonically. "I seem to recall you having the
impression that women couldn't add."

Now the poor man was coloring slightly. "I never
said that."

"Not in those precise words." She smiled at him.

He stared at her, uncertain the direction this conversation was headed. Didn't he know her by now?
Didn't he understand that she was not afraid of risk?
She turned her attention to Mr. McLeary. "How quickly
could the mine be reopened, and how quickly would it
make a profit?"

Mr. McLeary sat up eagerly. "We would need to as-
sess the deposits, but I estimate that within a year, the
mine could safely reopen, and perhaps a year after that
prove profitable. And remain profitable for a few years.
Maybe longer if we are lucky."

"We?"

"The bank would lend the funds for reopening the
mine and share in the profits. At a rate mutually agreed
upon, of course."

"Then, I think we should take a look."

Mr. McLeary looked to Mr. Horn for confirmation.

"Mr. McLeary?" Emma asked. "Did you hear what
I said?"

"Certainly." He smiled. "Pardon, Lady Dearborn. I've never conducted business with a lady before."

Emma settled back in her seat, allowing her perfect posture to relax. "Maybe you ought to get used to it. Well, then, I think there is no better time to start than now."

They talked for an hour or more. Mr. McLeary laid out what costs he thought would be involved, how soon they could deliver copper, how soon money would come into the estate coffers. When he told her how much they might make, giving her estimates that he considered conservative, Emma felt warm.

Adele would lose her mind to think of a bank involved in the sacrosanct Dearborn family estate. But didn't it make sense on this one venture to share the costs? If the mine failed, it would not ruin Butterhill Hall, as they would not assume all the risk. But if it succeeded as Mr. McLeary seemed to think it would, they would still make quite a tidy profit. She would make certain they retained majority ownership.

Emma turned to the window and thought a bit more. "We need to make this happen straightaway."

"I beg your pardon, my lady?" Mr. Horn said. "There is no need to rush."

There was every need to rush, which, of course, she couldn't explain to Mr. Horn. "One never knows when one's fortunes might change." Except that she did. It would happen in a matter of days.

When they were done, she invited the two gentlemen to stay and enjoy the party. Mr. Horn looked rather sad when he left the drawing room on the heels of Mr. McLeary's springy step. Why were people so resistant to change?

Emma couldn't wait to tell Luka about what she'd done and to hear his opinion.

Unfortunately, she'd run out of time this afternoon. She had to prepare for this evening's ball.

CHAPTER TWENTY-NINE

THE ORANGERY HAD been transformed into a garden wonderland, just as Emma had envisioned. The lights glittered against the windowpanes, and the ceiling was strung with ropes of flowers. Orange trees, purchased at a premium, and which had never borne any fruit that Emma knew of, were positioned around the room. More flowers and greenery graced the marble pedestals in the corners. By the time Emma made her entrance, the musicians had already begun to play, and people were waiting for Emma to begin the ball.

Her guests were dressed in a dizzying array of colors and fabrics—pastel silks, jewel-toned brocades, ethereal muslins. The gaiety was palpable, and laughter and chatter filled the room. This was exactly what she'd wanted, a night that no one would forget.

She sailed into the room, wearing a gown of gold silk with dark red trim and an attachment of rosettes along the train. In her hair, she wore gold silk ribbons and feathers painted gold. The bodice of her gown was tight, cut low, and her shoulders were bare. She felt invincible. She wanted everyone to notice her, to admire her appearance, to speak of how well she looked, how assuredly she'd managed all this time without Albert. She was pleased that so many heads turned in her direction.

She glided through their midst, all smiles, and noticed right away the man with his back to her. The black coat, the broad shoulders, the long dark hair brushing his collar. As she neared, he turned around. Luka's eyes took in every inch of her. He made no move to acknowledge her, but she could see the esteem in his eyes.

It was because of him that she failed, at first, to notice the other eyes on her. Those looking at her with something less than admiration. With suspicion, perhaps? With disdain?

No wonder Luka had made no move toward her. She realized now that people were looking at them both, watching. She suddenly didn't know what to do. She turned awkwardly, looking for a friendly face, and her gaze landed on Mr. Longbottom.

He grinned as if they were old friends. "Lady Dearborn," he said, bowing low, "I've been eagerly awaiting the opportunity to ask you for the honor of the first dance."

This was not done. She should start the dancing with Andrew. "Pardon?"

"As my lovely wife is not in attendance, I should very much like to do the honor."

But, on the other hand, she would be eternally grateful to him for this. The longer she stood, the more she felt her nerves. "Of course, Mr. Longbottom. I can't think of a finer partner." She held out her hand, and he slipped his arm under it and escorted her to the middle of the dance floor. Now that she had taken her place, other couples followed. It was only when the music started that she noticed Mr. Longbottom's black eye, and the perspiration beading on his forehead. "My goodness, sir, what happened to you?"

"Boxing, madam," he said, his smile quite broad. "You are in the company of the afternoon's champion boxer. Of the larger gentlemen, that is."

"Congratulations, Mr. Longbottom! I regret that I was occupied this afternoon. I should have liked to have seen it. But I hadn't thought the matches would be so violent."

"Violent? Oh no. All in good fun. At least, I thought so. I wasn't very good at the ax-throwing or the races. And archery, well—one needs a steady hand to excel. But it seems that what I lack with axes and bows, I possess in boxing. I can do the punching, and I can take the punching, and I remain standing."

Emma couldn't help but laugh. "An admirable quality, sir."

"I think so."

"May I ask you something, Mr. Longbottom?" she said as he attempted to twirl her about and unfortunately collided with another couple.

"Absolutely. I stand ready to serve."

"I have an opportunity to reopen an old copper mine, here at Butterhill Hall." She told him about the idea, about her thinking. Mr. Longbottom listened intently as he tried to maneuver them about. The music ended just as she finished explaining.

Mr. Longbottom bowed. "Thank you. And may I say, it seems sound to me."

"Does it really?"

He held out his arm to escort her from the dance floor. "It does. Copper is in demand."

"What would my sister-in-law think of it?"

"Oh, Lady Adele would need to be convinced. I don't think she likes to spend money under any circumstance."

He had taken Adele's measure, then. "I suppose she wouldn't. You'll keep it between us for the time being?"

"Absolutely." He dropped his arm, clasped his hands behind his back, and bowed again. "Thank you, madam, for a splendid weekend. I haven't enjoyed myself so much in a very long time. My only regret is that Mrs. Longbottom was not here to enjoy it with me."

She thanked him for the dance, and a moment later, Mr. Donhill asked her for the pleasure. He kept his gaze on her décolletage for the entirety of the dance. She danced next with Lord Iddesleigh. Beck was also sporting a black eye and busted lip. "On my word, I never imagined the boxing would end with so many injuries!"

"Let me tell you something, Lady Dearborn. It was the finest moment of my life."

She laughed at what she assumed was a jest. "You have five daughters, my lord."

"Yes, yes, all fine moments," he agreed. "But even they do not compare to the exhilaration I felt today. Something was unleashed, madam, and I am renewed."

He was speaking hyperbolically, but she also understood how he felt, the exhilaration of something within you coming forward and taking you to a place you never thought you'd be. She was clinging to that place in her heart with every fiber of her being.

After Beck, she continued to dance, each time, looking for any sign of Luka, but had completely lost sight of him. It was disappointing, but it was for the best. People were watching her. *Talking* about her. It felt like half her guests were waiting to catch her at something.

When she danced with Donovan, she tried to make light of her feeling of discomfort. "Have you ever felt you've got your trouser leg caught in your shoe and everyone knows it but you?"

Donovan smiled curiously. "Madam, have you been wearing trousers too long for you?"

"Not yet," she said with a grin. She glanced around them as Donovan led her off the dance floor.

He covered her hand with his and leaned into her. He said low, "Pay them no mind, Lady Dearborn. Unhappy people often look for scandal in someone else so they can ruminate about that instead of their own troubles."

"Do you think I am involved in a scandal?"

"Aren't we all?" His smile was enigmatic, and it felt to Emma there was much more to what he said, as if he knew her secrets. But he couldn't possibly. No one could. She was letting her anxiety invade her imagination. Still, it felt like a spider was crawling up the back of her neck. "It doesn't matter, really, as I am perfectly at ease with my life. All I want is to be suitably diverted."

"Then, I would say you have achieved your goal," he said. "Thank you for diverting me."

She thanked him as he bowed and walked away. She turned, and her gaze met Adele's.

Adele. *Addie*, as she'd once called her. She looked very pretty tonight, her gown an ice blue that went well with her black hair. It hugged her figure, which was generally unlike her modest sister-in-law. Emma couldn't help her smile of appreciation. "Adele, you look so lovely this evening."

"Thank you. So do you, Emma."

"Thank you." She noticed Mrs. White and Mrs. Terrance over Adele's shoulder. She suddenly realized the three of them had been talking as she'd come off the dance floor. "Are you enjoying the evening?"

Adele gave her a strange little smile. "In a manner. Feeney said that dinner was ready to be served."

"Oh." She wondered why Feeney had told Adele. "That's wonderful. I'll make the announcement." She started in the direction of the musician's platform.

"Emma?"

Emma turned back to Adele.

"Aren't you going to introduce your guest?"

Something unpleasant tugged in Emma's belly. A warning. "I hadn't thought of it."

"No? He is the guest of honor. It seems like you'd want to introduce him."

"But he's met everyone."

"Good evening, Lady Adele."

Fanny, bless her, had appeared. She leaned in and kissed Emma's cheek. "How lovely you look, darling."

"Thank you, Fanny. Your gown is gorgeous." Her sister was wearing pale yellow with bits of green and blue.

"The night is wonderful, Emma," Fanny said. "You've outdone yourself. Hasn't she, Lady Adele?"

Adele looked around them. "Of course she has, and it is to be admired…if one does not have to concern oneself with cost."

"Oh, Adele," Emma said. "Can't you simply enjoy it? If you like, I'll go over the costs with you."

"It's not necessary. What is done is done," Adele said primly and shifted her gaze to Fanny. "I was just suggesting to your sister that she introduce her guest of honor to her guests. Don't you think she ought?"

"And I was saying to Adele that I think Mr. Olivien has

met everyone, so there is no need," Emma said quickly. She couldn't imagine what Adele was about.

"Still, he's your guest of honor, and your husband's very dear friend come all this way. It seems to me that the proper thing to do would be to say a few words welcoming him. Perhaps when you announce dinner." Adele smiled again. That was what was bothering Emma, she realized. Adele so rarely smiled.

That uncomfortable tug in Emma's belly was stronger. She didn't trust Adele and looked to Fanny for help. But Fanny smiled reassuringly. "Perhaps you should."

"All right," Emma said hesitantly. She went to the orchestra platform.

The musicians stopped playing when she stepped up. "Ladies and gentlemen!" she called.

People began to turn in her direction.

"Good evening!" Emma said brightly. "Thank you all for coming to the Butterhill Hall house party. We are so very happy to have you."

There was a shift in the crowd, a touch of impatience. Emma was aware of Adele's eyes boring through her.

"Um… I should like to introduce our guest of honor. Mr. Olivien, are you here?" she called, looking around.

The crowd moved, some turning, eyes finding him where Emma could not. He was near a potted orange tree near the back and took a hesitant step forward.

"Mr. Olivien, the *Comte ve Marlaine* of Wesloria," she said, gesturing to him. "My husband's friend. He was kind enough to pay us a call."

Luka remained where he was. He bowed to Emma, then lifted his glass to her and the crowd.

"And now—"

"When will Lord Dearborn return?"

The question was called out by a man in the crowd. A familiar voice, Emma thought, although she couldn't place it. She looked around, squinting at the many faces. And then she realized it was Mr. Horn, standing behind Adele. She felt sick.

"I wish I knew, Mr. Horn. We all miss him so."

"Why don't you tell everyone where my brother is, darling?" Adele said, her voice treacly.

"Pardon?"

"Where is my brother currently?"

Emma tried to laugh. "He's in Egypt, but you knew that, dearest. He's on expedition. There are so many ancient wonders there. You all know how much my Albert likes to read. So does his brother, Andrew. Where is Andrew?" she asked. No one moved. "A family of readers, we Clarks, reading everything. But naturally, Albert wanted to see all that he'd read about. Wouldn't we all?"

"But when is he coming home?" That voice belonged to Mrs. White.

"I can't say. He's quite a long way from home, you know, and it takes a bit of time for word to reach me."

"It does," Adele agreed. "Perhaps Mr. Olivien can shed some light, as he was the last to see Albert. Presumably." Adele smiled and turned toward the corner where Luka was standing.

Luka gave Adele a very cool look. He stepped forward. "As I have previously said, Lady Adele, I would that I knew, but alas I do not. Lord Dearborn did not share his plans with me."

"That seems curious, that you've come all this way without any real news of Lord Dearborn," said Mrs. White.

"Mr. Olivien was kind enough to bring home Albert's prized pocket watch for safekeeping, Mrs. White. And I assure you, we shall celebrate my husband's return at the end of the year," Emma said quickly. "Now then, dinner is served. Our two cooks have gone to a great deal of trouble to prepare the venison. I think you will all be delighted. The dancing will, of course, carry on, and you may dine or dance at your leisure." She signaled the musicians to play, then hopped down from the platform, bypassing Mr. Longbottom's offer to help.

She thought briefly about running from the orangery, but Adele was there, smiling with a delight Emma had not seen in her in years. "Emma, darling, is something wrong? Your nerves seem to have gotten the best of you."

She didn't like the game Adele was playing with her, especially because she didn't know the rules. "Your concern for my health is touching, but I am quite all right. And now, if you will excuse me, I would like to dance." She looked wildly about for any willing dance partner. It was Luka who stepped forward. Luka, her savior. Luka, her lover. *Luka*.

"Lady Dearborn, would you do me the honor of a dance?"

"I would be delighted." And without another look at Adele, she allowed Luka to lead her to the dance floor. And dance she did. She was aware of eyes on her, the whispers, the rumors that were beginning to spread like fire. But for those moments dancing with Luka, she didn't care. Let them talk. Let them assume all the horrible things about her that they could think of. It wouldn't matter—she'd be gone soon enough. Adele thought she could shame her, and maybe, on a different day, she could have achieved it. But she would not allow Adele to do it tonight.

"Why must you look so beautiful?" Luka said as he expertly moved her around the dance floor.

"I would ask the same of you, Mr. Olivien."

"Ah, well. I am doing my best to impress you."

"You already have, in so many ways." She smiled warmly at him. "I would like to kiss you, you've impressed me so."

Luka smiled back. "I would like to kiss you back, but your friends are watching."

"Curious thing about that—I don't think they are my friends. Everyone is watching us, and I daresay without good will."

"Would you like to leave the orangery?"

She would not. She wanted to dance with Luka. She wanted to gaze up at him and feel his hand on her back and believe for a moment that she was a princess in a fairy tale. Nothing else seemed to matter when she was with Luka. "Not now. I think I rather like their jealousy."

He laughed. "Incorrigible temptress."

"Charming rake."

"Beautiful vixen."

"Handsome rogue."

With a grin, he twirled her around and around until the dance came to an end. He bowed to her. Emma curtsied. "I need to see you," she said.

"It's too dangerous for you."

"Maybe. And then again, maybe not. It is possible everyone will be well into their cups and not notice a thing. Or they will notice everything. But it doesn't matter, given that in a few days I will be wandering the road with my valise, hoping for a kind stranger to take pity."

Luka's smile faded. "Don't say that."

"On the ground floor, in the north hall, there is a small tearoom. It goes unused because Albert's mother liked to take her tea there. He could never bear to see it opened."

Luka placed her hand on his arm so that he might escort her off the dance floor.

"If you can imagine it, it is the fourth door from the main entry of the hall. The window faces the stables. I never thought that a very appealing place to have tea, but perhaps she enjoyed watching horses being saddled." She lifted her hand from his arm and looked around them for some indication of the time. "At half past midnight," she said softly.

"Emma, I—"

"No one will see us. The room is never used. It's closed off from the rest of the house, and the furniture is covered. Please, Luka."

Luka's gaze settled on her eyes. "As if I could deny you," he murmured. He bowed again, then walked away.

Now all Emma had to do was count the hours and minutes until then.

And when that hour was near, she walked around the orangery, admiring her guests. It didn't matter what they thought of her—she knew she deserved their disdain. But she smiled with envy at Lord and Lady Marley, who looked at each other with such devotion. And at Lord and Lady Iddesleigh, who laughed with each other and their many daughters. At Fanny and Phillip, who danced as if there was no one else in the room. At Prince Leopold and Lady Chartier, the latter sitting on the lap of the former, both laughing at something Mr. Donovan was telling them.

She looked at more couples who enjoyed each other, at young people who were dancing or speaking carefully to one another with a hope of love.

She wished it all for herself. She wished for that one true love that made each moment worth living. She wished for Luka.

She would not have him or love for the rest of her life, not with the scandal that would follow her. But she'd have it for one more day.

Emma intended to live every moment as if it was her last one on this earth.

She could feel the darkness of the future creeping into her thoughts, filling in around the edges of her mind. That darkness would come, she knew, but not for a few more hours.

CHAPTER THIRTY

THE TEAROOM WAS as Emma said it would be—dark and cold, the smell of mustiness in the air. Luka had been in this small room since midnight, staring out the window at the full moon, trying to make sense of his battling emotions. It was useless. He'd felt sick most of the day, a dull nausea that kept trying to climb to his throat.

He took the dust cover from the high-backed settee and set it aside. He sat, his heart as heavy as his body. This was his last night at Butterhill Hall. He would depart for London tomorrow. He had things to do before he left England—letters to write, affairs to sort, property to dispose of. His talk with Princess Amelia had sobered him dramatically.

His father, arrested.

In the last fortnight, Luka realized he'd lapsed into terrible irresponsibility, all for a woman. He was a scientist, a man who kept meticulous notes, noticed details, took his responsibilities seriously. And yet, here he was, acting like a young man with no occupation. How had he gotten so far away from the man he was?

He rubbed his eyes. His emotions, which generally lived in some subterranean corner of his soul, were eating him alive.

He was uncertain how to leave Emma. He wanted to take her with him, but to what? A potential civil war? A fight with his father? Worse, accusations made against him? He wanted to tell her he would come back for her. But how? He couldn't even convince himself that he wouldn't be hanged right alongside his father.

He heard a movement at the door and sprang to his feet. It opened a sliver, and she slipped inside. She'd brought a candle, her hand cupped around the flame. He thought that not a good idea—it could draw attention to them—and moved immediately to take it from her and blew out the flame. He set it aside.

Emma reached for him. "I have missed you so."

That was it, that whisper of longing, and Luka lost himself all over again. "And I've missed you." He kissed her, long and deep. But then he lifted his head. "There is something I need to say."

"All right."

He gazed down at her face, her features made milky by the moonlight. He wanted to tell her he loved her. That he didn't know how to carry on without her. He wanted to tell her he would forgo his country and his family to be with her—even though his head knew that wasn't possible. He wanted to thank her for adding this glorious summer to his life, but that sounded so final.

So he didn't say anything at all. He just kissed her again, which was the only language he had in that moment. He kissed her passionately. Deeply. With everything he was feeling. He hoped they had come to an unspoken mutual agreement—that they would love each other as long as they could, and when they could no longer physically love each other, they would from afar. That was the fantasy he told himself, the only thing that made sense as he let fate take him where it must. But until that painful moment, he was here, with her.

He could feel the heat of her body through her gown, could feel his blood warming his skin with every touch. He stroked her hair, wanting to not destroy her coif, but unable to stop himself. He pulled his fingers through, and her tiara toppled off into the dark. She laughed softly and slid her hands up his chest. "The toppling of my tiara feels a bit prophetic."

He pressed against her. The darkness made it easy to forget where they were, or the time, or the place. They were in another galaxy, another world, another life. The intoxicating sensations of hands and mouths on each other's bodies filled their senses. Her lips tormented him, making his blood run too hot.

He unfastened her gown, and pushed it down her body, descending with it, his lips trailing to her abdomen. When her gown fell to the floor, he stood and discarded his clothes as she removed her chemise. They were moving with each other, pushing aside clothes until their skin touched. He lifted her up and placed her on the settee and braced himself above her. He studied her face a long moment in the moonlight, wishing he could imprint the image in his memory in a way it would never fade. Maybe it already had—he could just make her out, but he knew every freckle, every curve, every lash. She was luminous.

She stroked his face and his lips. "You are the most magnificent man I have ever known."

He ran his hand roughly over her head. "And you are the most stunning woman I've ever known."

"I think we must have been very bad in a previous life to have found each other under these circumstances."

"It's not hard to imagine."

She smiled, and his heart melted. Just…dissolved into a puddle of warm, sweet molasses.

And then their hands and lips were on each other. When they came together, he felt an internal explosion of light and happiness and awe and sorrow. Their lovemaking felt profound in a way he'd never felt before. *This is love*, his heart whispered. She was the sustenance he required, the woman who made his pulse race and his heart pound and his muscles move. He was sick with love, and when he rolled onto his back and pulled her on top, Emma threw her head back and let her mouth fall open, the experience as shattering for her as it was for him.

His kisses turned hard with need. His release, caught at the last possible moment and spilled onto his belly, was so intense he was sheepish. She covered his face with breathless kisses then slid off him, draping her body over his. She tangled her fingers in his hair as she sought her breath.

"Magical," Luka said.

"*Magical*," Emma whispered. "You are magic."

He stroked her disheveled hair, tucking some behind her ear. "Emma Clark, you have surprised me in every conceivable way."

"Just as you've surprised me, Luka Olivien." She propped her chin on a fist on his chest. "And to think when I first laid eyes on you, I thought you were a highwayman."

"Or a preacher, as I recall. I wish I was a highwayman. I wish I had stolen you and ridden away with you."

"How would you have fed me? I am not the most agreeable companion when there are only berries and a few pieces of lamb and no wine."

"I would have slain a cow for you."

She laughed, and he could feel her laughter sinking into his chest. He remembered what he'd brought to this room and shifted beneath her, groping for his coat. When he found it, he fished inside a pocket and withdrew a small object.

He helped her to sit up, draped his coat around her shoulders. He kissed her softly, his lips lingering. "I want you, Emma," he whispered. "I want you with a strength I had never thought possible for me."

"Oh, Luka," she said, and cupped his face with her hand. "I want you, too. What have we done to each other?"

He opened his palm and presented his gift. It was the blue lotus he'd bought in the market in Cairo, a flower made of sapphires with an amber center. It was meant to be worn as a necklace, but he didn't have a chain. "In Egypt, the blue lotus is the symbol of rebirth, of life eternal."

She took the flower and stared down at it. She stood up from the settee and went to the window to look at it in the moonlight. "It's beautiful," she said. "Who is it for?"

"You. You are experiencing a rebirth. You are my rebirth."

"But—"

"When I saw it in the market stall, it spoke to me. I thought that perhaps, someday, there would be someone in the world who…" His voice trailed away. "I want you to have it."

"*Rebirth*," she whispered. "That's exactly what is happening to me." She looked up, tears in her eyes. "Luka."

"Don't do that," he said.

"I can't help it. I love you, Luka. I love you so much."

The words were daggers to his heart because he loved her, too. "Come here," he said, and led her back to the settee. He couldn't bear to leave her. "Come with me," he said. "It won't be easy, it could possibly be terrible, I'm certain of it—my father has been arrested."

"What?"

He picked up his shirt and slipped it on. "There may be a civil war. There may be a trial. I don't know what to expect. But I must go home. I've tarried long enough. But Emma, I will keep you safe. I swear on my life."

"Luka! I can't," she said miserably.

"But... You've said Lady Adele will abandon you—"

"She will," Emma said, and grabbed his hand, wrapping her fingers tightly around his. "But there is too much here that I can't leave like this. Andrew will be the earl, and he will need to understand things. I have agreed to reopen the copper mine, just today. I must see it through, for the sake of Butterhill. And for the sake of Andrew. And I must do it quickly, before Adele can end me."

A small piece of his heart broke away. It was slowly starting to crack, he could feel it. A physical sensation, a burning in his chest. "Emma, think—"

"I can't, Luka," she said firmly. "Just as you must do things you don't want to do, so must I. I have changed so many things! I can't walk away and see everything fall apart. I'd never forgive myself, and my ledger of misdeeds is quite long as it is. I care for Andrew. And he has only Adele to guide him if I am not here."

He understood, but it took several moments before it sank into him that there truly was no hope for them.

They stared at each other in the dark, their bodies still warm. She gripped his gift in a tight fist against her chest. Tears glistened like stars in her eyes. "We always knew," she said softly.

Yes, they had known from the beginning—that the beginning was really the end. And yet they'd ignored all the signs and plunged into this deep pool anyway without a care for how far below them the bottom was.

There was no point in making promises to each other. Neither of them knew what their futures held, other than bleak landscapes.

Luka swallowed. He scraped his fingers through his hair. He wished he could stop breathing like he'd run a bloody race. "I have to leave tomorrow," he said. "I've much to do, and the queen's escort will arrive for me Tuesday."

A small gasp of despair escaped Emma. A tear slipped from her eye and began to make its way down her cheek. "I understand."

He took her hands in his. "I will never know anyone like you ever again, Emma. I don't want to know anyone like you. I will always want you. I will always love you. Know that."

"Luka… I will always love you. For the rest of my days, you will be the one great love I long for."

He pulled her into his embrace again and leaned back with her on the settee. They didn't speak anymore, both lost in their thoughts and private hells.

Sometime later, Luka was awakened by the sound of a clock chiming three o'clock. He felt an emptiness where Emma had been beside him and sat up.

She was dressed. She picked up her tiara; it dangled carelessly from her fingers. She leaned down, whis-

AN INCONVENIENT EARL

pered in his ear that she loved him with all her heart. Luka grabbed her hand, feeling abruptly panicked that she was slipping away. He kissed her knuckles. "Is this the end of the story?"

Emma caressed his face. "It's never the *end* of the story, Luka. I haven't even told you about the time I fell in love." She smiled sadly, kissed him on the lips, and slipped out of the room like a spirit.

The ache in Luka's chest was potent. A sharp pain that sparked with every breath. He feared he might be sick.

He feared he would never recover from this loss.

CHAPTER THIRTY-ONE

THE FOOTMAN WHO deposited Lila and Valentin at the train station presented them with a small basket of food. "Lady Dearborn thought you might like something to eat during your journey."

"How kind of her!" Lila exclaimed. It was only two hours or so to London, which, Valentin had reminded her more than once, was much more desirable than a four-hour carriage ride with Lord and Lady Iddesleigh.

"They weren't as bad as that," she'd chastised him, but he'd looked at her over the top of his eyeglasses with a silent warning not to argue.

They sat on a bench to wait for the train. Lila inspected the contents of the basket. Pastries, which she was very pleased about. Cheese, some bread, and a bottle of ale that Valentin would appreciate.

"Well then, my love, what did you think of your first English country house party?" Lila asked as she nibbled a pastry.

"A grand diversion. My shoulder is rather sore from the ax-throwing, however, and my head feels like it's filled with buckshot after last night." He sat up and moved his shoulder all around, trying to loosen it. "I should practice."

"Drinking? Or ax-throwing?" Lila asked with a chuckle. "I think Lord and Lady Iddesleigh best prepare for the line of young gentlemen who will come round wanting to court their daughters."

"They did seem to be rather popular, didn't they? Do you intend to offer your services?"

"Perhaps," Lila said. "I would have to think very carefully about it. I'm not sure I could endure Beck or Blythe. They have all the ingredients to be the worst sort of meddlesome parents. And the two of them would never agree on anyone."

"You would only need to please Donovan. He would see to it that the Iddesleighs come along."

Lila laughed again. It was true that the Hawke family was terribly dependent on Mr. Donovan for his advice or services or secrets—whatever it was that endeared him to them so.

The train horn sounded as it drew close to the station. They stood, Valentin busying himself with the luggage, and Lila making sure the basket of treats came along. She watched the train chug to a halt and happened to notice Mr. Olivien preparing to board the train. "Oh my," she said, and poked Valentin in the shoulder. "Will you look at that? The Weslorian is boarding the train."

"What Weslorian?" Valentin asked.

"*What* Weslorian," Lila said with exasperation. "Mr. Olivien, darling."

"Oh?" Valentin looked up. "He's leaving? Too much frivolity? What about his affair with the countess?"

"Valentin!" she hissed, slapping his arm. "I said it was a *possibility*. I would wager he is leaving because of the political unrest at home. Lady Marley told me his father had been arrested for sedition."

"Good God," Valentin said. He adjusted his eyeglasses

and peered down the platform at Mr. Olivien. "A man cannot recover from such a charge."

They boarded the train with many others, and when they were seated and settled, Lila noticed Mr. Olivien sitting a few rows ahead of them. She tried to ignore his presence, but she couldn't help herself—he was staring out the window and looking forlorn.

Shortly after the train began to roll Valentin fell asleep as Lila knew he would. She stood up with her basket and went to Mr. Olivien's row. "Mr. Olivien?"

At his name, he started and jerked around. "Lady Aleksander." He moved to stand, but she put her hand on his shoulder and pushed him down as she took the seat next to him. She opened the basket. "From Lady Dearborn."

His head snapped up. "Pardon?"

"She had a basket prepared for our return to London. My husband is asleep a few rows back. Go on—there's enough to share."

He colored slightly. "She is very kind."

There was something in his eyes when he spoke. A longing. "You esteem her," she said.

He said nothing.

"Well, it seems to me that you do," Lila said, plowing ahead. "Don't look so surprised. I am a matchmaker and have a good nose for these things. You may not know that about me. I have arranged matches between Princess Amelia and Lord Marley, Lady Caroline Hawke and Prince Leopold of Alucia. Your very own queen was a particularly favorite client. And many, many more I won't bore you with. But several Weslorians in the end."

He looked out the window.

"My talent is in recognizing when esteem grows between two people. I generally notice it before anyone else does. Sometimes before the couple themselves."

Mr. Olivien reluctantly turned back to her. "And you want to tell me you noticed esteem between me and Lady Dearborn."

"Well, yes, I did. But I daresay everyone at the house party noticed it."

He looked so sad, the poor man, and Lila felt sorry for him. She pulled a tart from the basket. "It was nothing overt, I assure you. Just intense glances here and there. A dance where neither of you ever took your eyes off the other. You may think I am judging the two of you, as she is a married woman, but I'm not in the least. These things happen, especially when a husband is gone too long. A woman needs the attention of a man. And a man needs a woman for everything. You must have been lured into a false sense of security with her husband away."

Mr. Olivien sighed. He looked at his hands. "That's where you are wrong, Lady Aleksander. The earl will never return."

Oh dear, the things lovers told themselves. "I think he will, eventually. He has a huge estate and the need for an heir—"

"He is dead, Lady Aleksander." Mr. Olivien looked her in the eye. "He has been dead for some time."

Stunned, Lila gaped at him a moment. "I beg your pardon?"

Luka groaned and rubbed his face. "I hesitate to say it, but I think it will be widely known in a matter of days. The earl is dead. Of yellow fever. His remains buried in Egypt."

"When?" She dropped the tart she had been about to eat.

"Before I left Egypt. *Dia*, I should have ended this the first day I arrived at Butterhill. I don't understand her completely, the whys, her *thinking*," he said, sounding anguished. "But in truth, Lady Aleksander, I'm desperately in love with her, and it was as if I had no control over myself or what I did."

"What did you do, Mr. Olivien?"

He groaned softly. "I allowed her to pretend. No, it was worse than that. I...helped her to pretend."

Lila glanced back to where Valentin was sitting. He was still very much asleep. She put the basket aside and turned to face Mr. Olivien as the train rocked through a small village. "Let me help. Tell me everything."

For some reason, he did. He told her simply everything. How he'd come to Butterhill to deliver an inscribed pocket watch, but he'd been captivated by her free spirit, and the idea that he knew she *knew*, but for reasons he couldn't fathom, was working quite hard to pretend she didn't. That he didn't understand until he'd spent time with her, and while he didn't agree with the decision to hide her husband's death, he appreciated her reasons and her spunk.

He spoke like a man who was utterly besotted, excusing the woman's behavior, finding reasons she surely must have had for what she'd done. He spoke like a man in torment, who'd had to give up the love of his life to attend to dire matters at home and an uncertain future for himself, given his father's activities. He spoke like a lover who'd found the companionable soul he'd been looking for all his life but, like so many others, had found that soul in the wrong place at the wrong time.

If there was one thing Lila adored, it was a good love story, even when she'd not been compensated to make it happen. Which was why she inserted herself into this love story. "Why didn't you take her with you if you love her so?"

"It's not that simple, madam. We are facing a civil war at worst and, at best, my father's trial. I don't know where my family stands. I don't know how I will be received. Princess Amelia claims many think I am involved. And Emma...she has been working to modernize Butterhill Hall and feels a responsibility to her brother-in-law to help him see it through."

Lila nodded thoughtfully. "When will her family learn the truth?"

"She means to tell them when everyone has left."

Everyone would be gone tomorrow. Lila didn't have much time to help. And that was if she could think of a way to do it.

"You can't blame her, Lady Aleksander," Mr. Olivien said earnestly. "She found freedom for the first time in her life."

Lila smiled sadly. "You don't need to explain to me, sir." As a debutante, Lila had been practically banished from London after her father had embroiled the family in a terrible scandal. She knew how cruel society could be. She understood the choices women didn't have and the bad ones they sometimes made. "When are you leaving England, Mr. Olivien?"

"Why?"

"Where can I reach you? You'll want to know if I am able to help her."

"What can you possibly do?"

"Well, that I don't yet know. But one never knows what the morrow will bring."

He looked hopeful. He told her where he would be staying in London. Where she could reach him in Wesloria, assuming he was not accused of abetting his father and arrested.

When Lila returned to her seat, she thought that the first thing she'd have to do is convince Valentin that she had to return to Butterhill Hall for a few days. He wouldn't like it. But then again, he never said no to her.

And then she was going to enlist Donovan's help.

CHAPTER THIRTY-TWO

IT RAINED SUNDAY because of course it did—the heavens conspired against Emma to make the day the most miserable of her life. Luka was gone, the rain fell, people who did not care to be cooped up in the drawing room with her and others left. But then again, some people stayed—the guests most likely to drink all the wine in the hall.

Adele and Andrew left early that morning, Adele intent on church, even though Andrew was feeling poorly. He swore to Emma it was the best time he'd ever had in his entire life, and he'd danced *twice* with two different girls before Adele had forced him to go to bed. It was apparently too much for him—his pallor was gray again.

She wondered, in that way she had of wondering things at inappropriate times, how long Andrew would be the earl. And then what? She hugged her brother-in-law. "I love you, Andrew."

His laugh of surprise turned into a cough. "I—I love you, too, Emma."

She sincerely hoped he would still after this week.

She turned to Adele, who viewed Emma smugly. "Thank you for coming," Emma said. "I do hope you enjoyed yourself."

"Oh, there were parts that were *quite* diverting. Where is your friend?"

"Which friend? I have so many."

"I was referring to your special friend, Mr. Olivien."

Emma's skin crawled at the way Adele said his name. "He's gone on. Didn't he tell you? Wish you well?"

"He said farewell to me," Andrew said. "I saw him leave this morning."

"Well, he said nothing to me," Adele sniffed. "But I'm not terribly surprised. I have found him to be less than forthcoming on a few topics."

"Really!" Emma said, feigning shock. "And I found him to be very charming and very forthcoming. Oh well, I suppose we'll never sort it out. Would you mind terribly if I came round for tea on Tuesday?"

"Why?" Adele asked, her gaze narrowing with suspicion.

"To see about Andrew, of course. He looks a bit peaked." She slipped a finger under his chin and lifted his face. Andrew smiled.

"You are of course welcome to visit the dower house any time you like, Emma." Adele had already turned away, was yanking on her gloves, ready to be free of her.

"Thank you!" Emma said cheerily as her sister-in-law walked away.

The rest of the day was filled with remorse so big that it hammered against Emma's temples, giving her a terrible headache. Fanny kept looking at her across the drawing room, gesturing for her to smile, to lift her chin, to sit up. She eventually removed herself from a card game and came to sit next to Emma, to whisper a question of what was wrong.

"I'm tired, that's all."

Fanny frowned. "Where is Mr. Olivien today? I've not seen him."

"He's gone, Fanny."

Fanny gasped. "What do you mean?"

"Just that. He's gone, left for Wesloria. Why do you look like that? He was always going to leave."

"Yes, but…but I thought…" She shook her head, unwilling to voice what she thought. "Now what?"

"Now?" With a sigh of effort, Emma lifted her eyes to the ceiling. Her head felt as if it weighed a hundred pounds. "When everyone leaves, I will honor my word."

Fanny's eyes rounded. She pressed her lips together. "I understand."

Emma doubted she understood. Who could possibly understand? But Fanny eventually sent Phillip off to collect their boys and go home. She was going to stay. Fanny, steadfast Fanny, always by Emma's side, even when Emma didn't deserve her.

She was aware that some of her guests were still watching her as they had all weekend. Mrs. White kept a close eye on her. She could imagine that Mrs. White would hurry to Adele with her report when she left here. But Emma couldn't pretend she was happy when she was not. All those years with Albert, she'd perfected the talent of appearing happy and gay when her entire being was in turmoil. Today, it was impossible.

Lord Markham asked where the guest of honor had gotten off to.

"He's on his way to Wesloria, I believe," Emma said.

"Is he? Seemed rather content here, didn't he?"

Emma looked at him sharply.

"Your hospitality is unrivaled," he added apologetically.

"Thank you," she said warily.

Lord Markham carried on, presenting his empty glass to a footman, and then wandered back to the table where some were playing cards.

Emma sat near the hearth, staring into the flames. The rain was unrelenting. She'd been so eager to have this party, and now she just wanted everyone to go home.

"Lady Dearborn, you seem unwell." Mrs. White deposited herself next to Emma. "Is there something I can do for you?"

Yes. Leave. "I'm quite all right, Mrs. White. A bit tired, that's all. What you can do for me is enjoy yourself."

"I think you'll feel much more yourself when your husband returns. These parties are really just a way to pass the time, aren't they? Perhaps you ought to send someone to look for him."

Emma looked at the woman. "I don't think that would do any good."

"No? Perhaps not." She smiled in the same smug way Adele had smiled, and Emma imagined her and Adele going over every detail of Emma's life here. If Adele, with Mrs. White's help, could convince all of Rexford that Emma was having an affair, then she could convince Albert when he came home. If Adele couldn't get rid of Emma, she had found a way for Albert to do it.

Wouldn't she be surprised when she learned that Emma had been the one to get rid of herself.

She thought Monday would never arrive, but it did, as sure as the sun. She felt as if she'd been dragged behind a carriage. Feeney kept asking her questions that exhausted her even more. She didn't mean to be short with him, but when he asked what to do with Mr. and Mrs. Cassian, as their carriage wheel had broken, Emma snapped. "For God's sake, Feeney, do what you think is best. You know more about carriage wheels than I could ever hope to know."

"Yes, madam," Feeney said with a dark frown. He gave her the curtest nod in the history of nods and strode from the room. Emma thought to call him back, to apologize, but she didn't have the energy to do it.

On Monday afternoon, after everyone had left, Emma insisted Fanny go home, too.

"I don't think I should leave you," Fanny said. "You're despondent. I've never seen you like this."

"I don't think I've ever been truly despondent until now," Emma mused. "Even on the darkest days I spent as Albert's wife, I never felt as...*lost* as I do today." She went to the window and looked out. At the top of the hill, where the entrance to the Butterhill drive began, she could see the small gamekeeper's cottage. "What of the shop? I was so looking forward to it. And the copper mine. It will be a triumph, I think."

Fanny came to the window and forced Emma around. She wrapped her arms around her sister. "I know your heart is breaking, darling. I wish I could ease your hurt. I can't imagine what I'd do without Phillip."

Emma closed her eyes. Yes, Fanny and Phillip, the lucky ones. "I'll be all right," she said weakly.

After Fanny left late that afternoon, Emma wandered around Butterhill Hall, looking at it with fresh eyes. Memorizing the house and the features. The crown moldings. The ceiling medallions. The brocade drapes in the formal dining room. The gorgeous views from every window.

On Tuesday, Emma woke feeling as if she'd come down with an ague. But she got up, dressed as she always did, and took her walk around the lake. There, she cried enough to fill buckets. She cried for the loss of Butterhill Hall. For what she'd done to poor Adele and Andrew.

Mostly, she cried for Luka. How odd it was to sob for the loss of someone she'd known only for a short time. She'd never once cried over Albert in all the years she'd known him. She'd cried because of him, to be sure, but never over him. But after a fortnight with Luka, she felt an immeasurable loss that sank into her marrow. Her heart squeezed out every last tear for him.

She finally came in from the lake, her hem muddied, her hair windblown, her face tearstained. Feeney was waiting for her in the foyer. "A caller, Lady Dearborn."

She squeezed her eyes shut and groaned. "Haven't they all gone home yet?" Hadn't they all seen the scandalous countess and watched her fall in love?

"It is Lady Aleksander."

Emma was confused. "But…she and her husband returned to London on Sunday."

"She has returned."

Emma sighed and rubbed her nape. She honestly didn't have the strength for it—she was due at the dower house this afternoon. But she made herself go into the receiving room.

Lady Aleksander smiled as if they were old friends. "Lady Dearborn, I have interrupted your walkabout."

She had interrupted her dive into sorrow. "What brings you, Lady Aleksander?"

"Please, call me Lila."

Emma paused. Why should she? What reason would

Lady Aleksander have to invite such informality? "Is… is something wrong?"

"I can happily say nothing is wrong with me. But I'm afraid something is wrong with you."

"I beg your pardon?"

"I saw Mr. Olivien on the train to London."

Emma's heart squeezed. "Is he… Did something happen?"

"Yes, something happened. He told me the truth."

Emma didn't know what she meant by that—the truth about what? There were so many truths that could be revealed, and she panicked. "I don't…" No, she couldn't deny anything. "But you…" *No, no! Don't say anything, because she might not know* all *the truth.*

"He told me about your husband's unfortunate death."

Emma suddenly grabbed the back of a chair before she sank to her knees. Luka had betrayed her? What was the woman doing here? Was she going to accuse her? "What do you want?"

"You misunderstand, Lady Dearborn. I want you to call me Lila. And I want to help you."

"*Help* me?"

Lila gestured to the chairs. "May we sit?"

"No," Emma said immediately. "Just say what you came to say."

"Lady Dearborn, please. I really do mean to help."

"I don't see how you could possibly help me with anything."

"You won't see if you won't listen." Lila gestured to the chairs again.

Emma looked at the chair. She needed to sit if only because it felt as if her legs would give out at any moment. She sat, then sank against the chair back, sliding down like a petulant child. "All right, then, let's get to it. You must think I'm a terrible person, and I am, I won't deny it. I never wished for my husband's demise, of course not. But honestly, madam, after the shock of learning his fate, I felt nothing but relief. My husband was a cruel man. I got my wish. I was free of him at last, and I... I rejoiced in it. There. You may report it to whomever you like."

"I'm not reporting to anyone. You said he was cruel?"

Emma nodded. Eventually, Lila coaxed it out of her. Emma told her about his inability to perform. His cruelty to her. How he blamed her for the lack of an heir and gradually, for everything else. How he would ridicule her and taunt her. Humiliate her in front of others.

"I'm so sorry," Lila said.

Emma told her about his decision to go on an adventure and how she'd felt within days of his departure. "I could breathe," she said. "There was no fear of humiliation." She explained that she had lived simply, dreading his return. But that it wasn't her husband who had come. It was Mr. Duffy.

She told Lila what had happened the day the poor man had appeared in her drawing room. "I panicked," she said. "I realized that Andrew would be the earl and my sister-in-law...would lead him. I believed she would want to lead me out the door as soon as possible. So I said nothing. And I continued to live my life." She fingered the small blue lotus in her pocket. She hadn't been without it since Luka had given it to her. "I was reborn with that news."

"I see," Lila said.

Emma gave a sad laugh. "I rather hope you don't." She pushed herself up and tried to compose herself.

"Well, then, Lady Aleksander. Do you still believe you can help me?"

"Perhaps. When do you intend to inform your family of his lordship's death?"

"Today."

"And then?"

And then... "I hope to have time to prepare Andrew for his role. I've made some changes at Butterhill—for the better, I believe—but he'll need to understand before my sister-in-law intervenes."

"Ah. And *then*?"

Emma was growing annoyed with the woman. She had no right to ask such probing questions, and Emma certainly didn't have to answer her. Except that it was a bit of a relief to unburden herself. To speak aloud what had been in her heart for so long. "I don't know. I haven't allowed myself to think that far for fear of losing all hope. I thought I might go to London to visit a cousin. And, well...hope for the best."

"Hmm," Lady Aleksander said. She shifted forward in her chair to gain Emma's undivided attention. "I think you can hope for better. I want to help you."

"So you have said, madam, although I don't see how. You're a matchmaker, not a miracle worker, and really, I don't know why you care."

"Some would argue that a matchmaker and miracle worker are one and the same, but I won't pretend to have that talent. I'm not a miracle worker, but I'm quite good at puzzling through problems. As for why? Well, for one thing, I believe in love, and I saw in Mr. Olivien a man who was desperately in love. I think you are, too. I saw the way you looked at him all weekend. For another, I was once like you. I was a young woman trapped by societal rules who needed a helping hand. And finally, I don't see a long line of people at your door wanting to help you out of a terrible predicament. Now, it seems to me that you will need a place to live. Have you any money?"

Emma squirmed a little. Lila was not wrong—there was only Fanny to help her. "Some."

"Good. That will make it easier. I think I have an idea."

Emma hoped her idea was a good one, because she was fresh out. She felt strangely disembodied, as if she was watching herself trust a woman she hardly knew. But there was something about Lila Aleksander that seemed…true?

She twirled a bit of loose hair around her finger. "How was he? Mr. Olivien?"

"Quite despondent. And, as I said, very much in love."

That was a painful slap to her heart. Emma couldn't bear to think of him hurting. But she couldn't bear not to think of him. Her misery escaped her in a small moan. "He was magic," she said quietly. "The most wonderful thing to have ever happened to me."

"Oh, darling," Lila said sympathetically. "It will happen again."

"No, it won't," Emma said, and felt the tears rising in her eyes, a thickness in her throat, as if she couldn't breathe properly. She would never feel what she had for Luka again in her lifetime.

CHAPTER THIRTY-THREE

ADELE TOOK THE news precisely as Emma had imagined: not well. Rather violently, in fact.

Emma arrived in time for tea, feeling quite sick to her stomach. As she'd mulled over how to tell them, she couldn't help but marvel at the heinous thing she'd done. How had she lived with herself?

She had assumed that tea would be as it always was, Andrew regaling her with something he'd read and Adele asking probing questions. It wasn't that at all. When Emma came into the dower house drawing room, Adele was standing. Her hair was pulled in a severe bun, and she looked as if she hadn't slept.

Curiously, Mr. Longbottom was also present and looking as cheerful as ever. "You'll want to try the tarts," he said to Emma before she was even invited to sit. "They are exceptional."

"She will not be taking tea, Mr. Longbottom. Today, Andrew and I are confronting her."

Emma's heart hitched. "What?" At the same time Mr. Longbottom said, "Pardon?"

Emma imagined that Adele had learned the truth. For a moment, she felt a strange sense of relief that she wouldn't have to admit it. Unfortunately, she was wrong in that assumption.

"Andrew and I believe you are an adulterer. Frankly,

everyone thinks so. And as soon as Albert is home, I intend to tell him."

So, she'd been right in her suspicions about Adele. She hadn't thought she'd discover it precisely in this way. But her sister-in-law didn't approve of her and what she was doing at Butterhill Hall. What better way to rid them of Emma than accuse her of adultery after she made sure the rumors had spread?

Emma sighed and sank into a chair. "I am aware you think so, but you're wrong. That's the thing I've come to tell you."

Adele laughed. "You think to deny it?"

"It's not adultery because Albert is not coming home."

Adele stilled. Mr. Longbottom froze midbite. Andrew coughed and said, "What do you mean, Emma?"

"I am so very sorry. So *very* sorry, but… Albert has died."

There was, naturally, quite a lot of confusion. Adele called her a liar. Andrew begged his sister to listen. Mr. Longbottom went to the sideboard and poured whisky for everyone.

It was amazing, Emma would think later, how calmly she recounted the story of Mr. Duffy's visit and his death. How there had been so much confusion after he'd died, and how she had realized that she would have no place to go and had neglected to tell them, and then, when time passed, she couldn't think how to explain herself. She kindly—at least, she thought it was kindly—left out any reference to the sort of monster Albert had been. She took all the blame for herself.

When she'd finished, Adele said, "Mr. Duffy died months ago."

"Yes," Emma said simply.

Adele picked up a vase of flowers and hurled them at Emma. She missed her completely, but Emma felt the force of her anger quite sharply. She said nothing, remained where she was, as she deserved every bit of Adele's vitriol. Poor Andrew cried so hard that he couldn't breathe and was sent into rounds of coughing. Thankfully, Mr. Longbottom stepped in to keep Adele from latching on to Emma's neck.

"Now, now, Lady Adele, there is no cause for this," he said soothingly.

"There is *every* cause for it!" Adele cried. "How could you, Emma? Why did you keep this from us?"

Emma didn't know how to explain years of misery at her husband's hand, of the contempt and disrespect she had endured. She didn't know how to explain to a woman like Adele that she had longed to live freely, if only for a short time, and that she'd never intended it to go for as long as it had, but that it had been easy to do. "It's impossible to explain myself."

"Because there is no explanation! You have sullied my brother's good name. There was not a better man in all of England, and this is how you honor his memory? You spend his money and invite your lover to stay?"

"That's not what happened," Emma tried, but Adele would not hear it.

She whirled around to Andrew and told him to stop his wailing. "You are the Earl of Dearborn now, and you best act like it! The first thing you must do is banish your brother's adulterous wife!"

"I don't want to do that," Andrew pleaded, but Adele shouted at him to do it, and Andrew, dear Andrew, tearfully told Emma she had to go.

"I understand," Emma said. "Please, Andrew, don't trouble yourself. I truly understand. What I've done is unforgivable. I am unforgivable. But give me a week, dearest. I want to share some things about the estate with you."

"Andrew, you will *not* allow her to stay another moment!" Adele shouted.

Poor Andrew looked as if he might crumple. "By Thursday," he said, glancing fearfully at Adele. "You must go by Thursday. Is that all right?"

"It is," Emma said before Adele attacked him. "But the estate, Andrew—"

"You will say *nothing* about an estate you almost destroyed!" Adele roared.

Emma's shoulders sagged. She'd asked for too much. She was simply unforgivable.

Mr. Longbottom saw her to the door, her exit accompanied by Adele's sobs. At the door, as Emma donned her hat, Mr. Longbottom said, "Don't worry, Lady Dearborn. I'll show the young lord what you've done. You've turned a monolith that would eventually have begun to bleed money in its antiquated way into something useful, if you ask me."

She looked up at him. "Really?"

"Indeed. You've done a remarkable service to Butterhill Hall, and that young lad will know it, you have my word. Best of luck to you! I'm sorry Mrs. Longbottom didn't have the opportunity to make your acquaintance." He opened the door, and Emma, a bit dumbfounded, stepped out.

She trudged back to Butterhill Hall to begin packing her things. It was a new beginning, she told herself. How many times during her marriage to Albert had she wished for an ordinary life? Well, she was about to have one.

She clutched the blue lotus in her hand so hard that the small petals cut into her skin, leaving little pin-pricks of sorrow.

CHAPTER THIRTY-FOUR

LADY ALEKSANDER WAS, in the end, Emma's savior. Not only had she begun to pack Emma's things for her, with Carlotta's weepy help, but she'd convinced Feeney to send someone for her sister. Fanny arrived that afternoon, looking frantic.

Emma told her sister what had happened, how terribly hurt Andrew had been to learn of his brother's death, how terribly furious Adele had been. When she finished, Fanny looked ragged.

"Do you hate me?" Emma asked her.

"No, Emma. Never. I know how you suffered. I know you've a heart of gold, really. I wish you…that is to say, you shouldn't have…" She stopped and pressed her fingertips to her eyes. "I want to tell you it was badly done, but you already know that it was. But that's *you*, Emma. Always impetuous and free-spirited. You must be true to yourself." She dropped her hands and looked at her sister with anguish. "I will miss you so very much. But in a strange way, I am very happy for you."

"Happy!"

"Yes. Because wherever you go, you will be free to be you. At long last, you will be free to be exactly who you are."

Emma didn't know if Fanny was right about that or not. At that moment, the life ahead of her seemed bleak. She and Fanny clung to each other when it was time for Fanny to return to her own house and her own marriage and her own life, and Emma felt as if she'd lost another part of her heart when Fanny disappeared out the front door.

But then Lila came and put her arm around her shoulders. "The glorious thing about this life," she said, "is that one never knows what comes next. You and your sister will see each other again and under happier circumstances."

Emma dragged her hand under her nose. "You really do like to rattle off platitudes, don't you?" she asked shakily.

Lila laughed. "It's my nature. Come on, then. Let's finish up."

They arrived in London late Thursday afternoon, and Mr. Donovan met them at the train station. "Lady Dearborn, what a delightful pleasure to have you in town," he said, and bowed low.

"I think you might feel differently when you hear the news," Emma said morosely.

"I've heard every last bit of it, and I am delighted to see you. As you can imagine, it is the talk of the town. I have a wonderful accommodation for you if you like cats," he said, and picked up her bags.

"Cats?"

"Three."

He took her and Lila to a small town house on Bedford Square. It was narrow, filled with curios and books, and smelled musty and old. There was a thin layer of dust on most things. "What is this place?" Emma asked.

"This is the old Tricklebank house," he said. "The childhood home of the Queen of Alucia, where she lived before her marriage to King Sebastian. She and her sister, Mrs. Hollis Honeycutt, have kept it for sentimental purposes."

Emma blinked at him. "I've read about her."

"I am the caretaker and use it to house cats. Not strays, mind, but descendants of the original house cats. Impossible to stop them from procreating. There are currently three making themselves very much at home."

Just then, one wandered into the drawing room that featured faded draperies and a mantel with several burn marks. "Will this suit?" Donovan asked.

"Absolutely," Emma said.

And there she remained for a week. She was awakened every morning by a cat lying across her head or batting her nose.

A young woman named Marcie came each day to cook and clean for Emma. Emma didn't tell her who she was, and the young woman seemed not to know. She chatted easily about her babies, and her husband, and the woman down the street who had once accused her of taking some of her washing off the line.

During the day, Emma walked around London. She went to museums, she strolled in the park, she searched the markets for trinkets.

Mostly, she missed Luka. She wondered where he was, what he was doing. She wondered if he had seen his father, if there would be a trial or a war.

She wondered if he missed her as she missed him. If he loved her, *still* loved her, as she loved him.

One day, Donovan and Lila came to call. Lila said they had news. "Lord Iddesleigh has agreed that you may teach at the Iddesleigh School for Exceptional Girls!" she announced excitedly.

"Pardon?" Emma was stunned. She'd been a terrible student—how could she possibly teach? "Teach what?"

"Well, that's to be decided. But, I think, to begin you will teach comportment. How to be a countess, that sort of thing. Mr. Martin, the headmaster, will help you determine your talents."

"I don't have any talents," Emma said.

"I beg to differ! I've never in all my years seen anyone host a party like you!"

Emma looked at them both in disbelief. "That is hardly the sort of thing that's taught in schools."

"Maybe not yet, but perhaps they should," Lila said. "But—"

"I do beg your pardon, but there are no *buts*," Lila said firmly. "You must trust me on this."

Emma supposed she had no choice but to trust Lila. So she agreed.

She learned she would be traveling to Devonshire with Lord and Lady Marley. They had agreed to take her to Iddesleigh House, and from there she would be taken to the school.

On a bright Saturday morning, they set out from London. Lord Marley and their children had gone ahead by train. Lady Marley and Emma would ride together in the carriage. For the first hour, the princess said very little. But after a time, she seemed to warm to Emma and asked her about the *Comte ve Marlaine*. Lila did not understand her accent at first and asked her to repeat it. "Marlaine. You would call him Earl Marlaine, I think."

"Luka?"

"Well…yes," the princess said, and squirmed a little. "I take it you esteem him."

Emma considered there was no possible scenario

in which the woman had not heard the gossip. "I do. Quite a lot."

The princess sighed. She reached across the coach and put her hand on Emma's knee. "Be careful, Lady Dearborn. The Oliviens have been accused of treason. You know he's been arrested, don't you?"

Emma's heart seized with terror. "You mean his father."

"I mean both of them. For sedition."

Emma felt herself go weak. "But why? Luka has been out of the country for more than two years. He couldn't possibly have plotted against the government."

"So he says," Lady Marley said.

Emma gasped.

"Look here, I believe he is innocent. So does my sister, the queen. But you must understand that many people—advisers, ministers—don't. They believe the Oliviens are traitors and want to make sure they are never again in a position to attempt a coup."

Her heart was pounding so hard she felt breathless. "What will happen to him?"

"I don't know. He'll have a fair trial."

Emma's heart sank.

"My advice? Forget him," Lady Marley said. "That must sound harsh, but I would hate to see you pine for him. He may never be free."

Then, neither would Emma.

She stumbled around Iddesleigh House for a few days, surrounded by many young women, dogs, and Lord Iddesleigh, who was having a boxing ring built in one wing of the house. It was the subject of several arguments and debates among the Hawke family, with most of Hawke's daughters declaring him too old, his wife declaring him too foolish, and only one, Lady Birdie, enthusiastically supporting her father's desire to become a pugilist, because she wanted to be one, too.

Emma liked the laughter. She liked the company. She needed it more than ever, as it was the only thing that could lift the death shroud from her heart. She dreamed of Luka locked in a jail cell. She imagined him on the gallows. She cried when no one was looking.

After a fortnight, an elderly gentleman with a shock of white hair and a kind face came to call, driving a wagon. He introduced himself as Mr. Martin, the long-time headmaster at the Iddesleigh School for Exceptional Girls. "If you like, Lady Dearborn, we are ready for you," he said.

"All right," she said pleasantly because she didn't care what happened to her any longer.

The school, a refurbished abbey on the road to the sea, was a lovely setting, but the facility a little medieval. She was given a small, austere room, formerly used by monks. She had a window that looked out to the forest around them. She didn't need much. She had her clothes, some jewels, and her blue lotus, which Donovan had kindly put on a chain for her. She wore it around her neck.

Every morning she stood at her window and sent a hope to Luka that he was well.

She began to teach comportment to the girls. Most of them were eager to learn how to curtsy properly, how to address the titled lord they were all certain they would marry, and how to dance a waltz. Only a few girls took exception to being taught how to be a lady. "Boys don't have to comport themselves," remarked Joan Higgins.

"Of course they do," Emma said. "But in different ways. They are hardly ever allowed to sit, for example, as the seats must be kept open for the ladies."

"They can never *sit*?" asked another girl.

"Yes, they can," Emma said. "On a horse." She smiled with amusement at herself. "However, you may as well know now that girls will always be treated as weaker and inferior to boys. We're not, as we all know. But some lady discovered a long time ago that it's easier to let them think we are. Therefore, you must learn the rules of society."

"Did *you* comport yourself?" Joan asked.

Emma laughed. "Heavens, no! Why do you think I was brought here? For not obeying the rules."

The girls were rapt now. "What did you do?" asked Sarah Hillary.

"Well, I fell in love, for one. And then I forgot to mention a few things."

Some of the girls laughed, but most of them seemed confused.

When each the day was done, Emma would go to her small window and look at the sky and send another message through the heavens to Luka as she held her blue lotus. *I haven't even told you about my new position. I'm a teacher! You must be dying to know a teacher of what, and I'll tell you, but first I must tell you about a girl who came today...*

Emma didn't know how long she'd be at this school, dreaming of Luka, telling girls outrageous stories while she made them walk around the room with books on their heads, but it suited her for now. She loved the students. She loved that no one told her what to do. She loved that she was free to be herself. But she didn't know if it could sustain her.

Her heart ached worse with each day.

CHAPTER THIRTY-FIVE

One Year Later

THE TRIAL FOR sedition was particularly brutal for Luka's father. The old man seemed to age a decade in a matter of weeks. The evidence against him was startling—he'd been planning a coup against Justine for at least the two years Luka had been on expedition, if not longer.

Luka was tried alongside him. Nothing Justine did on his behalf seemed to help. But in the end, his father and three coconspirators, men all known to Luka, were found guilty of sedition and sentenced to years in prison. Their titles, holdings, and properties were forfeited.

Luka was found innocent. His hereditary titles were forfeited, his estate confiscated, too. But he was allowed to keep his personal holdings.

His mother died that year, the stress of her husband's crimes having been too much for her. Luka's sisters and their families moved to the seaside of Wesloria, as far from Astasia and the capital of St. Edys as they could get.

When all was said and done, Luka requested an audience with the queen and was granted one. When they were alone, he hugged his childhood friend and apologized not only for his father but for how long it had taken him to come home.

"Don't," she said. She had matured into a beautiful woman. She possessed a serene confidence she had not had as a child. "You are not your father, Luka, for which I am grateful. What will you do now?"

"Leave Wesloria. The name Olivien is now synonymous with treachery. My mother is gone. My sisters have their families. There is nothing for me here. I mean to go on another expedition and finish writing my book. I was fortunate to have some guidance from an Oxford professor before…everything."

"As much as it pains me, I think it's for the best. Have you any money?"

He had enough that he would live in comfort all his days. "I lost my parents and my pride. But my funds are untouched."

"That's something, I suppose," Justine said. "I envy you in a way. There are many days I wish I could flee Wesloria."

He could imagine that was true. She'd spent her entire reign thus far hearing how many people wanted her off the throne. "I hope that you never do. You are a perfect queen."

Justine laughed. "You've already been found innocent, Luka. There is no need to flatter me."

He smiled fondly. "The country is in good hands." His former country, he supposed. He was essentially a citizen of the world now.

But now here he was, walking in new boots (the shoemaker had assured them they were built to endure the hardest of expeditions) and his bag slung over his back. Inside were a few changes of clothes, his journal in which he'd taken copious notes during his stint in a St. Edys prison. It also contained letters he'd written to Emma that he couldn't send. Letters that told the story of his childhood. Of his fraught relationship with a father he'd once admired. Of his interests and the places he'd been. Of his arrest and trial.

Of falling in love so hard and fast that he still hadn't put the pieces together and didn't want to.

He knew where she was, thanks to Lady Aleksander. Somehow, she'd managed to get a letter to him while he'd been locked away. He'd learned Emma had been banished from Butterhill Hall immediately, just as she'd known she would be. She'd landed in Devonshire, engaged as an instructor at a girls' school. *You will undoubtedly wonder an instructor in what,* Lady Aleksander wrote, *and I can't say with certainty. As far as I have been able to determine, she teaches the girls how to live with abandon.*

That had made him smile. He couldn't imagine a better teacher.

He didn't know what to expect on this, his latest expedition. Perhaps she had met someone else. Perhaps she had put him behind her. Perhaps she had left the school and gone elsewhere. All he knew was that he couldn't go on with his life without seeing her.

He walked for hours, the school much farther from the train station than a stranger had indicated. He had his favorite hat pulled low over his eyes and a canteen of water at his waist. He had drawn some looks on the train—Englishmen were not accustomed to seeing adventurers, he supposed.

When the sun was directly overhead, he spotted the abbey in the distance.

As he drew nearer, that abbey looked almost golden in the midday sun. He watched as girls came streaming out of the entrance and turned into a field marked by a stone fence. He could hear their gay, laughing voices as they ran around that field, their gazes on the ground, clearly looking for something.

And then he saw Emma. She was wearing a plain skirt and blouse, a large sun hat, and her auburn hair in a thick tail down her back. He recognized her figure and could imagine every curve—it had been burned into his brain.

She was carrying a basket. She stopped and looked skyward. Then she caught up with the girls.

Wildflowers. They were picking wildflowers. Luka stood and watched from a distance. They put flowers in their aprons, pausing to examine what each other had collected. After a quarter hour, Emma began to direct them back into the abbey, walking behind them and nudging stragglers along. When the last girl went in, she paused to look skyward again, her hand at her throat.

And then, for reasons Luka would never divine, she turned and looked right at him. There was distance between them. And so much time. But right away he felt that pull between them.

She clapped a hand over her mouth. Luka dropped his bag. She began to run. So did he. He caught her and twirled her around. They didn't speak—they were kissing, clinging to each other, and it felt like they'd been separated a week instead of more than a year.

He did, finally, set her down. She caught his face between her hands. "I'm so glad you've come," she says. "I have so much to tell you. I haven't even told you about the time I was banished from Butterhill Hall!"

Luka picked her up and buried his face in her neck. He was home now. No matter where they were, if she was with him, he was where he belonged.

He was home.

EPILOGUE

Six Months Later

MR. AND MRS. OLIVIEN were married in a small parish church near Iddesleigh. Fanny and Phillip had come, along with Tommy and Theo. Lila and Valentin, too. The entire Iddesleigh family, including Donovan, of course, as they never seemed to travel except as an army. And Lord and Lady Marley, as Lady Marley somehow thought herself responsible for their happiness. Emma and Luka liked to lie in bed and theorize how she'd come to such a conclusion.

Andrew had come, too. He was a bit taller and he seemed a little healthier. He told her that Adele was still angry, even when Fanny had come round to explain what a brute Albert had been to Emma. "I'm very sorry for it," Andrew said.

"Oh, Andrew," said Emma. "You mustn't think of it."

"Adele won't admit it, but Butterhill Hall is better for what you did. The mine is open, and we are already seeing a profit. Mr. Longbottom says it was a brilliant thing to do."

"He does?" This delighted her. And she was pleased to hear Mr. Longbottom was still guiding him.

"I've missed you," Andrew said.

She hugged him tightly to her. "I've missed you. It

brings me joy to imagine that, one day, you will have a countess and an heir."

The mention of a countess and heir made Andrew blush furiously. "There is one girl," he said, and confided in Emma about a young woman who had come to live with her aunt and uncle, Lord and Lady Markham.

It gave Emma peace to know that Butterhill Hall was in good hands.

After their wedding, Emma and Luka stayed a short time in London at the Tricklebank house, courtesy of Donovan. They agreed they would live their life as they pleased, moving wherever the spirit took them.

Shortly thereafter, the spirit took them to India. Luka had finished his book about the Egyptian nomads, and it was in the hands of Professor Henley now. He had come to India to study the Bhil tribe, famous for their art in which scenes of their daily lives were depicted. Emma was studying birds. For no other reason than the birds were beautiful here. Sometimes, she passed the afternoons rereading the letters Luka had written her while he was in prison.

It was so warm in India that most days, she wore jodhpurs and a cotton shirt, her hair wrapped in a turban to keep it off her neck.

At night, they slept under nets to keep the bugs away.

This night, they lay naked, their limbs entwined and bodies damp with perspiration. It was the most wonderful feeling in the world to Emma, to be sticky, hot, and sated with Luka.

Emma like to tell Luka stories at night. Of a bird she saw that day. Of an orphan girl at Iddesleigh School for Exceptional Girls. Tonight, she told him a story of how the baby she was carrying kicked her today.

Luka put his hand on her belly. "I think it is too early for kicking."

"But I swear I felt it."

"Perhaps you did. Or perhaps what you are feeling is the two *dhokla* you ate." He chuckled.

"Our baby will be very strong because of those two *dhokla*. You will thank me."

Luka rubbed her abdomen, but he had a look in his eyes that seemed miles away.

"Are you happy?" Emma asked him.

He looked at her with surprise. "Abundantly. Are you?"

"Immeasurably."

"Any regrets?"

"That you didn't come to Butterhill Hall sooner. Years ago, perhaps. What about you?"

"That for more than a year I didn't have you."

She smiled with pleasure. "Do you love me?" she asked. She knew that he did, but she loved to hear him say it.

"More than life. Do you love me?"

"Oh, Luka." She sighed and settled in next to him, tracing circles on his flat abdomen. "Didn't I ever tell you about the time I fell in love?"

"Umm…"

"I'm sure I've mentioned it, but I don't think I've told you the whole story. It all started when I was eight years old."

"Wait. You fell in love when you were eight years old?"

"Yes. Not really, but…be patient. When I was eight, I had a dream about a stranger…"

* * * * *

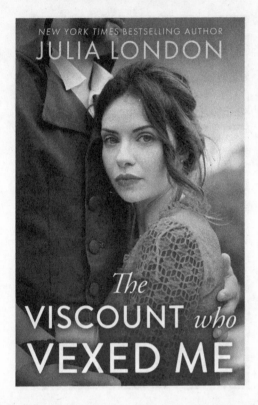

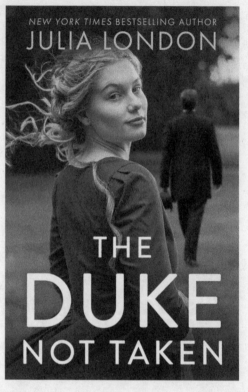

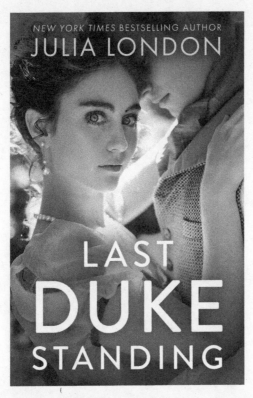

LET'S TALK
Romance

Follow us:

📘 Millsandboon

𝕏 @MillsandBoon

📷 @MillsandBoonUK

♪ @MillsandBoonUK

For all the latest titles and special
offers, sign up to our newsletter:
Millsandboon.co.uk